INTRODUCTION

HENRY WILLIAMSON was a writer of tremendous energy and tenacity. He wrote over fifty books, innumerable short stories and articles in newspapers and magazines, and literally thousands of lengthy letters. Most of his books were long and there were several typescript versions for each one. His compulsion and need to write ruled the whole of his life.

His first book *The Beautiful Years* was published in 1921. In 1951, thirty years and thirty-five books later, there appeared the first volume of his long novel in fifteen volumes, *A Chronicle of Ancient Sunlight*, whose hero, Phillip Maddison, is based on Henry Williamson himself. Apart from being an absorbing story of the life of an extraordinary man, the entire *Chronicle* is a fictionalized social history of the first half of the twentieth century.

The first volume, *The Dark Lantern,* opens with a scene where a man called Richard Maddison is out collecting moths on a summer night when he is set upon by two ruffians. Richard Maddison is based on Henry Williamson's own father, William Leopold Williamson, and this scene and most of the characters and incidents throughout the entire series are based on real scenes, characters and incidents from Henry Williamson's own life, and that of his family and friends. The element of fiction and transposing of real events with imagined ones does, however, mean that nothing can be taken for granted.

William Leopold Williamson was a bank clerk by profession who, in May 1893, married Gertrude Eliza Leaver in a secret ceremony. This dramatic tale is to be found in *The Dark Lantern*. Their first child, Kathleen Gertrude, was born in 1894, while Henry William Williamson was born on 1 December 1895 at 66 Braxfield Road in Brockley, south-east London. A third child, Doris Mary, was born in 1898. Soon after, William Leopold bought one of the new houses being built next to 'Hilly Fields' in Lewisham, and so the family moved to 11 [now 21] Eastern Road, where the main part of Henry Williamson's childhood and adolescence was spent. A blue commemorative plaque was placed here in 1984 under the aegis of The Henry Williamson Society and Lewisham Council.

Henry Williamson's mother came from a family who had been farmers in Bedfordshire and the young Henry was very friendly with his Bedfordshire cousins in whose home he felt more relaxed; we find all the relations woven into the tapestry of the *Chronicle*. An earlier branch of the family had originated from Devon, which Henry Williamson always claimed as his spiritual home and where he was to live for the greater part of his life.

In 1907 he obtained a scholarship to Colfe's Grammar School in Lewisham. He was not psychologically suited to the strict discipline of school life, preferring to roam the countryside collecting birds' eggs, but he was not a disgrace either: he became Captain of Harriers [cross-country running] and was in the school rifle team. His feelings, friendships and adventures gave him plenty of writing material and are marvellously captured in an early book, *Dandelion Days,* and later in *Young Phillip Maddison,* the third volume of the *Chronicle.*

On leaving school in the summer of 1913 Henry Williamson became a clerk in the Sun Fire Insurance Company, which becomes the 'Moon' Fire Office in the *Chronicle.* In the early summer of 1914 he went on holiday to stay with his Aunt Mary Leopoldina [Theodora in the novels], who rented a cottage in the tiny village of Georgeham in North Devon. This holiday made a great and lasting impression on the young Henry Williamson. He loved the wild coastal scenery of the nearby Braunton Burrows and the cliff promontory known as Baggy Point. This idyllic impression was further reinforced because shortly afterwards the First World War broke out and soon Henry Williamson was a soldier in the battlefields of Flanders.

He had enlisted into the ranks of the London Rifle Brigade the previous January, and was mobilized on 5 August 1914, embarking for the battlefields at the beginning of November. This period is related in the fourth volume of the *Chronicle, How Dear is Life,* where Phillip actually joins The London Highlanders, who also leave for the horror of the trenches. The ensuing volumes, *A Fox Under My Cloak, The Golden Virgin, Love and the Loveless* and *A Test To Destruction,* are all devoted to coverage of the war, interspersed with scenes of amorous and hilarious adventures of home leave, and service in this country training to be an officer, many of them episodes which were personally experienced by Henry Williamson himself. These books are considered by many critics to be some of the best that have ever been written about the First World War.

HENRY WILLIAMSON

THE POWER OF THE DEAD

Introduction by Anne Williamson

'Nothing is more corruptible . . . than the artistic
imagination living in mere probabilities.'

J. P. Stern

SUTTON PUBLISHING

To
Maurice Wiggin

First published in 1963 by Macdonald & Co (Publishers) Ltd

First published in this edition in the United Kingdom in 1999
Sutton Publishing Limited
Phoenix Mill • Thrupp • Stroud • Gloucestershire

British Library Cataloguing-in-Publication Data

A catalogue record for this book is available from the British Library.

ISBN 0-7509-2153-6

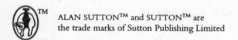

ALAN SUTTON™ and SUTTON™ are
the trade marks of Sutton Publishing Limited

Printed in Great Britain by
The Guernsey Press Company Limited,
Guernsey, Channel Islands.

The war affected him greatly, particularly the extraordinary Christmas Truce of 1914, when he discovered that the German soldiers – the enemy – were fighting for the same ideals as the British: God and their country. He realized the futility and destruction of war and this determined his life's work: to show the world, through writing, that truth and peace lay in beauty and the open air. This was reinforced when, in 1919, stationed in Folkestone with the Dispersal Unit, he discovered a copy of Richard Jefferies' book, *The Story of my Heart,* and read in rapt attention what was to him 'a revelation of total truth'. He began to write seriously from then onwards.

After demobilization in September 1919, Henry Williamson returned to live at his parents' house, where he behaved rather wildly for a few months. At the beginning of 1920 he obtained a job as motoring correspondent for the *Weekly Dispatch* and was soon having short nature sketches published in various newspapers and periodicals while he worked on his first novel. But he found life in the family home too narrow and frustrating because his father disapproved of everything he did. Finally they quarrelled irrevocably, and in March 1921 Henry left home for the cottage in Georgeham whose lease he took over for £5 a year. This period of his life is related in *The Innocent Moon,* the ninth volume of the *Chronicle,* although Phillip's courtship and marriage with 'Barley' and her subsequent death in childbirth soon after is a fictionalized version of what in real life was a frustrated love affair.

The Beautiful Years, the first volume of his tetralogy *The Flax of Dream,* was published that autumn. From then on Henry Williamson wrote and published a book (sometimes two books) more or less every year, almost to the very end of his long life.

In 1924 he embarked on an ambitious project: a novel depicting the life story of an otter. To procure material he joined the Cheriton Otter Hounds and at one of their meets he saw a beautiful young woman, Ida Loetitia Hibbert, whom he soon decided was his ideal partner. They were married in May 1925. She is Lucy Copplestone in the *Chronicle* and we first read about their courtship and subsequent marriage (and Henry's quarrels with her brothers) in the tenth volume, *It was the Nightingale.*

Tarka the Otter was published in October 1927 to much acclaim, especially after it was awarded the Hawthornden Prize for Literature the following year. A letter arrived from T.E. Lawrence, Lawrence of Arabia, who wrote to say he had 'sizzled with joy' on reading it, thus starting a correspondence and friendship between the two men.

With the £100 prize money Henry Williamson bought a field on the hill above Georgeham and built himself a Writing Hut which was to be his refuge throughout his life.

In *The Power of the Dead* Phillip goes off to learn farming from his uncle, Sir Hilary Maddison, who owns twelve hundred acres of downland with its own trout stream. In real life Henry and his wife and two sons moved to Shallowford in the village of Filleigh near South Molton in Devon, where there are, of course, several hundred acres of farmland and a trout stream. Henry set to work to improve the trout fishing and to write a book about another water creature, to be called *Salar the Salmon*. He published several more books and made two long visits to America, where his books had always been well received, at this time. His family increased and was complicated by the fact that his secretary, known in the novels as Felicity, also bore him a child.

In early May 1935 he wrote a letter to T.E. Lawrence asking if he might visit him to discuss a writing project for a friend, Victor Yeates, who had just died; Lawrence rushed out on his motorbike to send him a telegram in reply and as he returned had an accident from which he subsequently died. Later that year Henry was invited to visit his great friend Sir John Heygate, who was working in a film studio in Germany, and to attend the huge Nüremburg Rally being addressed by Adolf Hitler. Henry also saw and was greatly impressed by the German Youth Movement and the agricultural and industrial reforms Hitler was instigating. We must remember here that Henry had a German grandmother, and that his own ideas that 'truth and peace lay in beauty and the open air' coincided with what he saw happening in Germany. Later he was to call Hitler 'Lucifer', the fallen angel. This era is covered in *The Phoenix Generation*, the twelfth volume of the *Chronicle*.

Once *Salar* was published Henry Williamson felt he needed to move on to find fresh material. Two books, the charming *The Children of Shallowford* and the factual *Goodbye West Country*, relate the family's life at Shallowford in an interesting saga. Having seen the portents of war looming, he decided now to become a farmer and in 1937 bought a very run-down farm on the north Norfolk coast to which, amid much turmoil, the family moved. *A Solitary War* relates Phillip's [and Henry's] struggles to turn the 'bad lands' into a viable farming unit. Once in Norfolk Henry Williamson was persuaded to attend a meeting of the British Union of Fascists where he met its leader Sir Oswald Mosley. As a new farmer Henry felt the BUF's

agricultural policy held the answer to the country's troubles, and
Mosley became his new hero. Mosley is Sir Hereward Birkin in the
Chronicle novels. *Lucifer Before Sunrise* continues the story of the
farming struggle in wartime England. He also covers the farming era
in *The Story of a Norfolk Farm* and *The Phasian Bird*.

It was a harrowing time for the family. Henry was exhausted and
irritable, trying both to run the farm as a perfect system and to write
to earn enough money to keep everything going. At the end of the
war it was obvious that things could not continue as they were. The
farm was sold but the tensions were so great that the family broke
up. Henry returned to his field in Devon alone, although he always
maintained close touch with his ex-wife and his children.

The last volume of *A Chronicle of Ancient Sunlight* also has Phillip
returned to Devon, living alone on Exmoor. This tremendous novel,
The Gale of the World, culminates in an epic description of the storm
that led to the flooding and devastation of Lynmouth in 1953.
Afterwards, Phillip, finding himself still alive, decides that he can at
last start to write his Chronicle – opening with a shy young man out
with his dark lantern mothing on 'the Hill' and including all his
friends in ancient sunlight . . .

In real life, on his return to Devon Henry Williamson met and
soon married his second wife, Christine Duffield, and their son was
born in 1950. He built a larger studio in the Field, and bought a
large, comfortable and convenient caravan, but eventually also
bought a cottage in nearby Ilfracombe. And he began in earnest to
write *A Chronicle of Ancient Sunlight*, publishing one volume almost
every year between 1951 and 1969. His second marriage could not
withstand the pressure of his difficult personality and this tremendous
workload, and he and Christine were divorced in 1964.

Despite the attentions of friends and family Henry was then
permanently lonely. His last book *The Scandaroon*, the story of a
racing pigeon, was published in 1972. Many years previously he
had drawn up plans to build a large house in the Field and he now
achieved that ambition although he never lived in it. He finally
gave permission for a film to be made of *Tarka the Otter*. With his
life's purpose over he was now tired and ill and eventually was
taken into a nursing home on the outskirts of London run by
Alexian monks. The filming of *Tarka* went ahead unknown to him.
He died aged nearly eighty-two years old on 13 August 1977 on
the very same day that the death scene of Tarka was being filmed
in the exact spot that he had placed it over fifty years previously,

and a few days later he was buried in a simple grave in the churchyard at Georgeham, in a plot he had bought many years before.

ANNE WILLIAMSON

Readers who are interested in the life and work of Henry
Williamson might like to know that there is a Henry Williamson
Society. Meetings are held twice a year and the Society's *Journal,*
with a wide range of articles on his life and work, is published in the
spring and autumn of each year. For further information please
contact the Membership Secretary:

Mrs Margaret Murphy, 16 Doran Drive, Redhill, Surrey,
RH1 6AX.

Further Reading: *Henry Williamson: Tarka and the Last Romantic,* an
illustrated biography, written by Anne Williamson, was published by
Alan Sutton Publishing Limited in August 1995.

A CHRONICLE OF ANCIENT SUNLIGHT

1 THE DARK LANTERN
2 DONKEY BOY
3 YOUNG PHILLIP MADDISON
4 HOW DEAR IS LIFE
5 A FOX UNDER MY CLOAK
6 THE GOLDEN VIRGIN
7 LOVE AND THE LOVELESS
8 A TEST TO DESTRUCTION
9 THE INNOCENT MOON
10 IT WAS THE NIGHTINGALE
11 THE POWER OF THE DEAD
12 THE PHOENIX GENERATION
13 A SOLITARY WAR
14 LUCIFER BEFORE SUNRISE
15 THE GALE OF THE WORLD

Part One

A DRIVE TO PERFECTION

'Grief, with a glass that ran—'
ALGERNON CHARLES SWINBURNE

Chapter 1

TWO RHYTHMS

The early August sun burned upon the vale which lay, field upon field, to a line of downs under the southern sky. Distantly beyond those pale-green hills was a higher line of blue, the ox-drove of Cranborne Chase.

An elderly man, wearing a tweed jacket with the high velvet lapels of a bygone fashion, stood in a gate-way looking down upon the harvest scene. Beside him stood a young woman in a home-made print frock cut to conceal her pregnancy. They were resting on their way up the borstal dividing the upper fields of the farm. Thistle-seeds, arising with heated air from flints almost entirely covering the soil of an adjacent field, drifted past them. The web of a garden spider spun across the broken gate was a wheel of trembling floss.

"This field," he said, pointing with a silver-mounted blackthorn walking stick, "is not worth the harvesting."

Small sheaves, the corn heads almost hidden in thistle cardoons, irregularly lined the field. Goldfinches were busy feeding, a happy twittering filled the air. He continued, "The sooner Lobbett's is put down to grass the better."

Below the wretched field lay a land of gentle curving slopes. The earth upon a subsoil of chalk had been wave-smoothed by the sea in gradual recession in pre-historic times, leaving a marine deposit of shell and weed and fishbone to be rendered by the sun, moulded by the wind.

"But for the war, Lucy, the grazing up here would never have felt the plough. Down there the soil is a fat loam, up here it is merely the remains of a thin skin of rotted turf, forsaken even by the wire-worm."

The valley lying under their gaze was divided into large arable slopes by hedges, and by far rows of beech trees planted as wind-breaks. The nature of the ripening corn crops was revealed by

their colours—red-golds of the hard milling wheats, pale gold
of softer French wheat used largely for biscuits; rotten-ripe barleys
the weak straws of which were bleached nearly white, beside that
buffish brown of oats so pleasing to the eye of the countryman,
revealing a soil fertile after sheep in fold the previous autumn and
winter upon roots.

"Even with sheep this land up here would hardly pay, Lucy.
The war temporarily put farming on its feet, or rather it brought
back the ewe-flocks—what used to be called the golden hoof—
but for some years now the hoof has become leaden, with the
importation of frozen mutton from Argentina, which has undercut the home market for farmers. It will soon be the same story
with corn. Cheap barleys and wheats are now coming to the ports
from Central Europe, where the wages of the peasants in Poland,
Roumania, and the new state of Czecho-Slovakia are less than a
third of those paid to the English labourer."

"Yes, Phillip was telling me, Uncle John. Isn't the price of a
sack of wheat the labourer's weekly wage?"

"That was always the ready reckoning. Let me see, the wage
today is thirty-two shillings and sixpence; and since the repeal of
the Corn Production Act three years ago corn-growing, at least
on these upland fields, with their small yields, is a losing
game, I'm afraid. 'Horn and corn' to maintain the fertility of the
soil is a thing of the past. Free Trade is good for the towns, no
doubt, but it spells ruin for the country."

He looked at his watch. "We've half an hour in hand, Lucy.
Would you like to rest here, or in the shade of the hanger?"

Phillip had asked for the tea-basket to be brought to the rick
they were building at 5 p.m., in order to encourage the men to
work an extra hour before going home. The men liked weak tea,
he had explained to Lucy, with a little milk and plenty of sugar.
They also preferred it in bottles. They didn't want much to eat,
so would she bring some lardy cakes, split open and spread with
honey.

"Oh, I *love* the hanger, Uncle John."

The borstal, a sunken grass-road rutted by cart wheels, ended
at the beech hanger on a spur of the downs. Below the edge of
the wood, on the sward among carline thistles and late harebells,
they sat down. Here was peace, here the small blue butterfly and
the wild bee sought the late flowers in the light of the sun now in
the south-west. There was always a cool breeze up here, and

silence, broken only by the occasional chatter of a magpie and the querulous scream of a jay.

"Sounds like a fox afoot. The birds are seeing him off, I fancy."

He felt a sudden elation; he could hardly believe that he was no longer alone; that the years of solitary living were over; that Phillip and Lucy had accepted him as a friend, apart from the relationship; that they all got on so well together, his age did not seem to be any barrier.

John William Beare Maddison, rising sixty-six, looked at his niece by marriage, at the warm colouring of her cheeks, like the bloom on a ripe peach, the gentle line of the mouth, the grey eyes under the dark hair gathered in a bun at the nape of the neck. She was like one of the women in Botticelli's Primavera, beautiful with contentment that they were with child. He recalled the wedding day at the end of May, it was now August; her child would be born in the spring. Dear Phillip, with his understanding and sympathy, he would make the best of fathers. How would Billy, his son by his first wife, feel when the baby was born, he wondered. Billy would be two when the baby came. He hoped it would not put the little fellow's nose out of joint.

"Do you know, Lucy, this is the first time I have come here since the official end of the war? I walked here to see the beacons on the night of, let me see, it was July the Nineteenth, nineteen nineteen! I counted twenty-five fires in all, from those on the Chase"—he pointed south with his stick—"to those, so far west as to be mere spots of fire, on the Somerset hills."

"Phillip saw them in Kent that night, he told me." She wondered if she had said the wrong thing, for her companion was silent. Willie, his only son, had been with Phillip at Folkestone then.

"I've seen the beacons fired three times now, Lucy. The first occasion was the Jubilee of the Queen, then they burned again for the end of the South African War, and for the official end of the Great War in July 'nineteen. I remember my grandfather telling me about the beacons for Boney's defeat at Waterloo."

He fell into reverie. He had been alone on the three occasions; his wife had died giving birth to his only child, his son, the year before the Jubilee. Now both were lying in the churchyard. He wanted to put his arms round Lucy, to weep away all the unshed tears of the years—the phantom within himself crying out for all the past to be changed through love.

"Your home must lie to the south-east of Shakesbury, Lucy."

The town on the hill lay across the plain, half dissolved in mist.

"I was just thinking the same thing, Uncle John."

She wondered what Pa and the Boys were doing at that moment. 'Mister' had come over to see her that morning on his old motorbike, to tell Phillip that things weren't going too well.

"Many a time my brothers Richard and Hilary and I have walked across the ridge to the ox-drove above the woods of the Chase, growing on the southern slopes, and back again, when we were boys. We used to set out before dawn, and walk all day, returning dog-tired under the stars. There were more woods in those days, of course. The last of them went out to Ypres, to make the corduroy roads. The Chase is now little more than a grazing tract.

"Yes, it must be fifty years ago when we walked there last," he said, before turning to her with a smile. "And now, I see, Phillip is letting his beard grow. I cannot tell you what memories the sight of that beard calls up, for he has the same look about him that my brother Dickie had at his age.

"I can see Phillip's father now, with his light brown beard. All young men wore beards in those days, Lucy. Dick and I did, but it never appealed to Hilary. He preferred the shaven cheek and chin in keeping with the new idea, as it was then, of steam navigation replacing sail. When is he coming here, have you any idea, Lucy?"

"Yes, I heard by the afternoon post that Uncle Hilary will be here for the week-end."

They walked under the hanger, and came to the field which was being carted.

Phillip was on the rick, learning to lay sheaves like tiles upon a roof, keeping the middle well-filled to ensure that no rain would penetrate the heart of the rick. The visitors arrived during an interval between two waggons; the empty one was about to leave, its fellow was still being loaded in the field.

"Hullo," he said, climbing down the short ladder. His face was thin and sunburned; his arms and legs bore many scratches, he wore khaki shorts with shoes and socks. Thistle-seed clung to his hair, his eyes were blood-shot with dust. "How good of you to come."

He sat down and took off his shoes to empty them of small black seeds of charlock among shrivelled barley kernels. The horse

between the shafts was shuddering its skin. He walked over to
squash a number of gadflies which had eaten through the hide
and, with buried heads, were gorging on blood.

"I must do something about these keds, Uncle John," as he
squashed the bloated insects, taking care that no fly-heads were
left in the horses' skins. "There are plenty of old sacks in the corn
barn. I thought of slitting them to make a sort of blanket. I've
tried rubbing the hair with buckthorn oil, as recommended in *The
Stockbreeder*, but it doesn't keep these brutes away." Slap, slap.
"What we want is some tame swallows, or spotted fly-catchers.
Where's Billy?" to Lucy.

"He's sleeping, the pet," she said, softly. "I promised to bring
him out later in his push-cart, when you're carrying nearer the
premises."

John thought that his nephew looked very thin. His face had
the look of a sparrow-hawk. "You seem to have been working
hard, Phillip."

"It sweats out the vice, Uncle John."

"Well, don't go too hard, my dear boy. You've got a month
to six weeks before you."

"That's right, squire," announced a husky voice of the bailiff
from the rick above. "'Littles by littles,' that be what I told'n,
zur."

"Ned and I have been discussing the merits of a rick-cloth,"
went on Phillip. "I want one, to cover up at night in case it
rains. This blue haze looks like thunder."

"Naow," wheezed the voice from above. "It woan't rain, not
wi' the boo' 'aze on th' 'ill, it woan't. No need to meet trouble 'arf
way." Then peering over the edge, the rick-maker said in a
different voice, "Us'll leave'n well topped up, squire."

The bailiff was dressed in shirt, vest, waistcoat, khaki trousers
with thick pink woollen pants under them, and heavy boots with
rags in lieu of socks. He and Phillip had discussed many things
in the intervals of awaiting each waggon-load. They were in
agreement about one thing only—neither could go through, again,
what they had experienced on the Western front during the war.
As for details of these experiences on the Somme and at Passchen-
daele, both shared a deep reluctance to talk other than briefly
about them.

Just before the tea-basket had arrived they had had an argument
about the effect of the sun's rays on the flesh. The bailiff declared

that he kept cool by wearing many clothes, also his trousers stopped hawns and seeds from giving him blistered feet.

When his uncle and Lucy were gone, Phillip continued, "But Ned, supposing it does rain heavily—for a few days?"

"Look you a-here, guv'nor, I've a-seen nigh on fifty corn-carryings, man and boy——"

"Ned, my dear, you'm only forty-seven, and little more than a tacker."

The bailiff laughed with mouth askew, he was pleased; many of his nights were passed in mental struggle with the death-fears and what would happen to wife and children if he became 'past it'. He laughed askew because he had been shot through the face, the right jaw-bone had been shattered and the muscles of the other cheek destroyed. He received five shillings a week pension from the Government, and a further two shillings from the farm manager, Mr. Hibbs, for his services as foreman over and above the Wages Board rate of 32/6 a week. The other two men were also ex-Army men, but younger: a horseman and a cowman, both doing general farm-work for the minimum wage. There was no dole for the out-of-work farm labourer.

During the following days of bright sunlight, as he sweated to pitch the dishevelled and dusty barley sheaves, pictures of his past life passed through Phillip's head. He thought of the sweating, blistered marches of August 1914, of the near-agony of having to keep on, step after step, laden with rifle and fifty pounds of kit and ammunition. If he could stick that, he could stick this; and above all he must make a success of farming for the sake of the men who would otherwise be out of work. It was good to drive oneself; *mens sana in corpore sano*. He weighed, on the sack-machine in the barn, a stone less than when he had arrived on the farm in June. His muscles were hard, his riding breeches made in 1917 still fitted him, and—a triumph—his 1916 service tunic was short across the chest by five or six inches. The expansion had come from using arms and shoulder blades, and also breathing deeply. Never again would that germ of impotence, indecision, and degeneration—*tuberculum*—find a feeding place in his lungs.

Pictures of the war passed through his mind as he pitched: the friendly face of Mr. Kerr, his tailor, when he was on leave, and dropped into his shop in Cundit Street, to be given a reception as though he were almost royalty, with whiskys-and-soda in the little office, instead of a mere temporary gent. ("Mellow as milk, sir, you'll find; it's 'Dew of Benevenagh', thirty years in the wood.") Flossie Flowers' hotel; Teddie Gerrard and Jack Buchanan in *Bubbly*; *The Lilac Domino* at the Empire, *The Bing Boys* at the Alhambra; the leave train at Victoria; the rough, the deadly sea to Boulogne; the slow clank up to railhead; transport lines, distant rising flare, chlorinated whisky-and-soda in candle-lit dug-out. 'Spectre' West and his black eye-patch, black glove over wooden hand, and nine wound-stripes on sleeve. One day, one day—he dare not think further of the war. Let it lie hidden, until, one day——

Thrust of two, three sheaves on the long-handled pitching fork: eight feet of polished ash-shaft, enriched by linseed-oil, the two prongs burnished by emery paper: O, one day the farm would be the best in the district. It was good to be alive. What luck he had had, to have come through the war—all the faces he had known, enriching his life: a wonderful war, really, only two slight wounds, and a small dull patch in one lung which he had healed by walking hundreds of miles about the South Devon country after the war.

As he pitched sheaf after unending sheaf, he wondered when he would be able to re-create the wonderful days of the war. Yet were they *truly* wonderful days—that period before the post-war loneliness of youth? The real war of the front-line soldier had been a delirium of dust and heat and hell; the real war beyond the candle-light in the dug-out, beyond the rotting parapet, among the lip-to-lip craters of Third Ypres, water-filled, where the dead and the living slowly sank into the featureless swamp with tanks, mules, limbers, guns—how could it ever be re-created in words? And yet—in that time—the war as one experienced it was not the gashed and limbless trunks in shredded pink woollen vests, ruddy-swollen necks and faces of internal bleeding, strewn all across the old uneven grass-grown wilderness of the Somme country in the retreat of the Fifth Army in March 1918. One was somehow above, or apart from, that general post-war picture: the real war was the comradeship, the great chance to know the best of friendship; even as the war at home was hateful, mass-ignorance led and fed by lies that were the negation of the truth and beauty of the comradeship of war—comrade and enemy alike sharing the same spirit shining in the deep, dreadful night. Once—only once in Europe—only once the lesson, only one generation to pollinate with its spirit of self-sacrifice the lilies of the night. Not again, Englishman and German: that would be blasphemy.

"Take it easy, guv'nor, yar'll wear yersel' out if you go on like that. Yar all wire, Maister."

"Only part is wire, Ned."

"A-ah."

It was during the preliminary sweatings, after sedentary work, before the slow rhythm of body-work returned, that thoughts were like barb-wire within the skull. Whether of the personal scope, or the jump-off into the abstract of war, all thoughts were grievous at the re-start of the body being broken-in: complaints of the little ego.

Another waggon arrived. The young carter went up the ladder to help the rick-builder by passing the sheaves, a comparatively easy job. If he were boss, he wouldn't pitch, he thought. Hadn't the boss any money, that he needed to save a man's wages?

When Phillip was breaking himself in to hard graft, as the men called it, after a period of intense thought-feeling at his writing desk, mental torment was always most active. He had known for years that writing day after day despoiled the body; the creation of an imaginary world had its satisfaction, but it was gained at the expense of physical life. Whenever he started to work with his body after such a period, it was always with dragging reluctance; the work itself was so slow, the first sweatings weakening, the pores of the skin irritated, prickly; the mind was sharp and resentful of the slowness of others.

There were two ruling rhythms of his life that he was beginning to recognise: the one of body-work, the other of the perfectionist mind. Uncle Hilary was a perfect example of this mental attitude, with his insistence upon a sense of form—ever exhorting to tidiness, exactitude, observance of the letter of the smallest detail. But when Hilary was swimming in the sea, his body again naturally accustomed to an active life, he was quite a good chap: his over-bearing attitude was shed with his clothes. But did Nuncle see his previous exhortations as part of a bad dream which literally had vanished in sunlight?

The slow rhythm of the body, the insistent rhythm of the wit, were they becoming irreconcilable in modern civilisation? The sedentary life, frustration and irritability; work with the body, fatigue—and peace of mind.

"Shall Jim give you a spell, guv'nor?" asked the bailiff, leaning over the edge of the rick.

"Oh no, I can stick it. Sweats the nonsense out of me."

The sweat dried on his bare back and arms and legs, and was salt to the tongue when licked. He was getting clear, thank God.

After two more days in the harvest field his sweat was sweet, almost with the smell of Barley's tame otter, which had been faintly of violets. When winter came he would finish the book of the otter's wanderings; meanwhile he must strive to live in the actual moment, to be thoughtless, in the sense of having a calm mind, to deal with every moment as it came; and seal-off his retrospective mind, with its periods of melancholy, and at times despair that he would never again see Barley coming to him.

The sun in Virgo burned over the downs, and swinging above the plain of Colham, inclined to the south-west, so that every aspect of his body was made brown, and given strength to force tired muscles to lift beyond aching, to empty a waggon of barley sheaves without pausing—three, four, five together pushed up on the long polished handle of the pitching-fork, six feet over his head to the edge of the stack.

The carter took them on his shorter-handled fork and served the bailiff, who laid the sheaves, keeping the middle always well-filled as he trod round and round the sides of the rick, splaying 'chuffs' at the corners. Up—up—up—driving himself ever the harder, hoisting the long-handled fork. The barley awns were everlasting, creeping through his socks, pricking his skin, working round his belly, into his ankles and between his toes. By now arms and legs were impervious to the scratches of the harns; he had ceased to sweat with the final dissolution of his fat; he was sinew and muscle and bone, burned by the sun, the strength-giving sun of August.

Every day the welcome sight of Uncle John and Lucy with Billy and the tea-basket—nine days of burning sun and clear blue sky—the corn harvest nearly over—well-saved, thistles and all. Now he could get down to a spell of writing the book which had been dragging itself along through the pages, with constant irruptions, for more than a year.

How blessed was the tea interval, never early, never late, exactly at 5 p.m. every day. Lucy and her basket of lardy cakes, butter and honey, shared with the men to give them all a feeling of comradeship, as in the war.

Even so, the three men chose to sit apart, seldom speaking, along another side of the rick. They preferred it that way; as they wanted their own bottles of weak tea, with only a colouring of milk. It had always been like this for them; regularity was their security. They had seen masters come and masters go; the land remained, and without them the land was nought.

The bailiff regarded his new 'guv'nor' as a man too keen, who wanted to get everything done in a hurry; but he was a good man, he would learn. The bailiff knew the land, he had worked on it since boyhood; the land would remain, but the guv'nor wouldn't, if he didn't go easy.

Phillip, sitting on the other side of the stack with Lucy and Billy, felt that he was almost back in his boyhood again. He told himself that farming was the only life: that this was Father's country: his grandfather's and many forefathers' going back before the Wars of the Roses: he belonged to this land. And one day it would belong to him: Phillip Maddison, *Esquire*, painted on the waggons and carts. Why then was that thin thread of fear, as of a dry-rot fungus moving over airless wood, always at the back of his mind? It was nothing to do with Barley's death, to be honest; he had always felt like that. Why?

He told himself that he was a free man: he could sit at night by the open hearth of Skirr Farm where he had first sat in that wonderful time before the war with cousin Willie and Jack Temperley, Willie's great friend. The white owls still nested under the thatch at the eastern end of the roof, flying in and out of the dark triangular nesting hole as they had done for hundreds of years. Father had first told him of these owls when he had been a small boy, walking with his two sisters to Cutler's Pond, before the electric trams of the L.C.C. ran along the road, and the elms were thrown; he remembered the very moment when Father had told them, and he had shivered with a strange thrill, imagining the scene so vividly that it had remained the dominant of his inner life until, staying with another cousin, Percy Pickering at Beau Brickhill, and sharing the same bed—a wonderful experience, for they could talk in whispers in the darkness—he had heard an owl hooting just outside the window, part of the mysterious Night and the Stars entering his secret life. It was later on that he had visited Skirr Farm, and Rookhurst, in his seventeenth year.

Jack Temperley had been killed two years later, in 1914. Mr. Temperley had carried on, working harder than ever after the younger labourers had been called up after the battle of the Somme. In 1919 his elderly wife had given him another son; that had provided momentary hope, despite the loss of fertility in his fields, owing to war-time need to grow corn-crop after corn-crop without the essential potash and its equivalent of bullock muck containing the residues of linseed 'cake'.

Potash, before the war, had come from Germany; slabs of crushed linseed from the Argentine. By 1924 the farmer was exhausted, like his land; for a farmer's heart is the heart of his land. It had taken some time before the break-down, the acceptance of final defeat. Skirr Farm, a yeoman holding in his family during several centuries, had come on the market. Other farmers, selling up just after the war, had made good prices for their land; but with the repeal of the Corn Production Act land values had withered away, and with it had begun the decline of the old order of peasantry which had helped to put back into the land what had been taken out to feed the towns.

Hilary Maddison was driving east in his car, a 14 h.p. two-seater Wolseley painted a bright red. It was a fine day, but even the green solitudes of mid-Wales could not dispel unhappy thoughts about the future of the country, and the threat to his plans to complete the restoration of his estate should the Socialists get back into power and impose a capital levy. In his imagination he was driving through the growing desolation of blast furnaces and docks twenty miles or so south of the Black Mountains. This coastal area to him was more than ugly and squalid to look at: it was a hotbed of all that was opposed to the qualities which had made Britain a great nation. He could not forget the General Strike in May of that year. It had been called off, certainly, but only to postpone the final reckoning.

For the reality of the situation had to be brought home to the workers sooner or later: the inescapable fact that no one section of the community could be allowed to throw the productivity of the nation into chaos 'by holding a pistol to the head of the nation', as *The Daily Trident* had declared in its leading article. Had the General Strike in May run its full course it would have meant starvation, and worse, in the mining areas of Wales, Durham, and the North; but it would have saved a coming greater catastrophe.

The sooner agitators like Cook, Tillett, Bevin and others of their kidney taking orders direct from Moscow were shown up for what they were, the better it would be for the genuine working man.

Hilary had left the fishing village of Solva an hour after sunrise. Taking it easily, he arrived at the Chepstow ferry two hours before noon, with another sixty miles to go, just as one of the two paddle-boats was being warped to the little stone quay. The tide was nearly at the flood, making a pleasant prospect of pale blue water reflecting the sky; but he could not forget that the Severn estuary was everywhere foul with untreated sewage. Even so, by now he was less pessimistic; and leaning on the rail of the ferry boat as it crossed to the other shore, he looked forward to his arrival at Rookhurst in the early afternoon, where he hoped to hear good reports of the progress made by Phillip.

The fact was, this elderly man had centred all his hopes on his nephew. Phillip was, in part, an extension of his life, a compensation for a growing awareness of his own inner distress. He had bought Skirr Farm, to add it within a ring fence, when the inflated prices immediately after the war had gone down. The Fawley estate, with the woodlands, including the war-wreckage of Rookhurst Forest, consisted of a little over thirteen hundred acres. All this land, with the exception of Skirr Farm, had been sold by his father forty years before, under conditions which had led to the break-up of the family.

Later, his own family life had been broken. He had divorced an unfaithful wife, and disowned the two children by her previous marriage for whose education, the boy at Winchester and the girl at Eastbourne, he had provided, only to meet with, in his eyes, crass ingratitude from both. Neither had bothered to keep in touch with him—not so much as a postcard from either since the divorce, in which their mother had been proved to be the guilty party. There had been several men during the war, while he was away at sea, in service to his country; he had found out about one, the co-respondent in an undefended case. And for all that he knew, Phillip might have been one of her paramours, according to his sister Viccy, whose maid had seen Bee go into his bedroom when Phillip had stayed at the Hampshire home in the spring of 1915; only to leave, abruptly and without notice, very early on the morning following his arrival of the day before.

However, that was neither here nor there. If Phillip, his only nephew surviving from the war, showed himself capable of assuming responsibility as the future head of the family, he would in due course become tenant-for-life of the estate; and when his son or sons came of age, they would, if they proved themselves capable and of good character, become trustees and in time Billy, the heir, would become tenant-for-life in his turn.

For himself, Hilary, whose life had been spent first in a Glasgow shipping office and then on the high seas until he entered the Ministry of Shipping in the war, and incidentally made a small fortune in the buying and selling of tramp steamers, had no desire to play the squire. He had been driven by an idea to see his father's land back in the family, and thus, in part, to heal the despairing early memories of a father who had kicked over the traces and broken his mother's heart. Now the land was back in the family, the ambition of his life had been realised; but so far it had not yet given him any satisfaction.

Phillip saw the red car stop outside in the lane and ran down from his writing room. Nuncle was just opening the door to get out.

"Good afternoon, Phillip."

"Good afternoon, Uncle Hilary. How are you? Have you had a good journey?"

Hilary looked at Phillip's beard. He paused with his hand on the top of the door and said, "You can't go about looking like that, you know. That beard looks simply awful."

Phillip, as though complimented by this remark, waited a moment before saying, "May I take your bag? How are the trout in Wales?"

"Oh, local poachers have taken out most of Captain Williams' fish with a prawning net. He tried to stop them using a seine net for sewin at the mouth of his river, you see. How are the rainbows in the Longpond doin'?"

"I've seen several. They've grown a lot since they were put in. They like the deeper water at the bottom end, near the reeds."

"They're probably tryin' to get down with the stream to spawn," replied Hilary, as he squeezed himself out of the roadster. "Rainbows usually disappear in land-locked water, you know, after a year or two." There was a pause, then he said, "You must shave off that beard, you know."

"Oh."

"It doesn't become you."

"To tell the truth, I haven't had time to look. Where's your bag?"

"I can manage it, thanks. But be a good fellow and give me a hand with the wireless set."

At the back of the boot was the biggest loud-speaker Phillip had seen. "I say, that looks a magnificent job. The promenade concerts from 2LO are starting again. My little Cosmos crystal-valve set is very feeble, except late at night. How many valves has this?"

"Twelve. I can get America on the Welsh coast. I get New York sometimes very late at night at Bournemouth, but I don't anticipate it will pick up many foreign stations here, being so far inland. Well, Lucy, my dear. You look blooming."

He was about to kiss her when he heard Phillip's voice behind him saying, "Oh hell. Don't look up the lane, anyone. I'll take in the wireless set," and he staggered away with the cabinet.

Hilary turned to look up the lane and saw what was evidently a country gentleman approaching about two hundred yards away, walking with a shooting stick and a retriever on lead. He asked Lucy who he was.

"It's Major Crichel, I think."

"Why doesn't Phillip want to see him?"

"Oh, I don't really know, exactly. I think it's something to do with politics. He's the local Conservative chairman, I think."

Hilary went after his nephew. "Major Crichel has called. You must see him."

"But I don't want to have anything to do with politics. Anyway, I believe in socialism."

"Well, the sooner you learn sense the better. You've come to live in the country, so you must take your place in the normal life of a country gentleman. And politics apart, it's a matter of common courtesy to greet a guest, for whatever purpose he comes. You can't allow Lucy to stand there by herself. Come along."

They went out as Major Crichel raised his cloth cap. Lucy said, "How very good of you to come all this way, Major Crichel. You're just in time for tea! This is Captain Sir Hilary Maddison —Major Crichel."

After a few words Major Crichel excused himself, saying he had to be on his way, but might he include their two names on his list? Having made a tick against the names he enquired about the corn harvest and left.

Hilary approached his nephew on another course.

"I thought Crichel looked a thoroughly decent fellow. Why don't you like him?"

"He wouldn't let his wife read *The Constant Nymph*, which I lent her when she came to see us, but sent it back the next day by his gardener, with a terse note of thanks."

"That's a very slight reason for not wanting to see him, surely?"

"Just before I lent the book he asked me if he could count on my vote at the next general election."

"Well?"

"I told him that I felt I couldn't allow him to count on me, as I was unreliable politically."

"Why couldn't you say straight out what you meant?"

"I thought I had."

Hilary turned away impatiently. He faced his bearded nephew again. "What's all this nonsense about your being a socialist?"

"But mayn't I decide for myself at the polls, Nuncle? Probably I shan't vote at all in the next General Election."

"It's high time you learned sense. And don't call me by that awful name."

Lucy came in with the tea tray. The guest settled himself in the only armchair in the room—it had come from his old home— and read *The Morning Post*. Soon he was snorting about the unrest in the Durham coalfields.

"Here you are, Phillip. You ought to read Birkenhead's speech, and learn what your precious socialist agitators are responsible for—unsettling the men, so that the Geordies won't do an honest day's work." He looked round, "Hullo, where's he gone, Lucy?"

Phillip had crept quietly upstairs; he had heard what was said, and thought, Five thousand poor bloody Geordies lying out on July the First, in Sausage Valley. You're right, they hadn't done an honest day's work, the machine guns from Ovillers and the Glory Hole got them first. Then, not wishing to cross Nuncle further, he pretended to sneeze and returned downstairs after blowing his nose.

"I'm afraid there's a lot of doust, as the men call it, in the barley sheaves, Uncle. It gets in the nostrils."

After tea Hilary let down an aerial from his bedroom window, and pushed a portable copper earth into the flower-bed below. Having heard the 6 o'clock news, he disconnected the battery and said to Lucy, "I don't suppose you've had much chance of leaving the house while the harvest was on, why not drive with me over the downs, to Stonehenge? We'll take Uncle John with us. There'll just be room for Billy beside us."

Left alone, Phillip went up to his room, and tried to write, but his mind was crossed. He wondered where he could go. On the Norton to Stonehenge? No: he wasn't wanted—there had been plenty of room in the dickey seat. So he went to Colham, and sat in The Rising Sun, drinking beer and playing skittles with the landlord, a fish-poaching ruffian named 'Bosun' Tinker, whom he had found to be a kind man under his rough exterior. Once again he determined to leave the village more often, and mix in the world outside. After three pints of ale he rode home, and was putting the bike away when he heard the sudden blaring music of the loudspeaker, followed a few moments later by silence.

He stood in the sun, irresolute; then going through a side-door beside the neglected croquet lawn—both he and Lucy were waiting for a chance to restore and level the grown-out turf—he entered the parlour; and stopped abruptly.

Hilary was sitting in the armchair, doing his cross-word puzzle; while, held between his legs, was Billy. The child was striving to crawl away, heaving with red face which, turned in his father's direction, showed imminent tears of hopelessness. Phillip felt enervated; the sight recalled his own feelings of desperate weakness when his uncle used to hold him on the lawn at Epsom, chuckling at his puny efforts to escape.

"No!"

At the cry Hilary looked up. "What's the matter?"

"Shall I take Billy, if he's annoying you, Uncle?"

"Of course he's not annoyin' me. Billy and I are gettin' along famously, aren't we, you young rascal?"

"I rather fancy he wants to go to the lavatory."

Hilary uncrossed his legs. Phillip held out his arms, but the child gave him a mournful look before hiding his face on an arm and lying still on the hearth rug. Rusty the spaniel looked up, wagging his tail-stump, then crept to lie beside the child.

After supper Hilary lit two joss-sticks and stood them in a pot upon the chimney shelf. The ends fumed slowly; a pleasant scent spread into the room; bringing to Hilary an almost poignant memory of his early life in the Far East; and particularly of his first return home, just before the Old Queen's Jubilee, with souvenirs of travel, including lotus flowers (in paper) from the Feast of Homeless Ghosts, during the Seventh Moon. The lotus lanterns, each holding a tiny lighted taper, were launched upon the moonlit waters to guide lost souls to heaven. He had brought home a boxful, meaning to sail them on the Longpond, in the company of his parents, brothers and sisters: but he had found the estate sold, his mother forsaken by his father, and the old home in disintegration.

The shock of that homecoming was still active in memory. Hilary walked alone to the Longpond, to return and pour himself a stiff drink from one of the two bottles of the special malt whisky he had brought with him, and kept hidden in his portmanteau.

A beam, the trunk of a medium-sized oak shaped by the strokes of Elizabethan adzes, crossed the parlour of the farmhouse. On first seeing it, Phillip had spent a whole day in 'feeding' the wood with linseed oil. The beam gave a feeling of enduring strength, although its sap-wood was riddled by the death-watch beetle.

The walls of the farmhouse were thick, the new plaster smooth; but it had been distempered too soon, and after a few weeks had flaked here and there. The stone floors were liable to sweat; and were cold, even in summer, to the feet. Other defects became apparent. The bathroom, put in by a local builder, was too small. It had been part of a bedroom. The walls were of asbestos sheeting, a mere box. The bath, a second-hand affair of heavy enamelled iron and mahogany, had been carted from a Victorian country house which had been occupied by the military authorities during the war. The house had been bought by Hilary's agent and gutted for the panelling and fittings.

The bath was deep and it took most of the contents of the hot-water boiler to bring the water-level one-third up the sides. The flue of the boiler had been led into one of the wide, wood-burning chimneys, wherein the fumes of coke now wandered, to drift erratically with the wind. In the south-west gale the coke burned yellow-hot, causing the copper tank to rumble, while steam from the safety pipe bubbled through the cold-water tank in the attic. When the wind swept from the downs, eddying about the elm spinney to the east of the house, the fire went dull and sometimes out. It was not wise to think about preparing a bath without listening to the B.B.C. weather report. When the copper tank rumbled, look out! The water was liable to fizzle and spirt from the heavy brass tap, with its lever-like handle; again, when the N.E. blew, the boiler went sulky, according to Mrs. Rigg, who helped Lucy about the house. The water was tepid when one got in, to feel the cold iron under the soles of the bather's feet; the bather being Lucy, for Phillip always had a cold bath in the morning.

Even so, the cold tap was temperamental, like the hot-water boiler. When opened full-bore the water was liable to flood over the rim of the bath very quickly. It was stiff, to stop dripping; fortunately Billy could not turn it on.

Hilary, upon introducing them to the place the previous June, had explained that it must serve until markets improved, since the yield from his investment was already swallowed up by more urgent repairs to the estate.

He repeated this intention on the morning after his arrival. "I'm prepared to forgo, for three years, any return on my money, Phillip. I regard this farm as a capital investment for the future, which means your future, provided all goes well. To put everything in first-class order now would result in an inverted pyramid. The agricultural market won't stand capital improvements just now."

"What's an inverted pyramid, Nuncle?"

"Spending all one's capital at once, as Lucy's brothers have done in their so-called Works. And don't call me 'Nuncle'. I've told you before that I don't like it."

"Sorry. It slipped out. 'Nuncle' is the nickname of the king, or the lord, in some of Shakespeare's plays."

"Well, you're not Shakespeare. Now please pay attention. If we can hang on through this present slump—and, as I said, I'm prepared to—and you learn to do your job properly, you'll live to reap the benefit of what I am doin' for you. But put your heart into it, and chuck trying to write novels. Aunt Viccy tells me they're rotten."

"I agree. I wrote them. But what are we two against so many?"

This joke, in imitation of G.B. Shaw's reply to a solitary shout of 'Rotten!' from the gallery, after Shaw had held up his hand for silence following enthusiastic cheers and clapping at the first night of *Arms and the Man*, missed fire.

"Well, you yourself have told me that your books have sold only a few hundred copies all together, so why not regard this writing business as belonging to the past?"

"That's exactly where it does belong to, as a fact."

"Good. I'm glad you see the sense of it, Phillip. Now to get down to brass tacks. You will pay the half-yearly rent to the agent, Captain Arkell, at his office in Colham. My bank will continue paying sixty pounds a quarter into your account until next Midsummer, after which we shall be in a position to review the situation."

"Well, thanks very much, but I think I can manage without the allowance."

"If you'll kindly let me finish what I was going to say——"

"Sorry."

"There's Lucy to be considered, remember. After all, she comes of a good family, and it won't do to have her going about looking like a field woman. Also, you've got a position to keep up now. The Maddisons were here in the fourteenth century. That reminds me, I see you're wearing a signet ring with some sort of crest on it. Whose is it?"

"It's the Turney crest."

Hilary had his doubts about the so-called Turney crest. According to his brother Richard, old Turney was not entitled to a coat of arms.

"Well, it's your mother's family, and as such you're not entitled to wear it."

"It was my twenty-first birthday present during the war."

"Who's idea was that?"

"Mine."

"Why?"

"Many of the officers I knew had signet rings, so I thought I'd like one. Father said he didn't pay the armorial bearings tax, so I wasn't entitled to the Maddison one."

"Uncle John has several rings belonging to your grandfather, and I'll ask him to let you have one. It will cost a guinea a year, if you wear it. Anyway, such things are out of fashion since the war, with crested envelopes and writing papers. They belong to the last century. Now tell me, have you had many callers?"

"A few, all of them Lucy's relations."

"Of course you've returned the calls?"

"Lucy has."

"What sort of cards have you got?"

Phillip opened the drawer in the table, and showed the packets.

"H'm, Day & Co., Bond Street. What made you go there?"

"They were a wedding present from Lucy's father."

Soon after the marriage, when they had just settled into the farmhouse, a parcel had arrived with a London postmark. Inside were three packets of ivory pasteboard, one of large cards, and two of smaller cards, engraved and printed by hand from copper plates.

Mr. and Mrs. Philip Maddison, Skirr Farm, Rookhurst, Colham.

Mrs. Philip Maddison

Mr. Philip Maddison

"Why didn't you let Mr. Copleston know in time that your name was spelt with two 'l's?"

"I'd no idea he was going to have them done."

"Well, I suppose as they're a wedding present one shouldn't look a gift horse in the mouth."

"The gift horse was followed by a bill."

"What, from Lucy's father?"

"No, from Day & Co. However, it was a kind thought of Pa's. Perhaps he thought if it was left to me I might get some cheap ones done with fancy letters, all twirly, every other inch a gentleman, in fact."

"He's an old man, you must remember. Old men forget little details."

A butterfly wandered through the open window, and out again.

"Tell me, have you done any fly-fishin' since you've been here?"

"I really haven't had any time. Also, I find I'm more interested in watching birds and fish."

"You used to fish, I remember."

"Yes, before the war. But since then, somehow, I don't want to fish, or to shoot."

Hilary had bought, in March of that year, a thousand two-year fish from a hatchery on the Thames. Five hundred brown trout had been put in the brook, and the same number of rainbows in the Longpond, an artificial lake filled by the spring-head of the brook gushing out below the downs.

"If you don't fish, and it gets about that you don't, poachers will clear out the stock, you know. You should learn to fish with the dry fly, and get some trout for Lucy's breakfast. What sort of a rod have you?"

"I haven't any rod, Uncle."

"I'll let you have one of my split-canes. I did think of going out for the noon rise today, but it's rather late in the season, and the fish will be preparing to spawn. Have the papers arrived yet?"

"Yes, Uncle," said Lucy, coming into the room. "They didn't forget your *Post*."

"Ah, thank you, my dear."

He didn't feel like fishing; he was tired, his nephew always seemed to have that effect on him; so settling into the leather arm-chair, a whisky-and-soda to restore him, he read his paper, friend of many years, before switching on to hear the midday weather report.

The anti-cyclone was continuing; good, he would stay another day, and perhaps get Lucy to carry the net for him on the morrow. She must learn to fish, if Phillip was such an ass as not to enjoy some of the best dry-fly water in the county.

Hilary had always been an early riser. Phillip found him standing by the Ash pool soon after 7 a.m. the next morning. The cows had already been brought to suckle the calves in the yard, their tracks wandered through the red and blue dew-glints on the grass. Hilary was content; he had walked round the farm the previous evening and seen that all the corn-ricks were thatched. The sides had not been raked clean, they were decidedly ragged; but that would have been a waste of time, with all the thistles in the corn. He had decided that the arable must be ploughed quickly, and mustard sown. Mustard would hold the pheasants, he told Phillip.

"It's a catch crop, and provides good cover. Also it's useful as feed for a ewe-flock, before the tups are put in. A sort of aphro-disiac, if you know what that means."

"I've read about them, but thought they were a pornographic invention."

"Not at all. The most sought-after among African natives is powdered rhinoceros horn."

"I always thought that was a fourth-form joke. Have you had any luck?"

Hilary looked at his nephew sharply, suspecting sarcasm. "What do you mean?"

"Have you caught any fish?"

"Oh yes."

He showed Phillip a long, slim trout in his basket.

"It's a hen, I'm afraid. Pricked the tongue—no use putting a fish back when you see blood. Got it on a large badger. One of the native fish. No yellow spots, you notice, which the stew-fed hatchery fish retain until they assimilate a full gorge of summer flies."

"You know," Hilary went on, "I've an idea that we should regard this farm as in hand mainly for the sporting it provides, for the next year or two, anyway, until markets improve."

"That's what the foreman was telling me. He's afraid of losing his job, I think. Can you tell me why a Conservative Government doesn't conserve British farming?"

"Because we're mainly an industrialised nation, dependent on our export trade, Phillip. We also lend money abroad, in the form of loans. Part of the interest on those loans comes back in the form of foodstuffs——"

"Then a Conservative Government is a government mainly of usurers?"

"That's a catchpenny Labour phrase, Phillip. It doesn't alter the fact that Great Britain, despite the war, is still financially strong. We export the products of our heavy industries all over the world, and of course we require to be paid for what we sell. There's a great deal of British capital tied up in Argentine railways, for example. So we take a part of their agricultural products, in the form of maize, wheat, and frozen meat, which are sold in the City for sterling and so provide the interest to the stock- and bond-holders."

"Money comes first, then; in other words, the interests of the rich?"

"Money is merely a token of energy, properly applied. Now don't bother your head with matters you don't understand. And the sooner you get rid of all this socialistic clap-trap, and apply yourself to hard work here, on the land where you belong, the sooner you'll get your reward. By the way, how are Lucy's brothers doing with the Workshop?"

"Not too well at the moment, I'm afraid."

"D'you remember what I told you when I came over in the spring, just before your marriage to Lucy?"

"Yes, you told me, before they properly got started, that they were bound to fail. I'm afraid you were right, Uncle."

At the unexpected concordance, Hilary remained silent. Having dried the fly on amadou, he began to wave it gently to and fro, in order to spread the long fine hairs bound to the shank by yellow silk. Then, giving it a touch of odourless paraffin from a little bottle with a box-wood cap to the cork, through which a brush was fixed, he waved the fly again.

"That will make it float, with the hackles resting lightly on the surface. Now don't let me keep you from your work," he said, pulling out enamelled tapered line.

"Before I go, do you mind one more question—it's not about politics. Do you think the farm economy can afford a tractor?"

"You'll have to make do with what you've got for the time being, Phillip. I've looked at the range of tractors. They're no good. They're cumbersome things, and their weight pans the ground. D'you know what that means?"

"Yes. A few inches under the top-soil there's a hard pan of chalk which has been neutralised by carbonic acid brought down by the rains of centuries."

"Where did you get that from?"

"I've been reading *The Farmer & Stockbreeder* regularly."

"Good man. I agree that later on, bit by bit, we may have to break that pan, but it will be a gradual process."

"Well, I'll be off. I mustn't spoil your fishing."

"No great hurry. I think you should know that I've gone into the matter of tractors with Arkell fairly thoroughly. We've looked at the Fordson, the International Titan, and the Saunderson, and agree that they're all in the experimental stage. For one thing, their weight disposition is unsound. They tend to rear up under load. On this hilly land they'd be dangerous. You can't beat horses to plough with. The movement cracks and crumbles the furrows, if you notice. There's a lea-breaker still serviceable in the barn, by the way, you might try your hand with that."

"Yes, I'll do so, Uncle. Breakfast in an hour's time?"

"The fish won't rise any more after the sun gets over the hanger. I'll be leaving about ten, and if I can I want to take back a basket of trout for your Aunt Viccy."

Hilary returned with the solitary trout. After breakfast he said, "I'll be back for the shooting in late October or early November, according to how the leaves fall. I've discussed all matters concerning the farms with Arkell, and he'll pass it on to Hibbs, who will tell you. The arable will be scarified before ploughing, or cultivated as we say here, and mustard be broadcast. If sown soon, it should be well up by the time we shoot. After the shooting it can either be fed to ewes, as I've said, or ploughed in. I think, for next season, we'll probably bare-fallow all your upland fields, the marginal land. You'll have a small acreage for oats and feeding barley, and roots of course, for the stock. But Arkell will let you know all particulars through Hibbs, as I've said. Hibbs will continue to come round regularly as before to keep an eye on things."

"I see. By the way, if it isn't a secret matter, do your other farms pay? Or is that a delicate question?"

"Not in the least. I'm glad you take an interest. They're not showing a profit yet, and won't for three years. We may have to sell the ewe-flocks—this is confidential, mind—I don't want any trouble with the shepherd. With the sheep gone, the policy will be to grass down as much acreage as is practicable, for milk and stock rearing. That will reduce considerably the labour costs all round."

Phillip felt regret when the moment of departure came. He hadn't been much of a companion to poor old Nuncle. Hilary saw doubt and anxiety in his nephew's face, and when Phillip held on to his hand during the final shake, he said, "Don't worry too much about present difficulties. These depressions are inevitable, they come and go. Why not go out with Haylock sometimes, when he ferrets the rabbits? I've got a good little 28-bore you can have, in the gun-room at your Uncle John's. Ask him to let you have it. I used to shoot with it when I was a boy."

"Thanks very much, Uncle." He didn't tell him that he had a 12-bore of his own.

"'Twill help you get your eye in. Haylock will have to do a lot of ferretin', to keep the rabbits down, for I don't want village cads to feel that they have the run of the woods, which they will do if he has to ask some of them to do the shootin'. They take enough game with their lurcher dogs already, and also use sweep-nets for the partridges. What you shoot, of course, should be left for Haylock. Keepers feel that rabbits are their perquisites. He tells me he could trap five thousand every winter, if only I'd give him permission. But I've told him that this was a first-class partridge shoot in my father's time, and there's no reason why it shouldn't become so again. So go out after the rabbits with him. Have you got any friends you'd like to invite?"

"No, Uncle."

"Well, I expect you'll make friends in due course."

He turned to Lucy, and kissed her. "I've enjoyed my visit no end, and look forward to my return in the fall. I'll be bringing down half a dozen guests, but we'll all put up at the Royal Hotel in Shakesbury." He said to Phillip, "Try to get the ploughing done by the middle of September, broadcast the mustard, and you'll be surprised at the number of birds that will fly out when we put in the beaters."

"Yes, Uncle Hilary. By the way, I'm going to shave off my beard."

That evening Phillip re-entered the world of his inner self by which alone he could transmute the burdens of conscience and memory, a world which had been deserted since his marriage.

He began writing, at the point left off the previous June, with intense nervousness. First he looked at his notes; to reject them and wander round the dozen square yards of the room; returned to the low mahogany desk which had been his grandfather Turney's; left to rearrange the fire; returned to glance at the notes. So many pages: where to begin? He was reluctant to read them. They began with Lutra, her tame otter, going down the Maladine stream to the reedy mere, soon after her death . . . but all he could picture, with sighful despair, was a pale face within a coffin deep in the shaley soil of Malandine churchyard, the oak boards not yet rotted, so that she was waiting, waiting to escape from the cruel, restricting pressures of the earth, when she could forever be of ambient air, clear flowing water from moor and valley; rising again to be with clouds, to fall as rain into the tidal pulses of the sea, sharing the life of fish and shell, of rock and grain of sand. And thus to be with him, her pilgrim still held back from the elements. Lutra's wanderings were her wanderings, she was with Shelley, with Blake, and all the holy poets who knew that life was a Spirit.

It was no good: Lutra was too small, its spirit was alien. He must return to the battlefields, and lose himself 'in the silentness of duty'. Putting aside the bundle of manuscript, he took from a drawer a shilling hard-cover quarto book with ruled lines and began to write in a slow, tremulous hand.

At sunrise the next morning he was still at the desk; after a couple of hours' sleep on the couch under an army blanket he awoke with a feeling of happiness never known since waking of a

morning beside Barley, and went on with the narrative. Lucy, so
impersonal, almost remote, brought up sandwiches and a pot of
tea; he clasped her, with streaming eyes, but could not merge
into her spirit, she was apart. So on with the scenes in the autumn
of 1914, beyond another sunset and into the stars of night wheeling
slowly past the window. Towards dawn, at the hour of stand-to,
he opened the casement; the slight noise was a shock, lest machine-
gun fire open up; but the moment of fear passed; the stars were
brighter and clearer than any he had seen before. He felt a
strength in the breast, he was living again his true life. Then
suddenly weary, his eyes stinging, with the lids pressed hard together he groped a way to the couch and dropped asleep. When
he awoke Lucy and Billy were standing in a slant of red light
across the uneven oaken planks of the floor.
  "Have I been asleep all day?"
  "Yes, we didn't like to wake you."
  "Ni' ni' Dad," said Billy, smiling. "Ni' ni' room—ni' ni' fire—
oyl! oyl!"—this last a shout of glee as one of the white owls, which
roosted under the thatched roof, sailed across the yard opposite,
past the flint walls glowing with the light of the sinking sun.
  "I'll get you some food," Lucy said, after he had sluiced face
and arms in the deep bath. "Could you eat a plate of bacon and
mushrooms? How's the work going?"
  "Part One is finished. Hallowe'en, Messines Ridge. Enfer
Wood—the burning windmill—the Bavarians' band playing under
the rising moon—the withdrawal to Wulverghem—Menin Road
and Sanctuary Wood—Cranmer dead—the battle of Ypres broken
off in the November rains—'Bobs' death at St. Omer—the Brigade
marching back to Bailleul—Grenadiers, Coldstreamers, Camerons,
Black Watch, London Highlanders—less than four hundred all
told——" He stood on the uneven oak boards of the floor, a man
transfixed.

Chapter 2

IRON HORSES

Lobbett's having been marked out and the tops opened, the horseman then ploughed a furrow, Phillip walking beside the team
across the field to the headland. There the horses were turned, to

stop with the share in the new furrow. The horseman handed over
the stilts with their wooden handles, together with the two lines,
one attached to each of the outer ring-bits of the horses, to his
pupil. Then without a word he took the bridle of the near-side
horse and led it up the field, the off-side horse walking in the
furrow.

Phillip felt himself being drawn along, holding to the stilts for
balance; then quickly adjusting his weight he bore down upon
them, using the stilts as levers while watching the wave of earth
corkscrewing up and dropping over behind the breast of the
plough. It was a matter of keeping the unseen point—the share
—from dipping too deep. It was exhilarating; he got to the headland across the field as gulls began to arrive, one dropping a splash
on his coat sleeve. There stood the bailiff.

"Be you writin' your name?" he asked, pointing to the irregular
furrow.

Phillip had watched the headland being marked out all round
the field, parallel to the hedge and six paces from it; a boundary
within a boundary; but to establish the bailiff's prestige before
the horseman he asked, "Why do you have headlands, Ned?"

"To close yar work, sir."

"I think I begin to see what you mean. When all the up-and-
down ploughing's done, we enclose the 'work' by throwing the
furrows inwards, right up to the hedge, boxing in the ploughed
work?"

"You've a-got it."

"What good English you fellows speak. 'To close your work.'
Then, 'You've a-got it.' I feel I'll never be able to learn all there
is to be known about farming."

"Littles by littles," said the bailiff, going away. He came back
later to see how Phillip was getting on.

"Yar'll do," he said.

"Shall I take my osses away now, bailie?" asked the horseman.

"That's the idea, Jim. I'll show th' boss how to harness up
Donk and Daisy," referring to the two aged animals left in the
stable. "Come you with me," he said to Phillip. They walked
down the borstal to the premises. "Donk wor in th' Army," he
said, patting the neck of a long-eared mule.

"I had light-draught horses in my transport section in the
winter of nineteen-sixteen, Ned. Ancre Valley, Fifth Army.
Where were you, bailie?"

"'Appy Valley," wheezed the bailiff. "Cor, there wor' some mud thar, wasn't 'a, tho'."

"Then we went north to Ypres, to the Second Army. Were you at Third Ypres, Ned?"

"Aye."

"Moonrakers?"

"Aye."

The bailiff spoke no more: the war to him had meant an unwanted interval of misery, loneliness, endurance, and finally painful nauseating wounds which had made him feel a half-man ever afterwards, in a world which was gone-in.

"I'm looking forward to working with a donk again, Ned."

"Aye. They'm kind."

The bailiff was gentle towards the younger man's optimism. After a deep breath he made to lift off its peg a horse-collar for Donk. The leather was broken away in places from the stitches. Straw had burst from the torn flannel lining. He was not a tall man; he staggered after stretching up to the rows of pegs along the flint wall.

"Let me do it, bailie. Sit you down, you were up before I was. I'll harness Donk and Daisy. Traces—sails—we won't want the cruppers, will we—bridles, bits—where are the lines?"

The bailiff looked in a wooden oat bin. Then in the manger. Rats gnawed rope for the oil in it, the grease off a horse's coat or perhaps the salt of sweating; the carter had hidden his lines somewhere. Perhaps there wasn't another pair? The bailiff didn't know.

Phillip dashed away on the Norton to buy a new pair in Shakesbury. The bailiff was sitting on the same box, his face patient and thoughtful, when he returned.

"Yar bin quick, guv'nor," he said, approvingly.

"I want to get the ploo'n done bailie my dear. Then I want to get on with my writing."

"Us've only got th' old lea-breaker ploo, guv'nor."

They went into the barn, leaving the untied animals standing side by side in the stall. They were rising twenty years; long since the black beans in their teeth had been worn away. Both Donk and Daisy had known the glutinous grey mud of the winter Somme, one and sometimes nearly two feet in depth along the transport tracks. They had survived the yellow clays of Ypres, which had dragged the guts out of thousands during the exception-

ally wet and stormy summer of 1917. They were 'kind', in the
bailiff's laconic description: patient, enduring all things, brown-
eyed, gentle, gaunt, slow.

The lea-breaker had seen some years, too. How old was it?

"Mebbe sixty year, guv'nor—mebbe seventy—perhaps a
hun'ed. 'Tes a crab breast," touching the four-foot length of dark
wood, slightly curled like an opening sunflower petal. "Crab—
yar know—harn't yar ivver gathered up a capful o' crabs when
yar was a bwoy? 'Course yar did!" touching Phillip affectionately
on the sleeve of his jacket.

"Is the curve natural, or was it steamed, do you think?"

"Aw, natural. For stren'th, surely. Tes a master ploo, 'twull
bear up the vores (furrows) slowly-like, without crackin'n. Tes
what us yurrabout calls a lea-breaker."

"I suppose this sort of plough was originally used on the
downs?"

"Could'a."

"Why mustn't the furrows on a lea be cracked?"

"Flag'll grow through." Flag was grass; lea was pasture.
Phillip felt more confident.

The bailiff pulled out an old plough-skid on wheels: a rusty
iron trolley. Wobbling and precarious, the lea-breaker was taken
up the borstal behind the cranky team, and through the gap by
the broken gate into Lobbett's.

"I'll start yar off, guv'nor."

The lea-breaker had a long sloping iron share; the slightly
curved wooden breast raised the furrow gradually until it curled
over on its face. All forward movement was critical; one must
stare intently lest the iron share work out of the ground.

"Mind 'a don't score."

The bailiff was now almost enthusiastic, from a feeling that the
young fellow was a good man; yet he was sad under the feeling;
for what was Lobbett's but rubbish, the heart in the land gone?
You couldn't farm this land without a ewe-flock. This was bad
land, it would break any farmer.

Behind the return furrow Phillip felt that he knew what to do:
it was a question of an eye for steering straight, of balance to
counter the pulls upon the swingle-trees with the pressure of the
earth on the share. He was a ploughman! Behind him now were
screams as black-headed gulls lit on the new slice to seize worms,
beetles, and once a dazed mouse exposed to sudden day.

The mare began to sweat; he rested his team; and went on, furrow after furrow, not very even or straight furrows, not all the stubble put under—"writing his name" across the field, as the bailiff had declared. When Donk had had enough, he stood still. Nothing would make him go on until he wanted to. One drooped ear was a sign of weariness. Phillip stood by his head, arm on mule's neck, thinking of how often he had seen, in the mud, an ear go down; and when the donk's second ear went down it too went down in the mud and died.

Later in the morning John walked up with Lucy to see how he was getting on. He pointed with his stick at a small and rusty, very narrow iron object which had been turned up by the plough.

"That looks like the off-side half of a bullock's shoe, Phillip. We used to plough with bullocks not so long ago. Each beast required eight shoes, for the cloven hoofs. The horn is harder than that of a horse's foot, and holds the clenched nails."

The iron U, oxidised in pale loam, resembled one half of the brown mark on a partridge's breast. Bullock foot, two sections small and narrow: slow and delicate-stepping neat-stock. He must remember the details.

"I wonder if French peasants ploughed with oxen on the loam of the Somme uplands before the war, Uncle John?"

The old man looked at his nephew. The war lives in him, he thought; everything comes back to the war with Phillip.

"Would it be cheaper to plough with oxen now, Uncle John?"

"You might like to try. I seem to remember that a pair of ox-bows, by which the wooden beam plough used to be drawn, are still hanging on the wall of the Corn Barn, Phillip. There's also a 'drashel', or flail, with an ox-horn joint to allow for two-way movement, what I think today would be called a universal joint."

"Yes, I was looking at it with Ned. It's a pity that the holly-wood striker is eaten by the death-watch beetle."

The round holly-wood stave, white under its grime, was pitted with holes like a battlefield, Phillip thought, as he went on working into the dull afternoon. Then suddenly the plough went mutinous, skittering along the stubble; the iron share had dropped off. The front of the wooden breast was broken. He took his tired team back to the stables, unharnessed and watered them ready for the carter to feed when he came back. It was beginning to rain. He welcomed this decision of the sky, for now he might, without burden of conscience, write the introduction to his war book.

He began, as always, tremulously.

> The church in the peaceful village where I live has a tower of dressed flint, above which is a belfry. A clock with gilt hands and Roman numerals shines in the southern wall. It was built into the tower seven years ago as a memorial to the men who fell in the Great War. Their names are written in the porch below, on an illuminated scroll protected by glass from the damp winds of this south-western downland country.
>
> Sometimes, when the ringers go up into the room where hang the ropes with the coloured sallies, I go with them, climbing on up the worn stone steps of the dim spiral stairway, past the ringing chamber, to the bells. The ropes and wheels begin to creak; the bells begin to swing, and the tower trembles. Then with a dinning crash the metal tongues smite the deep bronze mouths, and an immense torrent of sound pours out of the narrow doorway.

He broke off and wandered about the room. Then sitting down again, while sweat dripped from an arm-pit, he took up the pen.

> The great sound sweeps other thought away into the air, and the earth fades; the powerful wraith of those four years enters into me, and the torrent becomes the light and clangour of massed guns assaulting heaven——

There was a knock on the door. The nib broke into the paper with the shock.

Lucy came into the room.

"Uncle John thought you might like to see this," she said, putting down a copy of *The Colham & District Times*. Marked with a cross was an advertisement headed in large type JOHNSON'S IRON HORSES. "Am I interrupting you?"

"No, Lucy," he replied, getting up.

"Uncle John says that they are two traction engines which work a six-furrow digger plough by hauling it on a cable across the field. He thought you might like to know that his father used to employ them for deep-ploughing, to help to weather and sweeten the raw soil brought up. Then they spread guano in the early spring. The Iron Horses used to do splendid work then, but he can't say much about them now, but it's the same family firm of contractors."

"You remember it all pretty well, don't you?"

"I wrote it down, as I didn't want to get anything wrong."

"Well done, Lucy. I'll telephone them at once."

He waited for the Colham number and a burring voice said it would ask feyther when the tackle would be available. He waited. After two minutes he said, "Is anyone there?" No reply. "Is anyone there?" he repeated. When there was no response to louder and louder repetitions he yelled in exasperation, "ARE YOU THERE, IRON HORSES?" in a voice that could be heard all over the house.

"'Ullo 'ullo," replied the burring voice. "I can 'ear 'ee, no need vor shout like that. You ban't crow-starvin', my dear."

"I'm sorry, I thought the line might be broken. Is that Mr. Johnson?"

"Aye. Who be 'ut? Aw aye, I knaws th' name. Zo you'm varming Frank Temperley's land, be 'ee? Wull wull. Aw, I can't tell 'ee exactly. Sir Roland's agent want me vor ploo at his place, sometime, and to thresh a number of carn ricks. When do 'ee want vor ploo?"

"As soon as possible. When do you think you can make a start, Mr. Johnson? Can you give me a date?"

"Aw, tidden possible vor zay exactly, y'knaw."

There followed a halting two minutes. Then the son came on the other end and said that Feyther wanted to know when the tackle was required.

"As soon as possible."

"Aw, I can't exactly zay about that."

"Why can't you come here, if you haven't a definite date to be elsewhere?"

"Wull, us can't afford to offend a big man, can us?"

When there was no reply, the voice asked how many acres were to be done.

"About ninety."

There followed a whispered colloquy between son and father. Then the son said, "Feyther says he might come, but only for cash on the nail. 'Tes the coal strike, zur, us nivver knaws exactly where us be nowadays for steam coal. And the merchant demands cash from us."

"It's rather urgent, Mr. Johnson."

"'Old on a minute, wull 'ee?"

He waited, making himself go limp, for patience. At last footfalls; bumps of the receiver being picked up.

"Us'll come soon as us can, zur."

"When will that be?"

"Aw, I can't exactly zay, but us'll do our best."

"Thank you, Mr. Johnson. I'll stand by to show you the way."

"Aw, us knaws the way up th' old borstal, zur."

Equinoctial gales flung away the first yellow leaves of the elms around the churchyard, peewits in close flock passed over the downs. Phillip sat by his cousin Willie's grave, before going up the church tower during the practice ring on Thursday night. He took pen and paper with him.

I take the weight and strength of the barrage, and grow mighty with it, until it becomes but a seam of sound nicked with flashes, and puny in space and time controlled by the vaster roar of stars in their age-long travail through elemental space. I see all life created by those flaming suns of the night, and out of life arises a radiance, wan and phantasmal and pure, the light of Kristos.

The wraith of the War, glimmering with this inner vision, bears me to the wide and shattered country of the Somme, to every broken wood and trench and sunken lane; among the broad, straggling belts of rusty wire smashed and twisted in the chalky loam; while the ruddy clouds of brick-dust hang over the shelled villages by day, and at night the eastern horizon roars and bubbles with light.

One morning he was up on the tower, with its flat leaden roof scored by initials, hearts pierced by arrows, and outlines of boots, when he saw over the parapet a white trail of smoke above the thatched cottages to the west. The Iron Horses were coming. He hurried down the steep stone steps within the cold tower, to greet them. Boys followed as the traction engines dragged their slow puffs up the borstal. The broken gate was lifted off its remaining hook, and one of the engines settled against its spades just inside the hedge. The other puffed away across the stubble drawing a trailer upon which was chained an immense plough, consisting of two sets of six staggered steel breasts, one set either side of the beam. The engines weighed twenty tons apiece. Across the field they were connected by a steel-wire cable with a breaking strain of fifty tons, he learned from the driver of the near engine. Five men in all came with the tackle. Beside the two drivers were two men to manipulate the ploughs, while the fifth man was in charge of a smaller engine to bring steam coal from the railway Halt, and water from the brook in a heavy iron tank on four wheels.

He began to understand some of the reasons for the delay: the steam coal had to be specially ordered at the Halt, a truck of ten tons. Each working day of nine hours required a ton of coal and a thousand gallons of water. The rate of ploughing was about an acre and a half per hour: fourteen acres a day. Ninety acres of stubble might be done in a week, providing the weather held. Then there was the Big Wheatfield of hay aftermath, if he could get out the muck from the bullock yard and get it spread in time.

The work could be done, said the younger Johnson, in a week, but it would mean overtime at the rate of time and a half. Phillip could not face the idea of asking what it would cost.

Mr. Johnson asked how deep he wanted the field to be ploughed.

"Well—let me think. We want to get rid of the thistles, and also to break the hard pan, while we're about it."

Phillip was told it would mean turning up a lot of chalk.

"Won't that be good? I mean, the hard pan is acid, according to our samples of soil."

"Aye, us can do that. 'Twill take a bit longer. Us'll raise the ploos if they vetch up too much chalk."

The two teams of horses were put on muck-carting, and the bailiff hired some out-of-works to spread the heaps on the Big Wheatfield.

The work was going well; he felt a sense of completeness. It was exhilarating to watch the six ploughs below their shining fellows quivering as though eager to dig into the ground on the return journey, to burst up the weedy litter of the field. So silently, too, below his eyes, as he sat with the two men on a plank tied to the superstructure of the plough. The soil came up in six waves almost silently, yet sometimes whispering as the shares were drawn through layers of gravel, to be followed by a grating changing to a crackle as broken flints came up and tumbled over, to lie upon six fresh new furrows braiding with new hope the poverty of the thin stubble. He wondered how he could re-create the scene in words: the hissing and chuffing of the engine, with its smoothly whirring flywheel to which was attached a drum: the noises of the steel cable in tension, sometimes holding a *whippering* quarrel with the drum which gathered its protecting coils so tightly.

The two men riding with him got off, and pulled down the shares for the return journey; the driver pulled his lever, the flywheel ran backwards, releasing the cable. He walked back beside the plough, sometimes breaking into a run, since the pace of ploughing was half as fast as a quick walk. It was wonderful to feel that he was on top of the work. He walked down to the Big Wheatfield, which adjoined the Shakesbury road, feeling freedom that the work there was being done well; returned up the borstal to the Iron Horses, eating his sandwiches under the hedge beside a fire; remaining out of doors until the engine fires were damped down with slack for the night, then down the borstal to the lights of the farmhouse in the vale below, a contented man, to sleep deeply, to awaken with keen anticipation.

"How lovely," exclaimed Lucy, standing by the beech hanger one morning towards the end of the week with Uncle John and Phillip. Field below field revealed a unity, each transformed from its shabby littleness to the aspect of a cloth woven of many autumnal hues, with white and near-white predominating. He led them over the furrows, pointing out here a patch of pale brown loam pied by broken flints and streaked with yellow clay; there an area of fawn sand ending in a saucer-like bowl, once a dew-pond when the land had been pasture before the war. Then the dewpond had been but a hollow overgrown with reeds and surrounded by thorns: a dumping place for dead animals. Now the deep plough had torn up the clay fretted by layers of wheat straw and streaked with a black compost amidst the bones of sheep and bullocks, fractured and decayed, breaking down into lime and phosphate to feed once more the thin mother-soil.

"The deep ploughing will bring in air and light, you see. This soil was enfeebled—sick. I used to feel when I was walking here that it was crying for help."

She was drawn to him by his strange expression, and moved to take his hand, but he preferred to walk back alone.

"He's been writing rather late at night," she explained to Uncle John.

"Ah." He had seen a look of his dead son on Phillip's face. He was disturbed; but concealed his apprehension.

"It looks to me to be a capital job of work, Lucy."

They followed down the borstal. Only the ragged hedges remained of the former aspect of poverty; but to Lucy they were

beautiful with their grey of traveller's joy, clusters of black-
berries among the red haws of the thorns and the brighter ver-
milion hips of the dog-rose. To John there was pleasure in the
sight of a covey of partridges flying over to the ploughed work,
not because he was a shooting man, he had long given that up,
but partridges brought the land alive again.

Outside the farmhouse stood a horse and trap. An aged man
sat beside the driver's seat, his son waited in the lane. In the
aged man's hand was a bill. He wore broadcloth, with a hard
square hat above a fringe of white whiskers surrounding an otherwise shaven face.

Mr. Johnson had a long memory, unspoiled by any fiddle-
faddle connected with the arts. His mind was the land, seen from
an agricultural implement dealer's world. The name Maddison
meant to him money lost when he had had to accept, when
Phillip's grandfather had died towards the end of the last century,
10/- in the £ for steam ploughing, and threshing. Now he
wanted his bill settled.

Phillip looked at the bill. Ninety pounds! It was a shock.
With horses it was reckoned that the cost per acre was 5/-. The
son spoke.

"Can you let feyther hev your cheque for fifty p'un', sir? Us'v
got thik coal bill vor meet, and then there be the men's wages——"

"I'm awfully sorry, Mr. Johnson, but a cheque I'm expecting
from London hasn't arrived yet. Can you wait until Saturday?
It ought to be here by then."

"How about fifty pun now, sir? Otherwise feyther will hev to
take thik tackle to once."

Several farmers had gone bankrupt in the district that Michaelmas, and Mr. Johnson was much worried by bad debts.

"Yew promised cash, zur."

"I ought to have inquired about the cost. However, you'll be
paid all right. I'll telephone tomorrow to my agent in London,
as soon as he gets to his office, Mr. Johnson."

There was the advance of £25 due for the Donkin novel.

Anders said that he was about to write to him to say that
Hollins didn't want to see the novel, since they were not proposing to take up the option. Had he done anything more on
The Water Wanderer? "That's the book that will sell, you
know."

Phillip telephoned Mr. Johnson. The contractor replied that
he was sorry, but he would have to take his tackle away, and he
couldn't do any more ploughing without something on account.

"Why not ask the Boys," said Lucy. "Shall I ring up Tim?"

"No, please don't. I simply couldn't ask them for money now
they're hard up themselves."

"But you helped Pa by giving him a cheque for the rates,
remember?"

Mr. Copleston had written a brief letter to Phillip asking for
£15/7/6, beginning, 'Needs must when the devil drives', and
Phillip had sent the amount by return.

"Why not? Pa didn't hesitate to ask you." She looked out of
the window. "They're taking the tackle away." There was a
plume of steam by the row of elms.

"Didn't even wait to hear about my telephone call. Did you
give the wages to the bailiff last night? I must call at the bank
and see what I have got in my account. Precious little I'm afraid.
What a fool I was not to find out the cost of that ploughing before-
hand. I thought it would be about eight bob an acre. Well, I'm
off into Shakesbury, and then on to see the Boys."

Billy had been listening to this conversation. He had not understood much of it, but had felt the anxiety in his father's voice.
The trundle of the traction engines came nearer.

"Iron Horsey goin', Dad." Billy thought they were his father's
engines, and grieved.

"Yes, how right you are. Well, Lucy, I'll be going now."

"Daddy come back?" said Billy, smitten with fear.

"Of course, darling." How anxious he was whenever Phillip
went away.

The Works were open, but silent. Ernest and Fiennes had gone
to look at an aeroplane which had landed under the slopes of
Whitesheet hill, and broken its air-screw; Tim was with Pansy,
'his young woman', said Pa, who offered him a bowl of Cox's
apples. Phillip took one and sat down.

After awhile Pa looked up and said briskly, with a kindly look,
"Anything particular brings you here? All well at home, I hope?"

"Oh yes, sir. As a matter of fact I wondered if you would care
to shoot with us in a month's time? I don't shoot, so you are
welcome to my place. My uncle is coming and it will be partridge
driving. It's the first shoot this season."

"They usually walk 'em up for the first shoot, I fancy. However, you know your business best. Unfortunately my legs won't
stand such walking nowadays, thank 'ee all the same. My shooting
days are over. But give your Uncle my thanks for the invitation,
won't 'ee?"

He had finished the apple, eating it to the stalk, when Ernest
and Fiennes walked in. Fiennes said, "Hullo, you here?" Ernest
said nothing as they sat down, looking tired. Phillip asked Fiennes
if Tim was likely to be in soon.

"Tim? I've no idea."

The bell for the petrol pump rang outside. All sat still. After
awhile Ernest muttered, "Bother."

"Why does anyone want to come here on a Saturday?" said
Fiennes. "Let them ring."

The bell rang again. "I may as well go and see what's wanted,"
Phillip offered.

Ernest murmured something; Fiennes went on with his reading.

Phillip went out and saw 'Mister' sitting astride his pre-war
worn-out 2-stroke motorbike known as the Onion. He recalled
that 'Mister' had borrowed some cash from him once: dare he
ask for it back? It was only £10, but that was something.

"Well, well, well," said the thin asthmatic voice. "If it isn't
the very man I wanted to see. I was on the point of coming over
to your place, to call on you and leave cards, don't you know.
How's Lucy these days?"

"Oh, everything is all right, 'Mister'."

Had he come over to borrow more money from the Boys? Well,
he wouldn't be able to tap *him*. There was only £7 odd in the
bank.

"Who's at home, anyone?"

"Pa, Ernest, and Fiennes. I really came over to see Tim."

"You've heard the news, I suppose?"

"What news?"

"Why, about the Works. Haven't you heard? The bank has
told the Boys that it won't meet any more cheques. And creditors
are pressing, I fancy. Among other things, it's a question of a
judgment summons having been ignored. And that's no joke, I
can tell you."

"What's a judgment summons?"

"Well, a creditor has got a judgment against them, and if the
money isn't paid into court within a stipulated time, the question

of contempt arises. Then the bailiffs are put in. If they come
here, they'll take possession for a knock-down sale of all this
machinery." He pointed at the Works, which had been built
and equipped earlier that year.

"How much is the sum required?"

"About eighty pounds, I think."

"Can't we rake round and find eighty pounds?" said Phillip.
He was thinking of 'Mister' paying back what he had borrowed
from the Boys, from time to time.

"The trouble is, old chap, I haven't a bean to bless my name
with. It's all tied up with trustees. In fact, I owe the Boys some
money, with no prospect of paying it back just yet, otherwise I
would."

"I've got only seven quid in the bank."

"The trouble is, they've no idea of business. Some of that new
machinery in the Works isn't paid for. From what I can gather
they lost a couple of hundred pounds on the Gasworks contract,
putting on that roof. Well, I must be off, I suppose." 'Mister'
sighed. "I suppose you can't come to supper? It's dashed dull at
home these days."

"Many thanks, 'Mister', but I must get back."

"When are you and Lucy coming to stay? Oh, before I forget,
the magneto of this beastly Onion has gone wrong again. Before
you go, ask Ernest to come over and have a look at it, will you?
Tell him to come to dinner tonight, will you? Now, be a good
fellow and let me have a gallon of petrol. I would have done it
myself, but the beastly pump's locked for some reason. The key
is in the office, I expect. They usually keep it on the top of the
till."

He found the office door locked and got in at the window facing
the railway cutting. The till was open and empty, the key lying
on top.

"Shall I book it, 'Mister'?"

The old man hesitated; then said, "Oh yes, you might as well,
I suppose, old chap. Now be a good fellow and shove me off,
will you? This beastly asthma always comes back in the autumn,
dash it."

When Lucy heard about the Boys' troubles she thought to ask
Uncle John's advice when she took Billy there to tea, as was the
Sunday custom, while Phillip stayed at home and tried to write.

Perhaps she could sell her share of the marriage settlement. Uncle John had been a barrister, and would know about such things.

"The Boys have had their share, I think about a thousand pounds each. I'd like to sell, well, some of mine, anyway."

"For an agricultural speculation, Lucy?"

"Well, partly," she answered, blushing. It had not occurred to her that Phillip did not want Hilary to know about the Iron Horses.

"Let me share in it, Lucy." He went on, "After all, it's a job well done. The weathering will do good to the soil. In the spring a scattering of what they call 'artificials' before drilling lucerne, or sanfoin—lucerne perhaps on the drier fields, since it puts down deep roots—with ryegrass and clover should result in sound grazing. That is what Hilary is after: when he was here last his idea was that all the farms should turn over to stock, and so the deep ploughings, which could not have been done with horses, are just the thing. With balanced grazing I am sure the land will be brought back into heart. Now with your permission, I'll take care of Johnson's account. Be sure that I will not mention to Phillip that you have been here to talk about it. Before you spoke of it, I had intended to propose to Phillip that he allow me to regard it as an investment for the future. After all, what little I have, beyond my annuity, will eventually come to Phillip. I'll telephone Johnson first thing tomorrow and ask him to bring back the Iron Horses, so that the Big Wheatfield can be drilled before the shoot."

"Iron Horsey come back?" exclaimed Billy, happily. "Daddy come back too, Mummy?"

"Of course, darling." Poor Billy, did he miss his real mother, without knowing it? She had heard that a breast-fed baby was usually more contented than one fed only on the bottle.

And everywhere in these desolate places I see the faces and figures of enslaved men, the marching columns pearl-hued with chalky dust on the sweat of their heavy drab clothes; files of carrying parties laden and staggering in the flickering gunfire; the waves of assaulting troops lying silent and pale in the jumping-off trenches.

Again I crouch with them while the steel glacier rushing by just overhead scrapes away every syllable, every fragment of a message bawled into my ear; while my mind begins to stare fixedly into the bitter dark of imminent death, and my limbs tremble and stiffen as in an icicle; while the sand-bag parapet above the rim of my helmet spurts and lashes with machine-gun bullets. The sky of that morning of July the First is an uncaring blue which cannot help us; I meet it the instant I climb up the trench ladder, to see in the flame and the rolling smoke men arising on both sides of me and I go forward with them, and the moment is prolonged as an ordinary moment held within a calm glassy delirium wherein some seem to pause and with slowly bowed heads sink carefully to their knees and roll slowly over and lie still all in one extended motion. Others fall with rifles flung forward, or stop abruptly, to hesitate before turning in a sort of spin before dropping down in a heap to lie still. Others roll and roll, and scream and grip my legs in uttermost fear, and I have to struggle to break away, while the dust and earth on my tunic changes from grey to red.

And when I am hit and lying in a shell-hole others go on with aching feet, up and down across ground like a huge ruined honeycomb, and the wave melts away, and the second wave comes up and also melts away, and then the third wave merges into the ruins of the first and second, and after a while the fourth blunders into the remnants of the others, and they begin to run forward to catch up with the barrage, in bunches, anyhow, every bit of the months of drill and rehearsal forgotten, for who could have imagined that the Big Push was going to be this?

They come to wire that is uncut, and beyond they see grey coal-scuttle helmets bobbing about, and the vapour of over-heated machine-guns wafting away in the fountainous black smoke of howitzer shells; and the loud cracking of machine-guns changes to a screeching as of steam blown off by a hundred engines; and soon no one is left standing.

An hour later our guns are 'back on the first objective', and Kitchener's 'First Hundred Thousand', with all their hopes and beliefs, have found their graves on those northern slopes of the Somme.

Phillip went over the next morning to see how he could help the Boys in their troubles. He found them lounging in the office. One waste-paper basket, stuffed with catalogues, lay on its side on the floor, half its contents spilled.

"I wonder if you will allow me to help you get all this in order."

The other basket contained envelopes and letters as though dropped into it without having been read.

"I don't care what you do," replied Fiennes, who had heard Pa, on more than one occasion, say that Phillip ought to mind his own business, and not interfere with affairs that did not concern him.

There was a mess of cigarette stubs trodden out on the new wooden floor; a scatter of paper files on the shelves. The till was open; dust on the typewriter. Several balls of white string lying about, with sheets of unused brown paper of the finest quality trodden and crumpled on the floor amidst the general disorder of the place. Ernest, the eldest, continued to touch a spider's web in a corner of the window, gently twirling a piece of string between finger and thumb, while intently watching to see if the spider would dash out to seize it. It was an old web, littered with the shucks of bluebottles and the torn wings of moths.

"The fact is, we have no more damned money," said Fiennes.

"And we don't know how to tell the men," said Tim, the youngest.

Phillip pointed at a folded blue form lying on top of the waste-paper basket.

"What's that? The judgment summons?"

"Oh no," said Tim. "That's a new one."

"May I see it?"

"Rather, anything you like," exclaimed Tim, moving forward to pick it up.

"And there are more summonses in the basket?"

"We didn't know what to do about it, so there seemed no reason to keep them," said Fiennes.

"As a matter of fact, we've talked the matter over, and on going deeply into the matter, find we are in a bit of a mess," said Tim.

"I see."

"It's extremely decent of you to come over," Tim went on. "Lucy telephoned to say you were coming. Really, we don't like bothering you with all this."

"Well, of course I'll help you all I can, but it will mean drastic alterations, I'm afraid."

"We're ready for anything, absolutely anything, but we don't know what to do. Also, we don't want Pa to be upset. It's his seventy-fourth birthday soon."

"Can he do anything?"

"I don't think so." Ernest spoke slowly and carefully. He had ceased to play with the bit of string. The spider was sulking down its tunnel.

"Then what does anyone suggest?"

"I don't see that we can do a damn thing!" exclaimed Fiennes, lighting another cigarette. "As far as I'm concerned the sooner the beastly thing is over, the better. I'll go back to sea again."

"But isn't the shipping depression still bad? Can you get a job as wireless operator, do you think?"

"I can work as a stoker. I don't care a damn."

The telephone bell rang on the shelf behind him. He took off the receiver and slid it away. "No point in answering the damned thing."

"Well, you know, it may be from 'Mister'," said Tim.

It was from 'Mister'. His idea was that the Onion should be decarbonised. The engine had done twelve hundred miles, he said, and he fancied the portes wanted decoking, and the rings clearing. It hadn't the compression it had had. When Ernest came over to dinner, would he bring the requisite tools?

"Bother, I don't want to go," muttered Ernest.

"Ernest is a bit busy," explained Tim. He listened. "Well, we're all a bit busy just at the moment, 'Mister'. Yes, I'll give him your message. Hold on a moment."

Phillip said, "Tell him that things here for a few days are going to be fairly busy. The Onion will keep, won't it?" Tim repeated this, and put down the receiver.

"Leave the damned thing off," said Fiennes. " 'Mister' and his Onion are bores."

"I think the first thing to do is to get out a column of what bills, including judgment summonses, are owing."

"A good idea," breathed Tim. "We'll try to get it done by tomorrow, Phil." He avoided looking at Fiennes, who was in charge of the office.

"Why not now?"

"Well yes, I suppose it could be done now, since you come to mention it."

Fiennes made no move. At length Phillip said, with emphasised politeness, "Do you mind if we examine the office records in your waste-paper baskets, Fiennes?"

"You can do what you like as far as I'm concerned," replied Fiennes, getting up to leave. Soon afterwards Ernest, humming tunelessly, moved away to the open door.

"We don't need these entered into the books, Tim," said Phillip, picking out apple cores and cigarette packets. "Got a pencil?"

"Pencil? Pencil. Now where did I see a pencil? Ah, Pa borrowed it for his cross-word puzzle. I won't be long." Tim hurried away to do his bit to help his hero Phillip.

The hero put the telephone receiver on the rest. Shortly after

Tim returned the bell rang. The Clerk to the Magistrates' Court inquired in the matter of the fee for stay-of-execution. He had rung up twice before, he said, but the line was engaged. He said the entry by the bailiffs could be delayed forty-eight hours by the promised payment of a fee of £2 which must be paid by six o'clock. Phillip said he would go to his office at once.

"By Jove, I forgot," exclaimed Tim, seeing him off. "I told the bank I'd take a cheque in. It was for that beastly Dynawurker vacuum cleaner I sold Colonel De'Ath, but Mrs. De'Ath refused to take delivery of it, when I called this morning."

"Did you or didn't you sell it?"

"I thought we had."

"Who is we?"

"A commercial traveller who called. He offered to take me in his car, to give a demonstration, and asked me if I had any friends who might be interested. So we went to the De'Ath's. The traveller offered to leave it with them, saying there was absolutely no obligation to buy."

"And did you leave it?"

"No, I was coming to that. Outside he said we'd really made a sale, and advised me to buy a machine from him at trade price, and have it sent direct to the De'Ath's."

"So he really sold the thing to you?"

Tim laughed dryly. "Well, now I come to think of it, I suppose he did, in a way."

"I'd better come and help you, I think, Tim."

"How frightfully decent of you, my dear Phil. We'll do anything you say. It's a simply terrific load off my mind."

"Will you ask Ernest and Fiennes if they agree? If so, I'll want to know how much you owe; how much you are owed; what contracts you have in hand; how many workmen you employ."

"I can tell you the answer to the last query now, Phil. There's the carpenter, the smith, his son the apprentice, and ourselves."

They returned to the office.

"What are the wages? What do the men do?"

"Very little nowadays, I'm afraid, there simply isn't any work for them."

"No contracts?"

"None."

"Then they must be given a week's notice."

"I don't see how we can do that," objected Fiennes. "We can't just turn them off like that."

"Then you'll pay them out of your own pocket?"

When there was no reply he said, "Do you or don't you want me as your temporary honorary manager?"

Fiennes shrugged his shoulders. Ernest seemed deep in thought. "We want you to be," said Tim.

"All right. Now I must return to my farm. I had a bit of a financial crisis, too, but it's cleared up, thank God. I'll settle the fee for the stay of execution. There must not be a knock-down sale of this machinery, which will happen if the bailiffs come in. I may be able to come over later on in the day. Au revoir, and don't forget the figures, Tim. And telephone the bank when they open, find out the amount of the overdraft, and don't issue any more cheques. Cheerho—see you soon!"

On his way through Shakesbury he called at the Clerk's office to pay a penalty of £2, learning with dismay that it would only cover that day. "There's another matter just arisen, sir, a writ has been issued against the Copleston Brothers by Bristol Foundries, Ltd., for sixty pounds."

"May I use your telephone?"

He got on to the Works. "I'll be over in a couple of hours or so, Fiennes."

"Right. You might collect the papers at Roper's bookshop, and enquire if the *Encyclopædia Britannica* has come."

"Who wants it, Fiennes? It'll cost a bit, won't it?"

"I don't know. Pa wants it."

"What about paying for it?"

"Oh, that doesn't matter, it goes on the bill. Hold on. Tim wants a word with you."

"I'm most frightfully sorry, but Miss Calmady was asking about the groceries," explained Tim diffidently. "She says they weren't sent out, as usual, last Monday."

"Who is Miss Calmady?"

"A new cook we have engaged. Just a moment, Fiennes has something to say."

Fiennes said, "While you're about it, you might get another case of beer. And a bottle of sherry. Pa likes Australian sherry, ask for 'Bushranger' brand."

"I see."

"Also some cigarettes. Empire will do. Rhodesian. Here's Tim back."

"I've an idea, Phil. You can't possibly bring all those things on your Norton, so I'll come in with the Trudge. Then I can find out if the transformer of the wireless set has come."

"Have you decided anything about giving the men notice?"

"Well, we haven't had time to consider the matter deeply, as a matter of fact. Hold on, Fiennes wants to say something."

"I'll come with Tim," said Fiennes. "I want to get my hair cut."

"Do you want any cash for it?"

"No, I can get it out of the till. We'll be with you inside half an hour."

Phillip telephoned Lucy. "Are the Iron Horses coming back, d'you know? Well, please telephone Johnson, and tell him the cheque is in the post. Try to get him to return his tackle this evening."

He waited in the town until the Trojan ground its way up the hill. Fiennes got out and went to the hairdresser's.

"Do you write down what you take privately from the till, Tim?"

"Well, not altogether, Phil."

"Then how d'you know whether or not anyone takes money from it?"

"Well, we don't think anyone would—except ourselves, of course."

"Why isn't there any record of money put in and taken out?"

"We're supposed to write it down, but Fiennes said the books got behind-hand, so there seemed no point in bothering about the till."

"Who signs cheques?"

"Oh, any one of us."

"No weekly balance struck?"

"The fact is, I attempted it, when Fiennes wouldn't, but having to work all the time on the bench, I got behind with it. I have tried, I assure you, to keep things in order, but somehow they have got beyond me lately. I've got all the data you want, here in my bag—what we owe, and what is owing to us."

"Good. We must put the accounts in order together, Tim."

"You can absolutely count on me for anything whatsoever, Phil! By the way, the others categorically agree that you can be Managing Director."

"Here's sixpence. Go into that coffee shop over there and balance up your accounts. You know, Creditor on one side, Debtor on the other."

"Who are we, in this context, Phil? Debtor or Creditor?"

"It doesn't matter. On one side add up a list of *What we are owed*, if anything, and in another column, *What we owe*. That means wages, bills, everything you have to pay out."

"Well, we can't pay out anything at the moment, Phil, I'm afraid——"

"Your *debts*, Tim," said Phillip, tersely but quietly. "Your liabilities. Such as the writ on the way to you for that eight-cwt. cast-iron louvre for the Gasworks down there, that nobody wants. Sixty pounds, plus twenty pounds costs. Put eighty pounds in the column *What we owe*."

"Good lord, I'd forgotten that cursed louvre."

"Eighty pounds, *What we owe*. Now do this while I see the bank manager. Can you occupy yourself in the coffee house meanwhile? Wait a moment. Perhaps you'd better introduce me to the bank manager, and tell him that I now have the necessary authority. He'll want it in writing, I expect."

The bank manager was a short man with a greying beard. He received them kindly in his office. Tim left after the introduction, when Phillip asked the manager to speak frankly. The manager said he was sorry for the brothers, but the position was that they were overdrawn in the neighbourhood of one hundred pounds, on no security. Their receipts did not balance their expenditure. It wasn't his affair to offer advice without it being requested, Mr. Maddison would understand; but he must say that he was glad someone was taking the matter in hand. He suggested that no more cheques be signed, as they would, he regretted, have to be marked *Estopped, Refer to Drawer*.

"They'll bounce, in other words?"

The bank manager went on to say that he would require the partners to sign a paper relegating their powers of signature to him, giving him power of attorney. The manager, after a moment's reflection, then asked Phillip if it were his intention to assume personal financial responsibility?

"Yes."

"You will, I am sure, forgive my asking, but are you prepared to lodge securities with us, should you intend to issue further cheques?"

Phillip said he had no securities. The manager then suggested
that a balance sheet be drawn up, to find out if the Firm was
solvent. Phillip replied that this was being done; Mr. Timothy
Copleston was working on them in the coffee shop.

"Ah, reminiscent of the eighteenth-century merchant ven-
turers," smiled the manager, showing him out.

He joined Tim at a scrubbed wooden table. Figures were pen-
cilled all round the borders of a newspaper, most of them crossed
out. Phillip took over and started again. The lists were short.

"Is this all?"

"So far as I can see, it is."

They returned together to the bank with the figures. The
manager suggested that the phrase *'Cannot pay'* be avoided.

"If you say to a creditor, 'I cannot pay,' that constitutes an
Act of Bankruptcy, which would further complicate what at present
appears to be a not very involved situation."

"I take it that you won't allow an overdraft?"

"On these figures, I'm afraid not."

They thanked him and went out. While Tim went to the wine-
merchant—he had removed the last coins from the till—Phillip
called at the bookshop to ask about the *Encyclopædia*. He found
Mr. Roper in a small office at the back of the shop. Phillip had
had several talks there in the past, and been shown Mr. Roper's
collection of first editions.

The bookseller was a man with a twin passion for music and
literature. He did his best to recommend good books in a district
which was largely composed of farmers, with a sprinkling of
retired soldiers, sailors, Indian officials and their wives and
daughters; and had long ago found out that the literary-minded
among them were very few indeed.

"I've called about the *Encyclopædia* for Mr. Copleston, Mr.
Roper. Has it come?"

To his surprise the other's face hardened.

"It's a somewhat expensive item, I suppose you know, Mr.
Maddison? We booksellers cannot afford to give long credit, and
by long I mean anything up to three or four years."

"I understand that. I'd like to pay for it myself. How much
is it? *Twenty-eight pounds?* I suppose you wouldn't allow me a
little time to pay? I could give you a post-dated cheque——"

"But why should you have to spend your hard-earned money
on——"

"I know what you mean, but I assure you that the Coplestons are solvent. They are an extremely kind and unworldly family, really."

Mr. Roper offered him a chair. "Part of my life of drudgery is made worth while when I can talk to a genuine literary person like yourself," he said. "Will you give me permission to speak frankly?"

"Certainly. Truth never killed anyone yet."

"Not your kind of truth, I agree. But I see such things from another angle, from the wrong side of the counter, perhaps, but that is my side as a tradesman, I suppose. Only this morning I had the manager of the Empire Stores in here, sitting where you are sitting now. He is a genuine poetic character, and like all such, suffers at times from association with average insensitive humanity. Do you know, he has been owed a bill for groceries delivered to the Coplestons during more than two years! Where is he, if he cannot get his account paid? Either he risks being dismissed as an incompetent manager by his regional inspector, or else he has to make up the bad debt himself. Thirty-nine pounds for two years' groceries. And yet they can afford, apparently, to order expensive encyclopædias for cross-word puzzles— those refuges of idle intellects—and also to go otter-hunting."

Mr. Roper began to look almost angry. "Why, my dear sir, I find an incompatability in the two view-points, and would give another name for what you call 'unworldly'."

His words shocked Phillip. The bookseller saw this, and continued in his normal soft voice, "This is entirely between ourselves, of course. Only I felt I must tell you what I thought, since you have done me the honour of confiding in me. Now I have lived here all my life, and have a vivid memory of myself as a small boy, being sent by my father, who founded this bookshop, with a book to the 'big house', as we called Colonel Chychester's place, in Tarrant Park, in those days. It must have been thirty years ago, but I remember it as though it were yesterday. I felt extremely proud to be taking a book to the Colonel, who was a hero to us boys, for he had fought in the Crimea, and had been badly wounded. Well, I walked up the drive of Tarrant Park, terrified by the great size of the place growing and growing before me and timidly rang the bell at the immense oak door. My heart beat in my ears as I heard it being opened, and then a footman looked down at me and said, 'What are you doing here? Get round to the back door with you!' in a brusque voice. Almost in tears, I hastened away, gave the parcel to someone, and ran home. And when I see this attitude of, well—I can only call it indifference —towards the feelings of small shopkeepers today among a certain class of so-called ladies and gentlemen, our betters, I remember the small boy's reception thirty years ago and my blood boils. I'm sorry, but I can't help it."

"But I am sure neither the Boys' grandmother, Mrs. Chychester, nor the Colonel, would have treated a small boy like that, Mr. Roper, had they seen him."

"Well, Mr. Maddison, I know it must seem trivial and even crass prejudice on my part, but there is something wrong with a system by which such things—slight as they are, they indicate the world as it really is today—are maintained."

"Lack of imagination."

"I call it selfishness."

"Lack of imagination is the same thing, surely?"

"How do you mean?"

"Bernard Shaw has a piercing line at the end of *Saint Joan*— 'Must a Christ perish in torment in every generation, because people have no imagination?' That is the cry of the poets of the ages."

"And what is the answer?"

"Education must be aimed at creating a wider imagination in the child, not at suppressing. The child's mind must be set free."

"But according to your theory, these people have known every freedom—with the result that they have grown up to please themselves."

"Well, I think there is also a duty, an idea of service, still remaining, you know. This case is perhaps not typical. A recluse —his sons growing up without proper direction—their mother dead—the old-boy broken-hearted. Inept, if you like: but not knowingly selfish."

"Inept is the word. Do you know that the youngest boy, Tim, played truant for a year and more from the local grammar school? What did his father do about it?"

"I don't think he knew."

"Not even when the bill for the term's fees failed to come in?"

"I think the Head Master thought he'd left. And the old boy was shattered after his wife's death. He'd retired from life. It was a tragedy, I assure you. Since then the Boys have worked

really very hard—often all night on the lathes. I've seen them—
and all without proper business direction. Their actual work has
been good, too—nothing scamped or shoddy. In fact, it's *too* good.
Well, I must away. I'll see the manager of the grocery stores is
paid very soon. And I'll collect the *Encyclopædia* shortly—and
pay cash for it—I've very nearly got an offer of fifty pounds for
a book from my agent——"

"Why should you waste your talent and your money on others?"

"Why do you waste your spirit and your sympathy on others—
the grocer, for example?"

"Ah well, Mr. Maddison, I see your point. You'll consider me
hard and unsympathetic, no doubt, but even grocers have to live,
you know. This one's a great man for poetry—Shelley especially."

At the Empire Stores Phillip spotted him at once—a thin-faced
man with a wide gentle mouth and a high forehead. Tim had told
Phillip that he had a habit of introducing the poet Shelley into
conversation with his customers on all occasions. This had caused
him to be considered locally as slightly gone in the upper storey,
according to Tim. Phillip knew, of course, that Tim's ideas were
in part formed by the fiction of popular magazines: in the pages
of which anyone who 'spouted' poetry was usually portrayed as a
long-haired eccentric character, sometimes with a butterfly net;
comic stock-characters of the Conglomerated Press, London, E.C.

This Shelley of the cheese cloves and weys, of butter firkins
and tubs, of bacon flitch and bolls of oatmeal, looked at Phillip
expectantly with an essentially innocent, child-like expression.

"'O wild west wind, thou breath of autumn's being'," said
Phillip. "How do you do. May I see you privately for a moment?"

"May I have your name, sir?"

"I am one whose name at the moment is writ in water."

"Do I not recognise the author of the Donkin trilogy? I do,
sir? Ah, may I congratulate you on a very fine performance."

"Thank you. I hope you are well?"

"Hitherto, 'a heavy weight of hours has chain'd and bow'd,
One too like thee—tameless, and swift, and proud', but with your
coming, sir, I am with the Cloud. Pray step into my office."

Phillip entered a cube of glass hung with clipped bills. Without
preamble he said, "I know I can trust you, since we have Shelley
as our friend. I want to tell you that the Coplestons are rather
unpractical, living in a dream world. They have now entrusted
their optimism and inexperience to me. They are, in a way, like

Shelley, but without his mental penetration into reality. Have you read Shelley's political pamphlets?"

"Have I not. He had to flee England for telling the simple truth. Godwin was the man, his father-in-law! Have you read *his* 'Political Justice'?"

"Not yet."

"Then I will lend it to you. Excuse me a moment." He hopped out of the glass box. "Yes, madam, we have the finest Danish bacon. Mr. Gray, your best skill with our new hygienic cutter. Thank you." He hopped back. "Your pardon, sir. The pig in Denmark does not suffer both mental and physical obscurity, as in darkest England. As I was presuming to say, Shelley absorbed much of Godwin's wisdom, just as Godwin absorbed much of Shelley's income."

Phillip felt it was his fault for starting this slightly pretentious talk, and got away after promising soon to settle the account. He must work all night at his writing to make up for lost time.

That afternoon mechanic, carpenter, smith and apprentice were given notice.

The smith grumbled. "Where am I now? What about my son?"

Phillip pointed out that his son had been getting £1 a week as an apprentice, and had been learning his trade into the bargain.

"The easy money will upset him for a while only. He should never have received it. Why, the farm labourer gets only just over thirty shillings a week. And most apprentices have to pay a premium, you know that—getting it back in wages of about five bob a week."

He offered the smith the use of the forge for shoeing; the smith to take one half of the money, the Works the other half for use of tools and all materials, including coal.

"All right," said the smith, after an unhappy silence. "That seems fair."

Chapter 3

THE WORKS

By the end of the week four new summonses had been delivered at the Works, making the total of money owing nearly £200. On the

credit side 'Mister', according to the cheque-book stubs, owed
the Boys £145; a parson's wife owed for a Dynawurkur vacuum
cleaner; the buildings of the Works was £600, and stock and
machinery paid for came to a further £180.

"It seems on the surface that we are solvent, Tim, but we must
do something to stave off the bailiffs entering to seize goods for a
knock-down sale to clear these judgment summons'. Damn, I've
just remembered something on the farm. D'you mind if I use the
telephone? I must know if Johnson's Iron Horses have returned
this morning."

Lucy replied that she hadn't seen them. Time was getting on.
A fortnight to go to the shoot. He felt impatient with these slow
minds.

"Now, Tim, for heaven's sake get on with your sac machine
contract. First, the Works must be tidied up. That will be good
for *morale*. The new lavatories are a disgrace. Come with me.
Look at them—strewn with newspaper, in a state of total in-
efficiency and neglect. The office must be cleared of rubbish. And
there's another thing. How much longer is the Tamplin cycle-car
going to stand sheltering nettles? I've seen it here for nearly
eighteen months, and it was rusting and rotting away before then."

"Yes, by Jove, the old Tamp. The fact of the matter is, my
dear Phil, that it is of no further use. It has no brakes, the belts
and tyres are perishing, the body is decayed."

"It was left with you to be sold, wasn't it? Then it should
be sold now. The engine's worth a tenner."

"It's not ours to sell," said Fiennes, coming up.

"Then whose is it?"

"A friend left it with us, to be sold if we could find a buyer,"
explained Tim.

"Why haven't you tried to find a buyer?"

"It really wasn't much use, it's out of date," said Tim. "You
see, the cyclecar is now superseded by the light car—Morris,
Humber, Trojan, Calthorp——"

"How long have you had it?" Phillip asked Fiennes.

"Oh, about four years."

"And in that four years it has become out of date?"

"Your attitude is intolerable," said Fiennes, walking away to
the office.

Turning to Tim, Phillip said, "Hardy wrote in one of his last
poems, 'If way to the better there be, it enacts a full look at the

worst'. That's what I'm trying to bring home to you three. If things are to be better, everyone here will have to alter the blue-print of his mind."

"Yes, I understand what you mean," replied Tim, earnestly. "But perhaps I ought to explain something."

Before his young brother-in-law's mild and gentle gaze Phillip felt that he had spoken too sharply.

"Do explain what's on your mind, Tim. Let's talk in the office. Fiennes should hear what I've got to say."

"We appreciate that you're trying to help us, and believe me, we are grateful. But you see, we don't regard money from a business sense only. I mean, we offered to try to sell 'Bongo's' Tamp for him when he went to Africa, if we got a chance. But we haven't had anyone here who wanted to buy it."

"Now as regards our money," said Fiennes, "we were only too pleased to be able to help 'Mister'——"

"I see what you're driving at. You didn't like me going after 'Mister' for that money he borrowed, while I felt it my duty to get him to sign a promissory note. After all, it is to be kept in the bank, to be claimed from the trustees of his estate when he dies. That way the thing is done properly, and leaves no ill-feeling. Don't you both agree?"

The brothers remained silent. "If you won't face facts for yourselves, I must for you. The truth is that you have several pressing claims, and I'm trying to stave off a knock-down sale by the bailiffs. The writ is still only being held off by daily payments. If they lapse, all this machinery will go at a knock-down sale with no reserve."

"Personally, I don't give a damn if it does, I'm sick of the whole thing," said Fiennes, going out of the office. "It's a low spring tide, and I want some prawns."

When he had gone, Ernest, with a mutter, edged his way out, leaving Tim and Phillip alone.

"As Fiennes tried to explain," said Tim, "the Coplestons have never exactly looked on money as something which is to be put before living. You yourself once told me that money for money's sake is a bad thing, in that it alters human nature, making people grim and hard. We really are grateful for all you are doing, and we certainly intend to pay you back one day, but I think Fiennes feels a personal note of criticism in your tone of voice. Please forgive me saying all this, but you said the truth was wanted."

"I, too, believe that people should be happy, but I've known a fair amount of people who borrow money, and friendship is usually spoiled by it."

Someone knocked at the door. The postman wanted a signature for a registered letter. While Tim signed, Phillip opened the envelope, and then showed him a demand that the sum outstanding for advertising in *The Model Engineer*, £36, be settled at once, otherwise a writ would be applied for.

"Dash it all, it quite escaped my mind. Our standing advertisement has been running on for four months, curse it. We forgot all about it, to be quite candid."

"I must go home and do some work, Tim. See you tomorrow."

A year drifts by, and it is the summer of 1917, the wettest summer in Flanders for many years. I am standing on a duck-board by the flooded and foul Steenbeke listening in the flare-pallid darkness to the cries of thousands of wounded men lost in the morasses of Third Ypres. To seek them is to drown with them . . . the living are still toiling on, homeless and without horizon, doing dreadful things under heaven that none want to do, through the long wet days and the longer nights, the weeks, the months of a bare, sodden winter out of doors.

The survivors are worn out; some of them, tested beyond the limits of human dereliction, put the muzzles of their rifles in their mouths, in the darkness of the terrible nights of the Poelcappelle morasses, and pull the trigger.

Those at home, sitting in arm-chairs and talking proudly of Patriotism and Heroism, will never realise the contempt and scorn which the soldiers have for these and other abstractions; the soldiers feel they have been betrayed by the high-sounding phrases that heralded the war, for they know that the enemy soldiers are the same men as themselves, suffering and disillusioned in exactly the same way.

And in the stupendous roar and light-blast of the final barrage which broke the Siegfried Stellung I see only one thing, as recorded by Field-Marshal Hindenburg, an incident which grows radiant before my eyes until it fills all my world: the sight of a Saxon boy half-crushed under a shattered tank, moaning 'Mutter—Mutter—Mutter', out of ghastly grey lips. A British soldier, wounded in the leg and sitting nearby, hears the words, and dragging himself to the dying boy, takes his cold hand and says: 'All right, son, it's all right. Mother's here with you.'

The next morning the Clerk to the Court told Phillip that another £4 for the Dynawurkur judgment summons must be paid in by six o'clock, otherwise he would have to distrain. That meant the bailiffs. Phillip went to his office and paid the £4 with his own cheque, then telegraphed to his literary agent in London. That would give them another twenty-four hours' grace. The sale price had been £15. 17. 6; the sum due, with fees for stays of execution, was now £49.0.0.

In the afternoon he gave his cheque for a further £14, being extra costs for the stay-of-execution of the writ, which was for £40, plus £8 accrued expenses. Then totting up the items in his cheque-book stubs he found that he was already £22 overdrawn. He paid £45 to the Court, bringing his overdraft to £67.0.0.

"I am afraid that, unless a further four pounds is forthcoming by noon tomorrow, I must distrain," said the Clerk.

"But can't some of this be used for that?"

"I'm afraid I've already made out the receipt."

When Phillip told Tim that they must find £4 somehow, Tim replied "Oo ah," and disappeared.

Nobody had made any attempt to clean up the Works, so he set about cleaning and tidying. Afterwards he thought to go down to the river and fish in the pool below the oak wood, and think what to do.

He took with him a long bamboo pole, a reel of stout thread, a float made of a swan's quill, and a length of 3-X silkworm gut; and having baited the hook with a bread-pill, lay on an elbow and watched the float. It was the first time he had fished since the summer of 1914; it brought back many memories and regrets, upon which mounted present thoughts about the neglected state of the Works; so he hid the rod and returned up the path through the trees.

Tim reappeared soon after six o'clock. He got out of the Trojan with what a writer for the Conglomerated Press would describe as a mysterious smile on his face. Taking Phillip aside he said, "I have managed to get the four pounds."

"How did you manage that, Tim?"

"I went to Exeter and pawned the Dynawurkur vacuum cleaner, getting four pounds for it."

"But why did you do that?"

"I thought it would help us."

"But it doesn't help if everyone acts anyhow on his own."

"Now please don't get upset, I only did what I could to help."

"But it isn't helping, Tim, to cut across someone else's command. Incidentally, why didn't you send it back when the first summons came in? Now the cost of the damned thing is over fifty pounds! And it's never been used! And *you* make about a hundred mile journey by car virtually to sell it for four pounds!"

"I only thought I was helping," said Tim, with an air of hurt dignity.

"Well, I'm afraid you'll have to get it out of pawn. I don't exactly know the legal position, but we may be pawning something that isn't ours."

"I can easily go and get it back in the morning. Have you had any tea? Miss Calmady says you didn't have any lunch, either. Speaking for myself, I'm dashed hungry."

"I must get back now."

On the way home he called on Mrs. Chychester. She said he looked tired, and ordered tea.

"Do tell me, dear Phil, what is worrying you," as she leaned forward in her chair with sympathy. "I suppose it is Adrian's boys? I have heard a little about what is happening, from Ennis. I was afraid it would come to that." She sat still, her face a gentle ruin. "Adrian is hopeless."

"It is difficult to know where to begin——" he said; then seeing that she was looking frail, he declared that it would be all right in the end; they owed only a little money, and their assets were greater than their liabilities. He would stop all further leaking away of capital. The old lady thanked him, saying she was so glad to think that someone was there to help her grandchildren.

"I am sure that things will come right."

She pressed his hand, saying, "But you must not wear yourself out over it, you know. You look so tired and thin, if you will forgive an old woman being personal. And after all, your first duty is to your Lucy and dear little Billy. I am always so glad to hear about him from his 'new mother'. Do give them both my love, won't you?" Then she smiled and said that he must give Billy an extra kiss for 'Grannie'.

He went on his way to Rookhurst feeling happier, determined to act so that Lucy's grandmother should be justified in her faith in him. If need be, he would sell the Norton. Should he telegraph to cousin Arthur, for the twenty pounds owed to him? But Arthur was—crooked. How about some of the Copleston relations? He had learnt that if a Bill of Sale were raised on the new machinery of the Works, the machinery would not come under the hammer at a knock-down bailiff's auction: if he could raise £100 it would dispose of the imminent major threats of writ and judgment-summonses.

A money-order by telegram awaited him from Anders Norse, as an advance against the otter book, of £30. Where could he get another £70—plus the £4 per diem wastage?

The next morning, as a last hope, he urged Ernest against his silent, reluctant will, to accompany him on a visit to his relations, declaring that he could not very well go alone to beg from people to whom he was almost a stranger.

Ernest got into the sidecar and during the journey into Somerset to see Aunt Euphoria, his godmother, he remained unspeaking. When Phillip stopped at a pub to get some beer, Ernest remained in the sidecar. He was a teetotaller, drinking only sherry and port, which he did not consider to be alcoholic.

Determined not to speak until Ernest spoke first, Phillip brought out a glass of port and gave it to Ernest. Ernest drank it, and broke the silence with an "Ah", to which Phillip replied "Ah! ha!"

Mrs. Champernowne of Champernowne lived in a house on the side of an oakwood belonging to the family of her husband, the eldest of a family of fourteen. It was part of a five-thousand-acre estate, Lucy had told Phillip, in reply to his questions before the journey. Major Champernowne of Champernowne was a heavy, thickset man who in youth had emigrated to Canada, returning to serve with the yeomanry in the South African War, where he had been hit in the leg, so that it became shorter than the other. When he inherited he spent his life planting trees, shooting, fishing, and running the home farm. He was a gruff, bulky man, wearing tweed clothes of wool spun from his own sheep. He left the visitors with his wife, who said at once, "But why do you come here? What is it to do with us?"

Phillip, putting aside embarrassment, told her of the urgency of the situation. £100 would ensure the possession of £500 worth of new machinery. Mrs. Champernowne, somewhat fluttery, said that she was sorry, but did not see what she could do. Uncle Champernowne came back, and said that the peal were running —he pointed to the stream at the bottom of the valley—and if Phillip cared to throw a fly he was welcome to do so.

"Thank you, sir, may I come one day with Lucy, and bring my rod?"

They travelled many miles in the next two days. The farthest point was to East Hampshire, where lived an uncle who was a retired sailor. They stayed the night. At dinner Admiral Copleston asked where they were bound; Ernest hardly spoke, and then only in monosyllables.

"Oh, we're touring round, sir," said Phillip, and thereafter found he could not broach the subject. After dinner, when the Admiral was talking to Phillip before a small fire in his smoking room, he turned to Phillip and said, "Damme, are all Adrian's boys like Ernest? He don't say a dam' word. How long have you been touring? What're you doin', gettin' local colour, what?"

"In a way, yes, we are, sir. You see, I'm writin' a book about Nature in Devon, among other things."

"By God, you seem to be goin' in the opposite direction to get it," replied the Admiral, pouring him a whisky and soda.

The next morning they went north to call on Aunt Kimmy, who said that the idea of buying £100 worth of machinery was quite out of the question, for she had nowhere to put it. She gave them some lemonade, and they returned to Dorset, where Phillip found a cheque for £18.18s. from his agent for a short story sold to a magazine.

This kept away the bailiffs for three more days.

Then, as a last resort, he telegraphed to Uncle Hilary in Bournemouth, where he lived with his sister Victoria. Hilary drove over in the afternoon. Phillip asked him straight out if he would lend him £100 on a bill of sale of the Copleston machinery. Hilary said he would see his solicitor in Colham and let him know when they would arrive at the Works, later that day.

He was as good as his word, and the two arrived at Down Close, by appointment, at 4 p.m.

The lawyer began by asking if there was a balance sheet he might see? Phillip showed him the list of debts and assets, with a rough copy of the value of machinery and stock. Afterwards the solicitor and Hilary looked around by themselves; finally Phillip was asked to go to the solicitor's office in Colham the next morning, Hilary said good-bye, and returned home.

The next morning Phillip was told by the solicitor that he had not been able to advise his uncle to invest any money in the Copleston business.

"They reminded me of the Babes in the Wood," he said. "Of course such inexperienced young men should not have been allowed to undertake such a venture. Whatever were their trustees thinking

of?" He remarked that the eldest boy possibly had the makings
of an engineering genius. "His design and lathe work is first-class.
Is he always so remote from life?"

"Yes, they're all rather like that, even Tim, the youngest. They
live in a private world. I find it almost impossible to communicate
with them, especially with Ernest."

"That eldest boy is wasted where he is. He should be in the
draughtsman's office of an engineering firm. Now may I ask you
a question: are you committed in any way—financially, I mean?"

"Only a few pounds to stave off the bailiffs."

"Helping relations is a thankless task, usually."

"I don't want any thanks."

"It might be as well," the lawyer replied. "Now tell me, how
do you like living at Rookhurst?"

"I quite like it. By the way, may I ask you a question—but
don't reply, if you'd rather not. Is my Uncle fed-up with me?"

"Oh, I don't think so. If anything, he regards it as a useful
lesson for one about to enter the business world of farming."

When he got back to Down Close, Phillip found Pa in his chair
doing a cross-word puzzle with the aid of the new *Encyclopædia
Britannica*, which had the little trade-mark name and address of
Robert Roper, Shakesbury. How had it got there? He hadn't paid
for it.

"May I have a word with you, sir?"

Pa looked up from reading about Red Indians and said "Shoot!"
His eyes were kindly and friendly, so Phillip found it easier to say,
"The Boys are in a financial mess, and I don't see how a knock-
down sale can be prevented."

"Oh well, if it happens, it happens, I suppose. No use worrying
oneself over what can't be helped."

"A hundred pounds would stave it off, sir. Forgive my asking
you, but could you possibly lend us that sum for a day or two,
security being the machinery, which is paid for?"

"I? Good lord, I've no money. It's all gone long ago, I'm
afraid. I'm still paying off sixty pun' a year on a debt to 'Mister's'
Deed of Settlement, for a hundred and fifty I borrowed from him
twenty years ago, before he went bankrupt—let me see—eleven
years ago this past July."

"How very strange, for Mister has borrowed that sum, exactly,
from the Boys during the last year. Actually it is ten pounds from
me, and a hundred and forty from them."

"That makes us quits then."

"Well, I got him to sign a promissory note, but interest isn't mentioned."

"Ah."

Mr. Copleston blew the stub of an Empire cigarette from his holder expertly into the fireplace, and carefully fitted another into the tube. "Cigarette? So they're in a mess, are they? I thought something like that was happening. Well, it's their look-out, not mine."

"You must think me an interfering busybody, sir, but I must try every means I can to stop a knock-down sale. You say you have been paying sixty pounds a year for twenty years, on a debt of one hundred and fifty. Isn't that a long time to pay? Would you mind if I looked into it? The Boys, you know, were misled by one lawyer; and it might be a parallel case with this payment you are making."

"I don't mind you looking into it, not at all. So far as memory serves me, I've been paying sixty pounds a year for the last three years, and thirty for eight years before that. It seemed a lot, but these lawyer fellows have their own arrangements. Come with me, and I'll give you the box."

Mr. Copleston took him to his room, opened the desk, took out a small japanned box, produced a handful of receipts, and left Phillip alone with them.

'Mister' had apparently gone bankrupt in 1915, when he made a deed of settlement with his creditors. On Adrian Copleston, Esquire's debt of £150, a 5 per cent simple interest had been charged for the twenty years. This interest came to £75 before 'Mister' went bankrupt. Add another £75 for the remaining ten years, and £300 was the outside total owed. Actually it was less, since the capital sum diminished with every payment. But call it £300.

Now for what Pa had paid back. The receipts for the last two annual payments of £60 were missing. Why?

"Ah yes," said Mr. Copleston. "The beggars never sent receipts for the last two cheques I posted to them. I owe another payment now, I fancy."

Phillip did a sum.

"But, sir, you have already paid a hundred and twenty pounds too much, making four twenty in all. Of course the lawyers haven't sent a receipt for the last two payments, but have they sent back the money?"

"Not to my knowledge they haven't."

"Then they're crooks!"

"Oh, I wouldn't go so far as to say that."

"Well, sir, on your behalf, as honorary investigator, I can assure you you have paid back your debt, both capital sum and interest, and £120 over, which has not been acknowledged by the lawyers, nor have the last two payments been returned."

"H'm, now I come to think of it I did wonder why they hadn't sent any receipts. Well, that lets me off paying any more, you say?"

"Sure thing. May I look into the matter for you? The cheques you sent will be with your bank, and endorsed by the payee, of course. It will be simple to trace them. May I write to Slaughter & Co., the Solicitors?"

"H'm—I don't think so—thank 'ee all the same. I'm disposed to let bygones be bygones. After all, these lawyer fellows know their business best. Well, I must go and water my hot-house plants. What they need most is some good sheep's dung soaked in a tub . . ."

"I can bring over a couple of pailfuls from the farm, if you like, sir."

"Hey? Oh no, thank 'ee all the same."

And muttering something to himself which might have been too many cooks the old gentleman shuffled away in his slippers.

It had been a fine dry St. Martin's Little Summer, but now clouds were gathering; good-bye to summer. The swallows had been flying wildly for days around the reeds of the mere known as the Longpond, Lucy told him on his return: such a wonderful sight, thousands of them all flying together, she said. He ought to see it.

"Billy and I have been there every afternoon."

"I'm afraid a farmer, as Ned said once during harvest, hasn't time to look at the view."

"Dad come too, Mummy?" asked Billy.

"All right, I'll come with you tomorrow."

But next day the Longpond was deserted, the swallows had flown south in the night.

Phillip went to a garage and asked what they would give for the Norton and sidecar. The proprietor said there was little demand for such an outfit, which was underpowered with its 3½ h.p. engine. He was offered £25, and left the shop feeling it was the end.

When he entered the Works office he saw Ernest and Fiennes there. He told them he could not do anything further; the bailiffs must come in.

"Be damned to that for a tale," replied Fiennes. "What's more to the po'nt, are you and Lucy coming to Pa's birthday dinner tomorrow? At the Royal Hotel in Shakesbury. We're going to the flicks afterwards. Didn't Lucy tell you? Tim telephoned this morning."

Phillip returned home. Lucy met him with a happy face. The baby was kicking inside her. She was content with thoughts of Billy having someone to play with. The baby was due in March, and would have the spring and summer on the new lawn, which she intended to keep cut after Phillip had brought down the heavy roller to level it. She had made plans for the garden, too, including a rockery just like Pa's.

"Oh, Tim rang up after you'd gone. It's Pa's seventy-fourth birthday tomorrow, and the Boys want to give him a dinner in Shakesbury, then to see the film at the Gaiety Theatre afterwards. What do you think?"

"I don't think I'd be very good company—you know, the skeleton at the feast. Besides, I really must do some work."

"Well, no need to decide now. Wait and see how you feel tomorrow. By the way, Mrs. à Court Smith rang up to say that she would look after Billy, and we can stay the night at Ruddle Stones if we like."

He felt like giving up, but after a walk on the downs returned with determination not to allow his lesser feelings to influence him. After all, the Boys and Lucy and Pa were different in kind, and could not be otherwise. He must try to get a regular routine in his life: a time-table: so much farming business: then a regular daily period in his study.

The next morning when he saw the Clerk to the Court he was told that all due payments had been discharged. The Clerk did not know more than that a cheque had been given and the bank had telephoned to say that it would be honoured.

"It must be 'Mister's' promissory note, Lucy. I suppose they've raised a loan on it."

When they arrived at Ruddle Stones with Billy, 'Mister' took him aside to say, "I suppose you know where the cash came from, with which to settle the Court's demands?"

"Well, I imagined it was from your promissory note."

"No, that won't be payable until after my death, old chap. Even if the Boys wanted to, I doubt very much if they'd be able to raise any cash on that. They'll have to wait until I'm dead, I'm afraid. Even if I'd wanted to, I couldn't have got the cash for them. No, the promissory note didn't make a ha'p'oth of difference."

"Then where did the money come from?"

"Oh, Ernest's other godmother died and left him a legacy of about three thousand. By the way, while I remember it, I'd very much like to see this film in Shakesbury, *The Somme*, you're going to. I hear it's the real thing. I can't risk the journey home on the Onion after dark. I suppose you couldn't give me a lift in your sidecar? Lucy will be going in the Trudge, I suppose?"

"I'll call for you on the way to Shakesbury after the dinner, 'Mister'."

Lucy, having seen Billy settled with Mrs. Smith, was waiting to continue the journey to her old home. When they were round the corner he asked when Ernest's godmother had died.

"Oh, I think it was about six months ago."

"Didn't you know that she had left a legacy to Ernest?"

"Oh, vaguely, you know. I really don't know much about the Boys' affairs."

He stopped the engine. "Lucy, don't you *know* what's been happening these past few weeks?"

"Oh, I suppose so. But you *did* insist on taking charge of the Works, didn't you?" There was a slight note of weariness in the voice.

The journey was continued in silence, while he drove slowly, as though reluctant to arrive.

Phillip found Ernest alone in the sitting-room. He waited. After a while Ernest muttered something, got up from Pa's chair, and with a comic booklet entitled *Cohen on the Telephone*, moved slowly through the open french windows, while from his lips came a sudden flute-like warble.

After a few blank moments Phillip followed him into the garden.

"I'm afraid I find that I have some urgent work to do, so will you make my apologies for absence to Pa at the dinner tonight, Ernest?"

"Very well."

Feeling that he was destroying the last illusion of what had never really existed, Phillip walked up the lane and waited around the corner until the mutter of the Trojan's exhaust faded in the distance, then he returned to the Works.

A low sun shone across the railway cutting, lighting lathes, gas-engine, milling machine, tools scattered on benches, coke-stove with dribbles of rust running down the pipe from the roof. So Ernest had known about his legacy all the time; and had kept mum about it. Why hadn't Lucy mentioned it? Was it a case of no imagination, a failure to connect—or what? Was it his attitude towards them? Didn't they *care*—as Fiennes had said? Was he, not only in their eyes, but in truth, an interfering bore?

Everything he had said to them, everything he had proposed, or tried to do, had been, to them, meaningless. Look at the condition of the Works—the untidiness—everything higgledy-piggledy —the wash-basins black-rimmed with oil—towels, as grimy as the basins, flung on the floor. The lavatory pans were pits of horror. He stood still, momentarily lost, all personality dissolved as a bleak, strained feeling possessed him like a petrifaction.

After a while he moved away to the store-room, where stood a half-opened case of one gross tins of grease-solvent soap, sold to a compliant Tim by some commercial traveller telling a hard-luck story. He opened one, and started to clean the basins. There was no water in the tank. He went outside, found two pails by the kitchen door, emptied their rotting garbage on the ash-heap, and walked up the lane to draw water from the well. He borrowed a clean pitcher to dip in the water, and returned with full pails.

Muttering to himself, he began to clean the lavatories. It took several pails of water to free the passages after removing wads of newsprint and scraping with a wire brush. Then the scouring with abrasive, while he kept all feeling under control, breathing steadily against a mounting sense of horror at the indifference, the neglect, the unawareness due to what seemed to be a total lack of sensibility—butterflies without antennae. It only wanted shell-fire to complete in miniature the appearance of the Somme battle-field where all the underlying purpose of life—the created order and beauty of the species—had been denied; life working back-

wards to chaos, far beyond the simple, the natural order of death
succeeding life.

He could no longer control his feelings, he began to shout at
himself. Taking a broom, he swept the floor of the machine room.
The inner self collapsed; with a wild scream he went to the Office.
Here was no relief; here everything was in chaos. A feeling of
despair rushed out of him, leaving a sense of appalling lifelessness
within. He stood still, knowing his real self to be destroyed beneath
the personality he had assumed during the war, covering the distraught inner core of his earliest years. In a frenzy he struck the
back of his right hand on the bench again and again until blood
came from the base of the fingernails. In the flaring moment he
saw the truth of his life which, despite all he did, could never
change its pattern. He was done for. A man's life, right through
to its end, was as his beginning. He never had done what he
wanted to do; it was always prostitution for others, who *did not
want his interference*. Therein lay the truth; he was like Father,
trying to change others, because he was weak and unable to
change himself. He had always *pretended* with Lucy. What would
become of him? Was he doomed to the same sort of misery all
his life, always more or less at odds with those about him, always
trying to explain, to make things clearer—Doris, Mother, Father,
Cousin Arthur, the Coplestons—Uncle Hilary and his damning
of the miners' leaders—damning strikes which were only a mass
demand for a decent life—damning the General Strike in the
spring. A European generation had died upon the battlefields in
vain.

No, that was not true. He saw Hilary's point of view. It was
realistic, as he, and the Boys, were unrealistic. They had tried to
make a boyhood dream come true. So had he; so had Hilary.

Again, he had accused Lucy, in manner if not with words, of
being insensitive to the point of stupidity in not remembering the
legacy left to Ernest. He was becoming unfair, intolerant. Good
intentions paved the way to hell. He must be only a writer, in
detachment from life. A writer *must*, with his last breath, strive
for clarity; he must never damn anyone, but see all human, all
natural events, 'as a child, or an idiot, sees them'. Conrad *knew*.

He sat down, telling himself that the fault lay in himself because
his intelligence had been clouded by feeling: he had been dicta-
torial, withholding himself from the Boys: he had camouflaged his
fear of them, and of Pa. Lucy was balanced: had she not said, in

her mild way, 'Bother the Boys, why can't they look after themselves,' which really meant, 'Why can't *you* allow them to look after themselves?'

His entire attitude towards the Boys had been wrong. They were easy-going, and natural: he drove himself, and was unnatural. Feeling clearer, he resumed the sweeping of the workshop floor, and recovered himself in steady progression. He would not touch the office; if they liked to file their papers in the basket and upon the floor, let them. If Fiennes wanted to leave off the telephone receiver, let him. While Ernest solemnly read, with inner glee, *Cohen on the Telephone.*

Miss Calmady, the optimistic cook, had heard the shouting from the kitchen and came out, dirty apron and untidy hair, wondering what he was about. This queen of the greasy pot and bubbling garbage pails spent most of her evenings down the lane with the Collies, small-holders whose secret ambition it was to own Down Close and its garden, three parts wasted, when 'Colonel Coperston' died. The hamlet always referred to him as 'Colonel Coperston' ever since, as a man of forty years, courting Miss Margaret Chychester at Tarrant, he had taken part in amateur theatricals at the Gaiety Theatre in *The Yeoman of the Guard.*

"I thought I 'eard a noise," she said.

"Yes, I was rehearsing my part of the idiot in a play, Miss Calmady. Now I must pick up Mr. Smith at Ruddle Stones and take him to the pictures."

The Gaiety Theatre had been built on the site of the Assembly Rooms, which had been burnt down during the reign of Edward the Seventh. Now the theatre was a picture palace.

While Phillip stood beside 'Mister' just inside the door, waiting for Pa and the Boys, children began to file past, ushered by school teachers to the front rows. The local committee of the Junior Imperial League had arranged for the audience of children; while in the centre of the hall old soldiers of the British Legion, some with artificial legs, eyes, and arms, were already seated.

There was a gallery above the entrance; here on the front rows of tiered seats sat local dignitaries with superior, long-established tradesmen of the town who considered themselves to be 'just below the professions and the county,' said 'Mister'.

"My dear Phil and 'Mister', I can't tell you how glad I am to see you both!" exclaimed Tim, his face showing pleasure. Pa said, "Ha. You missed an excellent dinner." Then seeing 'Mister', "Hullo. You here too?"

The film began well, with shots of the dumps, new roads, etc., and the preliminary bombardment taken by official photographers in the early summer of 1916. There the marching columns were, waving, smiling, and cheering as exhorted by the camera-men of those sweltering June days. There were the howitzers in their chalk pits, firing in recoil; the field-gunners; piles of plum-pudding mortar bombs; strings of mules being watered in long lines at canvas troughs; the Leaning Virgin of the basilica of Albert above the horse and lorry traffic of the Ancre valley. The night-marching scenes of the boys going up the line were fine and true against the light-play, like continuous summer lightning, of horizon gun-flashes. But the attack at 7.30 a.m. on Z morning was nothing like it; and spoiled by the incessant shrill cheering of children. There was a moving roll-call scene, when, in pauses of silence while the platoon sergeant looked around, one saw the unanswering names hanging on barbed wire, or lying sprawled upon the pitted downland sward.

Then the film took an ugly turn. The Germans were portrayed as fat and cowardly creatures; some of them almost Billy Bunters of the ha'penny poor-boys' 'libraries' of before the war, always running away. The misery of deep mud and hopeless cold of winter rain was made light of by the antics of a comic cockney actor floundering about before the camera in a new tunic with sharply creased trousers—straight out of the Ordnance Stores at Pimlico.

Phillip felt that he could not remain beside a passive Lucy as the shrill cries of the children changed to a terrible booing of everything German; the feeling became anguish, equal to that felt during the first hours of the opening battle when his platoon had been cut down by machine guns and he had lain in a shell-hole unable to help with two bullets through his left leg, when the children cheered in crescendo as a young German soldier, going through the British barrage to get water for a wounded comrade, was killed by a bursting shell. But he sat through it to the end and God Save Our Gracious King, while thinking of Willie, dead these three years, who had prophesied that unless a change of thought came to Europe, and particularly to Britain, the war would come again.

He must delay his book no longer. When he had taken 'Mister' back to Ruddle Stones he returned to the farmhouse, and putting a pile of logs on one side of the little open hearth of his study, and drawing a pint of beer from the 4½-gallon 'pin' from the one-man brewery in Shakesbury on the other side, sat down to finish the introduction to his war book.

The bells cease to hum in their cage, the power goes from me, and I descend again to the world of the living; and if in some foolish confiding moment I try to explain why I want to re-live those old days, to tear Truth out of the past so that all men shall see plainly, perhaps someone will say to me, 'Oh, the War! A tragedy—best forgotten. No use dragging in the skeleton to the feast,' or, 'There always will be a war: it's deep in human nature.' They may give me a friendly hint, 'Don't talk about the War before my boy, old chap, if you don't mind. I don't want him unsettled: you know what youngsters are—very impressionable. And after all there is such a thing as loyalty to one's country, you know.' This last remark was once made to me after I had said that the Germans were brave soldiers, and fighting for the same 'ideals' as we were.

Sometimes it seems even more hopeless, as when one hears a hundred or so school-children, marched to the local picture palace for patriotic purposes, cheering and booing a film which only at times suggests reality, called *The Somme*, frantically cheering the 'British heroes' in their immaculate uniforms, and booing the 'German cowards' who always seem to be hurrying away from the British (O wraiths of the 8th Division before La Boisselle). They booed even when one poor lad in *feldgrau*, who went to fetch water for a dying comrade, was knocked over by a shell.

The children, I know, are but mirrors of the mental attitudes of their parents, of their school and religious teachers, but surely, after the bitter waste and agony of a lost European generation, it is time that these people should begin to 'know what they do'.

Lucy had told Mrs. Rigg, who came in during the day to help with the work, that they would not be home again until lunch time the next day; but there was a light on in the master's room. As she told Lucy next day—"Whinivver I poked me 'ade up out of the badeclothes, I zeed the light still on, and I zaid to me 'usband, ''Arry,' I says, 'whathivver be 'm about, a proper ould oyl he be, 'a zaith, workin' by day and by night. Whathivver be'm up to, 'a zaith, 'tes this yurr writin' that he be ut, 'a zaith.'"

Mrs. Rigg went on to say that she went over early, and cooked the master some eggs and bacon, he looked very happy, and not a bit like a weary man, she declared.

"'A was smilin' like someone had given he a present, ma'm."

I must return to my old comrades of the Great War—to the brown, the treeless, the flat and grave-set plain of Flanders—to the rolling, heat-miraged downlands above the river Somme—for I am dead with them, and they live again in me. There in the beautiful desolation of rush and willow in the forsaken tracts I will renew the truths which have quickened out of their deaths; that human virtues are superior to those of national idolatry, which do not arise from the Spirit: that the sun is universal, and that men are brothers made for laughter one with another: that we must free the child from all things which maintain as pre-eminent the ideal of a commercial nationalism, the ideal which inspired and generated the barrages in which ten million men of my generation, their laughter corrupted, perished.

I have a little boy now, an innocent who laughs in the sunshine; he sings and smiles when he hears the bells on the wind. Must he, too, traverse a waste place of the earth: must the blood and sweat of his generation drip in agony, until the sun darken and fall down the sky, and rise no more upon his world?

"We'll have to leave the ploughing of the Big Field until after the shoot," said Mr. Hibbs, the manager of Fawley Estate Farms, Ltd. "I've left you alone, as there was little I could do, while you were carrying on with the seasonal jobs. But looking round with Haylock I see you've had Johnson's Iron Horses to do the ploughing for you. He went a bit deep, didn't he? I doubt if anything will grow in that rank soil. When we ploughed deep for beet-sugar during the war we found that an extra inch was all that was practicable, and every fourth year afterwards we could bring up, with safety, another inch. That gives the rank soil a chance to weather, and be assimilated. I fancy you'll have to reverse the process, and put back the meat-soil on your ninety odd acres, Captain Maddison."

"Oh. It was pretty awful before, you know."

"Yes. it was sucked out all right. Haylock is pleased, there are several coveys on the furrows. He plans to bring them down from the top fields and line his guns behind the hedge across the road from the southern boundary of the Big Field. There will be stops out, of course, and a gun on either flank, to prevent the birds from breaking back and veering off. I suppose you'll be one of the flanking guns, sir?"

"I don't shoot, Mr. Hibbs."

"A man with a walking stick will be enough to keep them from veering. Sir Hilary, I understand, wants to shoot over our other farms the first day, and get the birds on to your land for the final battue. Haylock reckons there are between three and four hundred brace o' partridges; we'd've had more, except for that storm at the end of May which killed a lot of chicks just as they were hatching."

"I remember that storm, Mr. Hibbs—it was my wedding day."

Hilary and his guests stayed at the Royal Hotel in Shakesbury. He had arranged for luncheon to be delivered by van, with a waiter, to the keeper's hut beside one of the rides in Turk Wood, about a mile from Rookhurst. There on the trestle table was a large steak-and-kidney pudding around the basin of which a deftly folded table napkin was tucked; potatoes baked in the jackets; a ham; an apple pie, a plum cake, bowl of cream, Stilton cheese. There was whisky, claret, and coffee. Among the guests was a large florid man who had been the commodore of the Mackarness Line; he couldn't shoot for toffee. Hilary wasn't much good, either, thought Phillip, drinking his fifth glass of claret. One wasn't so bad, he was something on the staff of the Governor-General of Australia. Except for this man, Phillip regarded them as a lot of profiteers. When, after lunch, the talk came to the trouble in the coal-fields he made an excuse to go out and see if the beaters were getting their bread and cheese and beer.

There they were, sitting in line, a lot of oddmedodds wearing calico smocks as much for their own safety as for scaring birds, happy that they were being paid to enjoy themselves, with a couple of rabbits from 'bird kipper' Haylock thrown in at the end of the day. Most of them were labourers on the farms, others were out-of-works collected by the under-keeper.

The next day stops were put out before dawn—men in smocks carrying sticks to which white pieces of cloth were tied—along the eastern boundary of Skirr Farm, which adjoined the property of Sir Roland Tofield. After three stands near and around the various coppices and woods, the plan was to walk up the stubbles and leys and put the birds into a 20-acre field of roots near the western boundary of the farm.

While the guns were getting into position behind the farther hedge, the beaters were already walking in line across the swedes. Next to this plot were ten acres of beet-sugar. A score of pheasants,

many hares, and a few brace of partridges were laid in the game
cart from this stand.

Then a buffet luncheon in the billiard room at Fawley, a table
cloth covering the faded baize and perished cushions. Lucy had
gone up with Mrs. Rigg previously to clean out what had been a
lumber room, unused for play since Uncle John's wife had died
towards the end of the nineteenth century. Once again the
caterers from Colham provided the food and drink.

Now for the big drive of the day, which would end the
shoot.

The beaters were already on their way to the beech hanger
under the down. There was no wind; the original plan was un-
changed: south through the trees to the ploughed work; cross it
in line, Haylock with a gun on one flank, the under-keeper on the
other flank with Phillip, now carrying a gun, to deal with any
birds breaking back. The advance was to be gradual, not to
panic the birds, but to 'lift' them off the arable and so to the Big
Wheatfield which adjoined the Shakesbury road.

Hilary led the way to the village, past the church and through
the thatched cottages to the Shakesbury road and the line of
hazel-sticks topped by numbered white cards lining the hedge
across the turnpike road. There, as they sat on their shooting-
sticks, sixty yards apart, some with Newfoundland retrievers on
leash in front of their feet, while the game-cart waited well to the
flank, Hilary blew a long note on the horn.

They waited. Tiny white figures came out from among the
beech trees. They moved forward, and went out of sight in the
dip under the crest of Lobbett's.

Lucy, standing by Uncle John, tried to identify Phillip as the
line reappeared; he would be on the right somewhere.

At the same moment she heard trundling and chuffing noises.
Mr. Johnson was bringing back his tackle. Turning round, she
saw drifts of steam rising above the thatched roofs of the village.
The Iron Horses were on their way to the borstal. Billy, lifted up
in her arms, pointed out the important event to Hilary.

"Iron Hosses. Daddy's Iron Hosses come, Nuncle. Oh good!"

Across the centre of the Big Wheatfield one engine trundled,
while Hilary yelled at the top of his voice for it to stop, holding
out his arms.

"What idiot arranged for that thing to come here today?"

Covey after covey of partridges were in flight down Lobbett's. Over the lower hedge the birds threw up, wheeled, and followed their leaders to right and left, breaking away from the monster chuffing across the Big Wheatfield. Another check before its fellow standing in the borstal and blowing off steam. Away the coveys sped south over the boundary and so to Tofield property.

Hilary was more than incensed. His father had had nearly a thousand acres of arable deep-ploughed in the 'eighties, spent a small fortune on guano—and then had to have the land re-ploughed to replace the sour subsoil.

Phillip, walking down with his unloaded 12-bore, saw the attacking waves avoiding the fortress of La Boisselle. Thank God they had outflanked the guns.

"You're a fathead, an absolute fathead, that's what you are," Hilary told him after the guests had gone back in the hired Daimler to Shakesbury. "And who the devil gave you permission to hire that steam-tackle? You're a farm-pupil, kindly remember in future. And let it be clearly understood that you are to get the agent's approval, through Hibbs, before you undertake any hiring, buying, or selling—and that includes both live and dead stock—and if you interfere with the established policy again between now and next midsummer, when your agreement with me for the first year is up, I'll have seriously to consider ending that agreement."

"I've already apologised for the muck-up of the last drive, sir. It won't happen again."

"I sincerely hope for your sake that it won't."

"The trouble was that that old wooden lea-breaker didn't last. It should have been in a museum."

"Then why didn't you ask Hibbs to lend you an iron plough?"

Phillip hesitated, not wanting to involve the farms' manager, before replying, "I suppose I wanted to do things on my own."

"Initiative is all very well in an emergency, but this wasn't an emergency. You do see that?"

"Yes, Uncle, I see it. By the way, talking of museums, I found this bullock shoe in one of the fields. Uncle John said it might have been used in grandfather's time. It's exactly like the dark brown mark on one side of a partridge's breast."

"Don't talk to me about partridges. Your damfool machinery, right across the drive, turned most of the coveys on to my neigh-bour's land."

"Yes, I'm awfully sorry——"

"Remember what I told you about young Tofield—keep clear of him—he's a waster."

"Oh, I don't want to meet anybody. But talking about another kind of waster, Uncle, have you time to hear my idea about the rabbits? I don't feel I want to spend any time shooting them while the keeper ferrets them. It's too slow a job. Yes, I know about the traps; but isn't there another way to get rid of them? Many of them are diseased. Their livers have got yellow streaks in them, due to inbreeding."

"I won't have any gin-traps on my land."

"I agree. Uncle John says that trapping has caused the plague. The gin-traps catch the old bucks, who are first out of the buries at half-light. If they were not trapped, they would dig up and eat nests of young rabbits, in order, it seems, to bring the does sooner into season."

"You don't want them ferreted, and you don't want them trapped. Then what do you want?"

"Don't let Haylock allow badgers or foxes to be dug out. They're the natural enemies of rabbits."

"And of all game-birds."

"But surely rabbits are their main diet? Wasn't the lack of natural enemies the cause of the devastating plague of rabbits in Australia?"

"Rabbits are a dam' nuisance, everyone knows that. Now no more interference in my plans, if you please. It's time you developed a sense of balance. Well, I must be on my way. Where's Lucy? Ah, there you are, my dear. It's been a great pleasure to all that you were with us, and many thanks for today especially. I'll write to you about my future movements. Hang the birds on a north wall for at least a week, they taste better then. Remember me to your father when you see him, won't you, and to your grandmother. Give them a brace of birds apiece, with my compliments, will you? Goodbye, Billy my lad. Look after your Mother, won't you, now the stork's on the way."

"Iron Hosses come back, Nuncle. Daddy's Iron Hosses come back," said Billy, from behind Lucy's skirt. "Oh, good."

Mr. Hibbs had been appointed by Hilary on the recommendation of the agent, Captain Arkell. Exempted from service in the Army as 'indispensable' during the war, the young man had worked on his father's farm; afterwards he had persuaded the old man to let him have a year at an agricultural college. On returning to his father's farm he found that new ideas were not wanted, so he had left home: to find himself, as he put it to Phillip, out of the frying pan into the fire, condemned to carry out a policy which he believed to be old-fashioned and therefore unsound.

About a week after the shoot he asked to see Phillip, with a view to putting his ideas before him. The two walked round the estate together.

If he could have his way, explained the manager, he would combine all six farms in one unit, to cut out overlapping. The day of the small farm was gone; most of the hedges he would grub out, and having got rid of the rabbits, which were vermin, would replace the hedges where necessary with barbed wire.

"I would grass down all but the best of the arable, get rid of the ewe flocks and turn the land over to milk. Look at your farm premises, Captain Maddison. They need extensive repairs, but it would be money thrown away to attempt to restore them. I'd have no truck with the present cowsheds, but milk where the herds are grazing. No, not by hand-milking, but by machinery on wheels. It's the coming thing. Most of our winters here are soft, the herds could remain out and lie where they feed except in hard weather."

"Would that involve a lot of food being transported, often in wet weather, Mr. Hibbs?"

"No, sir. To start with, I'd fold them like sheep on a catch-crop of vetches and trifolium, followed by a clover ley, followed by kale. Hay would be a stand-by, but put in portable racks. This way all dung and liquid manure will be dropped back and not wasted down the drains as in the yards at present. The fertility of the soil would soon be built up. I'd follow with a catch-crop again, then with a ley, then kale—put the arable under a six-course rotation, all held together by milk."

"How can you milk cows by machinery, Mr. Hibbs?"

"Nothing in it, sir. One of our leading downland farmers does it already. Draws the bail on wheels to the fields and milks by suction from a small petrol engine through pipes to half a dozen stalls. The suction is intermittent, acting through an interrupter valve which squeezes by means of a mechanical rubber band lining a cylindrical container. After milking"—went on Mr. Hibbs, as one having learnt the routine by heart—"the machine has to be cleaned, but that is done by steam injection under pressure through pipes sterilising all channels and working parts."

"I see."

"The six-course shift would supersede the obsolete eight-course rotation of catch-crop—roots—roots—wheat—barley—catch-crop. And since it takes the same labour and fodder to feed a poor cow as it does a good cow I would have pedigree stock from the start, and for the first few years would rear my milk-calves only. I would clear out the present dual-purpose rubbish, which are neither beef nor milk, and go in for the hardy breed from the Friesian isles off Holland, which are big baggers."

"You mean they bag most of the prizes?"

"Well, not exactly," replied Mr. Hibbs, allowing himself the suggestion of a smile. "With their big milk-bags they yield up to four gallons a day of two milking periods, as opposed to an average two or two-and-a-half of our present redpolls."

They were crossing the arable ploughed by Johnson's Iron Horses. Mr. Hibbs kicked a lump of yellow marl.

"That won't grow anything, not even carlick."

"But isn't that a weed?"

"Even carlick won't grow on sour soil."

He went on to explain that carlick had sprung up when some of the old pastures in the vale, which hadn't felt the plough since Napoleonic days, were turned under on compulsory orders from the Ministry of Agriculture during the war.

"But carlick didn't show itself much after the first ploughing. We had a plague o' wireworm, which bred freely in the rotting sods and left the wheat bulb alone the first season. Father's idea was to kill two birds with one stone the following season, when we adopted the then-new beet-sugar cropping. Beet-sugar requires deep cultivations, so he got the ploughing done by Johnson's Iron Horses set-in twelve inches deep. We had so much carlick in May and early June that father had to hire school-children to pull up the yellow weed in handfuls. We couldn't even use the horse-hoe, the drills were smothered."

"What a tremendous lot you know, Mr. Hibbs. Do tell me, why was there so much carlick? Surely wild mustard doesn't grow in grass?"

"The rind or shell of the carlick seed contains a lot of oil, which preserves it. The seed had worked its way down worm holes, and lain there for well over a hundred years. We got rid of it by hand-pulling, as I said."

"And you think that this sour soil is so barren that even if any carlick were here, it wouldn't flourish? What should one do?"

"You might try cross-ploughing in the spring, when the rubbish you put under should be well-rotted. But don't let it worry you. You're not the first who's made a mistake. Rain will bring down nitrogen, and frost will help to weather the sour soil. I'll see Cap'n Arkell and advise some artificial on the seed-beds."

"For folding cows on—vetches and trifolium?"

"That's the idea, sir. Milk. There's an idea among the farming community to form a co-operative society to market dry milk and other milk products. If you can persuade Sir Hilary, I'll work on the idea of milk with the agent."

"I think all what you've told me is extraordinarily interesting. I feel that I'll never be able to learn all there is to learn."

"The progressive farmer learns something every day, sir. And if I may venture an opinion, you show that you have the ability to grasp the necessity of ley farming with both short and long leys. My father won't have it, he says that milk will suck the fertility away, but I tell him that with the bail all the fertility is left behind to grow a profitable crop of wheat where before two rabbits fought for one blade of grass."

Chapter 4

WEEST WEATHER

The weather became grievous outdoors; so much the better when the north-west wind drove rain against the rattling casements, and at times the beechwood smoke wavered and bulged into the room. His farmer's conscience was at rest, he could concentrate happily on the writing of his story of water, reed, tree, cloud, and stone. In imagination he was living with the spirit of lost love, his memories of sand and wave and tideless Mediterranean sea, where the cub, in Barley's cage of hands, had known its first salt wave; where Shelley was of the corals and the dreaming weeds of the Mediterranean sea. Had drowned Shelley risen with her upon his Cloud, to outsoar, with Keats, the shadow of Night; to fall as rain upon the granite rocks of Dartmoor and nourish the starveling lichens, mosses, and grasses?

He knew that such derivative thoughts had no value, beyond release of constriction before the true flow began.

> When, to the new eyes of thee,
> All things, by immortal power,
> Near or far,
> Hiddenly
> To each other linkèd are,
> That thou canst not stir a flower
> Without troubling of a star;
> When thy song is shield and mirror,
> To the fair snake-curlèd Pain . . .

He sat at the table with a map of Dartmoor before him. There in the fen between Great Kneeset and Whitehorse Hill five rivers were born. Should he ask Lucy to go with him?

When she came upstairs with the mail she said, "I wish I could, Pip. But there's the Church Council meeting this afternoon, and I promised to go with Uncle John."

He reversed an envelope addressed in Hilary's clear writing. "Hide it! If I open it all feeling will go from me. What's in this one?"

It was from his literary agent. Cowdray & Smith offered £50 advance for *The Water Wanderer*, subject to contract.

"I must finish the book," he muttered, as Lucy took away the unopened letter; but he could not settle to work; and called down the stairs, "May I have some coffee, then will you open Nuncle's letter and tell me if it's adverse or favourable. No, don't tell me what it says. Just say 'adverse'—or 'favourable'."

The coffee took a long time to arrive, it seemed, while thoughts of Nuncle were his unsettling. He ran to the landing and shouted down, "Is it good or is it bad? Tell me, don't keep me in suspense!"

"I am reading it," she called up the stairs. "It's good I think. Do you remember asking Uncle Hilary——"

"What does Nuncle *say*?" he yelled.

"He says he will be able to arrange two passages for Fiennes and Tim to go to Australia, if they are willing to work. The *Laurentia* sails from Tilbury, let me see—when was it—oh yes, here it is—it sails from Tilbury——"

"You've already said that! When, when?"

"He says next April."

"Oh, good! I'll come down and we'll have coffee together. Afterwards will you cut sandwiches for two? I'll send a telegram, and ask Tim to come with me to Dartmoor. I'm sorry I shouted at you."

Lucy was happy. Fiennes and Tim were doing no good at home, now that the Works were more or less closed. The sooner they had jobs to go to, the better. Ernest would look after Pa; and Phillip need worry himself about the silly Works no longer.

While waiting for Phillip to arrive, Tim imagined the great liner *Laurentia* surging forward under the flashing stars of the Southern Cross, of which he had read in stories of his boyhood. Dolphins leapt out of phosphorescent waves as he leaned reflectively upon white rails shaking a little from the steady beat of the great engines. And then—Australia! He imagined himself building a homestead in the Back of Beyond for Pansy, his girl in the village shop, whom he saw secretly and shyly. Mocking Birds sang—or was it the Laughing Jackass? Anyway, there were kangaroos to bound away into the horizon of the setting sun. But when he thought that he might never see Pa again, and the home where he and Lulu had shared so much happiness, he felt sad, and then afraid.

Still, it would be some time before he would have to leave. And today Phillip was going to take him to Dartmoor, a most wonderful place, known since his boyhood for *The Hound of the Baskervilles*. What good luck that Phillip had come into their lives, a hero of the Great War. Tim always felt reassured when in the company of Phillip, who always knew what to do in any emergency. Not much could go wrong with the old home, with Phillip in the offing to keep an eye on things when he and Fiennes were gone. Oh no, there was no need to worry. Ernest would be able to support Pa with his legacy, and by Jove, when Pa had passed on, he might even be able to join him and Fiennes 'down under'. The Copleston Brothers were by no means a thing of the past! Engineers would be needed in Australia, 'the land of unbounded opportunity'. By Jove, he must telephone 'Mister' the good news.

They drove west into a dull morning threatening rain. There was a long drive before them, and then several hours' walking

up the valley of Taw Head to Cranmere Pool, the loneliest part
of the moor.

"I suppose Ernest will sell the Tamp after you and Fiennes
have gone, Tim?"

"I have mentioned the matter, Phil, and Ernest says he will
bear it in mind, when the fine weather comes."

"There's Fiennes' 'Peerless' motor-bicycle as well. It's almost
unused, what about selling that? You'll need every penny, you
know, when you get to Australia. Work may not be too easy to
find."

"Fiennes hopes to take it with him, but I understand that the
cost may prove prohibitive," replied Tim, in the mid-Victorian
idiom he had learned from Pa. "But Ernest will sell it, he says,
if he gets an offer."

"He'll have to *find* a buyer, you know, Tim."

"Yes, I agree. I must remember to mention the matter to
him——"

When they reached Exeter and turned south-west for the moor
the rain was beating into their faces with the force of half a gale.
Wet and cold, they left the outfit on a track of granite gravel
beyond Belstone, and followed the valley below which ran the
clear waters of the little Taw. The wind had dropped but it was
still raining. Through moss and bog plashes their boots squelched,
for they had descended so that Phillip might observe the mossy
stones, the amber water, the diminutive trout of the stream which
broadened where cattle and wild ponies had broken bays along its
course.

Walking beside the stream meant water chronically in their
boots, so they climbed out of the valley, coming to a dry wall of
granite marked Irishman's Wall on the map. A female sparrow-
hawk flew up from a small mound, its plucking place. There lay
the remains of her kill, the skull and long beak of a snipe, its wings,
feathers, and gizzard. The mound was also visited by a fox, Phillip
pointed out to Tim: pellets of greyish fur and bone lay near it.
"Perhaps the fox at night comes for what the sparrowhawk leaves
by day."

"By Jove, all this is most interesting, Phil. I used to be keen
on nature when I was young, Lu and I used to explore all around
our home before we moved to Down Close."

"You don't mind the rain?"

"Not in the very least."

The hillside rose steeper, and they went down once more to the river-bed, now a succession of boulders. While walking up-stream they heard a dull, far-away report, succeeded by a swishing noise, and with a loud plop a dud shell fell fifty yards away. Phillip remembered that this part of the moor was an artillery range; they were under the arc of fire. As they went on they heard behind them the familiar chromatic whining of heavy stuff. Near the summit of a tor on their left front there appeared the fan-shaped bursts of high explosive shells. *Womp-womp-womp-womp.* The heavy detonations of the salvo smote the air of the valley. It was a strange sensation, that of being two personalities at the same time: one in the past, the other in the present. He thought now that if the War came again, he would have no apprehension about death. It was only the very young who longed for immor-tality.

He thought himself back into the rain of Third Ypres, 'Spectre' walking beside him up to Zonnebeke, and beyond to the Passchen-daele ridge, by way of the railway cutting. When, when, when would he be able to finish his book of those days? God, over twelve years had passed since the British Expeditionary Force had fallen back in exhaustion before the right wing of von Kluck's army-group, and the London Highlanders were awaiting orders to go overseas. It seemed but yesterday that they were marching through the Surrey countryside, while villagers and farmers came out with baskets of fruit and jugs of milk and beer for the brigade. How hot was that August sun, how heavy their equipment, how sore their feet, how proud they were afterwards that not a man of the battalion fell out, although in the wayside shade many soldiers of other battalions of the London Regiment were lying there, pale-faced and exhausted. How they had longed for that burning sun three months later, standing all day and working all night in the flooded trenches south of Ypres.

Now the whining of the shells almost drew the heart out of his breast for those vanished scenes and faces. He *must* finish the otter book, and then write of the truth of the war. O, why had he allowed himself to become a farmer?

Then he was thinking how good it was to be alive and free on the wild moor, life clear and natural as the water running on the rock all around him.

A herd of ponies moved away casually yet surely from their approach. They were small, shaggy, with bodies like little barrels.

Or was this fatness an illusion due to an almost permanent dis-
tension, caused by cropping grass that most of the year was wet?
The entire moor was running with water. The soil was thin,
compost of ancient grass and rush and heather, growths which
slowly crept, thousands of centuries ago, from the sea to these
granite hills. Had it not been for the Atlantic rains, had these
granite hills been in another part of the world where rain was
infrequent, they would be gaunt and dull glittering with crystals
left by the crash of genesis.

Talking about these things to Tim, who listened and expressed
his interest with an occasional 'Ah!', they climbed steadily up
the narrowing valley of the Taw and came to a wilder and more
broken aspect of the moor: peat hags like little islands in a lagoon
of bog, extended everywhere across the misty summit of the Great
Kneeset.

At first Phillip feared to tread in the bog, mindful of the many
stories of strangers being lost on the moor and never seen again.
After some minutes of hopping from hag to hag, followed by Tim,
he trod gingerly on the black spread of bog, and pressing harder,
to his surprise found that it was firm peat, the nailed impress
of his brogues hardly penetrating a quarter of an inch.

"I remember reading now that the 'bogs' of fiction are the
green 'quakers', hollows in the rock which are filled with water
and poa grasses, with duckweed and starwort on top, Tim. This
'bog' is only dead heather layers, too soilless to rot down to genuine
humus. I don't suppose there are many worms up here to break
down the acid peat, and precious few bacteria."

"Ah," said Tim.

"After all, if one thinks it out, nothing but rain comes here to
increase the life of this high ground. However, rain or snow must
add to the nitrogen in the peat. Look at the wind-harried condition of these peat-hags."

He wrote in his note book, *Islands of desperate vegetation*.

With the 1-inch contour map set by prismatic compass, they
went on to find Cranmere Pool. A mist was drifting across the
hill; Tim acted as marker, advancing on the lubber line of the
magnet to the point of fading visibility, then to stand as marker
until Phillip caught up with him for the next advance. It was
rather fun, Tim agreed; they were explorers.

"I fancy Pa has cousin George's prismatic compass somewhere,
just the thing for Australia."

Soon they came upon the slight hollow which was Cranmere, an empty pool of about a rood, with broken grassy banks. There was a post driven into the turf, and below it an iron box containing a book with the signatures of former visitors, together with a post-office stamp and ink-pad.

"The idea is to post your letter here, and the next visitor takes it away to put it in a letter box, so Pa told me," said Tim. "He came here once with Cousin Suff, and they brought back a small bottle of water from Taw head."

"You mean the uncle of Mary Ogilvie's mother?"

"I think it probably was, but blessed if I really know, Phil. Pa once told me that he had reckoned up that he had over eight hundred cousins, but we know only about thirty or so."

They wrote their names in the book, a fairly new one; the original book, which had contained the signature of the Prince of Wales, had been stolen by some curio collector, Phillip told Tim. "I read about it in the *South Hams Gazette*, when I was living on the coast south of here. A pity; it should have gone to some museum."

"I agree, every time."

Phillip wandered around the dry tarn, while Tim waited by the haversack, not wanting to disturb Phillip's thoughts. Beside him was a hummock, on top of which was a slight yellow patch and small dark blobs with specks of white in them. By Jove, they were an otter's spraints! He walked over to tell Phillip of this tremendous find. Phillip hastened to the hummock and knelt down.

"You're right, Tim." He bent his head to sniff. "Yes, a sweetish smell. You know, Lutra may have crossed over the watershed here. We must look for his spoor."

They found no tracks. Phillip wrapped the spraints in his handkerchief. "When we get back I'll put them in a glass of water, as I used to do with owl's pellets, and find out what he's been eating."

"By Jove, yes," remarked Tim, gratified that he had found an important clue.

"Talking about eating, you start on the sandwiches, Tim. I want to take some notes about the source of the Taw, also of the Torridge, which must start near it—brother Taw and sister Torridge."

He found the rise of the Taw, a slight channel about four inches wide and six deep, a mere trickle of amber water, and followed it until it broke its first bubble upon a stone of white granite made yellow by algae. Not far off was the Torridge, a diminutive pool hardly big enough to bathe a baby. What a place to baptise Billy! He sat awhile in the heather, his mind living other days, until the inevitable sigh of resignation, and return to the present.

Now he must go to the southern slope of the hill, and find the sources of Tavy, Teign, and Tamar. Yes, he must carry Billy up in the spring and touch his forehead with the water where perhaps Lutra had touched, Lutra who had known the warmth of her breast, but not Billy.

While he was eating egg-sandwiches beside Tim the rain, which had held off during the last part of their climb, began to fall again. All was now obscured by mist; they plodded back the way they had come, while the afternoon grew darker with clouds thickening about them. The motor-bicycle outfit was still by the gate, a welcome sight. Along the granite track with its plashy potholes they bumped, through rain that poured steadily during all of the return journey. Their clothes were heavy with water. The only stop on the way back was for petrol.

Lucy was out when they returned. He asked Mrs. Rigg where she was.

"She's gone up to see Squire, sir."

"Did she say when she'd be back?"

"After tea, sir. Shall I get 'ee something to ait?"

"No thank you, Mrs. Rigg. Is the fire in, for hot water?"

"Us'v run out of coke, sir. Th'vire be gone out."

Phillip turned to Tim. "I'm afraid I can't offer you a hot bath." He added, "I should have ordered the coke myself. But one doesn't think of such things when writing."

"Ah," said Tim. "Anyway, I'm quite all right, I do assure you."

"I'll lend you some clothes, and you can wash in the bathroom. Mrs. Rigg, will you fill the kettle on the lapping crook? I'll build up a fire. It won't take long, Tim. Go you up, my dear, and cast your sobbled clout, then zit you down yurr, by the vire, do! How about that for a farmer, Mrs. Rigg?"

"Aw, 'tes proper, my dear."

When they had washed and changed their wet clothes, they had tea, sitting in the blaze of split beech logs, while Phillip thought what fun it would be if Tim, instead of going to Australia, were coming to live at Skirr, and learn to farm. He would have a deputy, an adjutant; and be able to write more often, instead of being chronically shocked out of a state of dreaming with his eyes open, which wasn't so bad a phrase, he thought, to describe the act of writing.

He was about to speak of this idea to Tim, but saw that he had dropped asleep in the heat of the flames; and going up to his room, he added to the notes which the rain had interrupted.

> Cranmere is a hollow with broken peaty banks. A horn winds out of its northern end, filled with stagnant water.
> It would not be true to write that the rivers begin as 'bright threads of water'. Taw slinks through turf in a narrow, winding, grass-covered channel which splodges out into peaty slides after twenty yards or so.
> The Torridge (Ockment on map) begins in broader channel. Water the colour of Irish whiskey. It becomes bright when it meets the slope of the hill, where granite makes its first bubbled music.
> Black-faced sheep appearing out of mist.
> Torridge rises in maze of broken humps of turf, rounded by grey moss—the otter rolls in moss in sunlight.
> The Great Kneeset is occluded. In cold wafts and hollows the vapour drags past. I sit among the clouds.

How to convey the *occluded* moor in rainy winter weather? How could he re-create, in words, the muffled silence—omitting the *cliché* muffled? Descriptive prose must be brief, it must startle with an immediate picture in the mind. It must feel cold.

> The waters wan, and the water wap

Malory's *Morte d'Arthur*: seven words of a necromancer, calling up the 'tarn in the hills', the ripples breaking on a sandy shore, sere reeds vibrating in the wind, amber waters 'lonely as a cloud'. 'Poets live on air', and nourish one another.

> Cranmere is a hollow with broken peaty banks——

No good. He went downstairs, and heard Tim gently snoring in the armchair.

The December month darkened with rain. Colder winds brought sleet, which wandered aimlessly over meadow, field, and down. The sleet foreran snow, which thawed; then from the north-east whirled a blizzard all through a night and a day and a night. Telephone wires lay distraught; a man, with strips of sacking tied to above his knees, and a corn-sack over his shoulders, his eyebrows melting icicles, called with a message that the ewe-flock on Turk Farm was buried. Wonderful, blood-warming action followed: the war without fear and dereliction. Phillip was out until only two ewes remained unfound. This was the life.

"I 'eard a raven," said the shepherd, "callin' another lewside thak barrow by th' ould thorn up Comberley. Reckon ewes be ther."

Stars, and the keen air of eternity, walking beside Joby the Shep with crook and dog—men in the moon—lantern casting grotesque shadows as their foot-pressures squeaking with wadded snow. The wind was gone, stars glittered, this was the life—and he had *a warm room to go back to.*

They found the ewes under a riven white-thorn growing out of the lee side of the barrow, burial mound of some ancient British chieftain. One ewe already had two lambs, the other was soon to give birth. He stared at the scene, eager for details; the ewe squeezing out its young head-first; the lamb slithering out, fish-like, seeming to be entangled in the jelly-like placenta streaked with blood. Entoiled in what was now cold slime, it rested while it breathed for strength. It became a fawn-head in the lantern light, piping weak cries in reply to the bass mutter of its dam lying still, save for slight head-movements, on her flank. There followed the first small struggle of the lamb to use its feet. It found them, struggled up, to sway on unfamiliar legs which had their own independent motions ending in collapse. It gave weak cries for help; answering mutter from the diaphragm of the ewe, urging it to come to her. The wet thing remained trembling on its knees; the ewe called again, encouraging it to use its own strength. 'Take up thy bed and walk.'

Another effort; lamb struggling upon small cloven feet, to sway about, to appeal again, to be encouraged to 'stand on its own feet', thus to get to her.

Joby the Shep was encouraging the ewe. She gains strength from his feelings, she feels the shepherd's kindness, she knows that her flanks are protected, she can go forward into the attack upon the world's latent evil with confidence. *Krok-krok-krok* of raven under the moon.

The ewe passed on her love to the lamb. *Baa-baa!* It tottered forward under its own stilt-like powers, going forward by instinct, that inherited spiritual resolve. Encouraged—the very word!— by that low mutter it grows in determination; it finds the dug; its exaltation shows in the throbs of satisfaction passing through its body and wriggling down its spine and out of its tail. Mother and child were joined in love; and all the time the shepherd's dog, silent and still, eyes lambent in lamp-light, was flairing its nose for scent of fox or badger.

The next ewe, a dozen yards away, lay with her 'double couple' of two lambs. He didn't like to ask Joby if 'double couple' meant that both had shared the same umbilical cord. The phrase was enough. The ewe had had her twins an hour or so, she was licking them to help dry their tiny pelts, the small curled wool of which looked like the burr of the walnut table top in Lucy's boudoir.

"Us must bring them whoam, young maister."

"Give me your orders, Joby, I am your 'prentice."

"Yar'll do, maister."

It was now Joby's turn to encourage the ewe. With a lamb in the crook of each elbow, he held them low while Phillip placed the lantern so that she could see them, for a cloud was over the moon. She lay still, calling them; but now it was time to enter a dimension created by man. She must forget her established shelter, her base of warmth, she must begin again. Her loneliness must be transcended; it must be shared, for her world was civilised. The shepherd walked slowly backwards, showing her the lambs, encouraging her to get on her feet. With a trace of protest, of weakness, of self-pity in her middle-range *baa-baa* she got up and after a moment of bewilderment took their scent, replied confidently to Joby's bleating.

It was now Phillip's turn to persuade the ewe with the single lamb. At first, perplexed by his scent, she was flustered. He touched her nose with the lamb, before withdrawing to walk backwards to make her get up. She arose in a flurry of wool and glinting water-drops of melted snow and ran to its bleat, eager now, bumping gently into the back of his knees as he carried the lamb beside Joby on the way to the lambing fold in the lee of the wood.

Sometimes the shepherd imitated the bleating of his couple snuggled under his shoulder sack to get his ewe to follow.

The fold, a double row of nutwood-hurdles, straw packed between them, was built in the form of a square. Within the square, under a roof of more hurdles roughly thatched with barley straw, was a range of cubicles, or cubby holes, whence came the happy cries of lambs warm with their dams, tenants of a now familiar city. The newcomers settled in, their natures full of proprietary regard re-established within the security of the flock. Phillip's ewe began to gnaw a swede root, after turning to give a happy sniff at the anus of her lamb. Then, snuffled in oat straw (Joby would have no barley rubbish within his fold) the newcomers lay with their lambs half hidden in their fleeces.

The writing *trauma* was disrupted at the dark end of the year. For Christmas they went to Down Close, Phillip to feel defeated by the same unreturned acid carboys, in their rusty cages, five of them worth £25; the Tamp, half embraced by brambles, becoming a skeleton under the Workshop windows; and Miss Calmady, good-natured, fat, and untidy, the front-half of her hair falling over her forehead, the back hair enwisped as a feather knot at the back of her neck. The garbage pails outside the scullery door were solid with ice. The dropped door of the derelict smith's shop stuck half-open to allow a sight of rusty anvils, new bellows, tools, clusters of horse-shoes lying about. Broken china and glass, tins, rags, and decayed cardboard boxes littered the yard.

More snow fell on Christmas Eve and covered all gently with white. Trooping to church in the morning; Tim leaving to spend the rest of the day with Pansy and her mother. The Christmas festivities, otherwise the roasting of the turkey, had been postponed until Boxing Day. The previous evening Phillip had overheard the reason.

"I knows 'ee won't mind if I spends me Christmas 'oliday with me friends up th' lane, will 'ee, Master Tim?"

"By all means, Miss Calmady, by Jove yes, that will be quite in order."

He had wanted to spend Christmas at home, before his blazing hearth; but Lucy, he knew, wished to be with her father and brothers; it was probably the last time the family would be together. After a partly silent and wholly indigestible lunch of the cold remains of a fragment of hard, overcooked cow-beef and acid yellow pickles, he went for a walk by himself, while thinking of his parents spending Christmas alone, since his sisters were still forbidden the house in that sad, drab suburb of London.

Usually the Coplestons had their Christmas dinner at night;

but at breakfast on Boxing Day Miss Calmady made a further request—Colonel Coperston wouldn't mind, would 'a, if 'er went, after lunch, vor visit her sister in Shakesbury?

"Oh, not at all, not at all," Phillip heard Pa's prompt reply. "I suppose you'll want to cook the turkey before you go?"

"Aw yaas, I'll cook'n, if you'm a mind to eat'n midday, like."

In due course, about one o'clock, Miss Calmady carried in a large dish and put it before Pa. The old gentleman stared at the sight of a 22-lb. stag-turkey complete with long skinny neck and baked head curled about a body awash with Beefo gravy. After this, in silence, arrived a tureen piled with potatoes hard-baked on one side and white on the reverse, followed by its twin piled with deliquescent sprouts faded of nearly all colour. Then Miss Calmady, wiping her large hands on her only 'apern', which she had worn ever since taking up her duties in the kitchen, wished a good time to be had by all and departed.

"I suppose we must be thankful for small mercies," said Pa, peering at the monument. "At least she has plucked the brute."

"Ah," replied Ernest.

Then Billy, watching from a high chair the removal of the bird's head, exclaimed, " 'At pore dickybird might want 'is 'ade one day. You put'n back, Pa!"

"Ha," said Pa. "Somehow I don't think it will be needed."

In the afternoon Phillip said he must go home to work.

After a pause Lucy said, "All right, we'll come with you."

"No need for that. I'm sorry, but I must work. The weather report says more snow."

"Well, don't blame me if there's no hot water. I *did* order some coke, but it hasn't come."

"I'll manage with wood."

"I think I'd better come, too."

They went back through a landscape heavy with unshed snow. He spent the evening sawing and splitting small logs with which to stoke the boiler. Then to his room, to take the manuscript from the wall-cupboard, with its rusty hand-forged strap-hinges, where he kept a few relics of Barley—a hair-ribbon, the wedding ring, the sand-shoes with the lace that had broken on the penultimate day of her life. He managed to write a few unreal paragraphs, each one slower than the last. What was the use of going on? Who would want to read such a dull account of rushes, heather, trickling water, ice, and draggled white blossoms of the cotton plant? His life seemed to be ebbing away without purpose. He was nearly thirty-two years old: he had achieved nothing that he had set out to do.

That night a second blizzard coiled out of the north-east. In the morning the casement windows were clogged. A pallid light filled the living-room. After breakfast Lucy took Billy on the lawn to make a snowman. Phillip went to see what the men were doing. They were smoking in the stables, the horses and stock were fed, there was nothing else to do, so he went back again. In the afternoon he was sitting at his table, pen in hand and living in the imagination when Rusty started to bark outside. Looking through the window he saw two young men standing by the snowman and talking to Lucy. She saw him; there was nothing for it, he must go downstairs. She came towards him with smiling, blushing face.

"Mr. Tofield has called with a friend. They hope they aren't disturbing you."

"I suppose I must see them."

"They're outside, talking to Billy."

Looking through the casement he saw that one of the young men wore a brown overcoat and a trilby hat, while the other, taller and slimmer, was clothed in a dark blue ski-ing suit, and wearing on one side of his curly head a grey Tyrolean felt hat. His skis stood upright against the yew-tree on the lawn, beside his sticks.

"I'll come out now."

Phillip went out in his slippers, a bandanna handkerchief round his neck to keep in the warmth of a corduroy jacket.

The plump young man began with an apology for intrusion, explaining that he was staying in the neighbourhood and, having read an article in the *Crusader*, and being told that the author lived in the neighbourhood, he wondered if Mr. Maddison would consider giving a talk for the B.B.C.

"My name is Plugge. May I present Mr. Piers Tofield?"

"How d'you do."

Plugge went on, "Piers and I have temporarily escaped from the turmoil of life at the Coal Hole. I expect you know that pot house in the Strand?"

Phillip took the soft hand, and shook it enthusiastically, liking Plugge's large, benevolent, and almost entirely round face upon the upper half of which was fixed, in conjunction with his ears, a pair of American horn-rimmed spectacles with lenses which enlarged a pair of dark brown eyes so that he had the appearance of an owl; but unlike an owl, always ready to enjoy the brighter world.

"I never managed to get so far west of Fleet Street when I was helping to draw *The Weekly Dust Cart*, otherwise *The Weekly Courier*."

At this remark the plump young man screwed up his lips and laughed almost girlishly; but the laughter ceased at the next words.

"Would you care for a pint of beer?"

"Would I not."

"We have a Wood Hole upstairs," went on Phillip, leading the way to his writing room. There, in the middle of a wall of logs, rested the pin of home brew. A set of pewter mugs, ranging from quart pot to half-noggin, hung across the chimney piece. These had been bought from the landlord of the Rising Sun in Colham.

"My word," said Plugge. "A most excellent sight, if I may say so."

Phillip stooped to fill the quart pot. Plugge stood by to take it, but Phillip offered it instead to Billy.

"I say, can he manage all that?"

"Ah, I hear the voice of envy. Can you manage a quart, Plugge? Tofield, do you mind the pint pot?"

The other man hesitated, while giving a modest half-look at Lucy.

"I'm afraid beer is wasted on me," she murmured, colouring at this defect, as she thought of it, while lowering her lashes.

"I must see to the tea," she said, and left the three men sitting with the child around the fire.

"I hope I'm not being most frightfully inquisitive, but who is Nuncle?" asked Plugge. "I heard Billy saying something about Nuncle and an Iron Horse."

"Nuncle comes yurr, don't 'ee?" asked Billy, appealing to Phillip for confirmation.

Again Plugge laughed loudly; then seeing the child's face he stopped as suddenly as he had begun. "I say, do forgive me, I *am* so sorry, but honestly, I thought it was all a joke of your father's." He looked at Tofield before saying, "Who, or what—if it isn't most awfully rude of me to ask, is 'Nuncle'?"

"Well, the name really illustrates an everlasting human problem
—*the* problem, I think. Which side of a man's nature is the real
one?"

Feeling that he had gone beyond the depth of his audience
he told them about the shoot, and how the appearance of the Iron
Horses had diverted all the birds of the best drive.

"I heard about that," said Tofield. "Brilliant. Every bird
out-flanking the guns."

Phillip admired the way Tofield talked, always with understatement, and usually making a point obliquely. From what was
said he and Plugge appeared to belong to the London set of young
men and girls who had grown up just after the war, and so had
had all the reaction to the war years without any of the action.
He had read of some of their original, daring, and occasionally
outrageous (to the older generation) doings in the gossip columns
of *The Daily Crusader*.

They stayed to supper. Phillip had three bottles of champagne,
kept to celebrate the birth of Lucy's baby due at the end of February. He opened one, they drank to 'Lucy, and the trout', Phillip
reminding them that *Pisces* was the zodiacal sign for the end of
February.

Plugge seemed puzzled; but Tofield turned away any possibility
of further questions by asking Phillip, Did he ski? He would be
glad to lend him a pair if he cared to borrow them. Phillip said
that he had never skiied; whereupon the other replied that he
would be delighted if Phillip would care to accompany him on
the downs. By the end of the evening they were using Christian
names. Archie Plugge said he had to go back to the office next
day, unfortunately.

"Yours is quite the jolliest party I have ever been to, Lucy,"
he said. "May I come again?"

"Yes, do," replied Lucy. "Phillip and I so seldom see anyone."

"I am a great admirer of his work," continued Plugge, who had
read one newspaper article half-through. "I do hope that we
haven't interrupted it too deeply."

"On the contrary," said Phillip. "All is fish that comes into my
net, Archie."

"I say, am I to appear in another book? I'm in one already,
you know, Tony Cruft's new novel—it's to appear in the autumn,
I hear. Well, it has been *most* enjoyable, Lucy, and I *do* thank you
most awfully."

Gone were the first-day perplexities of balance, the fear of
toppling with crossed skis which could only be freed by lying on
one's back, lifting up aching legs with heavy elongated wooden
feet above one's head, precariously, then to one's flank to lie on
one's side to set them parallel in order to push sideways and try
to squat and then rise again.

The secret was bended knees, and one ski a little in advance of
the other after the push off with sticks, down the long slope, faster
and faster, juniper bush covered with snow in the way; stop by
sitting down and using one's wet behind as a brake. The technique
of rising was once more repeated. By the late afternoon, in
sharpening frost and the first glitter of stars, he could sail down
quite fast in a straight line, while the snow rose in little fountains
about the curved prows of his wooden feet and the wind softly
roared in his ears—Oh, this was the life!

The next morning they had the new world to themselves, as
they plumped up to the crest of the downs, leaving chevron-patterns
diminishing far down to the head of the borstal. *Plomp-plomp*, all
the way up to the sky-line, first one out-turned foot, then the other;
the body glowed, sweat cleared the mind. How welcome was the
crest, with its view of the vale below, black trees and hedges
spreading away under the sun to the loneliness of the Chase under
the sky. This was his own land—his people, before him, had lived
here. Then the sailing rush down again through keen air. He
learned to stem in a cloud of snow, to jump over small clotted
objects. The fingers, recently numb with cold in the valley,
glowed with warmth that filled his whole body with a feeling of
life lasting for ever.

They travelled the crest of the downs for miles, pushing themselves along with their sticks, wearing nothing above the waist in
the midday sun except dark snow goggles which Piers had brought
from Austria. Phillip made a fire one afternoon, in the lee
of a dilapidated bullock yard, its thatch half fallen, the flint
walls dropped away in patches. They lay on straw, eating
bread and smoked garlic sausage which Piers had brought from
London, and drinking red wine. They spoke about the war;
Piers said he read all he could get about it, having heard so
much about the fighting while at school, and wondering, with
the O.T.C. during field days, if he would be able to stand the
strain. The war had ended a few months before his sixteenth
birthday.

One late afternoon they followed the ridge way down to Colham, and the Rising Sun.

"I've been here once or twice," said Phillip. "'Bosun' the land-lord is quite a character."

The landlord was leaning both elbows on the mahogany bar-counter, visible from the waist up in thick blue worsted jersey and shapeless peaked chief-petty-officer's cap. A pint glass of beer was beside one elbow. On the floor of the bar-room, a fathom from the counter, stood a brass spittoon.

"Good evening, gen'l'men," he remarked, with movement only of eyes and lips.

"May we have two hot Irish whiskeys with lemon and sugar?"

"Missus!" bawled the landlord, swivelling his head through forty-five degrees. "Bring thik kettle o' hot water."

There came from behind the curtain the scrape of flattened slippers, followed by a pale face looking round the curtain hiding the barrel room.

"And may we have some eggs and bacon?" asked Phillip.

"Oh, it's the gentleman who came yurr in the summer on a motorbike. Yes, I can give you both a fry."

The two friends sat at a three-legged cricket table in front of a coal fire, drinking mulled claret, two musty bottles of which the landlord brought up from his cellar, explaining that 'two gents what went water-whippin' left'n there in the summer the war broke out and never came back to drink'n'', with thick fried slices of home-pickled gammon with eggs.

"I must say I find this an excellent place," remarked Piers.

The room was decorated with glass cases of stuffed birds, beside masks of badgers, various weapons of foreign make including spears and wooden clubs which might have come from the South Seas, rigged sailing ships in bottles, and hams wrapped in brown paper hanging from the beam that held the joists of the floor above. "Archie Plugge would feel very much at home here. How long have you known it, Phil?"

"Only since the summer."

"Have you done any fishing yet?"

The landlord, who had remained leaning over the bar, leaned forward. His cheeks tautened, and a salivary torpedo struck the brass spittoon amidships. "Whippin' water. Huh." He seized a bottle, squeezed away the cork, poured rum into the half-empty glass of beer, and tipped it down his throat. Then turning his face, with a cunning look in the salmon's eyes, chin thrust sideways as though inviting a lead from a boxing opponent, he said to Piers, "I suppose you think I don't know who you be, eh? Wull"— another torpedo into the spittoon—"I do know, see? Whippin' water gent, you be, totty li'l ole fish you takes 'ome, I knows, see?"

He held out his right arm, placing the index finger of his left hand between elbow joint and shoulder. "Scores and scores of fish I've took. Not by this yurr whippin' water——", his voice becoming exaggeratedly refined as his smile broadened with cunning, while his eyes were nearly enclosed below hairless brows— "this yurr toffs' way of *whippin'* water to get a totty li'l ole fish to take 'ome and get stuffed in a glass case." He poured rum into his glass. "Many and many's the time I've took trout four and five pun in weight and sold them to the toffs, and zeed in next week's *Col'am Times* a photygraff with the toff and 'is catch! And I zold'n th' booger."

"I suppose you did it with night-lines?" asked Phillip.

"Ay. Water-bailies or no water-bailies, I've had'm, y'knaw!"

"Did you ever try acetylene in bottles?"

"No, I never holt wi' that. I seed it done wance, and all the totty li'l fish in the river for a mile an' more down was turned up next morning. I don't holt wi' that kind of caper." He stared at Phillip. "I've a-seen you afore somewheres, I reckon."

"You sold me those pewter mugs."

"Ah, I've got you now. Very plaized I be for tew meet you agen. I hope you'm very well."

"Couldn't be better, after such an excellent supper." Mrs. Tinker, who had been listening one side of the curtain, now came out to give her husband a kick on the behind. "There you see, you ould toad. Someone likes my frys, see?"

"I don't trouble," replied Mr. Tinker, getting his third salvo on the brass target.

Midnight struck from the stable clock of Field Place. The whisky bottle on the table was half empty. The leather armchair was deep and comfortable, the hearth in play with lilac ember flammets.

"I suppose you heard the usual propaganda stories about 'Huns' at school?"

"I don't think we took any notice of them. There were a number of German boys at Eton throughout the war. They couldn't get back to Germany after the summer half, so they stayed with their housemasters' families during the holidays and were there when the Armistice was signed."

"What a wonderful school Eton must be. But then you had an exceptionally able Head Master, or is it Provost, in Lyttelton. I saw a caricature of him, beside Bernard Shaw's, done on a wall in a billet at Cambrin, near Loos, in nineteen fifteen. Both were hanging from a gallows. The guardsman who drew it was probably, like most of his regiment, killed a few days later in the attack on Hill 70. I watched the attack of the Guards Division from the Tower Bridge, above the Double Crassier. They fell in straight lines, one after another."

He told the story of how he had spent his light duty after the first two days of the battle looking round the front line.

"You must write that."

"I hope to, one day."

"No, soon. My generation knows nothing about the war. We want to know exactly what it was like. I suppose it was pure hell?"

It was now Phillip's turn to reply to Piers' assumptions.

"I rather enjoyed most of it, apart from the few real bad times. One didn't *realise* them at the time. How can I put it. Well, we all lived in an accepted idiom, after the first shock in action. And the 'horrors' of home-thought were not 'horrors' to us. They were always just a little apart from us. Only at moments was one overwhelmed; dead before death, as it were."

Piers listened with tactful silence, realising that his friend was not yet detached from what had happened in the past.

"I can show it, I mean reveal what I'm trying to say, by the popular, 1915 scorn and 'hate' against your Dr. Lyttelton, and G. B. Shaw. Even if the chap who drew the pictures had truly known that both wanted to stop the hell, he would still have felt righteous scorn against pacificism, side by side with his secret fear of death, and his sense of desolation so deep that it appeared to be ordinary life. It *was* our ordinary life. It was only *after* the war that we began to realise what an awful thing it was."

"Yes, I suppose that explains the paradox. I'd never thought of it like that before."

"I was lucky to be in a county regiment which was one large family. I suppose that was a substitute for a more or less unhappy childhood. I was glad when the war ended, in one way, but sorry in another."

"The party was over?"

"Exactly."

"Talking of parties, I do hope that when you come to London you will let me know, so that I can arrange one for you."

"I shall, certainly; but I can seldom get away nowadays."

"I can understand how happy you must be. I suppose it is fairly rare for husband and wife to be exactly suited."

Phillip wondered if he knew about Barley. "Did you know Lucy was my second wife, and not the mother of Billy?"

"I'd no idea."

Phillip told him his story, while the fire was made up, and the glasses refilled.

"Well, that's my dilemma. Art is a private world, I suppose. One seeks it from loneliness. But when I was with Barley I felt so clear and happy that I never wanted to write about the war, or anything else belonging to the past."

Piers said presently, "But Lucy, surely, loves you? Those lips, those eyes——" He went on in his level voice, "I've never found a girl I want to do more with than get her into bed."

It was 2 a.m. when, under sharp stars, Piers took Phillip home in his green racer over roads crackling with ice.

"Out tomorrow, Maddison! Meet at the beech hanger, zero hour ten ack emma, haversack ration."

"Zero hour ten ack emma. Message acknowledged, Tofield."

Lucy was in bed, but awake. "I'm so glad you've got a friend at last," she said. "It must be fun, ski-ing. I've always wanted to do it. Perhaps we shall together, one day. I've left you some sandwiches in your room, and a Thermos of coffee."

"Thank you. Good night, dearest Lucy."

The beech hanger was sealed in the north-west side by snow lodged there during the blizzard. Here under the skyline the flakes had whirled in eddy, and in the wind's delay had formed a tall and whitely carven cliff at the edge of the wood, beautiful with flowing lines as a Rodin sculpture. Upon the bare topmost branch stood a raven, floating off with a low *krok-krok-krok* of warning as they stomped near. Then about face, to fly down the borstal in travelling clouds of snow, faster, faster, head and shoulders well above the tops of the hedge on either side. It was marvellous to glide downhill with the keen-breathed wind thrumming in one's ears; faster and faster, with apprehension about the bottom, where the lane curved sharply to the left.

Fortunately the gate at the bend was open, and a friendly dung-heap by the cattle-shed made an appropriate buffer.

The next day Piers brought a letter to Lucy from his mother. Lady Tofield asked to be allowed to drop formality, she had heard such delightful accounts of their little boy from Piers, and would they all come to tea on the morrow. The three went over to Field Place, and sat before a great fire with a back-stick of half an ashtree as thick as a man. Lady Tofield was quiet and gracious, she seemed to be much taken by Billy, but often, in a pause in the talk, to be away in thought. Later, from Mr. Hibbs, Phillip heard that she had never got over the death of her elder son, who had died at two years of age.

Piers came to supper on the last evening of his holiday, and Phillip read some of the otter book to him while Lucy made a nightshirt for her coming baby on the other side of the hearth. Piers said afterwards that it was most moving; and when Lucy remained silent he turned to her, "Don't you think so, Lucy?"

"Yes," she said, while the colour came into her cheeks, and she looked on the ground.

Captain Arkell rang up and invited Phillip to a 'tree-shooting party'. They had three fine Douglas firs—he called them stands— in one of the woods, and the forester wanted scions to be taken from their topmost branches, to be grafted on to stocks already planted in the nursery.

"I don't know if he told you, but Sir Hilary is going into the costs of replanting the Forest with mixed hardwoods and conifers. The Forestry Commission give grants, in approved cases, of £2 for soft woods and £5 for hard woods, per acre. A year or two back we laid out a nursery behind Haylock's cottage."

Phillip took along his 12-bore. Piers did not shoot, he arrived on skis. Haylock the keeper had a bag of brass cartridges loaded with swanshot—fifteen to the ounce. Smaller shot, he said, would maul the tips, which must be broken off clean.

They took turns to shoot at the ends of uppermost branches. Down floated dark green feather scraps. The cleaner tips were selected by the forester and laid endways in a wicker basket. While Phillip was raising his gun, the keeper saw a red squirrel. "Get'n, zur!" he cried. Phillip let it go. Somewhat disturbed,

Haylock explained that it would cut off the tips of the growing grafts.

"They're de'ils for my saplings," said the forester.

"When will they be grafted? After the thaw comes?" Phillip asked Captain Arkell.

"Grafting of scions is usually done just before sap-rising. Until then, they'll be kept in an ice-house."

They saw some roe-deer at one end of the wood, small animals which fled in a flurry of snow. The agent explained that they were strays from some park, since the war. The new plantations, when set out, would have to be fenced with wire-netting five feet high.

"It'll cost a pretty penny if the whole Forest is to be replanted and fenced off, sir," said the forester. "Reckon forty pun the acre will hardly see it done, fencing, planting, and cuttin' out. There's nigh on four hunner acres to the Forest, then there's the scrub clearing, and blastin' of the old stubs."

"Planting is a long-term investment. Spruce parcels mature at forty years, and can be regarded as capital for death duties."

"And the oaks and beech, Captain Arkell?"

"The beech normally takes a century to reach maturity, the oaks about half as long again."

"So my uncle is looking ahead. What will happen if all land is nationalised?"

"I imagine there will be compensation—of a sort." And on the way back Captain Arkell mentioned that the War Department was considering an extension of military training ground, and one of the areas under consideration was, he understood, the upper area of the vale in a line extending north-east from the Longpond to a mile beyond the Rookhurst Forest.

"Does my uncle know about this?"

"I don't think so. Nothing is official, you understand, so I think it better not to mention it at the present time."

Soon after the thaw, when Piers had gone back to London, Lucy and Phillip helped to graft the scions. It was between the rising of the sap and the flushing, as the Scots forester called the time of leaf-breaking. He did the grafting, while Phillip carried a tray of scions, and Lucy a basket with softened bees-wax and lengths of bass. The forester worked fast. He made a T-cut on the side of a sapling, then opened the bark to lay bare the cambium, before holding the cambium of the scion to the cut. The bark enclosed it, then it was bound with bass and covered with wax to exclude air.

The needles of each scion had already been cut back to a dozen above the bud, the upper needles trimmed like a fighting cock's pinion feather, and dipped in warm wax to seal the ends. Thus the sap would enter the scion and thrust forward its growth. Eventually each scion would bear 'fruit', otherwise cones holding strong seeds for planting out in the nursery.

"How many years before the saplings will start life in the forest, Mac?"

"Och, several."

"I suppose Billy will be paying my death-duties with these scions, Lucy," said Phillip as they walked home.

Chapter 5

ROSEBUD

Soon after she returned from the nursing-home with her baby, Lucy went to bed with fever and micturition pains. The doctor came out and later a bottle of medicine was collected at the 'bus stop on the main road. Phillip nursed her, preparing simple food; milk, boiled eggs, and bread and butter. The baby appeared to have a bowel or stomach infection. Its stools were thin and yellow. Since it always cried after being at the breast he gave it bottles of diluted cows' milk and sugar added. The baby still cried, as though in protest. The doctor's advice was to get it into good habits by feeding only during the day. "Put it in a room by itself, and let it cry itself to sleep," he said. Phillip tried this for an hour, and then took on the job of night nurse.

Peter, as the mother called the baby, lay on its back across the father's thighs at night, while the mother was supposed to be sleeping to keep up her strength. It continued to cry after the first few sucks at every bottle. It could keep down nothing. Dill water was tried; its mother's breast; a stick of barley sugar; a dissolved soda mint; diluted Swiss milk out of a tin. Screams; froth; screams; choking—the father standing by with feelings of helplessness while it was apparently about to choke, or worse.

Supposing it sucked, during a paroxysm, stomach froth into its lungs? He carried it about the kitchen with its head hanging over his shoulder lest this happen, up and down where the dark waited all around the sad little flame of the candle. The baby quietened; the father lowered himself into a wooden chair, slowly placing the mite, with its death-like pallor, across his knees until it lay upon its belly. No use; it cried again, its face distorted, its screaming tearing into him. What could he do, beyond praying voicelessly for help, in the dark cavern of the kitchen warmed by two circular rings of blue flame behind the mica doors of the chimneys.

In her bedroom upstairs Lucy lay still, to preserve what little strength she had. She heard him saying, "Poor baby, poor baby, please don't cry. There—there." Tap tap. "Up it comes. That's better, isn't it, little fellow?" How history repeated itself, she thought, recalling what Mother (Hetty) had told her of Phillip's father nursing him when he was born, until the right food, the milk of a jenny-ass, had been found. She was wondering where such milk could be got when she heard Phillip stop his pacing of the kitchen floor, and his voice muttered, "That's it. That's what you need, my son. Donkey milk." She felt warm with happiness. they *did* think alike. In the morning she must write to Grannie; Ennis would know where to get some. She kept this idea from Phillip, lest in his impetuous way, he set off at dawn; and he must get some sleep.

As soon as Mrs. Chychester heard of the situation she wrote to Phillip inviting him to see her at her home. He had not shaved for a fortnight, he was growing a beard again.

"Do you think I should shave before going to see Grannie?"

"I think you look very nice with a beard." She thought it helped to offset his thin, rather delicate appearance.

To Shakesbury he went on his motor-bicycle, to hear a proposal that Miss Priddle, who had nursed Lucy's mother through her last illness, would, she felt certain, look after Lucy and the baby, should he approve the idea.

"I would be so glad if you would allow me to arrange this, dear Phillip, as a small return for all you have done for my grandsons."

"Thank you, Mrs. Chychester, it is most kind of you."

She leaned forward to take his hand. "Oh, but why do you not still call me 'Grannie'? Now let me ask Ennis to bring you some tea."

Neither Mrs. Chychester nor Mrs. Rawlings, her lady's-maid

of fifty years, appeared to have noticed the beard. He felt, as always in that house, at his best.

In due course Miss Priddle arrived: a raw-boned, thrusting woman of about fifty years of age, with a thin nose ending in a sharp point between two watery eyes. The first thing she did was to complain of Mrs. Rigg's presence in the kitchen. "I won't have her dirty ways about me, I can manage best by myself." So, with the departure of Mrs. Rigg, Phillip thought it might be more sociable—or civil as Uncle John would say—if in such a small house he suggested that they have their meals together; but very soon he ceased to digest any food while Miss Priddle was in the room, she was so emphatic in her dislikes.

"What do you think about this idea to have the common children's school in Shakesbury fitted with wash-basins and a place where wet overcoats can be dried in winter at the tax-payers' expense? I consider it *disgraceful*! Why, some of the little creatures come from back street homes where they've never seen a bowl of clean water! And here we are giving them all this luxury for nothing! Don't you think it is a perfect scandal?"

He made the mistake of replying to these emphatic opinions seriously, with the result that Miss Priddle assumed a haughty silence. The food remained half-eaten on the table. Soon he made an excuse to go to his room. There, unable to bear his feelings, he sought relief with Lucy.

"She's feeding the baby on *boiled* cow's milk. He can't keep it down. Boiling kills all nourishment."

Lucy managed to get him to see that Miss Priddle knew what she was doing; his thought took another line.

"'Spectre' West said, 'The slums have died in Flanders'. He meant that conditions for poor people would be different after the war. They've remained the same. Will the eyes of the stay-at-homes never be opened? Oh, why aren't I writing my war instead of 'Peregrinations in search of an Otter'—for that is all it is. Why am I 'farming'? It's all a waste of time and money. As Hibbs said——"

"I know how you feel," she replied, lying there with a yellow face that awoke fear in him: for Barley dying had had that look on a face more wasted. He took her hand, it was hot, not cold, thank God.

Her voice went on gently, "Try not to let it affect you. I am sure that if Miss Priddle was younger, and had to do with poor

children, their well-being would be her first concern. She was the
one who looked after Mother, you know, until she died."

"I'll try and be more sympathetic towards her."

The efforts were not successful. There was the matter of the
oil stove. Under Miss Priddle's management the kitchen was
frequently filled with floating smuts.

"I wonder if the wicks should be turned low when first lit, Miss
Priddle. The vaporiser is then cold, you see. Then, as it gets
hotter, it draws more oil up, and this turns to gas and burns with
an intense heat. The increasing heat——"

"I've seen plenty of oil stoves before I came here!" declared
Miss Priddle. "I wasn't born yesterday!" and out she went.

Alas, youthful good intentions for the improvement of age were
lost in the smell of oil-smoke the next morning; and running down
to the kitchen he saw flames rising nearly two feet above the
enamel chimneys of the stove. The iron frame was too hot to touch;
a gallon tank of oil was fixed to the base above iron legs. It was
warm, nowhere near flash-point, so he called Miss Priddle to see
what was happening, pointing out that the temperature of the oil
beneath was gradually rising to flash-point. She turned on him
with stony fury of face and said the wicks had been turned up
deliberately to spite her.

"You want to burn us all up! I know all about you! I've got
my copy of *The News of the World* home, for all as likes to see what
you are! You went to prison after the war was over, for arson,
we all know about *that*!"

When he was calmer he said to Lucy, "I begin to see what
Father meant, years ago, by my action in not standing up for my
family. I suppose that one wretched example of my conceit, in
shielding that idiot Tom Ching in nineteen nineteen will follow
me through life, like the incident of the pilgrim ship in *Lord Jim*.
There's another thing—why does she throw all the rubbish into
the hedge outside the kitchen door? I've put a new dustbin there
—part of 'a new world after the war'. Don't you see there's a
connexion, as Willie said? Not only should Great Britain be one
nation, regarding its people and resources as one for and with the
Empire, but everyone's aim should be to improve, improve,
improve!"

Miss Priddle complained to Lucy that he gathered her garbage
at night, and buried it. He cleaned the glazed earthenware sink
of grease, bacon rinds, and tea-leaves when she was not about.

"Is it my kitchen, or is it not? Did your Grannie send me here to look after you, Miss Lucy, or didn't she? I won't have any man trying to teach me my business! If it wasn't for you, and your dear dead mother, I'd pack my bag and leave immediately, that I would!"

"I think my husband is afraid of germs," said Lucy, weakly.

"Well then, let him look to the cows' milking, and the dirty udders they bring home to the cowshed, instead of finding fault with my kitchen and scullery——"

"I think the herdsman does wash them before milking, Miss Priddle."

"Yes, in rainwater from that insanitary water-butt, all a-wriggle with red worms."

Lucy said to Phillip, "Try not to let little things worry you, I'll soon be able to look after the house myself, so be patient a little longer."

"Yes, I'll concentrate on my writing. I want to re-create the early summer scene on the Chains of Exmoor. Remember how we walked there on our honeymoon, that day? The heather and ling were in flower, and the furze—purple and gold. I'd never dare to use those words in my description—but they would be true."

"You carried me for miles through the heather, when I had a blister."

"It was those heavy marching boots I forced you to wear."

"They were Lotus boots. I've still got them—they *were* a bit small, I'll admit. I'm keeping them for Billy."

Avoiding kitchen, scullery, and Miss Priddle, he spent most of his time in the small writing-room, going on the motor-bicycle to Colham to buy bananas, chocolate, and biscuits. While in the town he asked the doctor to take a specimen of Lucy's blood, or whatever was needed to test for typhoid. The doctor said, "She's got cystitis, that's all. It will clear itself up when the warm weather comes. Keep her well wrapped up, meanwhile. Nurse Priddle is a bit of a dragon, I know, but she's sound."

Then, abruptly came the climax: the village talking about a robbery. Phillip first heard of this through Ned the bailiff. Apparently one afternoon Miss Priddle, wheeling Billy in the mail-cart round the village, had stopped at door after open door to complain that 'that awful man, who had been in prison for arson', not only tried to burn them all up, but had gone to her bedroom, opened her trunk, and stolen ten pounds in notes. That was the reason, she declared, why he had not gone downstairs for his meals.

"Oh, I don't suppose they took much notice of her, Phillip," said Uncle John, adding, "After all, they know you—and they don't know her. You could of course take some action, but perhaps it would be best to ignore it, if only for Mrs. Chychester's sake."

"Yes, I'd thought so myself."

While he was seeing Uncle John, Miss Priddle was packing her bag.

"I feel I behaved badly," he said to Lucy, after she had gone. "You are right, I put her back up by putting that rubbish in the dust-bin. And I should have explained, at the start, about the way the Valor vaporisers hot up. But I wonder where the money went to? It couldn't have been 'Riggy', because she wasn't here."

"Oh, Miss Priddle will probably find that she left her money at home in its usual hiding place, a spare tea-pot or something like that. Anyway, Grannie likes you very much, and so does Uncle John. So don't worry any more."

When he had gone Lucy lay still, worrying about what would happen to him and the two little ones if she, like her mother, had tuberculosis. It all came back with startling clearness: Mother had died just before she arrived back from school for the summer holidays. The telegram had come on the last day of term, she had been called to Sister Agnes' room and told the news, with Sister Agnes' hand on her shoulder. There was no train home that night, it was war-time economy. She saw again the figures of Pa and Tim, then fifteen, looking lost as they stood together by the chalet on the lawn, where Mother lay dead. She saw their eyes, Pa's looking faraway in his gaunt face, Tim's swelled with weeping. Miss Priddle was crying, too. Tim had a Bible in his hand. Poor Tim, his hand was rather grubby. Later Pa told her that Mother had, just before she died, said to Miss Priddle, 'Will you bring the lamp, please, it is getting so dark.' Miss Priddle had at once fetched Pa from his rockery, where he was working in bright sunshine. Five minutes after asking for the lamp Mother had sighed as she held Pa's hand, and was gone.

She remembered the funeral, it was a rainy day, the last day of July, she had not been able to sleep the night before, and in the first grey light she had heard the dull booming of the guns in Flanders. It was said that the sound came through the chalk of the downs. She remembered that there was little in the house to eat, but that did not matter. It was the helpless look on Pa's and Tim's faces which had made her cry for the first time in her life. She could see Pa and Tim now, standing together, waiting for her to come home.

Earlier scenes of childhood arose, with never a cross word in her home, except from her governess, but that had not affected her, for she had Tim to think about. He and she had been inseparable during the holidays; while Ernest and Fiennes had always gone about together.

Lucy had cried only twice in her life. The second time was when she had gone to have lunch with Phillip in the postman's cottage, where he had his meals. They had just become engaged. She had gone into the cottage, and passed Mrs. Mules and Zillah the daughter without saying good-morning: she thought that one did not say good-morning to servants in a strange house. Afterwards Phillip had explained that the Mules were put out by it; Lucy thought she had let him down, she had turned away her head and wept.

They were married the following year, and very soon she realised that her former dream of Phillip and herself being like Mother and Pa was not to be. It was her fault, because she was not clever and quick like Barley, his first wife who had died when Billy was born.

Her baby cried, it was in torment. Early in the morning she had an idea, but she kept it to herself until Phillip came up with her morning cup of tea.

"Do you think you could spare the time to go to see Mrs. Smith? She's good with babies. She may know of something."

Within a quarter of an hour he was knocking at the door of Ruddle Stones.

"Babies vary, you know. What one thrives on, another can't take. Has Lucy tried Flowerdew and Heath's? It might suit Peter. Now you must have some breakfast."

"Well, thank you very much, but I think I ought to get the baby's food."

He went into Colham, and returned with a tin to Lucy. That afternoon the baby slept after its bottle, and again at night.

"I'll never criticise Mrs. Smith or 'Mister' again. Everything fits into the human scene, if only one has the wit, and the patience, to discover it. I'll write her a letter of thanks immediately."

Mrs. Rigg came back again, the kitchen was a happy place once more. Lucy's fever abated. Primroses were fading, bluebells rising in the hanger. Phillip continued to sit at his desk during most of the day, and sometimes at night. He was near the climax: Lutra was killed by hounds; it was free. Now Barley could arise from the grave.

He wept, thinking, I am an icicle, whose thawing is its dying.

The air was filled with birdsong, cloud-shadows moved over the downs. Lucy's first visit, after she was out and about, was to Uncle John. As she walked to the house she thought, What a friendly place it is. It stood in two acres of ground on the lower slope of Fawley down, just the right size, she thought, for the family of seven children who had lived there when Uncle John was a boy. She would like to have seven children, too.

The foundations of Fawley House were laid in the 14th century, when it was known as 'the barton'. The coigns of the original fortified square building were of limestone, the walls of dressed flint; the original barton was now all but invisible, the walls having been cut into to provide windows, passages for additional rooms and courtyard buildings—larger stables, laundry, brew-house, and various storehouses. What remained of the flint walls had been plastered over in the 18th century, patched and repatched during the 19th century, until in the 1870s the outside walls had been uncovered and re-stucco'd with a mixture of cement, sand, and blue lias lime. Phillip's grandfather had terraced the front and planted two cedar trees, one on each lawn, and wistaria in the wall-beds; now, half a century later, the dozen windows in the paint-flaked south front were overhung by the shrub, the roots of which twisted out of the foundations of the walls. The box hedges bordering the flower-beds were overgrown, with brambles winding among them. Lucy loved the garden's half-wild appearance, the very place for whitethroats, finches, and nightingales among the nettle-beds. It was a lovely house, not too large, and it had a colony of martins under the wide eaves. Jackdaws, too, built in many of the chimneys of the shut-up rooms. Uncle John had told her that there were ten bedrooms, not including the servants' rooms in the attic, and four rooms downstairs, two of them shut up; the billiard room, and Uncle John's smoking-room or study, where his meals were brought to him on a trolley by his house-keeper, who lived in two dark little rooms beside the servants' hall.

The affection which Lucy had for Uncle John was reciprocated. He thought her to be a beautiful young woman, in nature like his dead wife Jenny. How fortunate was Phillip to have found her, so soon after the death of Barley. How strangely family history was repeated; for Phillip, like himself, had lost his first wife when his son was born. In Time existed the great irony; if only one could recover Time, how differently one would behave. If only he had been more understanding of Willie's nature and ideas. Now his hopes were for Phillip and Lucy, and their growing little family.

While awaiting tea she spoke about the christening of the baby.

"Billy hasn't been christened yet, so Phillip and I thought of having a joint baptism with Peter when Uncle Hilary comes down for the mayfly fishing."

"A most sensible arrangement, my dear. Have you chosen the godparents?"

"Phillip wants to ask your advice, Uncle John. He wondered if you would be Billy's godfather, and do you think we might ask Uncle Hilary for Peter?"

"I'm greatly honoured to be asked. And Hilary will be, too. A little note to him from Phillip would be much appreciated, I'm sure."

He went on another line of thought. "Phillip with his beard has a look of my brother Dick, but his beard is a shade darker than Dick's at his age, I fancy. How does Phillip get on with his father nowadays?"

"Oh, very well, Uncle John."

"I'm so pleased to hear it. Dick hasn't been down this way for years, and I've been wondering if Phillip would care for me to invite his parents down for the christening?"

"I think it's a splendid idea."

"Perhaps, in a week or two's time, when you are feeling stronger, you would advise me about redecorating a couple of bedrooms? I'm proposing to have the eastern roof repaired shortly, the rain has made quite a patch down one wall. Now tell me, how does Phillip like the idea of farming?"

"Oh, he's looking forward to sowing the arable, Uncle John. I think the idea is to get some fields ready for grassing down, for an eventual milking herd."

"Oh, I hadn't heard about that. Has Hilary written to him?"

"Well, not exactly, Uncle John——" Bother, her face was getting hot. "I don't really know much about the plans——" She must say something. "I think he's *hoping* that, if his book succeeds, he'll be able to pay for things himself. Mr. Norse, his literary agent, did say that one day they would bring in—I think it was ten thousand a year." She blushed again, and half-laughed as she burst out. "He's just finished a perfectly *lovely* book about his otter."

The tea tray rattled in, a mahogany stand on cast-iron wheels upon the treads of which the rubber was cracked and hard.

"Well, Lucy," he said, when they were alone again, "to return for a moment to the farm projects. Hilary, Phillip, and the agent will be having a conference before very long, no doubt, to get something settled so that Phillip will not need to act on his own. Now, before I forget, has Phillip thought of adding the family name of 'Beare' when Billy is christened? Or was he registered as 'William Beare' at Queensbridge, when he was born, d'you know?"

"I think he was just called William, Uncle John."

"Well, it will be too late to add another name now to the Register of Births, but it can still be done by deed poll; and of course there will be the parish record at the christening. Put the suggestion to him, will you? 'Beare', as you probably know, means 'wood'. The four hundred acres of the Forest"—he pointed to the 25-inch Ordnance map framed on the wall—"were thrown during the war, to help provide the baulks for the timber tracks across the swamps below Passchendaele."

"Yes, Phillip did tell me."

"Hilary intends to replant a hundred acres, as a beginning. The idea, I understand, is to grow alternate belts of conifer and hardwood."

"How lovely to see the trees back again."

"Yes, it will be like old times," he replied with equal happiness.

Lucy was optimistic about most things. As she poured tea she felt happy that at last she was able to help, after the long enforced idleness in bed with a temperature that had moved up and down for no reason, irrespective of the daily douches given by the parish nurse. Now, for three whole days, ever since getting up, her temperature had been below normal; her precious, her darling Peter was doing splendidly, thanks to Mrs. Smith and 'Mister' at home.

Lucy still thought of her old associations as home; while Phillip, when he did dare to think, felt himself to be homeless.

One Saturday morning Lucy said to him, "Wouldn't it be nice if we could have our very own Jersey cow for Billy and Peter?"

Phillip had returned from his usual 7 a.m. visit to the premises. "Why not? Ned has asked me to buy two bull calves for one of the old screws used for rearing."

It was a sunny day. The men were making seed-beds on some of the arable deep-ploughed by the Iron Horses; then 'artifissals' were to be broadcast on the rolled work before drilling a mixture of tares, rape, cow grass, lucerne, and wild white clover. If a milking herd wasn't decided on by the time the 'seeds' came to flower, ewes could be folded there in the late summer, and on the lucerne and alsike in the following winter, and so restore the fertility by means of these walking dung-carts.

The nitrogen left by the snow, Mr. Hibbs had said, might help the take of the seeds to be broadcast by the fiddle. Phillip felt optimistic about the milk to flow from his new 'seeds', and wondered what a Jersey cow would cost, as a present for Lucy after producing Peter. Nuncle could hardly object to Lucy having her own private cow, paid for by himself.

"And I'm going to treat myself to a rick-cloth, for when my new fodder crops are ready to cut. I'll pay rent for the land—it's worth only half-a-crown an acre—if Nuncle objects. Then I'll be buying my own experience, and not living out of his pocket."

Having gulped a cup of tea, he set off on the Norton, keen to buy a Jersey cow as a present for Lucy. He drove fast, often lifting the empty sidecar 45° round right-hand bends for the thrill of it, and reached Colham in six minutes. In the Corn Hall he ordered a rick-cloth of a grade under the finest quality from a man with a smiling red face who greeted him like an old friend. He had never seen the fellow before, but was grateful for the greeting. It was a heavy-weight jute cloth impregnated with wax water-proofing. It was to be made in two sections, the sections to be laced together on top of the stack. A single cloth fourteen yards long and ten wide would be, he thought, too heavy for one man to carry on his back up the ladder, especially as the ricks of new fodder would probably be fairly tall.

A fanciful scene arose in mind as he left the Corn Hall.

Nuncle (wonderingly): 'By Jove, Phillip, you've got a wonderful shear off Lobbett's. How ever did you manage it. Hibbs tells me he's seen nothing like it in all his experience!'

Self (modestly): 'Oh, I think the snow helped. It was Hibbs' idea, really.'

Nuncle: 'But it was your idea to hire Johnson's Iron Horses, don't forget! Aunt Viccy *will* be surprised when I tell her.'

Self (imitating Ernest): 'Ah.'

With determination he went on to the Cattle Market, a place which he disliked, even dreaded. It was on the side of a hill, a congestion of iron railings set in concrete, a chaos of parked cattle-floats, driven sheep and bullocks, shouting shag-haired drovers with sticks thwacking red, white, and black four-legged bodies with dirty, slopping hindquarters and heads set with horns at various angles above distraught eyes. The day was hot. Men with hard faces were pushing and gathering everywhere about the various auction rings. Walking with resolution, he went to one of the sheds—a circular building with corrugated iron roof painted green, with seats around the ring, heavy iron tubular gates for entry and exit of the cattle, and the auctioneer's raised platform above. A sale of cows was in progress.

Most of the cows sent to market had been sent because of some defect, he knew. *Caveat emptor*—let the buyer beware. He moved into the acre of massed animal fears, human staring eyes and ruddy faces, past rows of cows standing mournfully tethered, sometimes belving for lost calves. Their bags were swelled; some were spirting with milk that the unhappy animals had let down in anguish for calves tied by their sides, cord binding the small muzzles lest they suck, and so diminish the bag. Many of the calves' backs were curved with exhaustion, their bellies hollow. Milkmen in search of a bargain wanted a big bag, to give the largest yield of milk. We're not in business for our health . . . but to make money—that was real farming. So the vendors usually left their cows, recently calved, unmilked and unsucked since the previous night, to get a swelling bag; and in the market place, awaiting sale—calves bought for a few shillings, perhaps for the glue factory—they shivered by the flanks of their dams, jaws tied, bellies pinched, backbones curved with cold and hunger, tails between infirm hindlegs. Some had ceased to cry for milk; they lay collapsed upon the concreted ground dirty with urine, loose straws, and squittered dung. On the rostrums above the

cattle rings auctioneers stood beside their clerks, taking bids
rapidly, their eyes roving imperceptibly, raising the bids at nods
from secretive emptors—secretive lest the owner of the animal
run the buyer, by adding bids, also covertly. 'You never know
who's out to do you, do you?' more than one fellow at market had
said to Phillip. *Caveat emptor*—don't go beyond your price—have
a good breakfast before going to market—or you may find you've
bought the worst screw in the place, probably with 'hurden hill'
—udder ill—a sort of coccus disease, he supposed.

Hopeless idea, to buy a cow there. Anyway, only dud milkers
from good herds, at the best, were sent to market. There were
no Jerseys. The proper thing to do was to buy a good Jersey calf,
and let Lucy rear it, if she fancied yellow cream and rich milk
for the children.

He went up the hill to the calf house. Here reigned comparative
gentleness. The calves were not so bedraggled, their coats less
staring than those of the wretched infants destined for the glue
factory, beside their hopeless dams lower down. Here the calves
stood, with full bellies, in line together, standing on clean straw,
their hind-quarters near the railing, so that buyers could see
whether or not they suffered from squitters. They were of all
ages, from new-born to veal-size. He saw two Ayrshire-cross
heifer calves, standing side by side. Good, clean little creatures,
bloom on their coats, they would just fit into the sidecar, if both
were put in sacks, as was usual, to prevent kicking and escape.
They could live in a box adjoining the yards from October to
April, while the water-meadows were being 'drowned'.

Ned had asked for bull-calves. Why? Beef did not pay. 'Meat
for manners'—the butcher got the meat and the farmer got the
manners—the dung. The dung grew the barley, which didn't pay;
the barley nursed the 'seeds' of clover and ryegrass, to grow the
hay to feed the bullocks to get the dung to grow the roots to feed
the sheep which didn't pay. Labour in vain!

Bullocks in yards fed on mangolds and sugar-beet pulp, barley-
and-oat straw and hay, with a little linseed or ground-nut cake
daily, while treading litter into good dark muck, and growing
into money for the butchers' bank balances. Carting hay and
straw to the yards—a ton of straw an acre, a ton of hay an acre—
all for manners.

Why not begin now, with milk calves? Lucy's private cow could
suckle them—the house didn't want four gallons of milk a day.

And yet, he knew he was doing wrong in going to that calf-ring for milking calves: they were a mixed lot, most of them throw-outs. The trouble was, he was always in a hurry, always with so much to do; and after a spell of writing he was scatter-brained, unable to assemble himself properly to find out, before-hand, where to buy really good milk-calves.

He looked again in the pens, and having noted the number stuck on the backs of the two Ayrshire heifer calves, shiny of coat, mild of eye, with good frames and clean tails, he waited to bid for them. He knew about the 'rings' at most auctions, ruled by one or two dealers, who bought for regular customers, charging commission, and that they did not bid against one another: but they were likely to 'run' a stranger who bid against them, to scare him off next time, and so induce him to buy through them.

He bought the two calves, paid for them, and gave his sacks to one of the regular shag-haired drovers. The calves were lifted up, each put in its sack, hind-legs first; and while they struggled, the mouth of the sack was twisted about their necks, and tied there, and again by the hind-legs, so that they could not kick free. And thus each little beast was kept warm and wrapped up for its journey in the sidecar beside its new mate.

The auctioning of calves had started about 12.30 p.m.; the sacking-up was done by 1.30 p.m. Now for a drink and a sand-wich. During a former visit he had had a pint of beer in The Drovers Arms, and a ham roll; the two bars were crowded on Market Day. He liked being among the small farmers, dealers, and drovers rather than in some hotel or café. He had his pint, with a beef sandwich; and was about to get astride the motor-bicycle when a low green sports-car passed him and drew into the kerb ahead. Phillip had time to notice the leather flying helmets of driver and passenger, and the two exhaust pipes, sheathed in coils of polished brass, coming out of the side of the bonnet, when the normal market din of squealing pigs and blaring cattle was increased by the clatter of cloven hooves, and a redpoll cow ran down the middle of the road followed by a shouting drover. It stopped near the sidecar, skidding on the cobbled surface, and let out a long bellow.

The animal's bag was swelled, milk dripped from its quarters as it looked about it, horned head raised and blood-shot eyes distraught. The two calves lying in the sidecar, only their heads free, began to struggle within the sacks. The cow saw them and uttered a short cry sounding like *merr* as it went to them.

The drover came up, stick raised to prod the cow, shouting "Hi! Hi! Garn! Garn!" The cow lowered her hornless head, four streams of milk now spirting from her quarters.

"No!" cried Phillip, as the drover thwacked the cow upon the point of hip. "Don't do that. Whose animal is it?"

"Her be mine."

A short man in breeches, gaiters and cheap coat of dark fustian, came across the road. Phillip particularly noticed the celluloid collar of red and black stripes without a tie. A large cap was set at an angle on his head.

"Want to buy her?"

"Well, I hadn't thought of it, to tell you the truth. My idea was that she might suckle these calves, and so do two good jobs in one."

"Aye, her'll do thaccy proper. Will 'ee make me a bid?"

"Is she all right?"

"What's wrong with her?" The man pointed at the overloaded milk bag. "They'm your calves?"

"Yes."

"What'll 'ee bid me?"

The driver of the sports car, pulling off his leather helmet and tossing it into the back of the car, got out. His passenger followed, after fluffing up her hair and adding lipsalve by the aid of the car mirror. Then the two, bare-headed, strolled over and stood talking together outside the Drovers Arms. Piers had a Byronic look, with his dark curly head. He laughed suddenly at something the girl said. How like him, thought Phillip, to appear to be unaware of any bargaining a dozen feet away from where he and his friend were talking.

"Before I make a bid, why are you selling her, if you don't mind my asking you?"

"Ban't you wanting vor buy her, tho'?"

"Well yes, I suppose I do. But if you've just bought the cow, don't you want to keep her?"

"Aye, if 'ee doan't want 'er. I'm ready vor take a profit."

"You mean you can buy another instead, if you sell this cow?"

"Aye. I be a milkman. Ask anyone i' th' market. They all know who I be. Wo, wo, my b'uty!" He held off the redpoll with his stick, while the drover stood by expectantly, feeling that it was partly due to him that his boss was doing a deal.

"How much will you take for her? But first let me make sure: will she suckle two calves at once?"

"You could rear four on they quarters," pointing at the bag. "What'll 'ee bid for'n?"

"I've no idea of her value, to be frank. But what I do feel should be done, is that she should have some relief." He turned in the direction of Tofield and called out, "I'm thinking of buying a cow, Piers, I won't be long."

"We're in no hurry."

"You know that gen'lman?" asked the milkman.

"Yes."

"Where be 'ee farming, sir?"

"Rookhurst. My name's Maddison. Look, we must do something about this unhappy cow."

"I'll tell 'ee what, sir. I paid eight pun for 'er, I'll take a profit. 'Er's a good coo, I won't let 'ee down. You give me ten pun, that won't see 'ee wrong."

Phillip still hesitated. "How old is she?"

"'Er be 'efer, just 'ad 'er first calf."

"How can I get her to Rookhurst?"

"Give me another crown an' I'll arrange it for 'ee." The short man waited, right hand poised.

"What's her name?"

"'Rosebud'."

"All right," said Phillip, and received a light blow on the elbow with the hand. Thus the bargain was struck.

The drover lifted out one red-and-white calf, removed the sack, and carried it into a pen, followed by the cow, which with a low *mer-r* accepted it. While Phillip wrote out a cheque, Piers and the girl watched the second calf being placed at another quarter by the milkman wary, for the calf, of a possible side-kick from the cow.

"Bootiful li'l 'efer," he said, when both calves were feeding. "Well, zur, I must be off to the ring. If my miss's sees me come 'oom wi'out a coo, 'er'll wonder what I've been up to. I'll see they'm delivered at your place before six o'clock. I knows it well —I've bought many a heifer from Mr. Temperley in the old days. They'm gone now, more's the pity. No disrespect to you, sir."

"I knew Frank Temperley. *And* his son, Jack."

The drover was waiting expectantly. "I'll keep an eye on they for 'ee, zur."

Phillip gave him a shilling, and turned to the waiting couple.

"We thought of having a drink. Won't you join us? Gillian, this is Phillip Maddison."

She had brown eyes and a brilliant smile revealed even white teeth. He was a little afraid of those artificially red lips; but felt easier when she said, "Isn't she a love?" as she patted the cow's shoulder.

"She's called Rosebud."

"How too, too sweet."

They strolled past pens filled with mournful cattle up the other side of the hill to an hotel. While the girl was away Piers said, "I'd no idea you were such an expert judge of stock. All done so quickly, too. How much more easy life would be if one could get a wife like that, and sell her again if she wasn't up to form."

Phillip was a little surprised at this; it wasn't like the courteous Piers he had known so far. Did the remark apply to his companion? He was wary when she rejoined them, the more so that the girl drank neat whisky, pouring it down her throat and following it immediately with water. Piers was soon signalling for the waiter.

"You prefer beer this time, Phil? Rather than a short one?"

After his third pint of draught Bass he felt that he would come to market every Saturday; the room was buzzing with the talk of yeomen, a few gentlemen farmers among them. Why hadn't he come here before? The hour passed quickly. He would be late for lunch at home.

"Must you go? Won't you stay and have luncheon with us? We're going on to the Yacht Club this afternoon, to look at my new racing eighteen-footer being built. I suppose we can't persuade Lucy to come too?"

"Well, thank you very much, Piers, but I ought to get back and see to the calves." He meant, I must get back and finish my novel.

"Another time, perhaps. Give my love to Lucy and Billy."

The time came to take Fiennes and Tim to London. The brothers took turns to sit on the carrier. They were due at Tilbury at noon the following day. It was a dull journey; the end of all they had known together. They arrived, by way of the northern suburbs, at Liverpool Street station.

"Well, let's have some tea."

They left the sidecar combination among the taxi-cabs, and went into the buffet. Phillip paid for two pork pies and cups of tea and asked if they would mind him leaving, since he wanted to visit his parents before returning to Rookhurst.

"Well, goodbye, chaps. All the best to you both."

He spoke bleakly, he felt drained by the formless city streets, the noise, the multitudinous movements before his eyes. It was a relief to enter the house in Hillside Road and sit with his parents, to whom his coming, although he did not fully realise it, had brought harmony.

Father and son were soon on common ground. Richard wanted to know about the various fields, and landmarks—recalling their names—Booley, Lobbett's, Copse Pasture, Galley Copse, Hangman's Marsh, the Longpond—with a mind revitalised by boyhood memories.

"Ah, I remember Johnson's Iron Horses," he exclaimed, the light of past days coming into his eyes. "We boys were forbidden to ride on the plough, on pain of being sent to bed with a tanning, and bread and water for supper. I hope you don't allow young Billy to indulge his fancy in that direction?"

"Oh no. A child falling off could be cut to pieces. Uncle John told me that it had happened when he was younger. I'm afraid I got into Hilary's bad books by that bit of ploughing, but——" He told his father of the plan to sow catch crops on the sour soil.

"The snow may make all the difference to the take. I've borrowed a heavy Cambridge rib-roll to conserve the moisture, and then work up a seed-bed. It's not exactly the policy as laid-down, but the only thing to be done, as I've reported to Hilary in my last letter."

"Well, old chap, you have to remember that Hilary is used to having everything cut and dried beforehand."

"But it was pretty useless land as it was. The sensible thing is to lay down sheep-feed and so restore the fertility. I agree that the golden hoof has become the leaden hoof, and the only remedy is to have some sort of control of imports of mutton from abroad. But Baldwin's just an old figurehead with a pipe. It's the financiers of the City of London who are the real government."

"Ah well, I'm afraid the Socialists' universal panacea for all our ills won't work in practice, Phillip. Also, they're hand in

glove with Russia—remember the Zinovieff letter? After that you
surely don't want a Socialist Government back in office. You, as
a prospective landowner, must know that under Ramsay Mac-
Donald all land would be confiscated, and then where will you
be?"

After tea Phillip said to his mother during a brief time together
in the kitchen, "My book is coming out in the autumn. But I
can't write nowadays. One needs to be a sort of sleep-walker, day
after day, never to be shocked out of one's semi-trance."

Hetty could see that he was still thinking of Barley, and hoped
that, in his new life, he would be able to settle down with Lucy,
and forget the past.

"You must think about your family responsibilities now, you
know. Do tell me about Lucy and the baby. I am so looking
forward to the christening."

"Lucy and the two boys make a happy little world of their
own. I'm not really wanted."

"Oh Phillip, whatever you do, don't let yourself feel that.
Your father did, when you children came, and accused me of
neglecting him, but it was not true, you know. He seemed to
want to be left alone——" she said, with a sigh of resignation.

He set out for home thinking a little sadly of Tim and Fiennes.
If only he had been a little less irritable with them—

Part Two

THE SOLITARY SUMMER

Chapter 6

A SIGN OF REGENERATION

Phillip determined to concentrate on farming. He got up every
morning, now that it was midsummer, at 5.30 a.m. and was at
the farm premises before the stockman arrived to bring in Rosebud
from the meadow to be milked in the stall, while the calves called
in an adjoining box. Afterwards Phillip fed them out of a tilted
pail. At first he had to put a finger in each calf's mouth, while
it was learning to suck, but now they drew up the milk unaided.
Their coats were glossy with bloom, their eyes, with full lashes, a
clear brown with dark pupils. Rosebud, now in what the stockman called profit, gave an extra gallon for the house, from which
Lucy made butter, remembering the lesson of the farm-wife on
Exmoor during her honeymoon.

The deep-ploughed arable had been cultivated, and left rolled-
down after several harrowings. The seeds for the layers—cowgrass, wild white clover, sanfoin, ryegrass, black medick, alsike,
and vernal grass—his own idea for successive grazings—stood in
five sacks in the barn, weighing nearly sixteen hundredweight
between them. White owls regularly flew in through a circular
hole in the eastern gable, for the mice and young rats beginning
to gnaw through the jute sacking.

Ned had given him an old fiddle for sowing the small-seeds.
This was a contraption of a shoulder sling supporting a canvas bag
above a small circular tin tray into which seeds fell from a funnel,
fast or slow according to a simple adjustment. The seeds were
'broadcast thissy way', said Ned, giving a demonstration as he
sawed with the bow, a light iron rod to which was secured a
leather cord, twisted round a cotton reel fixed upon the spindle
of the tray.

Simple! Ned walked once up and then down the field, sawing
with the bow which worked the circular tray, so that the seeds
were whirled in a fan before him. It was with a feeling of delight

that Phillip, walking beside him, watched the seeds, each describing its little parabola as it fell through the sunlight. The clover-family seed—sanfoin, medick, and alsike, red cowgrass—each compact and kidney-shaped, dropped fast, to bounce; the Irish rye and vernal grasses, like wingless bleached bodies of miniature song-birds, drifted down upon the earth, to lie among the pale brown and yellow clover seeds already at rest. There they were, ready to grow into green leaf and blossom—pink, yellow, and white the trifoliums, below tall grasses waving in the summer breeze.

The bailiff, having paced out the first line, set four hazel wands, with paper stuck in their split tops, two upon each headland. The overall sideway cast was a rod, he explained. "So set you up they sticks a rod apart each time, and you can't go wrong."

"I wonder how long this field will take."

"Lobbett's be twenty chain be five wide, so wark it out, guv'nor, how far yar'll be square-bashin' under my 'fiel' punishment number one'."

This was a joke, Ned seeing that the rookie sweated it out.

"Oh dear me, Ned, I wish I'd paid more attention to the Weights and Measures tables in the schoolroom."

"Nuthin' in it, guv'nor. A chain be dwenty two yards, ten square chain to an acre, Lobbett's be ten acres. Wark you that one out."

"But is a rod square measure?"

"Nivver 'appen. Four rod be one chain, yar knows that."

"I see. How long is a chain?"

"A hunner links, bain't it?"

"How long is that?"

"Dwenty two yard, a' reckon. Why d'yar ask? Yar doan't need to know."

"But I must know if I am to work out your sum."

Ned obviously enjoyed tantalising him. He sat down with pencil and paper.

"You don't need no theory. See you here, mester, Lobbett's be dwenty chain long and five chain wide. That's a hunner' square chains. That's ten acres, bain't it?"

"I see. The fiddle covers a rod, or quarter of a chain sideways each time up and down?"

"You'm on the right track now."

"I walk up and down four times to cover a chain of width, or twenty times to cover five chains across the field."

"You've a-got it."

"And the field is twenty chains long, or a quarter of a mile. So I walk five miles to sow the field."

"Wisht I 'ad your 'ade."

"Wish I had yours. You know it all without messing about with all this cross-word puzzle nonsense, Ned."

The bailiff, his measuring chain clinking upon the flints behind him, disappeared over the line of the hill. Phillip moved steadily across the field. Larks flitted up before him, finches flew down to alight and take what their sharp eyes instantly perceived. Extra seed had been allowed for the 'bards', including partridges. Later the light cylindrical sheet-iron roll was coming up, drawn by Donk, to be followed by six zigzag harrows in line to cover the seed.

When would the job be finished? Ninety acres seemed an appalling task. How far would he have walked when the last seed was sown?

Gulls floated over in oar-like flight. Nothing for them, all ploughing done; back to the coast they flew. Were they males? Surely the hens would be on their eggs.

A kestrel appeared over one corner of the field, to luff and hang, wings flickering rapidly to maintain its weight in windless air as it watched for movement of beetle, butterfly, or mouse below. It hung there, flapping loosely as though the wings had just been attached by Leonardo da Vinci. Then it dropped lower, and volplaned to earth to a beetle. The bird was up again almost at once, rising to swing round and glide down the next field and luff above the borstal.

This was the life. He sang to the bowing of the fiddle, making up words as he thought of the fine green hairs of the ryegrass, the first paired-leaves of clover and cowgrass, and later the delicate yellow flowers of medick, cover for lark and partridge.

> The wind-wave hissing in the grass
> The pollen come to blow
> And dream arises, but to pass
> To regions where man cannot go.
> So I who tread this fallow earth
> Must think of 'fulness after dearth'.

Striding up and down from hedge to hedge he began to calculate
how many paces would cover the field, taking a pace to be one
yard. If Lobbett's took five miles to walk, that was one mile to
every two acres. So he would have walked forty-five miles when
the last of the ninety acres was sown. Say four days in all. He
went on happily, until his thought attached itself to the number
of seeds he was sowing. A stroke of the bow every pace, say a
thousand seeds a yard. He sat down, and with pencil and paper
began to calculate, allowing one seed to fall, on average, upon
every square inch. He figured out 6,272,640 square inches to the
acre. By the end of four days he would have cast ninety times that
number of seeds—564,537,600.

The weather was fine, the work was done by the end of the
week.

Now rain was needed.

The plain of Colham, seen from high ground, was changing its
hues perceptibly; the wild roses of the hedges—Shakespeare's
eglantine—had shed their petals; the cuckoo was singing out of
tune. No rain fell.

On the last day of the month he did not return to breakfast at
his usual hour of 7.30 a.m. There was nothing to hold him up
on the farm; the men were waiting for the dew to dry off before
turning the hay. It was the rising heat and light, the sudden
memory of July the First which drew him on past the borstal to
the rim of the down beyond. As he climbed the western slope to
the site of an ancient encampment a phrase quoted by Aunt Dora,
long ago, from Euripides, 'danger shines like sunlight in a brave
man's eyes', came into his mind; and when the sun blazed
suddenly upon his face he sank down upon the sward and hid his
face in his hands for a few moments before turning to run home
with an overwhelming impulse to write down, while the im-
mediacy of memory lasted, that which had overwhelmed him.

The post had been delivered when he got back to the farmhouse.
There was a letter from Uncle Hilary to Lucy, which she thought
he should see, since he insisted that they always have what he
called liaison between them.

"All right, all right, read the damned thing if you must!"

"You did ask me always to tell you——"

"Well, tell me. Quick."

"Uncle Hilary says he is arriving on Thursday afternoon,

bringing Aunt Dora from Lynmouth with him. He wants to stay
here for the christening, since Uncle John hasn't been able to get
the bedrooms ready yet. Well, 'Mother' will be here on Saturday,
with Billy's other grannie, so I'm afraid it will mean turning you
out of your study, but it'll be for two nights only."

"How can we get them all in?"

"Well, Mrs. Lushington can have our bedroom, for one, and
I can manage in the boxroom with the little boys. That will
leave the three other rooms for Mother, Aunt Dora, and Uncle
Hilary."

"Where do I sleep, among the owls?"

"Oh, poor you. Of course, I can have a tent in the garden with
the children. I'd simply love it."

There were five upper rooms in the farmhouse, not counting
the bathroom: the main bedroom occupied by the children and
Lucy, Phillip occasionally joining his wife in the double bed; two
smaller bedrooms; a boxroom, and the study.

"Oh damn, I've forgotten to get the distemper and brush for
the walls of those two replastered bedrooms. There's no time to
lose. I must get off an article for the *Crusader*, and put it on the
afternoon train to London. The middle page is being made up
now for tomorrow's paper. I must telephone it. Sorry, no time
for breakfast. Not now, Billy—Daddy's busy."

"Bug off, Daddy."

On July the First, eleven years ago, the sun rose up out of the east
across the thistly chalk fields of Picardy known to us as Noman's land.
A great battle was imminent. Over 250,000 English, Scots, Irish, Welsh,
and Colonial troops, nearly all amateur soldiers, waited in chalk trenches
along a twenty-mile front for the final bombardment to open.

This, it had been declared, would annihilate the German redoubts
and trenches opposite and prepare the way for a general advance to
the high ground several miles into enemy-held territory. There, along
the Pozières—Bazentin—Longueval—Gillemont ridge we were ordered
to dig in and prepare for the counter-attack. Then, the enemy having
broken, the cavalry would go through the gap, and so the end of the
war would come in sight. Such were the hopes of the new, the proud,
the untried Kitchener's Army.

The final bombardment started at 6.30 a.m. Across the hundreds
of yards of Noman's land rising smoke and dust turned the sunshine
brown. At times the sun's disc was occluded. Surely no German could
live in that inferno of shells bursting like waves on a distant reef?

Roaring and screaming overhead, shells of all weights and sizes, from 13-pounder shrapnel to ton-weight 15-inch howitzer shells, and 12-inch armour-piercing stuff from naval guns mounted on multiple bogies on the railway behind the valley town of Albert, fell for an hour. The rising sun glinted on the Leaning Virgin holding the Babe in arms on the campanile of the shell-broken basilica, built of grey stone and red-brick—what the newspapers called the 'Golden Virgin of Albert Cathedral'.

For months this attack had been rehearsed in back areas. Every man knew his job. Coloured ribands were tied to shoulder-straps to distinguish bomber from bayonet-man, Lewis-gunner from rifle-grenadier. Patches of coloured cloth sewn upon tunic backs, and again in paint stencilled on steel-helmets, distinguished battalions and infantry brigades. Each division had its device of animal, shield, flower, butterfly, or other 'sign'.

Each infantry soldier carried about 66 lb.: rifle and bandolier of ammunition, bayonet, shovel or pick, bombs, extra water, food, barbed wire, sandbags, and so on. It was to be, as the phrase went in those days, a cakewalk—a popular Edwardian dance.

The General commanding the attacking Army—the Fourth British Army—Sir Henry Rawlinson, whose banner bore the sign of a wild boar (he had a tame boar at his H.Q. at Querrieu château near Amiens) based his plan on an overwhelming bombardment which would destroy all the 10-foot enemy trenches, bury what barbed-wire obstacles were not torn to pieces, and smash-in all German dugouts. 'All opposition will be overwhelmed in the preliminary bombardment' ran part of the orders to the Corps' commanders.

So the troops making the assault were used virtually as carrying parties. They were to go forward in six extended lines with 100-yard intervals between the 'waves'. The first waves were to deal with any survivors of the bombardment, the second would support the first and supply escorts for prisoners to the rear; the remaining waves were to advance to the Pozières Ridge, three miles to the east, dig in, put out wire, and await the counter-attack.

The bombardment concentrated on that morning of July the First, 1916, lifted at zero hour, 7.30 a.m. The sun, low in the clear eastern sky in which larks were singing, blazed into the eyes of the men of nearly 200 infantry battalions of fresh troops, many now white-faced and trembling, others swearing and shouting to free themselves from fear as they climbed up the trench ladders above the sandbags filled with chalk. The parapets in places were already spurting and breaking with German machine-gun bullets. Each soul found itself as though naked and alone in the dreaded Noman's land where, strangely, men were dropping rifles and sinking to their knees. While those remaining upright advanced in line, monstrous shells began to burst blackly and

noises like a hundred engines blowing off steam in a railway terminus
filled the air——

The door of the writing-room opened and Lucy came in.

"The 'bus is going into Colham in about forty minutes. If you
tell me the colour you want for the distemper I can go in and
get it as well as a brush."

She saw his drawn face, with its fixed stare, as he turned round
to say, "What are you talking about? Who cares a damn about
distemper or brushes." Then throwing his pen against the wall,
where it sprinkled ink and fell, he shouted, "I shan't be here for
the christening anyway."

"I can just as well brush off the flaky bits, you know, if you'll
let me."

He picked up his pen. The point of the nib was at right angles
to the shoulders.

"I'm so sorry to break-in on you like this. I'll fetch my pen,
I won't be a moment."

When she returned he was contrite. "I'm sorry, Lucy. Don't
take any notice of what I say."

"Well, you've got so much to think about. Now don't worry
any more about the rooms, leave them to me. I'm sure the walls
don't really matter, not for the moment, anyway. I've asked
Mrs. Rigg to bring you a bacon sandwich, and a cup of coffee."

After the many raids, to identify the regiments and therefore the
Divisionen opposite the 4th Army front, only one report from all the
infantry battalions taking part mentioned that the German dugouts
had as many as 40 wooden steps leading down into the tunnels below
and that the dugout rooms, with walls and ceilings similarly boarded,
lay at a depth of 30 feet. In the battle of Loos in the preceding September the enemy shelters had been more or less open, with heavy timber
baulks shoring up roofs of layers of sandbags filled with chalk. They
were seldom more than 10 feet below ground level; and most of them
in the front line had been wrecked by our 6-in. howitzer shells. Now,
during the final rehearsal of our Division at Querrieu, my Commanding
Officer, Lt.-Col. H. J. West, who had been wounded twice during
the abortive attacks of early 1915, and again (badly) at Loos, protested
to the 4th Army Commander, present as a guest of the Corps commander,
that the plan was based on a fallacy: for the German dugouts were too
deep for any shell of less than 9.2-inch to penetrate by a direct hit,
he declared.

For this breach of military etiquette he was relieved of his command.

During the preliminary bombardments, and the final concentrated bombardment between 6.30 a.m. and 7.30 a.m. on July the First the enemy dugouts, deep in the chalk, were not smashed in. German machine-gunners, sheltering below in comparative safety, came up at 7.31 a.m., as they had rehearsed many times. Some carried parts of their *Maschinengewehre* into shell-holes in Noman's-land, in some places before the tumble of their own wire, where they re-assembled these weapons, and awaited the slow advance of six waves of British infantry.

He put down the pen and walked about the room, trembling, while tears dripped from his eyes. Lucy returned very soon, it seemed.

"How is it going?" she asked, happily.

"It's stopped, except on our left, where the Ulster division has got into the Schwaben redoubt. They had better brigadier-generals, who got them up out of Thiepval wood and across to the wire during the bombardment, and so into the enemy trenches, while the more amateur officers in the southern divisions obeyed orders. The machine-guns flanking Ovillers started firing before zero hour, and our lot has copped it. In a few minutes, or hours, I'll be seeing Father Aloysius sliding down into my shell-hole holding his 'little book' in his hands, reading his 'office', while I can't feel my legs at all." Looking up, he went on quietly, "Not that I gave a damn for myself, but I wasn't able to do anything to help my platoon. They were laid out almost in a row, among innumerable others looking as though they'd come away from a Cup-tie final, blind-drunk, and were sleeping it off."

"I'll bring you up a bowl of soup, and some toast, in a minute or two."

In one part of the line, opposite Ovillers, a downland village among shattered trees, there was a gentle declension south to the Albert-Bapaume road. Lined by poplars, its metalling weed-grown, this road led direct through what had been corn and beet-sugar fields to the distant ridge. Within a few minutes all officers of our battalion which had gone over—25—were casualties. Mash Valley, as the declension was called on the trench-maps, looked to be filled by a Crystal Palace cup-tie crowd lying down to rest, some on their backs, others on their faces, after the long wait and excitement of the game.

Durhams, Green Howards, Staffordshires, Devons, Middlesex, Gault-shires—these and other county regiments had failed to reach their

first objective. Farther south the infantry had better luck, as the saying
went, and took the fortified village of Mametz. But north of the
straight Albert-Bapaume road, across the gently rolling downland to
its decline into the Ancre Valley, over the marshes and up again to the
rising ground to Beaumont Hamel and onwards to Gommecourt, the
most northerly bastion or flank of the attack—a dozen miles or so of
the 20-mile front—the assault was everywhere shattered. By evening
nearly 60,000 British soldiers, most of them of the new keen Kitchener
divisions, had gone down under the mort blast of Spandau rifles and
machine-guns. When the sun's rays were from the west the survivors
were back again in their own trenches.

Opposite Mash Valley—lying north of Sausage Valley, where Tyne-
sider troops lay almost as thickly as their comrades in Mash—the
Germans lost about 150 men, most of them wounded. Their British
opponents, belonging to the 8th and 34th divisions, lay outside the
German wire, 12,000 of them. When the firing ceased German doctors
and Red Cross orderlies came out and helped bind up some of our
wounded; but there were so many that for the next three days khaki
figures were still crawling, or being carried, back to the dressing station
below the Golden Virgin of Albert.

Thus began the Battle of the Somme.

Hilary was on his way from Pembrokeshire, having left his
caravan behind in a cove near Solva Bay before dawn. He had
arranged to bring his sister Dora from Lynmouth, which meant
a long, slow, out-of-the-way journey from Chepstow ferry down
the southern coast of the Severn Sea from Bridgwater to Lynmouth, and back again to Bridgwater—an extra seventy-four
miles.

He had insisted on fetching Dora by motor, although she had
written to say that she would not find the journey by rail too
much for her. The real reason for her not wanting him to come
to the cottage was on account of her 'Babies', two small and aged
spinster sisters, one blind, and the other suffering from delusions
which sometimes made her suspect that her food was poisoned.
When Hilary had last visited the cottage she had screamed and
hurried upstairs to her blind sister, crying out that a strange man
wanted to murder them.

That incident had led to an unhappy discussion between brother
and sister; for in his 'direct sailor's manner' Hilary had asked her
how long would she insist on looking after those two idiots. She
was wasting herself, he declared. What sort of life did she have?
What they needed was a professional nurse, who would stand no

nonsense; but not in a small cottage. They should be in an institution.

Hilary knew the story of how a neighbour, soon after the war —a relation of the two old women who was in charge of them— had asked his sister to look after them for a week-end and had never returned. Good God, that was now nearly ten years ago. Something must be done about it. He couldn't have his kidlet sister working herself prematurely into the grave.

This time Dora had arranged with the parish nurse to take over the care of her 'Babies' before Hilary was due to arrive; and a rendezvous in Lynton, at the top of the water-lift, she wrote, would save him a journey down the steep hill to Lynmouth and up again.

At first the motor-ride was enjoyable for Dora, the feeling of freedom brought back youthful memories, leading to keen anticipation at the thought of seeing Hetty again. Hilary remarked that she seemed to have found a new lease of life, and optimistically began to talk about a subject which, he declared, was very close to his heart.

"You ought not to continue having the responsibility for your two old ladies, Dora. Surely they'd be better off in a home? You'd find no trouble in getting them certified under the Lunacy Laws, you know."

"Well, as I have said before, dear brother, I feel for them as though they really are my own."

"Well, you know what I feel about it, Dora."

After that the meadows and paddocks of Somerset, divided by rhines and planted with withies, held only fleeting interest for Dora. Over the Dorset border, when they stopped for lunch, she was not able to eat the lettuce sandwiches she had brought with her. More nervous energy was lost while she tried to persuade her brother that she would be happy to be left to sit in the shade of the field beside which they had stopped, instead of going into the hotel Hilary had chosen from his A.A. book.

After vain persuasion he went in to eat alone without enjoyment a full meal of pea soup, roast beef, baked potatoes, cabbage, and batter pudding, followed by apricot pie with cream, and bread and cheese. Dora was cracked; he gave her a generous allowance, and instead of enjoying what was left of her life she had made herself a slave to a couple of imbecile strangers, who repaid her by . . . etc., etc.

The journey was continued, both enduring one another and partly sustained by thoughts of Lucy's face greeting them.

Ignoring the lunch awaiting him downstairs, Phillip blinded on the Norton to the railway junction and gave his envelope to the guard. It was to be collected at Paddington. Returning as the clock struck four he set about distempering the bedroom walls, which had been colour-washed by the builder before the new plaster had dried out, so that the distemper had powdered in patches. He worked fast, driven by the need to get the work done. Creamy drips fell on his jacket, trousers, and hair. Having done the walls, he thought to use up the remainder of the second tin by putting it on the ceilings, not knowing that the petrifying liquid would fail to key to the soft, porous whiting already there. As soon as the distemper had dried out, above the blue flames of the oil stove, it began first to crack, then to flake and hang down in small loose scales.

"Perhaps Uncle Hilary won't notice," said Lucy, hopefully.

"He notices everything. God knows what he'll say when he sees how all my seeds failed on the arable. He'll give me the sack, I hope. Why, when *one* brush mark showed under the varnish when he had his car repainted, he told me that he intended to make the painter take it all off and do it again. I bet the poor devil lost money on the job."

Lucy said suddenly, "Here they are."

Looking through the window, they saw two figures sitting still in the red car. Hastening down, Phillip opened the door and helped out his aunt, who said almost inaudibly, "Well, Boy— how are you?"

"I'm so glad you could come, Aunt Dora."

He was going round to shake hands when Hilary said, "Take in your Aunt's bag, will you? You'll find it in the boot." Meanwhile Dora was walking slowly towards Lucy, who with Billy was coming down the garden path.

Dora smiled wanly, and managed to say, "Lucy my dear, how well you look. And how your little boy has grown."

While the two ladies were going into the house, Hilary turned to his nephew and asked if he had such a thing as a wheelbarrow.

"I've got the very thing for a nursing mother," he said confidentially. "The crate can go in the larder, on the slate floor."

Surveying two dozen bottles of Dublin stout, Phillip said, "Well, Lucy isn't exactly nursing the baby now."

"It will help build her up, Phillip. Here she comes, not a word. Lucy, my dear," as she came in. He kissed her. "And how is my godson? . . . That's good news." He drew a deep breath. "Well, it's good to be back again." They went into the parlour. Billy was hiding under the table. He came out only when Lucy held out her arms; and when his great-uncle approached to touch his cheek with a podgy finger, Billy retorted by pointing at him and saying, "Bug off, Nuncle."

Hilary disregarded this remark together with the child, and said to Lucy, "What's become of Dora?"

"She has a headache, Uncle, and is lying down in her room."

"She's not used to motorin', that's only part of her trouble. As nervous as a cat, and I came along at a steady thirty. It's those two old women she insists on lookin' after. They're leeches. She ought to get them into a home. Have you seen them?"

"Phillip has told me about them. Are you ready for tea, or would you rather wait a bit?"

"Just as you wish, my dear. I don't want you to vary your usual routine for me in any way."

"I'll get the tea trolley."

When she had gone to the kitchen Hilary said to Phillip, "Where did Billy pick up that expression?"

"From me, I expect."

"Oh."

"He can't talk properly yet."

"So I observe. Now fetch me a glass, will you, like a good fellow."

He opened the corkscrew on a multi-bladed knife, and having held up the glass to the light to see if it were clean, poured out some stout.

"I'll leave it here, for the barm to settle. Lucy can drink it before her tea."

Knowing how Lucy hated stout, Phillip said, "I'm forgetting my duties. Let me show you to your room, Uncle. Mind your head on that beam."

"My dear chap, I knew that beam when I was a boy."

"I thought you might have forgotten."

"Why should I forget?"

He followed his nephew upstairs into the larger of the two

bedrooms. "Hullo, whatever's happened to the ceiling? What? But why didn't you find out before you attempted to do it? 'No time'? What d'you mean, 'no time'? You could have asked the oil colourman, he would have told you, surely? Well, you'll have to take it all off. Rub it with a damp cloth until it's smooth and clean—but don't put on too much water, or you'll have the plaster down, and heaven knows how many starlings' nests as well." He turned away. "I must go to the bathroom. I'll join you downstairs."

"Right ho."

Phillip ran down to tell Lucy about the stout. "I took him upstairs to get him out of the way."

"I can't drink it. It makes me shudder. Won't you drink it for me?"

"It's a poor heart that never rejoices. Cheerio."

After tea, Hilary walked to Fawley House, to see his eldest brother John, who was indoors with one of his attacks of bronchitis. Since the winter his breathing had been uneasy; the warm weather had not, as he had hoped, improved the inflammation; for the past three days he had remained in bed in order to be fit for the christening.

On his return to the farmhouse, Hilary fixed up his wireless set, watched by Billy, who remembered how Nuncle had trapped him between his big, big legs when Nuncle had come a long, long time ago; so Billy went into his hide under the table, and watched what was going on by the movements of boots and trousers. He cried when he was carried away to his play pen by Mummy, and became hysterical when he heard that she was going away in the car-car with Nuncle.

"I'll be back soon, Billy. Uncle Hilary is only taking me for a little ride."

He managed to get out, between sobs, the words, "Daddy—going—away—too?"

"No, darling, Daddy's staying here, to look after you and Peter. Be a good boy, and play with Teddy and Jacko"—the child's woolly bear and monkey with moveable limbs—and real monkey skin and almost human glass eyes—gift of Hetty and Richard in a parcel for his second birthday in January.

"Where—be—Daddy—to, Mummie?"

"He's working in the garden, my pet."

"No—goin'—away?"

"Daddy will be in the garden, Billy. Riggy is in the kitchen, she'll look after you." She put him back in the play pen.

The garden was neglected. Phillip had begun to dig in weeds when he heard a sudden roar from the loudspeaker, which continued shatteringly. He hurried into the house as the noise subsided. Billy, having climbed out of the play pen, had pushed a chair forward to get up to the cabinet, and was now fiddling with the knobs, delighted that he had, by this simple method, sent away the noise. Phillip carried him into the garden and gave him a trowel and some seed potatoes, which had long pale stalks growing from shrunken skins.

When he returned, Hilary went to see how Phillip was getting on in the garden. Billy escaped back to Lucy. Phillip found himself, willy-nilly, in the role of rear-guard, awaiting the inevitable attack. This time he told himself that he would be tactful.

"You should be trenching that weed, you know. Have you got a line? If you bring it here, I'll show you how it should be done."

Phillip got the line.

"The first thing is to get the line really straight. That's it. Now give me the spade. Push it in deep, cut clean, like this. Try it. No, keep the blade upright, not slanting. Here, let me show you once more. Now finish along the line."

Hilary asked for the mattock. He had made Phillip a present of a new set of tools, which had had very little use, by the look of them.

"Skin the rubbish like this—short, clean strokes. We'll put the weeds in a heap—they'll be carried, last of all, to the final trench, with the soil you take out, and so heap beside the weeds, well apart. Try it."

Presently he said, "What do you propose to use this ground for?"

"I thought of putting out potatoes."

"Your main crop? Rather late, isn't it?"

"As a matter of fact, they're my first earlies—Sharp's Express."

"You'll get them about September. Anyway, don't let's waste the seed. Carry on with the shovel. No, that's a spade. You need the long-handled shovel I gave you to save bending your back. A spade is too tiring, also it's inefficient. Oh, give it to me—now watch—this is the way to use it."

After another lesson, he told Phillip to carry on, and went away to look at the rest of the garden. The first thing he saw was a heap of green weeds in a corner, unnaturally wilted.

"Did *you* put paraffin on this pile of weeds?"

"I tried to burn them."

"But why? They're valuable dressing. And in any case, oil poured on damp weeds is useless. They can't burn."

"Oh, I was just mucking about."

He had known it was impracticable to light a fire like that. His act had been that of a personality scattered—'scatty' as boys had said of him in his early days in a London suburb—by too many things on his mind.

"Well, you shouldn't 'muck about', as you call it, at your age."

I haven't used that expression since I was a boy, thought Phillip. "Well, I haven't given it much thought, to be truthful."

"The proper way to deal with these weeds is to let them rot, either in a compost heap or trenched under. When you've trenched this bit, we can put them in."

There was an old eschalot growing among the grass and weeds. Phillip pulled it up and tossed it in the trench.

"Don't waste that, it's a perfectly good shallot."

"What shall I do with it?"

"Eat it, of course."

Seeing Billy looking out of the nursery window, Phillip waved to him; and picking up the shallot held it above his head, dangling it until the white roots were ready to drop into his open mouth.

Without further words Hilary left the garden. Phillip put the tools away and followed him into the house.

"I only meant it as a joke."

Hilary appeared to be reading his newspaper.

"I've been doing a fair amount of writing," went on Phillip. "In my own time, of course—and after writing one is inclined to do idiotic things."

Hilary continued to hold the paper before him before lowering it to ask what the men were doing.

"Cutting hay. The hoeing is done."

"Have you been writing during the day?"

"Yes."

"Wouldn't the men work better if you were with them?"

"I shall be with them during the hay carting."

"Don't you think that one should learn to do a job oneself before one can understand what the men have to do?"

"But there's really nothing to do at the moment. Ned sits on the cutter, and drives, while the other chap scythes the laid patches and sharpens the knives. That's all. After the cutting, Ned turns the swathes with the tedder."

"Couldn't you do that, and free him for something else?"

"I could, yes, but then he'd find nothing to do."

"There's always something to do on a farm. What happened to your small-seed sowings on the arable?"

"I'm afraid most of them have failed in the drought."

Hilary changed the subject. "What are you writing about this time? Not another novel, I hope?"

"I've had an advance of fifty pounds from a publisher. The book is due for publication in the autumn. It's not a novel."

"What's the subject?"

"Oh, the elements, generally speaking."

"That doesn't tell me much."

"It's hard to describe, Uncle Hilary."

"You're a rum chap, 'pon my soul. You don't help to make conversation, do you?"

"I don't quite know what to say, to be frank."

"You told me you were going to shave your beard. A small thing, but a straw shows the wind's direction, Phillip. Isn't your word your bond?"

"I did shave that beard. This is another one."

"Anyway, I must say I'm glad you've chucked your novels. D'you remember I gave you your Aunt Viccy's opinion about them——"

"Really, Uncle Hilary, is there any need to worry about my writing? I quite realise that it isn't of the least interest to anyone in the family."

"All I'm trying to bring home to you is that no-one can do two jobs properly, at the same time. I know what I'm talking about. I tried it once, and it didn't work. Now sit down and listen to me, I've had more experience than you've had. My career as a sailor clashed with my fruit farming interests in Australia. My partner was an easy-going sort of chap, and it wasn't good enough, leaving matters to him. So I chucked the farm, before it chucked me. All I'm trying to do is to give you the benefit of my experience." He looked at his watch. "Nearly time for the six o'clock news." He saw Billy standing by the table. "Come here, little man; come and switch on the news. Just turn this knob."

The child moved to be just out of arm's length. Phillip, who had little interest in the news, considering it to be unrealistic, went into the kitchen, where Lucy was giving the baby his bottle.

"This is 2 LO calling, 2 LO calling. Here is the news."

During the broadcast Billy came silently into the kitchen. He looked at his father, then walked past him, to stand against the far wall. Phillip went to him and picked him up. The child struggled. Phillip put him down, feeling rebuffed; at that moment Lucy came into the parlour with the baby.

"Billy, darling, you're tired," she said. "Here's a barley sugar. I've only got to put the joint into the oven, then I'll give you your bath." She looked at Phillip, her head held uncertainly on one side. "You mustn't mind my saying it, but if you *could*, when I'm nursing baby, find time to play with Billy—any little game would do——" Seeing his face she went on, "There now, I didn't mean to hurt *your* feelings. But I think a young child can often feel out of it when the second child comes. The damage can be done so quickly, without one realising it."

"Don't I know it. My father always showed that he preferred Mavis to me. Not that I minded that so much as the way he was always criticising my mother, much as I do you. Well, I must go up and write."

He left the kitchen with a slight feeling of self-destruction, as often he had felt during his boyhood.

After the news, followed by his favourite Flotsam and Jetsam programme, Hilary went into the kitchen, leading Billy—who had successfully switched off—by the hand. With the air of one performing a rite he took the silver-handled knife from his pocket—blades, tweezers, spike for killing trout, scissors for nipping off ends of gut after tying a fly, corkscrew, hook for getting stone out of horse's frog—and letting Billy hold the half-empty stout bottle, twisted the screw back in the original hole. Billy was allowed to turn it before Hilary drew the cork. Billy insisted on filling the glass.

"Now then, Lucy, let me see you put this down like a good 'n."

She coloured as she took a sip, and laughed. "I'll keep it until Billy has had his bath, I think."

Hilary went away with his new friend Billy; and almost immediately jazzy music, of a softened, sweet variety, filled the parlour. It stopped abruptly. "We don't want that dreadful stuff, Billy my lad, do we?"

"Ning-a-ning!" cried Billy. "More ning-a-ning, please, Nuncle!"

"All in good time, young fellow. And don't call me 'Nuncle'. I'm 'Uncle'."

Hilary turned a knob; orchestral music filled the parlour. Hilary disliked all music and turned the switch. "More! More ning-a-ning, please, Uncle!"

"I'll allow you to switch it on yourself when you've had your tub, if you're a good boy, and do what your Mamma tells you."

"Mummy dead," said Billy, having overheard Mrs. Rigg say this to Miss Priddle when she was staying in the house.

Phillip ran down the stairs. "That's the *New World Symphony*. May he have it, please, Uncle?"

"Oh, you don't want that sort of thing, surely? Also too much noise isn't good for children. I've told Billy he can switch on when he's had his bath, if he's a good boy."

The usual Victorian mixture of bribe and threat, thought Phillip. Did Nuncle ever *think*? A good boy was the result of good, natural treatment, of good leadership which allowed freedom. His next thought was that in criticising Nuncle he was criticising himself.

Feeling almost entirely in disintegration, he went into the kitchen. Lucy was holding the glass of stout. "Ugh, I can't drink it," she whispered.

He was drinking the stout when Hilary walked in, to stop abruptly at the sight, and without a word return to the parlour. Would Lucy explain to Nuncle why he had drunk it? He waited while she went on with her work and at last, thinking how like Pa she was, he went through the kitchen door to the garden, to dig without interest and momentarily without hope.

Within the parlour, in pyjamas and blue dressing-gown made by Lucy, Billy listened to the Stock Exchange Summary, which he enjoyed enormously by means of his own mental pictures of dust-bin lids blown off by gusts of wind (Contango, Rio Tinto) fairies ('Imps eased a little') ploughing (Broken Hill Silver) washing clothes in the outhouse and breaking sticks for Riggy's fire (Furness, Withy) his own recent birthday party (Tea, Sugar, Coffee). Uruguay (soap in eyes) reminded him of Miss Priddle and getting up he switched off, remarking cheerfully to Uncle Hilary, "All gone. All gone now," before clasping his hot-water bottle and going upstairs before he could be held within ha-ha legs.

For two days Dora lay in bed, with aspirin and a hot-water bottle. Just before the others left for the junction to meet Hetty and Irene, who were travelling down together, Lucy went into her room, to be told by Dora that she was quite happy to be left alone, but would Lucy make her excuses.

"It's my stupid migraine, Lucy dear, it always lasts for forty-eight hours. I'll be better by this evening."

"We won't be long. Mrs. Rigg will be downstairs, to see to everything, including the children."

Billy, in bed in the next room, heard this; and the party was about to leave when he appeared in his pyjamas, bear and monkey under one arm and dragging his blue dressing-gown by hand.

"Let him come," said Phillip, at once. "I'll tell Mrs. Rigg," and he ran into the house.

It was a fine evening, a warm scented air lingered below the downs; bee after bee from flowers of thyme and bird's-foot trefoil lost honey and life against the windscreen. Phillip, in the backseat, saw that the speedometer needle was 35. When a pair of turtle doves, picking up grit, flew away before them just in time, he leaned over the leather seat and said, "I don't think many cars come this way, Uncle."

"They weren't in any danger, Phillip. And they'll learn what to do next time."

The motor ran on at 35 m.p.h., leaving a cloud of dust of chalk and flint behind it. The doves had a nest in one of the thorns on the slope above the winding lane; Phillip had visited it several times, he knew the birds as his own. He thought of Jefferies' essay read recently in one of the books that had belonged to cousin Willie, *Pigeons at the British Museum*, describing the scholars within the dome, while London's pigeons were outside.

They have not laboured in mental searching as we have; they have not wasted their time looking among empty straw for the grain that is not there. They have been in the sunlight. Since the days of ancient Greece the doves have remained in the sunshine; we who have laboured have found nothing. In the sunshine, by the shady verge of woods, by the sweet waters where the wild dove sips, there alone will thought be found.

And while being driven back, slowly from the station along the same route, sitting between Lucy and Irene on the back seat, he felt that his mother, in front and holding Billy, her small, child-like face a-dream, was unlike his father because she could get beyond memory, she was able to feel that the beauty of the early summer evening was really part of her present life: that it was never too late. W. H. Hudson in *Nature and Downland* had said that Jefferies was 'slain by cruel fate before his time': like Jefferies, Father had never been free within himself unless he were away from streets and houses, away from memories in the sunshine, or under the stars.

To be beautiful and to be calm, without mental fear, is the ideal of nature. If I cannot achieve it, at least I can think it.

And in an essay on going by train to Brighton, away from wearisome London, Jefferies had written:

The dust of London fills the eyes and blurs the vision; but it penetrates deeper than that. There is a dust that chokes the spirit, and it is this that makes the streets so long, the stones so stony, the desk so wooden; the very rustiness of the iron railings about the offices sets the teeth on edge, the sooty blackened walls (yet without shadow) thrust back the sympathies which are ever trying to cling to the inanimate things around us. A breeze comes in at the carriage window—a wild puff, disturbing the heated stillness of the summer day. It is easy to tell where that comes from—silently the downs have stolen into sight.

Was Father doomed, like Jefferies? Was that why Mother looked so frail and worn?

He leaned over the folded hood and, touching her shoulder, said as he pointed to the grey-green slopes, "Jefferies said, 'There is always hope on the hills'."

"Yes, yes," she exclaimed, and momentarily the thin, worn face took on a gentle, abstract look.

"What a pity Father didn't come, Mother."

"I was just thinking the same thing," she sighed. "He nearly did, you know." Dickie had wanted to come; but since neither Phillip nor Lucy had mentioned him in the letter he had felt unwanted; and had withdrawn once more into his armour of pride, saying, Well, I have to be at the office, you know.

"I did think of asking him to come, too, but felt he would refuse, Mother."

"Oh, what a pity. Then the three brothers would all be together again."

"I'm afraid Uncle John's rather poorly. He's in bed with bronchitis."

Mrs. Rigg, the amiable, dumpy little cottage woman who enjoyed herself immensely in the kitchen, helping Lucy with invariable cheerfulness, had the dinner ready for them on their return. It was roast shoulder of lamb, ordered by Hilary in a letter to Mr. Hibbs, who had brought it with the wages that morning. To help Lucy, Hilary offered to carve when Mrs. Rigg came in with the large Willow Pattern dish which, since there was no sideboard in the parlour, was put down at the head of the table. This was an oaken affair, nearly twelve feet long, built some centuries ago.

At one end of the table stood the yew-wood chair which, once belonging to his grandfather Turney, Phillip had intended to occupy as host; but unknown to him, Lucy had already accepted Hilary's offer to carve. Seeing him standing there, examining the edge of the carving knife, Phillip kept in the background while Lucy, left alone, exclaimed, "Oh, do sit down anywhere, won't you?" Then, seeing that 'Mother' and Aunt Dora were hesitating —six places had been laid, with rush mats between knives and forks—she recovered from her fluster, due to Phillip's sudden withdrawal, and said, "Mrs. Lushington, will you sit next to Sir Hilary? 'Mother'—let me see—oh, you'll be on the other side, of course."

"Which is your place?" asked Hetty, appealing to Phillip.

"Where would you like me to sit, Lucy?" Phillip enquired, with exaggerated politeness.

"Why not at the other end of the table?" replied Hilary.

"I rather fancy that's Lucy's place, sir."

Before his uncle could reply Phillip went forward and drew out the chair for Lucy; then, a little ashamed of his attitude, he helped Dora to sit down before seating himself beside Irene, with whom he had hardly spoken so far. He had looked forward greatly to her coming, feeling that it was a link with the old days; but she appeared to be aloof. Could it be only that Billy, on seeing her, with Irene's arms held out to him, had turned away to watch the train?

Now, sitting beside her, he said that children grew to their parents, and others, gradually. "I mean, Billy—at the station———"

"Of course, my dear P.M. It must be so strange for him, so many faces high above him." She smiled into his face.

"Yes, Billy likes to feel free, and usually tries to squirm away when I lift him up."

Irene thought that he took after Barley in that but all she said was, "I hope he won't be 'temperamental' at the christening tomorrow."

"Oh, I don't think so," said Lucy. "Although it will be rather a lot of strange faces. For him, I mean," she said, recovering herself. "He will be all right by tomorrow, with Uncle John here for lunch, and my father and brother. Oh yes, Piers is coming too, isn't he. Billy will feel at home with us all by then."

"Piers is a neighbour of ours, Irene. He's my best friend, and is the other godfather," explained Phillip.

"D'you mean Piers Tofield?" asked Hilary, pausing in the act of making a good thick cut into juicy meat under a crisp brown skin.

"Yes," replied Phillip. "He's the only decent fellow in the neighbourhood."

"I'm so glad you have a man friend," said Irene. "Does he farm, too?"

"Not exactly. His father's a City gent, whose land adjoins ours. I haven't met him yet. It's rather a long story, there was almost a family feud with the Tofields, two generations ago. Good material for a novel one day, perhaps. Everyone suitably disguised, of course, like the characters in Thomas Morland's *Crouch-end Saga*, but no satire, which is the refuge of the destitute."

The shoulder of lamb was from the Dorset Horn flock; it went well with Hilary's favourite Chateau Latour claret, of which he had brought six bottles, in addition to the Dublin stout, and a couple of bottles of his preferred brand of malt whisky.

Towards the end of the meal, when Hilary had gone to the 'throne', Hetty took the opportunity to ask Dora, who had had nothing but a cup of beef tea, about her charges.

Dora smiled a weak smile and said, "Oh, my Babies occupy my days, you know. Indeed, I would not know what to do with myself without them." She turned to Irene. "Both my charges are now approaching eighty years of age, the elder is blind, and her sister is liable to delusions, usually at the full of the moon. At other times they are the dearest little children imaginable." To Hetty, "Our District Nurse is very good, so I am able to leave them for a while now and again."

Swallowing his fourth glass of wine, Phillip pushed back his chair and cried out, "I'll be back in a moment. Don't go away. I'd like you, Aunt Dora, to hear what I wrote in my note-book after my visit to you last year."

When he came back, Hilary was seated at the table.

"Here it is. 'Two pawns on a chessboard, virgin figures dressed in black early Victorian clothes: timid, impulsive, young-girlish manners: two butterflies gone black with protective colouration after escaping in vain from the dark killing-bottle of early love-lessness. Not even the light of Hellas can save them now.'"

Silence followed these words. There was a knock on the door: Mrs. Rigg came in to pile the plates on the trolley. When she had gone away, followed by Lucy to see about the strawberry tart and cream, Dora said to Phillip, "Surely you are not intending to write about my 'Babies', are you?"

"What I've just read is no reflection on you, Aunt Dora. After all, the killing was achieved before you knew them. Who were their parents, I have often wondered. Although it isn't important, except to explain how they came to be what they are. Were they smuggled away, to be hidden for the sake of Victorian 'respectability'? 'Farmed' out as lost little children, to cower all the rest of their lives in Dostoieffskian dreads and fears—like Mavis," he said, to Irene. "My elder sister, who calls herself Elizabeth in a desperate attempt to grow a new and happy personality——"

"Hush, Phillip," said Hetty.

"Mother, are you still 'hushing' me? Surely we're all grown up here, and can face the truth? After all, we have it on the highest authority that only the truth can make an integrated personality. This is also Freud's belief. Some people abhor Freud. He is a Jew of genius, like Jesus of Nazareth. What a pity, Aunt Dora, that you haven't read cousin Willie's notebook. *He* was a great man."

Hilary pushed back his chair. "I consider the subject to be a poor one, and I for one will not sit here unless you apologise at once to your aunt for those idiotic remarks."

"Very well, I apologise, Aunt Dora."

This prompt acceptance appeared to upset Hilary the more. He sat, breathing deeply. The silence was broken by Lucy's voice

saying gently, to Hetty, "I do so hope it will keep fine for the
christening tomorrow."

"Oh yes, I am so looking forward to it."

"Don't forget that we want rain to bring up the small seeds,"
remarked Phillip. "'The gentle rain, that down doth fall from
heaven.' Still, I hope it won't rain tomorrow."

"You haven't answered my question," said Dora, looking
steadily at him.

"Don't worry," he replied, "my talent, like the rest of my
generation, is buried," and taking the note-book from his pocket,
he removed the page and tore it up, putting the pieces in the
fire.

Rookhurst parish church was built of dressed flint, with lime-
stone coigns; the Norman tower, holding six bells, was stubbed
by a steeple not unlike the tower of Clayborough which was such
a landmark above the sea near Malandine in South Devon. Whenever Phillip saw this likeness, he sighed; but the fresco on the north
wall within, that of the giant Saint Christopher, gave some kind
of fortitude. This coloured painting had recently been discovered,
or rather uncovered, after lying during nearly four centuries since
the Reformation under a score or more coats of lime-wash.

Sitting with the others under the vaulted chancel, waiting for
the village children's Sunday school to end, Phillip wondered if
Piers' theory of Saint Christopher was true: that the Neolithic
giant, seen from the road north of Dorchester one day, club in
hand and genitals in full pride, was the base from which the figure
had been borrowed. The demi-god of the Neolithic people,
fructifier of the Great Earth Mother, who carried a club forty
yards long with which to bash out the brains of the Celtic newcomers, had been transformed by them to Helith, an idea borrowed
from the Greco-Phœnician symbol, Heracles, Piers had said at
luncheon. The Neoliths had not feared death; the Celts had
feared both the living and the dead; the Christians tried to bear
the burden of all and to love both, Aunt Dora had replied.

While they were discussing it, Phillip saw light in Dora's face;
she obviously liked Piers. He had been charming, in his modest
manner, to Nuncle, Uncle John, and Pa in turn, listening atten-
tively to all they said. Irene, too, had brightened in his company.

Now it was time to stand at the font. The godfathers and god-
mothers, on behalf of the infants, duly promised to renounce the

Devil and all his works. The baby was held at the font, sleeping despite the drips on its skull covered by dark hair, its eyes closed. Thus Peter was changed into Hilary Copleston, an utterly strange happening watched with puzzlement, concern and finally alarm by Billy, who suspected that the giant on the wall was going to take the baby away afterwards. When his turn came to be changed into William Lushington Beare he tried to struggle out of the parson's arms, and, his legs being held by Nuncle, turned a tearful look on his father, shouted in sudden rage of betrayal, and collapsed sobbing.

After the service, and a cheque for two guineas discreetly given to the vicar, together with a pound note for the Ringers' Fund, Phillip sought the child, who as usual had gone into a corner. Only when more tears had fallen, as from a broken resolve to stand alone, did Billy allow himself to be picked up by a parent whose emotions were as water spilled in the font. The father's cheek-bone rested on hair the hue of ripe barley, which lay warm and soft to his quiet caress. The child yielded, face hidden, an arm went round the father's neck, soon to be followed by the other arm. Hetty watched with shining eyes near to tears; and when her son said, "Grannie, will you carry the baby, because I must look after my best boy?" she felt that her prayers had been answered.

"Now Peter has got two real names, Billy darling," said Phillip. "So have you, Billy—you're a big boy now, William after Uncle John—Lushington after your other Grannie, and Beare after the Forest below the downs—where all those pretty pink flowers are, for Beare means 'wood', the man of the wood, the tree man."

Billy connected the wood logs in the writing room with the beer barrel, and said, "Me Pin, too?"

"Yes," said Phillip, thinking that Billy had enough to go on with for the time being.

The bells in the tower were now ringing out. After tea, Phillip urged Pa and Ernest to stay to supper, then he would be able to invite Piers as well. Pa was quite happy to stay; apart from enjoying the jolly party, he had no love of Miss Calmady's so-called cooking. In due course they all sat down at the refectory table, for Billy had been allowed to stay up, sitting beside new Grannie Lush. Hilary again carved; Phillip asked him if he would be so good as to do this while the table was being laid, thus restoring the initiative to himself.

"I'd half a mind to ask Uncle John to do the carving, Lucy,
but thought he looked rather tired."

"Yes, poor dear. Aunt Dora says he ought to try a cure by
fasting."

"I must find time to take him for walks on the downs. I know
it isn't the same thing when one forces oneself to take exercise."

"Oh, *do* ask him. He'll love it."

"I shall. I say, isn't this fun? Our first real party."

"I'm so glad you're happy, Pip."

Lucy, at Phillip's direction, had put Piers next to Hilary at
table; Piers seemed to know a lot about sailing. By a lucky shot
he had asked Nuncle if he had ever rounded Cape Horn; and
so interesting was Nuncle's account of the six-master's attempt to
make the passage, finally to be put on course for the Strait of Le
Maire, and so to the open South Atlantic, that soon all the eleven
faces around the table—including Billy in what had once been
Phillip's high chair—had turned to listen.

In his late middle-age, had he not lacked imagination, he
might have been able to extend sympathy for the younger generation: instead of merely passing on the criticism he had received,
so harshly, in his early period at sea. With imagination he might
have communicated some of the truth of his experiences, for he
had lived an adventurous youth, of which he seldom spoke.
When (for example) going round the Horn in winter, during his
first voyage on the 'Frisco run, it had taken three weeks, with
three masts fallen and cut away by axes, to round that terrible
black headland, with the vast fissures in its face clotted by centuries
of salt. Day after day and night after night the ship had stood off
a lee shore, Hilary joining the crewsman aloft, a hundred and
forty feet above the deck, in darkness; thrusting himself up rat-
lines of ice to edge his way along a yard and to claw at stiff canvas
threshing and booming and cracking in a full gale, his feet burning
with pain upon an unseen foot-rope. After three weeks they had
rounded the Horn, to run before the wind almost under bare poles
until on awakening in his bunk he had been dazed by a glowing
porthole, for the sun was above the mountains of Chile. Before
them lay the great swells of the open South Pacific; running
before breezes bearing strange scents all the way to Valparaiso,
where they put in to refit.

When Nuncle ended his tale Phillip said, "I wish I could write
as well as you can talk, Uncle Hilary," words which induced

Ernest, hitherto silent, to say, as though from the deeps of his being, "I went round the Cape twice during the war," while his face took on a dusky pink hue.

When the guests had left and the others gone to bed Hilary said to Phillip, as he was lighting some joss-sticks on the shelf above the fire-place, "Young Tofield has plenty of ability. I wonder what caused him to play the giddy goat with that set—what is it the papers call them?—those young people in London."

"Oh, I suppose it is their sense of fun, Uncle Hilary."

"Well, some of their acts I've read about are downright bad form. That bogus marriage, with a bogus priest, for example. They even sent invitations to their parents. That reminds me, I've not yet heard from either of Lucy's brothers, no word of thanks for finding them free passages to Australia."

"I must apologise for not writing to you again, after they had left."

"Has anyone heard?"

"Lucy had a letter. Tim said they had an important job electrifying Sydney, or something."

"'Electrifying Sydney'! It's been electrified before they were born."

"Anyway, they've got good jobs connected with some temporary fair or other."

"'Some fair or other'! Would you call the opening of Parliament, and the illuminations for the festivities, 'some fair or other'?"

Hetty and Dora were sitting in the little breakfast room that faced the morning sun, waiting to walk with the others to the Hanger Coppice. Uncle John was to take them there, he was due at eleven o'clock. It was now a little after ten. A spirit of contentment filled the house.

The scent of the joss-sticks still lingered, bringing back happy memories to Dora. Irene was in the garden with Billy, in flow of love to him; she had seen, for a moment, her darling girl in the little boy's face.

"It's been an awfully nice visit," said Hetty. Looking around to see if they were alone, she went on, "Well, dearest Dora, I don't suppose there's any harm in saying it now, but for a time I was very worried that Barley's death might have intensified—how can I put it—Phillip's tendency to live in the past."

"Yes, Hetty, my dear Father had that characteristic, which can so easily lead to an unawareness of the feelings of others. But it will not happen, I think, like that with Phillip, now that he is living an open-air life. If only my brother Dickie—— Tell me, Hetty, when is he due to retire?"

"Dickie thinks when he is sixty-five. He was due to retire at sixty, but volunteered to stay on for a further period. Now he is talking of looking for a cottage, far away from London," she sighed.

Dora could see that she was troubled about leaving Doris and Elizabeth.

"I've often wondered what is the *real* reason why my brother became so set against his daughters."

Hetty felt her strength ebbing. "I suppose it is the strains of City life; but I cannot understand him." She smiled as though cheerfully. "Perhaps now that the time for his retirement is due, he will see matters a little differently. What then will become of Elizabeth—she no longer likes to be called Mavis—and Doris, I hardly like to think."

"I understand how you feel, Hetty. I have my 'Babies', and often I wonder what would happen to them if I fell ill, and could no longer be with them. So do not feel that you are alone—we have each other, and now that we have come together, we must not drift apart again." She hesitated, and went on, "You know, I think sometimes that Dickie has fallen into the error of caring *too* much for his own. It is a paradox that love ceases to be love when we become *too* concerned in the lives of others. For a dominant concern leads us into trying to convert others into the image of our own righteous feelings, which arise not from love, but from fear."

Lucy came into the room and said, "Uncle John will be here in a minute or two, to take us to Hanger Coppice. Peter has gone to sleep, thank goodness, and Mrs. Rigg will look after him."

During the christening party, Dora had decided to stay an extra day, and return by train; while Hilary was leaving in the afternoon, after taking Hetty and Irene to the junction.

Hanger Coppice had been a favourite place for picnics when John and Richard and Hilary had been boys together. Hetty, seeing her son walking between his uncles, thought again what a pity it was that Dickie had not come down with her. The way led up the borstal, branching off along a foot-path below the beech hanger. There, in a fold of land at the foot of the down, were a couple of acres of hazel and sweet-chestnut, the greater part of which had been cut to the stoles during the past February. The sounds of knocking came from the far end, where hurdles were lying in heaps, with cords of cut stakes.

Wood smoke arose through the remaining trees and bushes, in whose green shade nightingales, now voiceless except for harsh notes of warning, were leading their fledged young.

For Hetty the walk around the Coppice was one of enchantment. Her country-bred eye, dulled for so long among bricks and mortar, saw again dry skeleton leaves on the woodland floor; the few late blooms of primroses, blue-bells making their green seed-cases, the blue-and-white feather of a jay hanging in a spider's web. And from afar, from beyond the skyline of the downs, came the sound of sheep-bells.

"The rotation is usually twelve years between cutting," said Phillip, returning to them. "This season the coppice-wood was sold for a shilling the lugg, otherwise the jolly old rod, pole, or perch of our schoolroom days," as he took her arm, to lead her to the brothers who were making the hurdles.

Hetty and Dora shook hands with them after he had introduced the brothers. "They make the best hurdles in the district," went on Phillip, as he left them to their work, which was done fast, since they were their own masters. "While one cuts out rods, the other stacks them ready for the making of hurdles after the pheasants have hatched off their eggs. The keeper doesn't like the hurdle-makers on principle, but it's been done by the same family for nearly a century, isn't that right, Uncle John?"

"Probably longer, Phillip."

"They make them in shape moulds, here's one," went on Phillip, pointing to a heavy length of oak with a slight bend in it. "The uprights, or sails, are knocked into those holes to keep them steady while rods, which have to be split first, are woven in and out of the sails. A good man can make one in an hour. The trouble is that most farmers use wire netting now. The best is hand-woven, made in Scotland."

"You seem to have acquired a countryman's knowledge very quickly, Boy," said Dora.

He felt he was back in her good books again; but could not resist saying, "Yes, I remembered your words about 'treading the primrose path', and changed direction in time! By the way, I realize now that, speaking only from a writing point of view, the entry in my note-book was superficial and worthless. Such a superficial portrait is no good because it implies mere indignation, and does not truly divine. There is no difference, really, between Billy and your Babies. Put at its simplest, life without love is lost life."

He looked at his mother's face; he thought of Barley, while his hollow middle seemed to fill with blackness; he wanted to move away from them, swiftly—but where could he go? He stood there without moving, a smile on his lips, his eyes on the ground, waiting for them to move along the footpath to the spring-head, and then back beside the Longpond.

Chapter 7

SECRET WORLD

Hilary was due to leave in the early afternoon for Wales; he had arranged to take Hetty and Irene to the junction and leave them there to await the Penzance train to London. Dora was staying on for another day, before going back by train; and while she was resting with Hetty in the garden before lunch, Lucy walked to where the two elderly women were sitting in the shade of the mulberry tree and said, "Irene thinks she would like to go on to South Devon, and visit Malandine while she is down here, and Uncle Hilary says he will drive her there immediately after lunch. He proposes to telephone for a taxi to take us to the afternoon London train, so dear Mother, I'll come with you, and shall we take Billy with us? Aunt Dora, would you care to come too? The train doesn't leave until five this afternoon, so there's plenty of time to decide."

Phillip, trying to write upstairs, with the window open, heard this and, looking out, said, "What's that? Irene going to Malandine with Nuncle?"

"Yes, Phillip," replied Hetty. She had learned, under her son's persistence, and with regret, not to call him 'dear'.

"Those two together?"

It was a shock. He did not know what to say, or think, as he sat

on his bed. Those two going to see Barley's grave without him!
He felt active dislike of Nuncle. But no: Nuncle had his feelings:
and perhaps, after all, he would be asked?

Irene and Hilary were fishing. They returned with two trout
which Hilary had killed in the pool below the Longpond,
watched by Irene, who had carried the long-handled net. Phillip
heard him telling Lucy that he would cook them for luncheon, an
offer to which she readily agreed.

Whose house was it, that Nuncle behaved as though he were the
captain of a ship? Still, what did it matter? All the same——

The fish, gently simmered in the tinned copper kettle with the
lid on, were allowed to cool in their own liquor. Uncle John
brought in a couple of cucumbers, to be thinly sliced; the mayon-
naise was made by Irene; an excellent meal, all agreed.

Afterwards Lucy said, "Well, dears, I hope you have a nice run
to South Devon."

Phillip waited to be invited.

Nothing was said.

When they had gone—and Aunt Dora was lying down in her
room—Phillip walked up the valley beside the brook, feeling
ashamed of his bad behaviour on the first evening of their arrival.
If only Willie were alive. With a little shock he realised that Willie
was nearer to him than Barley. Ah well, it was done now. He
must accept life as it was.

How swiftly the spring had gone—and he had hardly seen it.
Long since the blossom of the downland thorns, haunt of magpies,
had fallen. 'For faces fade as flowers, and there is no consolation'.
Dear, lonely Jefferies, he thought, as he walked beside the brook,
following its course through the water-meadows to the Longpond.

The Longpond—a stretch of ornamental water—had been made
in the 'eighties by damming the brook a quarter of a mile below its
source at the foot of the downs. At the base of the hill a spring
gushed forth to flow at the rate of hundreds of gallons a minute.
The spring-head was confined within a ring of limestone blocks,
with a spillway of paved stone carrying the water to the 'broad',
which was shallow and narrow at this entry but became deeper
as it widened to fill six acres of the little valley.

The Longpond had never silted, since the flow of water was from
out the chalk-bed composing the downs, which lay several hundred
feet above the vale. The flow was crystal and everlasting; no
floods disturbed it. The water issuing from the spring-head had

fallen as rain upon the upland pastures anything up to eighteen months before, taking so long to filter through the flint-beds underlying the chalk.

Here had stood Hilary and Irene—while he had remained aloof: and now it was too late. If he had only behaved as a true host, instead of inwardly grizzling about his 'position', like some uneasy little official fancying himself snubbed. Well, was it fancy, after all? Did Irene prefer Hilary to himself?

Ornamental shrubs and trees had been planted round its banks when the stream was dammed, part of a scheme to bring picturesqueness to a bare countryside by a North Country industrialist who had bought the land and come south to found a family. His only son, a soldier, had in due course inherited; his marriage had ended with the drowning of his wife. Thereafter the place had slowly become ruinous. It was sold after his death to speculators, a syndicate of anxious lawyers' clerks who had failed to get their price for the house. It had remained empty until the outbreak of the Great War, when it was taken over by the War Department. The trees were cut down, including those around the Longpond. During the post-war shortage of building materials, the house, which had been bought by Hilary, was stripped of its panelling, doors, floors, staircases, banisters, and all metal fittings, including the lead roof.

Hilary had waited to buy the place cheaply. His idea had been to build a small, labour-saving lodge on the site of the dilapidated shell, using two of the outer walls; but they were found to be rubble, and infirm. Plans were drawn but nothing built. Hilary was too comfortable with his sister Viccy at Bournemouth, and his caravan was enough for the spring and summer months.

During the years before the war many fish—roach, jack, rudd, perch, and carp—had increased in the Longpond. The year before the arrival of Lucy and Phillip, Hilary had had the weed-beds cut with chain-scythes, and pulled out, several score tons to be heaped beyond the banks. The water was then netted. Cartloads of fish were removed, some to be fed experimentally to pigs, but the main mass, of over a dozen tons, was rotted down with waterweed between layers of straw and bullock dung. This he called compost, and Mr. Hibbs called trash.

In fact, declared Mr. Hibbs, it wasn't worth the carting: every rat came for miles, some of them in droves led by old king-rats, to the heap, to dig in and tunnel away from crows, daws, and gulls in conflict above. Soon the heap was literally a heaving and squeaking mass, and Skirr farm acquired a new name—Rat Town.

In due course the decayed heap was carted to the arable in the autumn and spread, six tons to the acre, experimentally upon four acres. The following spring—just before the time of Phillip's marriage to Lucy—plants of wheat upon the area, with 'stalks like bamboos and heads like maize laid themselves down', in Mr. Hibbs' words, 'and rotted in sympathy with the skeletons of the fish'.

Sitting on the bank, Phillip wondered how the Longpond could be tidied up. Perhaps if his books made some money, he could engage men to do it. And—here was an idea!—he could write a book about how he had restored it to its former beauty. Some credit must be given to Hilary, of course, since, during the month of March, a year previously, he had purchased a thousand fish at the Hungerford Trout farm, at a cost of £75. The trout had arrived by lorry in four galvanised tanks, with ice afloat to dissolve and release oxygen in the water. Half the trout were brownies for the brook; the two remaining tanks held rainbows, and went into the Longpond after tank and lake water had been equalised, to avoid shock.

Everything had been done to ensure that a good stock of game fish would replace the former coarse fish. Herons were shot, and Haylock even put down an otter trap, which 'disappeared' from the entrance to one of the overflow pipes. It still lay hidden in nettles where Phillip had thrown it.

Several large trout had escaped the net by getting below its leaded drag in deep water. These were not cannibals, as Hilary had supposed, but being feeders in the shallows (minnows) by night, and in deep water by day, had avoided the rushes of monster pike, some of them nearly thirty pounds in weight, which ruled each area of the Longpond, raiding from the cover of its particular weed-beds—those strongholds castellated in early summer by white flowers of water-crowsfoot.

After the pike had gone, the big trout began to cruise, each a lord within its own waters as it seized 8-inch rainbows across the back and swallowed them head-first, with an occasional roach and rudd; but the cruising became general and careless when the mayfly was up and all fish thought only of those objects of crisp and cream.

Phillip remembered the big trout in the fish-ponds at Wester-
ham, when he was a boy—the bluish-green tapered fish, some as
long as a man's forearm, and spotted, in the clear headwaters of
the Darent, scores of them to be seen at once, unafraid of figures
on the banks, seizing creamy mayfly after mayfly; sometimes the
crisp crushing of an insect between prickly fish-tongue and palate
was distinctly audible. And here he was, no longer a fervent
suburban explorer on a *Swift* 3-speed bicycle, but the heir to a
thousand acres—as yet a desolate area to the mind. Yes, he could
include that in his book.

Willows sprawled unkempt beside the Longpond. Reeds choked
the margins, half-concealing in one place the ruins of a boat-
house. He could not bear the sight of the dead stumps of ornamental trees, felled for the few pounds they had brought to the
local speculators during the war; and the appearance of ruin
extended by the army—brick sills of huts long since robbed of their
window-frames and doors, the asbestos walls broken, pieces still
lying among the nettles. These fragments, and an occasional dried
green boot, its sole a mass of rusty hob-nails, were all that was left
of a vanished life.

He felt tired; his strength went suddenly; perhaps his tubercular
lung was infected again. Or the excitement of the past forty-eight
hours. He looked at his watch: time had passed quickly: it was
already six o'clock. Would Nuncle and Irene be at Malandine
by now? It was possible. Was his sudden fatigue due to trans-
ference of Irene's emotion at the grave? He had meant to go and
tidy it, plant flowers, and also a bush of rosemary; but had never
gone. O God, what must Irene think of him. He had meant to
ask her to stay many times, to see Billy, but had never written.
A feeling of being unreal overcame him, of being somebody not
himself. Perhaps nobody was ever really himself, as labelled and
known to others: the real self was that upon which the personality
was grafted; the blossoms of the graft coming from the pollination
of others. Piers had added to his personality, he had copied the
manner of Piers, the oblique Etonian idiom of speech; it came
out at times. Ernest dissolved that part of him, by shutting himself
off. But these were superficial influences; the true begetters of
the mind were the poets, musicians, painters, and writers; one
had grafted them upon oneself—or rather, had 'grappled them
with hooks of steel'. And the hooks pierced not only oneself, but
others in one's life.

Feeling now empty and nearly without hope, he left the thistles, nettles, and burdocks growing out of uncleared heaps of pink bricks and rotting roof-felt, and went home, while the thought of Irene's unspoken criticism possessed nearly all his being. Or was it all his imagination? If *he* had been more expansive to her, would she not have responded to him? Surely she would have responded anyway, if she had divined the condition between Nuncle and himself?. And now she had gone off with him.

Irene! he cried, *I did not forget Barley!* She was gone; it was too late to tell her now, to so behave that she would be once again the Irene he had known at Malandine, in those far-off care-free days (as they now seemed) when the Barley-Irene friendship was the very sunshine of life. Nuncle and Irene had made friends, and he was left out! They had gone to visit the grave of Barley; he had longed to be asked to go too; but they didn't want him.

The fact was that Irene had suggested that Phillip might feel hurt if he were not invited to go with them, but Hilary had replied, "Better not open old wounds, dear lady".

And the truth was that Hilary wanted to be alone with Irene.

Phillip went for a long walk on the downs with Rusty, to tire himself out; and descending along his usual route to Colham, went into the Rising Sun and drank several pints of beer there, to arrive home just as Lucy was going to bed.

"Aunt Dora went up an hour ago," she said. "We thought you'd gone for a walk, to clear your head after all the happenings of the past three days. It was a lovely party, wasn't it? I think everyone enjoyed themselves."

The next morning there was a letter from Anders Norse, his literary agent, together with a parcel of the typescript of his book. Mr. Quill, of Cowdray & Smith, did not feel disposed to publish it unless the author, who appeared to have some con-nexion with the sporting fraternity, he wrote, would undertake to guarantee a sale of 500 copies, on laid paper and buckram bind-ing, among his friends, at £1/1/– the copy. This would enable the publishers to cover the cost of setting, so that a popular edition at 7/6 could be run off the type for the trade. Meanwhile, Cowdray & Smith were prepared to consider any copy for a prospectus which Mr. Maddison might care to submit for their approval.

Phillip was still thinking about this as he drove Aunt Dora in the side-car, at 20 m.p.h., to the junction later that morning.

Dora, too, was preoccupied with her own thoughts. She still
suffered from her brother's attitude towards her 'Babies'; she had
observed his interest in Irene, who was still attractive; and hoped
that Hilary would do nothing rash.

"Goodbye, Aunt Dora. Thank you very much for coming all
this long way."

"Goodbye, Boy. Be good to Lucy, won't you? She is such a
gentle creature."

Having seen her off, he went to Down Close, to ask Pa's advice
about getting lists of subscribers to the numerous Otter Hunts in
England, Scotland, and Wales.

That old gentleman suggested that he get hold of a copy of
Baily's Hunting Directory, where no doubt he would find the
addresses he required.

"Perhaps it would be as well if you made no mention of any
particular connexion with any of the local hunts."

Phillip pondered thisremark, this hint: did Pa think it best to
keep any local light under a bushel measure? So, avoiding the
home hunt, he wrote formally to the honorary secretaries of a
dozen distant packs. In due course he received lists from four
of them; made his copies of the listed names, and returned the
originals with thanks.

From the secretary of a pack in Sussex—'the portly pole-
carriers' of Martin Beausire, his Fleet Street friend—Phillip got
a startling letter about *The Water Wanderer*.

> Your ears would burn if you could have heard what I and some of
> my fellow members, including the Master, said on reading a short
> story of yours about an otter hunt at Lynton, which recently appeared
> in *The Sporting and Theatrical World*.

Phillip had written about the water 'carrying the ream', in the
sense of scent. He had heard someone among the pole-carriers use
the expression. His correspondent declared that the 'ream' was
a wave, or travelling ripple, pushed out by the otter's nose when
surface-swimming.

> I advise you to give up all attempts to write such a book as you
> contemplate, for it is obvious you have no talent as a sporting writer.
> Also, I would inform you, there is neither room nor need for a book
> such as appears to be your declared intention to write, since the field

is already covered by Tregarthen's *Life of the Otter*, a capital work by a Cornishman who knows what he is writing about, a thing which it is made apparent by your article, you lack knowledge of.

When he had recovered equanimity, Phillip wrote to say that he was most grateful for the kind help and advice he had received: that he fully realised he knew nothing about the hunting of otters. He had once observed a tame otter for a short while: and he was always striving to learn from his superiors. The correction regarding the erroneous use of 'ream' was a most valuable criticism. His letter ended by asking Mr. Hon. Secretary Sheepshanks to read the revised typescript for further errors before publication.

Mr. Hon. Secretary Sheepshanks' reply, written in a different tone, proved to be most useful.

I am in receipt of your letter, and am afraid you have taken my criticisms rather too seriously, but at the same time, I am glad you have given due consideration to my remarks, and in substance, agree with them, which shews me at once that you are prepared to accept the advice of those who have had perhaps longer experience of otters, their ways and habits, and the hunting of them, than yourself.

Had I not been sure of my ground, I should never have written you as I did, but after nearly 30 years' active participation in otter hunting, and in close study of the animal's habits and ways, I think you will agree that my remarks are those gained by long experience.

Yes, I know the Lyn quite well. I have seen it hunted by Littleworth, Martin and Waters, and when I was Master of that pack, took hounds there once, but as I had several hounds badly injured by slipping off the boulders, decided that the game was not worth the candle.

The water is hunted however above *Watersmeet*, and the present Master has had several good hunts there during the last two seasons.

I too, have kept tame otters, having brought up a bitch cub on the bottle, keeping her for 5 years and getting the loan of a dog otter from the Zoological Society, of which I am a Fellow, with the hope that they would breed, as no record exists of otters breeding in captivity, but although the surroundings were as natural as I could make them, with a pond, holts, trees, and a constant supply of their natural food in the form of live eels, frogs, varied by small birds, earth worms, etc., my hopes were never realized, as they did not breed.

I could write you pages of interesting stuff concerning the habits and ways of otters both tame and otherwise, but I entirely agree with you that the otter is a savage, relentless beast that will kill anything within its capacity when pressed for food, and when hunted, shows little sign of fear.

I have seen otters attack hounds (not bitches with cubs) but big, old dog otters, and the Culmstock when hunting on the Irish coast some years ago, swam an otter to sea, when he attacked a hound and drowned him in full view of the hunt.

The words ream, or wave are not to be confused with wash, as the ream or wave indicates the otter's movement through the water, while the wash is the scent carried down stream from the otter which is in a holt or some place of hiding.

With regard to your expressed wish that I should look over the type-script of your book, you do me an honour, which after my somewhat drastic criticism I do not feel myself to have merited. However, if when the book is recast, you still feel the same way about it, please consider me to be at your service in the matter. I have a certain experience of publishing, having written a book about a Wiltshire Hunt, and may be able to help you also in this connexion.

Phillip replied to this saying that he would not take advantage of the kind offer by sending the typescript, feeling that he had already made too great a use of his correspondents' considerable knowledge; but the real reason was that now he felt sure of his subject. It so happened, a few weeks later, when Hilary looked in on his way to Bournemouth, that he spoke of the letter, and mentioning the name of the writer, discovered that Nuncle had been at his private school with him, and they had been inseparable as boys. This was a point of contact between uncle and nephew; they got on better after Phillip had told him how grateful he was for the help his old chum had given him.

The hay had been carted, stacked, and thatched; there was little or no work to be done on the farm. The sowings of clover and grass seeds having failed, alternate fields had been cultivated and drilled with mustard.

"Come with me while I throw a fly, and carry the net," suggested Hilary. "I want to have a talk with you."

Phillip thought he knew what was coming. Lucy had had a cheerful letter from Irene two days after her departure, saying how much she had enjoyed her visit, and been delighted with the appearance of her grandson.

I must see more of the little pet, and get to know him properly. He is the dearest little boy, and constantly reminds me of his mother at that age, especially his sudden smile, giving all of himself to happiness. Skirr Farm is delightful, I cannot imagine a more beautiful place for the children to grow up, nor a kinder mother. My dearest love to you all.

Hilary's talk was not quite what Phillip had expected. It was short and to the point, taking the form of questions.

"She's a nice woman, Irene Lushington. How did you come to meet her?"

"On the sands at Malandine, during my first summer. I got marooned on a rock, and she and Barley tried to help me."

"She'd left her husband then, hadn't she?"

"I didn't ask."

"Weren't you curious about her?"

"No."

"Then why did you cotton on to her?"

"Barley and I were keen on walking and exploring, and she took an interest in my work."

"I see by *Who Was Who* that Lushington was a judge in India, and was educated at Harrow and Trinity, Cambridge. Why did she leave him, d'you know?"

Phillip avoided that one. "She came back to find a school for Barley."

He wanted to ask about the grave, but could not utter the words.

Hilary went on, "I left her at the Clarence, in Exeter, and then motored north to stay the night at Bristol."

In his relief Phillip said, "I must go down to Malandine one day, and plant some flowers on the grave."

"There won't be any need to, Phillip. Irene said she would see to it. She realises you have enough to do here, and won't think any the worse of you. In fact, she thought the stone you put up, with the carving of sickle and rosebud, was just right. But I'll tell her that it's been on your mind when I see her in London next week. We're going to dine and do a theatre while I'm up."

Phillip was still wondering if he dare guarantee the sale of five hundred copies of a non-sporting book at a guinea each, by buying them himself at trade price and storing them as future valuable first-editions, when Anders wrote that he had learned that Mr. Quill's publishing business was in a precarious condition: and would he consider having the book submitted to another publisher, Mashie & Co? Anticipating his agreement, Anders said, he had already taken the typescript round to Mr. Driver of that firm.

Three days later Anders wrote to say that Mashie & Co. would take over from Cowdray & Smith, pay an additional £50 advance

now, and hope to publish the book in time for the Christmas
season, paying a further £25 on publication.

> I put up the question of a special limited edition, and hear that they
> are prepared, at their own expense, to put out, before publication, a
> limited edition for subscribers, one hundred copies on hand-made
> paper, to be printed by the Eyot Press and bound in vellum. Meanwhile
> Mr. Driver, the managing director, has a few queries to submit to you.
> He says he read the typescript most carefully, and, if you accept his
> terms now, he will post the typescript direct to you, to save time.

Phillip accepted with glee. Later in the week the Tss. arrived,
with a letter signed *Jasper Driver* saying that the writer had carefully gone through the story and made notes of what he considered
might possibly spoil the book as a good seller for school prizes.
Glancing through the pages, Phillip found that the chapter he
liked best, describing the prolonged hard winter, was the one
most blue-pencilled. Mr. Driver's criticism was, *Cosmic references
to come off must be very good indeed. These do not quite come off.*
Phillip threw the bundle of typed sheets over his head, and
rushed down to tell Lucy, whose hands were scaly with dough
being moulded for a currant pudding.

"Mr. Driver wants to make a bran-mash of the best chapter, my
winter chapter! Look, for God's sake."

"Oh, what a nuisance," she said, peering at some pencil marks.
"Why not rub them out and send it back again? He'll probably
have forgotten what he wrote. And as he says in his letter, he
went through it while in bed with influenza."

The supra-sensitive perception which was the basis of his writing,
reinforced by the visual sense—a handicap in ordinary life which
had made him so poor a manager of the Boys' affairs—now
induced a searing inner disintegration which he could not control.
He ran upstairs, and sitting at the typewriter began to dash off
a letter, *Dear Mr. Driver, I have received your plate of mash but where
is the sausage*; then ripping the sheet off the roller he flung it into
a corner. Another attempt went the way of the first; followed by
a third, a fourth, a fifth, a sixth, a seventh, all varying in content
and style from understatement to overstatement, with ideas ranging from a declaration that he did not wish to compete with Bumper
Annuals to a suggestion that their two names should appear jointly
on the title-page, together with that of the compositor, should that

official find it necessary to misprint any sentences. Thus an entire morning was wasted in rubbish: but it served to clear his feelings for the next day, when he was able to benefit from the publisher's advice: for he set about revising the criticized chapter, crossing out, altering, shifting, and clarifying until it flowed to a crescendo with the appearance of the Dawn of the Winter God, a passage which he knew was better than the original.

One afternoon towards the end of the month, while he was hoeing weeds between the rows of late-sprouting potatoes, he saw, over the hedge, the hooded top of an apparently new motor-car stop in the lane outside the farmhouse. He was peering through a gap in the hedge to see who it was when Lucy's voice from her open bedroom window exclaimed "Ernest! How perfectly lovely! Where *did* you get it?"

From the other side of the hedge he heard a gentle murmur of "Oh, I just got it."

Phillip went on with his hoeing while telling himself that if Ernest wanted to spend all his money at once on a brand-new motor car it was nothing to do with him. Nevertheless, a heavy feeling spread up from his diaphragm. How could Ernest be so feckless as to chuck away his remaining capital like that? And after all that had happened?

After a while, brother and sister came to where he was working. Lucy carried the baby, who had one sock and shoe on, Billy having pulled off the others. Phillip did not like the children wearing socks or shoes, wanting their toes to be broad and strong like Barley's, not cramped as were his own; but Lucy enjoyed dressing the baby. Sometimes Phillip had taken off both the children's clothes and let them lie naked in the sun, he beside them. Billy usually went away into shadow when his father leaned over the baby to let it pull his hair.

"Ernest and I think of going for a little ride around in his new car," said Lucy. "Would you like to come, too?"

"I think I ought to get on with the garden, thanks all the same." He leaned his hoe against a damson tree full of wild wood. "What make is it, Ernest? Oh, Crossley. I'd like to see it."

How *could* anyone have the hood and celluloid side-curtains up in such blazing sunshine?

"Isn't it very hot inside, like that?"

"Oh, you don't notice it when you are going along."

"It looks jolly nice, Ernest," he said, relenting. He took a deep breath. "What's happened to the dear old Trojan?"

"Oh, I took 'Mister' into Salisbury, and the beastly thing broke down, so I decided to get rid of it."

Phillip couldn't help saying, despite the knowledge that it was tactless, "I suppose you got an allowance for it, in part-exchange?"

"Oh, I didn't bother. It wasn't worth considering, so I just parked the Trodge and left it there."

"Still, as you're in the trade, I suppose you got fifteen per cent discount on the Crossley by showing your business card, so it amounts to the same thing."

"I didn't bother."

Ernest by now was tired of being questioned.

With an effort Phillip persisted, "How much did it cost?"

"Oh, about six hundred."

"Jolly nice motor, the Crossley."

With this Phillip went back to the garden, working out the lost discount—15% of £600 was £90—as he struck at weeds, cutting some of the potato haulms. Didn't Ernest realise that the money he, Phillip, had paid out to help save the Works had not been repaid? O, why had he ever been such a fool as to try and help them? Still, he had promised Grannie Chychester, and had tried to keep the promise.

"Are you coming?" asked Ernest through the hedge.

As he washed his hands under the pump he realized how Ernest must hate being mentally disapproved of. Was he like Hilary? Nobody liked being overlooked. Was that the origin of the witch's *overlooking*, the cursing of someone the black witch disapproved of? And yet, wasn't he, in a way, being overlooked by the very name of Copleston? Why did he feel his stomach sink whenever he thought of the Works, of the stagnant Tamp, of old Ernest? Lucy was much nearer to Ernest than she was to him. They really had nothing to talk about, beyond the children. He had known it before his marriage, but had stifled his intuition. Lucy was kind, gentle, and—like Pa. No, it was his *own* fault, for not entering into *their* world.

He went to the car. Ernest was telling Lucy that he had joined a flying club, and was learning to fly at two guineas a flight.

At that rate Ernest would soon be broke again, and the same ghastly situation would arise. Was he resenting Ernest's extravagance because it meant that his own work was wasted? Or because, when the crash came, Pa and Ernest would, of course, have to come and live at Skirr Farm. Where else could Pa go, if there was no money?

"We thought of having tea first," said Lucy's happy voice.

He noticed that his hands were not properly clean, so went back to the pump, to soap them thoroughly, rinse them in the cold spring-water, and dry them slowly in the cool and shade of the outside wash-house, or laundry, with the hart's tongue ferns growing out of the north wall.

Now he really must try to get to the truth of his own actions and thoughts. Was he growing like Willie—trying to alter the thoughts of others? Or more like Nuncle, who insisted on everything being done *his* way, the money-making way? Anders had not liked the last of the Donkin novels: like a fool he had sent it to him when only three-quarters written. Anders had argued with him about Donkin's beliefs, declaring that he, Phillip, had not seen Donkin in the round. The fault of the novel, Anders had written, was that the author had not admitted the value of suffering as a divine or ordered means of regeneration, as the only way to truth.

Phillip had replied that surely suffering was not necessary if people would see clear and plain. The idea of this had come from Willie.

Back came the answer: We can learn only through suffering, which brings clarity.

There the argument had stopped, Phillip thinking that Anders thought like that because he had not been through the battlefields. Back to Pa and Ernest.

Both considered him to be interfering, and, no doubt, said among themselves that he was a bore. They wanted to be left alone to live in their own way. They did not want their lives to be ordered by someone else. Yet when they got into a muddle they had to be got out of it—at the nervous expense of someone else. Grannie Chychester knew it: she had suffered from it: that was why he always felt easy and clear with her. She understood. Pa and the Boys, and their blood-loyal sister Lucy, did not understand.

He longed for them to understand. So good—so kind—if only Lucy was understanding, what a happy, happy time they would have together. But as it was, he had to live more or less in a vacuum. And he was trying to pour her into the vacuum of his personal memory, or experience. He was trying all the time to alter her.

Lucy probably accepted that he was not what she had hoped for; and so her whole being was given to Billy and Peter. And his moodiness had affected Billy, who no longer went to him with happy cries of "Dada-dada." Ah well, like his own father, he must make the best of a bad job. He must devote his life to writing. He would ask Hilary to end the contract, and go away by himself, find a cottage somewhere, and live alone.

"Tea's ready," Lucy called out, from the table in the shade of the mulberry tree. "Come if you like, but I don't want to disturb you, of course."

That was the trouble: she left him alone, she didn't really care. And yet, how could she? How much did he *really* care for her? Only so much as she was convenient to him. Appalling thought!

He sat down at the weather-warped table, next to baby Peter in the high chair.

"Where's Billy?"

"Oh, somewhere about," replied Lucy, happily.

The klaxon of the new motor-car sounded. *Err-err, err-err.* Phillip went to the gate. There was Billy sitting at the wheel, twisting it. He made to lift him out. Billy resisted.

"Uncle he said yes."

"Well, Daddy he say no. It will spoil the steering if you try to turn the wheel while the car is standing still. Come on in, you're going for a ride after tea."

"Peter comin', too?"

"I think we're all going."

The boy sat still. Phillip gave up and went back into the garden. *Err-err, err-err,* went the klaxon. Lucy went out and said, "Such a nice tea for you, darling, then we'll all go for a ride with Uncle, shall we?"

"Will Daddy come in Uncle's car-car, Mummy?"

"I expect he will."

Lucy held out her arms, and he yielded. She knew how deeply he loved Phillip, from his first conscious moments, the nurses at the Malandine Cottage Hospital had told her.

Phillip rode with them to the top of the downs, while feeling that he could not breathe inside that dark prison while the sun was shining outside. On the crest he asked Ernest, who had hardly spoken during tea or afterwards, to stop and put him down. He wanted to walk up to Whitesheet Hill.

Here, on top of the world, with the extended hump of the Chase rising along the southern sky, and the vale to the west, its human hopes enclosed within hundreds of dark hedges and taller hedge-timber—each family life bounded by a few meadows and pastures, ruled by them indeed—he saw his previous conceptions to be petty, and due to his own frustrated feelings scape-goated upon Pa and Ernest. Why be dissatisfied, when he had been given the chance to live the life he had always longed to have? He had felt that he did not belong to Wakenham; or belong anywhere, indeed; now he belonged to this country, he was no longer rootless. There in the church were the proofs of what he had always longed to have; the Maddison chapel with its effigies and memorials, eroded and defaced by Time; and it meant nothing to him. Indeed, in some way he could not determine, it was a petrifiction upon life—upon Hilary's as well as his own.

And yet, what was the alternative? He couldn't let down Hilary after all his kindness. He worried Hilary, he knew; even as Ernest, and that unsold Tamplin cycle car, now entirely hidden in nettles, worried him.

A string of small white clouds was stationary in the sky beyond the Chase. Below them, in his mind, he saw the blue waters of the Channel, and the summer wavelets on the sands of Malandine. Barley now seemed infinitely remote from his life; and yet, O God, she was ever-present.

He lay on the sward, with its scent of thyme, but no tears came. He was what he was; he must accept it; he *had* to live his secret life apart from the ordinary world. But that world had its claims; and he must not avoid them. Indeed, the secret world must sustain the ordinary world. In the application of that faith was freedom. O God, he prayed, help me to do the right thing.

He arose, feeling clear.

Now for a view upon the ordinary world. If the wander book sold well, as Anders said it would, it might solve his problem, as well as Hilary's. There was not much future in farming, and land prices were dropping steadily. Those farmers who had bought their farms just after the war were finding it hard to make ends meet. Why live against the grain? Time was passing; he was already in his fourth decade. He must write, or perish. And literary success would mean that he could keep the land going. The problem was soluble.

Striding over the close grey turf, he found freedom in impersonal

ideas arising as though on the breeze which shook the carline
thistles, and lifted the wings of linnets flitting before the wind.
Wheatears ran ahead of him, pausing to watch before flying on
with low measured flight, to drop again as though they had tired
suddenly, or abruptly changed their minds. His life was like that:
often broken across, impulse after impulse. As soon as the final
Donkin novel was finished he had intended to begin his suburban
trilogy, the central character his father, sympathetically presented
in every aspect of that unhappy, irritable, dreaming man. But
now he had virtually promised never to write about any of his
relations—not even with love, and its hovering spirit, compassion.

London was to have been the villain of *Soot*, not his father.
And yet, with the full focus upon truth, how could 'London'
really be the villain? London was living soil which had been
harmed, debased, made sour; its river polluted by the spirit of
unenlightened commerce: but even as he decided upon that, were
material, otherwise unspiritual, minds really to blame for what
they did not know? Had the Luddites been right to smash the
machines, which made the Satanic mills of William Blake? All
life was impelled by trial and error; there was no absolute good
or absolute evil. The steam-engine brought the wheat of the
destroyed prairies, as Jefferies had written; and English wheat-
fields went down to docks and thistles; labourers starved while
the finches rejoiced. The cheap food cry was one of genuine bene-
volence for those working in the mills, and the factories; whence
the slums, the rookeries of the feared East End, and that shocking
story once told by Father about Gran'pa Turney, and an out-of-
work cab-runner at Liverpool Street station carrying his bag to
London Bridge and being rewarded with a cigar stump. *Fear* of
desperate, out-of-work men had been behind that act. For, at
heart, Gran'pa Turney had been a kind, even generous man.
'Must a Christ perish in torment in every generation because
people have no imagination?' Nuncle's opinion of nearly two
million unemployed, most of them ex-soldiers: *Those fellows could
get work if they wanted to, only they don't want to* was matched by Pa's
complacent, *I've no use for the fellow*, meaning Dick Sheppard of St.
Martin-in-the-Fields, who was ill with asthma, Martin Beausire
had told him. Asthma was the disease of the sensitive, frustrated
by what Arnold Bennett called *le bloc*.

Where then, could a regenerating point be found? In revolution,
as in Russia? *When I hear Beethoven being played, I want to stroke*

people's heads Lenin had said, *until I remember that today heads must be split open.* Jesus had refused direct action at the Passover, and had gone to his death. So had Father Aloysius, on the Somme, shot while moving among the wounded. He could hear his voice now, against the distant hammer of machine-guns and exploding shells. *The Virgin and Child is a symbol of what is . . . Love is in the world always, waiting for all men.*

What guts, to push the entire bloody war away in thought, and proclaim the spirit of love while tens of thousands lay dying in Noman's Land. Such were the lights of humanity.

He strode on, joyfully. He saw human life clearly. Man was the dreamer; his seed drove him to dream. Woman was practical, the home-maker. The dream in man's seed was for her; he dreamed first of her beauty, which could never be, *should* never be, totally possessed. Even with Barley he had felt at times lonely: perhaps all dream, the life of the spirit, must be in secret. And yet, when with her, he did not dream: or rather, living was dream itself: one was through to the other side of life, as it were, beyond the barbed-wire and the barrage, into open country, the war between heaven and hell was over.

Was the part of Barley which had fulfilled his nature, completed his life, the companionate male part of her in a female body? She *understood*, she was a friend first, a female afterwards.

Why was he growing towards Lucy like Father to Mother? Lucy was always willing to help, to listen, to go for a walk, to do this or that—when she was free of the nursery—but he had to do all the talking. With Barley there was no need for words. She *knew.*

With Lucy it was always the same: he had to be the leader, the explainer. She followed out of kindness, generous for his sake. Like Mother to Father. So Father had always felt that Mother was a burden; and his irritability was due to loss of nervous energy. Had he not shouted out once, during a row, years ago, *You force me to play the rôle of the bully.*

Consider the case of Lucy. She was seldom, if ever, free of house-work: her time spent in cooking, collecting the eggs, pouring the milk into large shallow earthenware pans to stand first in the larder, then on the stove so that the cream on top of the milk began to crinkle, and turn yellow as it clotted: to be scooped off, and the scalt milk put outside the kitchen door for the pigs. On the go all the day and half the night. Then church work; visiting old

cottagers; taking eggs and jelly to the sick; riding on her bicycle
to return the calls of local people who had left cards.

In fact, Lucy was happy to be left alone. In her own way she
was neat and methodical, and enjoyed ending one job to begin
another which was equally enjoyed. She did not mind how hard
she worked, or how long; she would drop what she was doing to
help Phillip, although by now when he called her up to his writing
room to hear what he had written, she went with a shade of
apprehension lest she be unable to answer a question quickly, or
to give an immediate opinion. His mind worked very fast, she
knew, and she admired him for it; but her mind was slow, like
Pa's, and if people expected her to reply quickly, she felt flustered,
and then foolish.

When Phillip began to walk every afternoon she was glad, not
that he was out of the way, but because when he came back he was
calm, and liked to sit quietly in a chair with a book, or play with
Billy. It was his writing, she knew, that worried him; whenever
he had been able to write, he was always happy.

Sometimes of an evening when the children were in bed he would
run down from his writing room to call her upstairs to hear music,
or a play, issuing from the six-inch tin horn of his Cosmos 5-valve
wireless set. One night she heard him crossing the floor above
rapidly, the door opened and he called out, "Come quickly. It's
Peer Gynt, with Russell Thorndike as the poet! I've never heard
it before, it's marvellous!—come now, drop everything. This is
how writers really are—mixtures of selfishness and greater love."
He was startled and vitalised by the play's penetration of reality
to the spiritual truth beyond.

"Isn't it marvellous?"

Lucy had stayed for a while, he looked so young, his whole
face appeared to be shining: but she must go down, or the cake
would spoil. She was making it for Pa's birthday, and had been
wondering how she could get so many candles on the iced top without damaging the pattern. So Phillip heard *Peer Gynt* alone, the
poetry—the spiritual truth of events—unshared. He felt devas-
tated. The set could not be moved down to the kitchen because
the aerial came in through the window and the earth-wire was
fixed to the pipe bringing water from the new ram beside the
brook. *Peer Gynt* ran on until well after midnight, when he walked
up the borstal alone, seeing the autumn stars flashing over the

downs, and feeling himself to be part of the greatness of the earth;
but alone, and returning, the afflatus gone, he felt himself to be
aching with unshared love.

This longing was paramount in *Tristan und Isolde*, he alone in
his upstairs room, deeply moved by the theme of honour, love, and
death, while longing to share the noble music with Lucy. But
her iron, upon the kitchen table, went thump periodically as she
worked to make his shirts look like new.

"Can't you spare a moment?" he pleaded, looking round the
kitchen door. "The music of Tristan's delirium, as he tears off
his bandages and stumbles to meet Isolde in his mind, is marvellous. Drop everything! *Who* wants shirts? Nothing matters but
this."

Lucy hurried up, to listen quietly as though patiently, then
she said, "Oh, the milk for your coffee is boiling over. I forgot
to turn down the wick!" and down she went again; the music
spoiled, as well as the milk.

After the *Liebestod* he was irritable from exhaustion, and wondered if the real reason was that the music was based on unnatural
feelings, in that it led to the longing for death. Or was it *true*,
from the spiritual world; was heavenly love a reality? Yes, yes,
every feeling in him, beyond those of his little ego that chilled
poor Ernest, said yes, yes, this is the truth.

He joined the men on the farm at irregular intervals, his mind
beyond the horizon. Yet in both field and writing-room self-
reproachful thoughts arose, because he was not doing what he had
set out to do; neither a real farmer nor a real writer, but that
barren thing, a hybrid. His guilty conscience persuaded him to
that harsh judgment; but as a fact he kept an eye on the work which
at this time was mainly of improvement and reclamation: miles
of overgrown thorn hedges to be cut to the stub; the borstal ruts
levelled with flints picked off the arable. At other times the men
were used by a professional builder making new cow-sheds, relay-
ing rotten rafters; retiling; thatching. This work was under the
supervision of Mr. Hibbs, whose cultivations following the bare
fallows on the land ploughed by the Iron Horses had produced a
fine tilth in which the new leys of rye-grass and clover mixtures,
between those fields sown with mustard, had taken well, following
the rains.

Phillip's bad conscience in the matter of his 'neglect' arose from deeper impressions of himself, relating to the irritable, yet at times justified, anguish of his father when confronted by the mental inability of his mother to face facts where his father was concerned. To avoid a direct clash with Lucy, who so resembled his mother, he had to suppress the truth of his own nature; in bed with Lucy he had to act the infant, imitate the little boy; her sexual tenderness could only be aroused by diminishing himself to the level of her child. With Barley it had not been like that; she had enjoyed love-making for its own sake, and even encouraged him by laughing at his occasional bawdy jokes, sharing his desires and nearly always welcoming them in a way which had remotely shocked him, although he knew the slight feeling of disapproval arose from his early repressive upbringing.

Lucy was too good for him; she did not share that side of him; he lived basically withdrawn from her, and had to suppress in his mind comparison with Barley, whose imagined presence when he was making love to Lucy was often a necessity; a spur.

The draft of the prospectus for the private edition of the wander book had been sent off some weeks before to Mashie & Co. One morning, to his delight, the proof of the prospectus arrived. He returned it with a list of all names to be canvassed, including those likely relations and connexions of Lucy and himself. In due course Hetty sent a cheque for £3/3/-, so did Dora and Hilary; on Lucy's side Mrs. Chychester, Ernest (whom Phillip jostled into giving him a cheque), Mrs. à Court Smith, and four others subscribed. Pa, declared Phillip, should have a special copy, in white vellum quarter-bound in dark blue, the colours of the hunt of which he was the oldest member.

At the end of a month, when the copies were stacked in their cardboard boxes in a ramshackle building in Paternoster Row, he had had orders for twenty-nine. One morning he saw the name of the Colonel of his Regiment in the newspaper. Would the Duke of Gaultshire have known about the wretched manner in which he had left the first battalion at Cannock Chase in September 1919? And about his month's imprisonment, later? And if he wrote, wouldn't the Duke think that he was 'using' a war-time acquaintanceship to further his own career (as indeed he was)?

Supposing, instead of to the Duke, he sent one to the Duke's cousin, who had commanded the reserve battalion on the East Coast during the last year of the war? Lord Satchville, that tall

Viking of a man, Henley rowing champion, genial and imperturbable, veritable paladin and patriarch with his large china-blue eyes and golden beard streaked with grey—the only colonel, with the exception of a few specialist doctors in the R.A.M.C., to have worn a beard during the Great War in England. Dare he? He asked Lucy.

"Why not? I am sure he will be glad that you have remembered him."

"What an admirable level mind you have, Lucy. I wish I had your common sense."

The £50 advance in royalties for the book had been accepted, at Phillip's insistence, by Uncle John as part repayment of the loan for the hiring of the Iron Horses. He was equally determined to pay the bill for the fodder seeds which had failed at last year's sowing. He was determined to get clear of debt as soon as he could; so while the wander book was being set-up in Caslon Old Face Type, he wrote to Anders about the Donkin novel. Could he get Hollins to pay the £25 advance now; he realised that Hollins only had an option on it, with no liability to accept the book.

Please tell them they won't regret publishing this novel, it is far superior to my early efforts. I can't send the manuscript just yet, I am revising it day and night.

His agent replied enclosing a copy of the letter received from Hollins, who thanked Mr. Maddison for his offer to send the novel later, but they did not propose to exercise their option. They were about to remainder the other books, and would Mr. Maddison let them know if he wanted to buy any copies at remainder price for himself under the terms of the agreement? The price was 6d. a copy.

Phillip bought a hundred copies for £2/10/-, meaning to keep them until they were worth something, and then give sets to all his friends and relations.

The ordinary 7s. 6d. edition of *The Water Wanderer* was published late in November. It had a good reception among the critics. Encouraged by that, he determined that the novel of the ex-soldier Donkin should be finished. Nearly three years had wasted away since he had started to write it, and seven since the idea had grown into his life. He sat in the small room while the rain beat on the window, feeling secure in the dumpy little chair his mother had given him for a wedding present—the very chair he needed to keep him at his desk: for, once drawn up at the desk, it was impossible to get out, since it had no castors. One could wriggle oneself out in stages, each with a lift and a hop and a shove all in one movement, while the flat wooden feet rucked up the carpet, and his knees, raised in each effort to push backwards, lifted the top of the desk and threatened to shower pens, papers, and ink-bottles upon the floor. So it wasn't really worth while trying to get away from the job, until it became urgent to leave; then, calmly, one might, while sitting still, lift up the desk top, set it back on its two supporting rests of drawers—excellent for strengthening the stomach muscles—and then writhe out like an eel. It really was more effective as a work-compellor than Carlyle's cobbler's-wax on the seat of the trousers.

A pin from the local one-man brewery stood on a box beside the desk, within arm's-reach. Now and again he drew ale into the battered pewter pint-pot. The poker was already in the fire, ready to be plunged in to mull the ale. All done while fixed in the chair.

It was at night, when the darkness came, that the story really began to flow. The beech-logs gave out slow lilac flames; three candles burned on a diamond-shaped base of dark oak, part of a Jacobean floor-board which had been taken out, to split and fracture, when hot-water pipes were laid under the floor. The lozenge of wood was thickly coagulated with grease: it looked like a frozen ship, a star above each white funnel. As the candles burned down, so they were replaced; and a new light shone upon the gutters of the old.

One midnight of the dark of the year, with a feeling of the appalling imminence of fate as the B.B.C. went off the air, he pressed down fresh candles, and braced himself for what was to come. The tapers burned, steady and faithful, like the riding lights of the ship in Conrad's *Secret Sharer*, while the tide that was to bear Donkin away began to flow in from the Atlantic. He wrote steadily, unconscious of time: the tragedy was nearly over. The candles came down to wick-falling stage, dark particles were swimming about in the liquid grease. One wick fell over and died as the last word was written. It was done, Donkin was drowned.

"Willie! Willie!"

He pushed back his chair, tears streaming down his face. The top of the desk lifted, scattering pens and paper. He went to the window and opened the casement, to look at the stars and to feel their greatness in his breast. It was ended; now Willie could rest.

This feeling gave way to the thought of what would he himself do now? What was there to look forward to? Could he get back among ordinary people, and change the trend of his thoughts? Was he not on the same pathway as Willie had been, and perhaps others of their generation who had survived the war?

He crept into Lucy's bedroom, to stand beside the dim-seen head breathing softly on the pillow, and to whisper, "Are you awake?"

She did not stir. He looked down at Billy sleeping in the cot on one side of the bed, then at the baby in the cradle on the other side. There lay her whole thoughts, her love. No, it would not be fair to awaken her, and to tell her—what?

Downstairs there was the noise of claws scratching wood. Rusty was awake, and wanting to come to him. Did animals feel emotion, without power to rationalise their feelings? Had he broadcast his emotion to the dog? He went down quietly and the dog went happily up the stairs and into the writing room, to lie before the fire, head on paws, eyes upon Phillip getting under the rug of the couch. Only when his master's head was on the pillow did the spaniel give a sigh of relief, and settle to sleep.

Phillip lay still, feeling the flow of time to be rushing silently in the room, while the embers made their small tinkling noises, and the old aching sadness possessed him as he thought of Barley, lost for ever and for ever. Yet love *is* resurrection, the thought came: love is from everlasting to everlasting.

Chapter 8

LITERARY LIONS

One spring morning, on his return from setting-off the men, Lucy gave him an envelope in an unknown handwriting. The envelope of thin grey paper was addressed directly to him, not redirected from the publishers. He asked Lucy to open it, since he felt it was

something extraordinary; and so it proved, for within was a brief
note from a manor house in Buckinghamshire, signed by the name
Corinna Arden, which at once sent an extra beat of blood through
his head.

"I knew it! I knew it, though the thought never came to my
conscious mind. I've always known my true place in the world."

Nevertheless, it was with a shock of surprise that he read that
the Committee of the Grasmere Memorial Prize had unanimously
awarded it to *The Water Wanderer*, and that she hoped to get
Thomas Morland, O.M., to make the presentation. The writer
asked him to keep the secret, as it was hoped to announce it for
the first time at the award in London during the coming June.

"Seven years to be famous! Walter Ramal told me in J. D.
Woodford's house in Inverness Terrace in March nineteen twenty-
one that it would take seven years. He too has second-sight,
which is only clear thought. The prize is one hundred pounds,
so I'll be out of debt to Nuncle." He suppressed a feeling of
panic by taking a deep breath and respiring slowly. "I must
revise *The Phoenix* at once. It will be timely in the autumn, and
get the publicity of the Grasmere Award. Look how Robert
Graves' *Goodbye* has gone. The war-interest is coming back, but
the real war this time. I can't help the farm, it must look after
itself."

He danced with Billy and Peter on the rush mat, while the
spaniel in affectionate excitement gripped Phillip's leg. "Poor
old Rusty, he wants a wife. He's given all his humanised self to
us."

He went to tell the good news to Uncle John, and was congratulated; but under his gracious manner John was disturbed
by the thought that Phillip's success was the beginning of the end
for Hilary.

While he was revising the book Phillip wrote to Mr. Driver
asking him to pay £50 advance for the novel.

I promise you that you will never regret it. I can't send the *Tss.* now
as I haven't finished it. I want it to come out in the late autumn. I
can't tell you why, but ask you to trust me. I guarantee a good sale.

Mr. Driver replied at length, saying that it was generally agreed
in his office that the otter book was so far and away superior to the

novels that he did not think it in the author's interest to accept an unread novel. Phillip answered that it was a good book, and now that the old novels published by Hollins were out of print and the copyright lease returned to him, he intended to rewrite them in direct line with *The Phoenix*.

Mr. Driver wrote again to say that he really ought not to accept a book like that, but would rather wait to read it. By the same post came a letter from Anders Norse saying that he had had a telephone call from Coats, a comparatively new and successful publisher, offering £250 for his next book, whatever it was to be, if he were free to give it to him.

This was a situation which could only be resolved by writing again to Mr. Driver, begging him to reconsider his decision.

> I am rather hard up, but that has nothing to do with my request that you take *The Phoenix*. I have certain knowledge that this book will have a successful sale. You will never regret taking it now.

Again Mr. Driver wrote to ask, What is this knowledge? Phillip spent 5s. on a telephone call, saying that he was not free to tell him; but if he would trust him, he would not let him down. Mr. Driver still maintained his opinion that the novels were far inferior to the story of the otter, and after a further wait of two weeks, during which time he hoped that Mr. Driver would change his mind, Phillip wrote to Anders.

> You are my agent, will you decide for me?

As soon as Anders got this authority he telephoned to Mr. Coats who formally accepted the novel and asked that the manuscript be sent direct to him, since he wanted to include it in his Autumn list, then being made up. Anders telegraphed this request to Phillip, who posted the Tss. of *The Phoenix* from Colham within an hour of getting the telegram. Three days later the agreement came for his signature with Anders' cheque for £225. By the same post was a book called *Dubliners*, with a letter from Edward Cornelian: the famous critic, and discoverer of Conrad, had written to him, Phillip told Lucy.

> I have read your story, and it is good, very natural and inevitable. But of the climax I shall have something to say when we meet. Are

you ever in London? I go there, to Coats' office, every Friday. Meanwhile you might care to read some of the stories by James Joyce, particularly *The Dead.*

Again the Norton raised the dust on the Colham road; the cheque was paid in, then a visit to Captain Arkell's office with a cheque for the seed-bill.

"What am I supposed to do with this?"

"I'd be glad if it could be paid into the farm account immediately. I want to pay for my own mistakes."

"As you wish, but I don't know what Sir Hilary will say."

Feeling all light and air, he returned fast to his home, thinking how he would now be able to give up the monthly allowance from Nuncle, and perhaps help to pull his weight by paying the wages of the farm men.

He found Lucy looking more than usually happy: she had heard again from Tim. The temporary electrification work in Sydney had ended unexpectedly. Tim's part in the wiring had been extremely interesting, he wrote; it was fairly important, too, for all Sydney was to be illuminated to celebrate the arrival of the Duke of York to open Parliament. But something had gone wrong somewhere with one of the switches he had fixed up; anyway the foreman had put the blame on Fiennes and himself.

The foreman absolutely despised both of us for being Britishers. He frequently referred in a disparaging way to the clothes we wore, our attempts to be polite, our youth, and most frequently to our soft, white hands. Well, Lulu, since Fiennes and I spent the entire voyage, sixteen hours a day and seven days a week for nearly two months washing plates, cups, and saucers for the 2,700 emigrants on board, with our hands continuously in soapy water, I consider he was a little unreasonable. His contempt, I regret to say, made me not a little nervous while in his presence, and under his fault-finding eye. But to my story of the Fiasco of the Illuminations. Our company had the job of fixing up the switch-board, including the Master Switch, for the said Illuminations. One change-over of the switch, and Sydney would be a city of light, a signal to which all ships in harbour would respond. Well, as the Lord Mayor, or whoever it was, pressed the Master Switch, there was a big blue flash followed by darkness.

After a stunned silence, which you can well imagine, I heard the foreman shouting out, "It's that XYZ Forrise." 'Forrise', I must tell you, is the name he invariably bestowed upon me, because of my spectacles—'Four Eyes', I think. "Forrise, where the etc. is that (ahem!) Forrise!" I need hardly tell you that both Fiennes and I agreed in the matter of not answering his call, then or later. In fact we both lost a week's pay because we didn't turn up the next morning, but wended our way out of Sydney, carrying our swags. We heard, incidentally, that the current which should have gone into the Civic Festivities went instead into the town reservoir some distance away and killed a number of swans thereon, but I honestly don't think the matter had anything to do with our wiring.

Well, to cut a long story short, Fiennes and I walked several hundred miles, and very cold it was at night, being winter. We found the best places to sleep were farmyard manure dumps, but we had to be careful of dogs. You have no idea how much warmer they can be than the surrounding air, particularly during frosty weather. Well, here we are, camping out just outside the town I've put on the top of my letter, and adjoining the aforesaid coal-mine. The work down below is fairly hard, but we feel we are getting somewhere at last.

Before going to London, Phillip went to see Mrs. Chychester, to tell her the news.

"I am so happy for you, my dear. And I can see a splendid career lying before you. So you may be going to meet Mr. Thomas Morland, whom I have long admired for his country house stories. I wish I could feel the same way about his Crouchend family chronicle, but then I have never known anyone like them. Now go you to London, my dear, and enjoy your holiday after all your hard work on the land."

On the train he saw Piers Tofield, who left his compartment and sat with Phillip in a 3rd smoker until it was time to have lunch together. They drank a bottle of Burgundy, and Phillip had to dissuade Piers from ordering another.

"Come to my flat and dine with me," Piers proposed at Paddington station. "I can put you up if you want a bed. I'd like you to meet some friends of mine afterwards. We'll dine at my club."

Now that he was about to be a man of means, Phillip took a taxi from Paddington to the Adelphi, to tell his agent of Miss Arden's letter. Anders' face broke into a smile, his eyes shone.

"This is going to be your year, you know. I told you that you were going to the top soon after I met you in the Parnassus Club seven, no eight, years ago, d'you remember? Now before I forget: are you free at two o'clock tomorrow? Coats rang up this morning and said that Edward Cornelian, his reader, would like to see you.

Cornelian's day for coming to town is Friday, tomorrow. He says he can't ask you to lunch with him because he has a long-standing engagement with Thomas Morland to discuss a private matter, but he and Thomas Morland would be able to see you afterwards for coffee, at Romano's.

"Well, you'll be safe in Cornelian's hands," went on his agent, "but he can't care for your work more than I do. Remember, it was I who first knew that you had the potential to be a great novelist."

"Will Coats be disappointed if *The Phoenix* is the last novel I write?"

"Your *last* novel? But you've only just started, man! What about those novels you once told me about—the one to be called *Soot*, for instance?"

"Oh, I don't know."

"Well, these things resolve themselves in their own time. Are you doing anything tonight? If not, would you care to dine with me at my club, the Barbarian?"

"Thank you, but a friend has offered me a bed, after dining with him, Anders. Then we're going to see some friends of his."

"Well, lunch with me at the Barbarian tomorrow, will you? Meanwhile I'll telephone Coats to say that you'll meet Edward Cornelian at Romano's."

At 7 p.m. Phillip arrived at Piers' flat in Blue Ball Yard.

"I thought we'd go to the Voyagers, they have a decent grill and the best claret in London. You look surprised."

"Oh, nothing really. Only my Uncle Hilary belongs to that club, and as you know we don't get on awfully well. However, he's spending the summer in Wales—— You must think me very rude——"

"Not at all. I'm all for the generations keeping their distance. We might go to the Game Pie—or a restaurant if you'd prefer that."

"May I change my mind? I'd like to see the Voyagers again. I had lunch there with my uncle years ago—before the war."

The lobster soup was good, so was the mixed grill, the wine was exhilarating. Phillip told Piers of the decision he would have to make about continuing to write, or to farm.

"How odd. My father wants me to follow your example, and learn estate management. I'm afraid I prefer London life to that of the country. He gave me a pair of guns for my twenty-first birthday, and complains that I haven't used them yet. If ever you should want to borrow them, do tell me. I was measured for them, and the cast-off might suit you, since we're about the same height."

"Thanks. I'm rather like you, I think. When I was a young man I longed to live in the country, and to shoot, and now—I don't care about it. Birds and animals feel the same about death as we do."

"I have thought about selling my Purdeys. I'm rather keen on an Aston-Martin. I know of one for sale at four hundred pounds. I suppose I might get half that amount for my guns."

"Oh, don't sell them, Piers. Your son, one day, might appreciate his father's guns."

Phillip was thinking of the small saloon garden-gun which Uncle John had given him when he was a schoolboy, but Father had confiscated it as dangerous. How he had dreamed of knocking over a pigeon, or even a wild duck, in a countryside of mysterious lakes and forests. Perhaps Billy, one day, might covet the little gun. Billy, of whom Uncle John sometimes spoke as the heir. No, he mustn't give up the Maddison land. He must discipline himself and go to bed early, regularly, and get up every morning at 5, to write until 7 a.m.

"Anthony Cruft is going to make a name for himself, I fancy," said Piers. "He and Virginia have a flat in a little-known part of London." He avoided the word suburb. "It's in rather a pleasant square. Early Victorian. I suppose City merchants once lived there, and took a 'bus to the office and back. Or more likely kept their mistresses where no-one would have heard of the place."

The taxicab was going up Gray's Inn Road.

"How did Tony Cruft find it?"

"Tony is interested in 16th-century architecture, and went to see the site of the country residence of the Priors of St. Bartholomew, or rather the tower which remains, and has a carved oak room. He decided that an adjoining Square was the place for a writer to live, far away from traffic and people."

The taxi passed King's Cross Station and turned east.

"Has he published anything yet?"

"Yes, a novel of Oxford, a very funny one. I liked it. Desmond Macarthy told me he thought that Tony Cruft was an original writer. We're not far from his place now."

The taxi was going up Essex Street. It turned into a small quiet square, with a garden and trees in the centre.

"He we are. Wonderfully hidden away, isn't it? I'll ring twice, and they'll throw down the key. They've got the top flat."

A window opened, a man's face appeared, a key tinkled on the flag-stones, the face withdrew.

"Quick work," said Phillip.

They searched for the key, while a smaller face watched from above.

"If it had a white streamer it would be seen easily, Piers."

"Can you find it?" a girl's clear voice called from above.

The Crufts were delightful. The author was a young man of modest aspect, cool, self-contained, with a quiet manner concealing an intent watchfulness. He was remotely friendly. He had a face of good proportion, the brow reminding Phillip of the Polish boy chess champion he had interviewed during his Fleet Street days: a double-plated brow, as it were, like that of a miniature Napoleon, the temples in balance: a thinking brow in the sense of immediate awareness, of sharp perception, but lacking, perhaps, the supreme gift of divining the concealed truth of another made pretentious by fear.

The four sat at a small square table and played cards. Mrs. Cruft, who looked to be about eighteen but with the self-possession of a woman without age, told Phillip that she had bought the table in the Caledonian market for a shilling, and Tony had repaired it, making it firm on its feet. It had a glass top which he had fitted to cover an old map of the district. On a side-table was a cluster of humming birds brilliant of hue under a glass dome, near another dome of waxed fruit. An odd clock in a dark wooden case ticked on the wall: the cover revealed an original impression of Parliament Square by night, in mother-of-pearl. The full moon above the river, the tiny circle of the clock face in the tower by the bridge, the flowing tide below, all faintly reflected the electric light bulb set in an early Victorian chandelier with dependent glass prisms.

"The barrow boys are *so* sweet, to find such heavenly things for me. The trouble now is that I simply dare not go there any more, one simply cannot disappoint them. The room, as you can see, is so small." She sneezed. "Oh dear, I'm going to do the nose trick again. Give me your handkerchief, Tony." She pulled the bandanna from her husband's breast pocket, and used it loudly. "You forgot to say 'Bless you'," she said, stuffing it back into the pocket.

Cruft continued to sit still. His face was composed and expressionless.

"Have you by any chance read James Joyce's *Dubliners*?" Phillip asked him. Phillip had read *The Dead* by the decayed boat-house beside the Longpond, on the way home from visiting the sheep on the new layer of Lobbett's. The story had held him, moved him deeply. The scene at the evening party given by the old ladies, the livingness of all the characters, the unstressed drama of the writing—here was life transmuted by art: and the final scene of the snow falling in the streets as the party-goers went home, filled with memories of the past—the snow falling all over Ireland, 'from the Bog of Allen to the mutinous dark waves of the Shannon estuary' lifted one into the very spirit of life. He knew that he, too, had the same gift, the same power to bring back a lost world.

"Joyce is a writer of genius. *The Dead* is a marvellous short story—the last one in the book. Edward Cornelian told me that every young writer should read it."

There was a silence which might only be described as respectful, as from a good-manner'd host to an enthusiastic stranger.

It was time to go. Piers got up, saying, "I always enjoy myself here, Virginia. It's been great fun."

Cruft, without a word, telephoned for a taxi.

On the way back Phillip said, "I suppose I was too emphatic about *The Dead*?"

"Not at all. But Tony's talent is for satire." He leaned forward. "Driver, stop at Pardew's, will you." The taxi took them to a wine cellar.

"Let's crack a bottle of port, and forget our problems. I suppose of the four of us sitting round that table you're the only one with the real urge to create."

"I thought Cruft had a fine head. Oh Piers, might we have a half-bottle?"

"He's a social critic, first, I fancy. But very funny."

When the half-bottle was gone Piers said, "How right you are about education. I must write a book about Eton. Virginia also wants to write about her stifled childhood. Tony thinks that it should be satirised. His favourite book is *Alice Through the Looking Glass*. I told her to read your *Pauper Spirits*."

"Oh, that terribly crude humour!"

"I like your high spirits. Would you care to come with me to the Game Pie for eggs and bacon? Do say if you would prefer to go to bed."

The night club was at the end of a small courtyard, in what might once have been a coach-house. A score of young men and women were inside: among them Phillip saw Gillian, whom he had met with Piers at the cattle market. She was standing by the table which extended almost the entire length of one wall, and pouring stout down her throat. It was a slightly shocking sight: that young and pretty girl holding her head back and appearing to get rid of the liquid without swallowing.

"Hullo, Gillian," said Piers. "Won't you join us?" She sat down between them, and turned to Phillip.

"How is Rosebud?"

"Oh, she gives the best milk."

"And those two darling calves?"

"They're on the meadows, 'growing into meat', as the herdsman says."

Across the room a girl with fair hair was standing beside an elderly man and looking at Gillian, who beckoned her over.

"Here he is," Phillip heard Gillian say. Then, "Piers, do you know Felicity Ancroft? This is Piers Tofield. And Phillip Maddison——"

"How d'you do."

"How d'you do."

Piers' voice said, "Waiter, bring a bottle of Veuve Cliquot and four glasses, will you." He turned to Gillian. "Won't you and Miss Ancroft join us for eggs and bacon?"

"Will I not," she replied, with false gaiety. "Not a crumb or a drop has passed these lips since a half-pint and a sandwich in the Coal Hole at one o'clock. Have you seen Stephen? He's supposed to be taking me to the Waterbridges', and said he'd be here at half-past ten on the dot."

It was now nearly half-past eleven.

"We've been with the Crufts."

Phillip thought Gillian looked startled. For a moment she lowered her guard of gaiety and looked empty. Was she in love with Piers?

Piers said, "I always think that one's first glass of champagne is like one's first mistress, to be taken in gulps, which means I suppose that the bottle gets empty rather quickly. Zum Wohl." He drank.

"There's always another bottle, I agree," she replied gaily. Then turning to Phillip, she said as though sharing a secret, "Felicity adores your books. She's been telling me that Beatrice Harrison's nightingale was simply marvellous tonight. We're at Savoy Hill, together. Don't you adore the nightingale? In Wiltshire just now she says you must be simply *ringed* with song. Isn't that the *mot juste*? Such a clever gel. What are you, of *all* people, doing in London now?"

"What are *you* doing in London?"

"London is my bread and butter."

"Oats, too," said Piers. "Don't forget the oats."

Phillip felt the shyness of the fair girl upon himself. They sat on the form beside the table. Four places were laid for the food. The room was beginning to fill up. A short fat young man with a pink face and dark calculating eyes smothered in a smile came over to them, and without look or nod at Piers said to the fair girl, "Hullo, darling. What a very great pleasure it is to me to see you here again. I've been here every night specially on purpose to see you ever since we did that dance together, the Black Bottom if I'm not much mistaken? Are these your gentlemen friends—if so, will you all take a drink with me?"

"Another time," she said, with a smile of lips only.

The pink face disappeared.

"Who's your bounding friend?" asked Gillian.

"I don't remember seeing him before."

This modest reply caused instant merriment in Piers, whose laughter was so loud that heads turned their way. "Ha ha ha! I'll try that myself one day. Gets a rise once in a while, no doubt. Called you darling, too, I noticed. Been reading Mr. Anthony Cruft's paragraphs in the gossip columns, I shouldn't wonder."

The waiter arrived with a tray of eggs and bacon.

"Get that down you," said Piers to Gillian. "Stephen's always late after the second night shift. The back door of the Coal Hole is too much to pass on a warm night. Keep the girls waiting, that's the idea. Let me fill your glass."

"God, I was hungry," said Gillian. "I felt myself beginning to go back into Time like Prousty-wousty. Have you read Prousty-wousty?" she said to Phillip, looking into his face beside hers.

"Don't talk. Eat," said Piers. "If one doesn't sleep, one must eat."

"I'm drunk," she burbled happily, looking into Phillip's eyes. "They're such a deep blue. True blue."

"It's drinking on an empty stomach," said Piers. "All you girls are alike, starving yourselves in order to look as flat as boards. Hullo, Stephen."

The escort had arrived. After a glass of champagne and a plate of caviar spread on biscuits the newcomer left with Gillian.

"Goodnight. Thank you so much," said Felicity, with a startled look at Phillip.

"Must you go?" replied Piers, half getting up. "Well, good night." Then he said to Phillip, "Gillian worries too much. The great thing is to take life easily."

"The cut worm must forgive the plow, as Blake wrote."

"Better to join up with another worm."

"I suppose all living creatures need stability and reassurance. All the species work together in a true partnership."

"Let's have another bottle. The Ancroft girl likes you."

"D'you mind if I don't drink any more?"

"This place is far too crowded nowadays. Too many hangers-on. Nancy boys, too. Let's go to the flat and I'll make coffee. Can you bear to wait while I drink some brandy?"

They drank brandy and coffee. Piers began to look actively happy.

"Extraordinary how women have an instinct for romance. Gillian said that when the Ancroft girl was reading your book she thought that the otter was a symbol of some tremendous secret love."

"How strange. I thought she looked rather like my first wife."

"I noticed how she kept looking at you."

Piers swallowed his brandy and said, "Could you bear to wait a few moments while I telephone?"

A saxophone was playing beside the piano at the other end of the room. Couples began to dance. The pink-faced young man had attached himself to a girl with remotely frantic brown eyes. The tune was a mixture of dreaminess and sauciness.

> *My baby says yes-yes*
> *I'm glad she said yes-yes*
> *Instead of no-no.*

"Hullo," said Piers, returning immediately, "I thought Brenda had gone lesbian, but perhaps she's only bored. Or he may be the chap who delivers her snow."

"Cocaine?"

"She usually gets hot water from her radiator and gives herself a jab sitting in her car. No beak could very well ask what a girl's doing by herself in her own motor. The line was engaged. I wonder who was on to Virginia. I'll try again now."

Phillip looked around for the fair girl, but could not see her. Piers was telephoning for ten minutes. Coming back he said, "Let's have one more brandy." His eyes were unusually bright. "I've been talking to Virginia," he said, in his impersonal, almost casual voice. "Tony has begun his book on Cranmer the martyr, and she can't do anything to upset his work. So she can't see me for the next few weeks. Let's leave this place."

On the way back to St. James Street he confided in Phillip. "What would you do, if you were in my place?"

"I'd wait, and not rush into anything."

They sat up talking until dawn, Phillip lying under the table, his feet above his head, completely relaxed as he told Piers about Eveline Fairfax, and how, if he had gone off with her, he would have missed meeting Barley.

Piers said, "It must be hell for Tony, knowing that his wife wants to go off with someone else."

Phillip said goodbye to Anders at the Barbarian Club at 1.45 p.m., noting that some of the members were still noisy at the bar, and walked east to make a reconnaissance, as he thought of it, of Romano's restaurant. Arriving at its green incurved glass front he imagined the splendours of the 'nineties, and wondered if its position had caused its decline after the spacious Edwardian age. For it was situate in the narrow neck of the Strand, where traffic blocks occurred, with their engine noise and smoke.

He walked up and down until the hands of the clock above Charing Cross station pointed to five minutes to two. Once again he went towards Wellington Street, with its memories of the Royal Opera House gallery, eight years ago now: it seemed a lifetime. Those days in Fleet Street had become poignant with their passing; so it was with Romano's—with everything made by hands, thought over, longed for, failed, and achieved. What writers had once laughed and found happiness in Romano's! He knew of it only from articles in popular literary weeklies, from the pages of which he had lived in scenes that were vanished; this happy rendezvous of writers, rare beings whose awareness of life had been based on loyalty and maintained by a few simple virtues, as Conrad had written. Life for an artist must always become poignant once it was passed: here the sad, lost-child Barrie had dined with Hardy the silent, but revered for his proven quality; here Conrad had come, from Hythe in Kent, to meet H. G. Wells; later with Stephen Crane, and W. H. Hudson who had escaped awhile from an immewed life—immewed the exact word, from falconry: the falcon shut up in a dark stable, held by its jesses to a stump in the floor, no longer lord of the skies—poor Hudson, who 'writes as the grass grows', Conrad had said, living his last years in a London boarding house.

Standing outside the restaurant he thought that here, too, had come Ernest Dowson, in hopeless love with 'Cynara', the coffee-house-keeper's daughter, flinging 'roses, roses riotously with the throng, To put thy pale, lost lilies out of mind'. And through this very doorway had walked J. M. Synge, remote from his western world's childhood ever harping in his mind. And John Davidson, who had waded into the sea, and out of life at Dymchurch, never to be seen again. Suddenly to remove himself from the air—to live only in the occasional thought of a friend, or in the mind of a reader of poetic anthologies, in the spirit of some woman who had cared for him! O God, he himself had sat on the same sea-wall along the Romney Marsh with Barley, on the way to Dover and the Rhône valley to the Mediterranean; and later he had taken Lucy there, to imagine Barley smiling as she watched Lucy playing so gently with Billy . . . 'Drive my dead thoughts over the universe' —Shelley's cry to the West Wind. These holy poets, these saints. . . . Francis Thompson seeing the reflections of life passing in the window as he was seeing them now—the poet in rags, his boots broken, his mind hazed by laudanum, crying to his Mistress of Vision . . .

> Her song said that no springing
> Paradise but evermore
> Hangeth on a singing
> That has chords of weeping,
> And that sings the after-sleeping
> To souls which wake too sore.
> "But woe the singer, woe!" she said; "Beyond the dead his
>   singing lore,
> All its arts of sweet and sore,
> He learns, in Elenore!"

Dear Francis Thompson, companion of the spirit in that swampy
summer of 1917 in Flanders: his poems had stood up to the reality
of Third Ypres: they had revealed grace beyond the disgrace of
life moving backwards into chaos.

'Pierce thy heart to find the key;
With thee take
Only what none else would keep . . .
Learn to water joy with tears,
Learn from fears to vanquish fears,
To hope, for thou dar'st not despair . . .
Plough thou the rock until it bear . . .
When thy seeing blindeth thee
To what thy fellow-mortals see;
When their sight to thee is sightless;
Their living, death; their light, most lightless . .
When thy song is shield and mirror
To the fair snake-curlèd Pain,
Where thou dar'st affront her terror
That on her thou may'st attain
Perséan conquest: seek no more,
O seek no more!
Pass the gates of Luthany, tread the region Elenore.'

It was two minutes to two by the clock. He thought of how he
had first known Romano's in company with several other young
members of the Parnassus Club in 1920. G. B. Shaw had come to
lecture in the little upstairs room in Long Acre hired for one
evening a week for 5s. The great man had entered with a slightly
marionettish stride, but to talk with bright penetration, his
reddish-grey beard held well up. He had remained after the
address and discussed his early life with surprising, and endearing,
frankness. Here was the phoenix arisen from the ashes of disaster
in those early Dublin and Liverpool days: his two sisters mocking
'Sonny's' tears, mother ever upbraiding father. To Phillip it had
been a revelation. He had thought, It is just like my early life,
except that Father was always so cross with Mother. I, too, must
always try and bear with, and transcend, mortification. In
Romano's upstairs supper room, where G.B.S. had taken them,
he had eaten a nut chop and drunk fruit juice and water, whereby
to hold himself lightly and well in body against the later 'battle

of the brain' in those terrible small hours, each a miniature Passchendaele, which temporarily destroy the poet's fortitude.

A church clock struck the two hours. He drew a deep breath,
and stood still to collect himself before going in to enquire for Mr.
Edward Cornelian; to find that he was expected. A waiter took
him upstairs, and there at a far table, overlooking the street, sat
the man whom he recognized at once as the famous critic, and
beside him the remote, almost chaste, countenance—a word more
apt than face—of Thomas Morland, world-famous for his sequence
of novels, generally supposed to be based upon the older generations of his own family.

Phillip walked forward lightly, eagerly, feeling that he was about
to be recognised by his own kind at last. He heard Edward Cornelian say, "Well, my dear fellow, to sum up: we both agree that
Evelyn Crouchend will have to die; but not the way you have
arranged his death in your first draft." He looked at his watch.
"We have a moment before the young man is due, and I think
I can recapitulate in that time."

Phillip sat down at an empty table, to wait. How awful, he was
too early. He pretended to be writing in his pocket-book, while
overhearing what the famous critic was saying. This was the stuff
of literary history!

"Let me be frank. The so-called virtue of tolerance," said
Cornelian with a loosening of already loose lips as he smiled at
the creator of *The Crouchend Saga*, "can lead not only to the death
of art, but to the extinction of society. Nature advances by tension,
not by relaxation of physical laws. In your book as it stands, my
dear fellow, your over-extended tolerance not only trembles on
the verge of sentimentality, but brings one perilously near to what
Oscar Wilde said of one of Dickens' characters—'Only a man
with a heart of stone would fail to laugh at the death of Little Nell'.
No, my dear fellow, Evelyn should die appalled by the terrors of
his mind arising from within, the materialist without sensitivity
come at last to realise that his property cannot save him, and that
he has nothing else to fall back upon. His final loneliness should
purge the reader with pity and terror. As now written, his death
by a picture falling on him when his house is on fire is a mere
accident happening outside the story. He might as well have
fallen under a train at Waterloo Station, or had a chimney pot
drop on his head."

At this moment Thomas Morland observed a thin young man getting up from a table to approach them with a smile. To Morland the eyes were the arresting feature: deep blue, with a look about them suggesting a capacity for reflection beyond the normal; but which now were in free play upon the living scene. Here was modesty, here was that rare quality of balance, he thought, that had gone to the creation of the world of the otter.

"You have had luncheon?"

"Oh yes, thank you, Mr. Morland."

"Will you have some coffee, and brandy? A cigar?"

"May I have some coffee, sir?"

Edward Cornelian said, "I have been reading your new novel. It is good stuff. But I'll talk to you about it later. How is the farm progressing?"

Phillip told them of his dilemma; they listened; Cornelian with one ear thrust towards Phillip, Morland looking like a benevolent judge, his eyes alight with understanding and sympathy.

"There's a novel in what you have told us," said Cornelian.

"Part of a novel, as I've seen it, sir——"

"Oh, for heaven's sake drop the 'sir'. We are all writers here," retorted Cornelian, testily.

"'Emotion recollected in tranquillity'," said Thomas Morland softly. "I don't think any writer can see a subject in perspective while he is one of his own characters. 'Ripeness is all'."

"Oh, he won't make your mistakes, Tom," replied Cornelian, a little maliciously. "Maddison's characters in the novel I have just read are objectively created, that is with compassion, because he has no axe to grind, or old scores to pay off."

Phillip thought that Cornelian had aimed this remark at the characterisation of Evelyn Crouchend in *Possession*, said to be based on the novelist's cousin, whose wife Morland had married. He kept an open expression on his face.

"What do you want to do, most of all?" asked Thomas Morland.

"To write a series of novels beginning at the end of the nineteenth century, eighteen ninety-three, and leading up to the Great War," said Phillip, feeling a slight constriction that he was exposing his subconscious mind.

"Why go so far back?" Cornelian cut in sharply. "Why not plunge directly into nineteen fourteen?"

This was a shock. Why had he exposed his most secret idea,

which even to himself he sheered away from formulating? He kept his gaze on the table-cloth, and felt the cold drip of sweat under his arm-pit.

Thomas Morland's lips were now slightly pursed; he drew in a breath as though to speak, but held it. Then he said in a soft, controlled voice, "I must tell you, Maddison, how greatly I enjoyed your book. The prose flows like water from a spring on one of your high moors. You are a West Countryman?"

"Only by adoption. I was born in Kent—now part of London."

"But your forbears lived in the West Country."

"Yes."

"My forbears originated under Cranborne Chase," murmured Thomas Morland. "We were small copyholders. There is a Morland Down near the border of Wil'shire and Dorset."

"I can see the dark-blue tree-line of the ox-drove on top of the Chase from our bit of land, Mr. Morland. My father and uncles used to walk there and back, making a wide circle, when they were boys."

"How came you to write about the moors and rivers of Devon-shire when you are a 'moonraker'?" asked Cornelian.

Phillip told them about his cottage in South Devon after the war.

"And you had a tame otter living in your cottage with you?"

Both noticed that the young man lowered his gaze at this point. Hitherto he had been frank and open about himself: now he seemed to close up, the sight of his eyes becoming unfocus'd.

"Have you still got the otter?" asked Cornelian.

"It escaped one night."

"Did you track it down, as you describe in your book?"

"Yes. But it escaped from hounds, the last time I saw it, into salt water, which carries no scent."

"I remember the tide-head scene. It actually got away then?"

"Yes."

"Then why did you kill it off at the end of the hunt?"

Morland, who had seen that the young man's eyes had filled with tears, said gently, "But otters are still hunted to death by hounds, in spite of a growing revulsion after the blood-shed of the war."

The critic continued his own line. "What puzzled me when I read it was a feeling that your beast was more than an otter.

You appear to have had an extraordinary affection for your beast, in fact, the search for its mate after she had been torn by hounds might almost be the animal equivalent of *Tristan and Isolde*." He peered hen-like at his wristlet watch. "Good gracious, I must soon be on my way to Coats'." He turned to Phillip. "Will you be able to meet me there later—Satchville Street, you know it I expect —at three-thirty? I must have a word now with Morland about a private matter——"

Phillip was already on his feet, thanking Mr. Morland for his hospitality, and then the critic for 'making such a meeting with both of you possible'; and with a bow, he left them.

"Of course it was his wife's tame otter," said Cornelian. "Coats heard about it from Norse. His wife was very young and had a remarkably clear intelligence. His book is the result, almost, of the transmigration of souls."

"But if you already knew that, Eddy, why did you persist in questioning him?"

"To see to what extent he was prepared to be truthful, my dear fellow." The critic peered again at his wristlet watch. "Now let me briefly recapitulate my points about your novel, *For Rent*——"

Thomas Morland suddenly felt tired. He reflected that Eddie Cornelian had set out, in youth, to be a creative writer, and had never brought it off.

"My main objection is that you have cheated us of the inevitability of Evelyn's death scene, in his bed, a lonely old man— fearful, anxious, tormented—the inevitable nemesis of failure ever to have shared his personality with any living person." He looked with sly innocence at his old friend. "So you're in the know too, about Maddison having got the Grasmere? We'll meet again at the Aeolian Hall, then."

Phillip saw Mr. Cornelian again later in the afternoon and, after an exhilarating talk about *The Phoenix*, went away carrying the bundle of typescript under one arm, to call on Anders Norse. As he took long, confident strides towards Adelphi Terrace from Satchville Street he recalled that the Duke of Gaultshire owned a great deal of London, W.C., and would it be taking advantage of a war-time acquaintanceship if he sent him a copy of the otter book? After all, the Duke was a great man for natural history. Yes, he would send a copy.

Arriving at Anders' basement, he told him that Edward

Cornelian had praised the novel, but suggested that the climax, just before the drowning of Donkin, should be strengthened.

"He said that everyone takes it too calmly, that no tears are shed. Of course you haven't read it, but I didn't want to stress the irony, as Hardy did sometimes in his novels. To tell the truth, the ending moved me so much that I was afraid of sentimentality."

Anders knew that Phillip's cousin, and great friend, had been drowned; but all he said was, "What are you going to do, take Cornelian's advice?"

"I'm going back by the evening train, and will bring it up to you after the week-end."

"Are you in a great hurry now?"

"No."

"I wonder if you'd run your eye over this for me." He took a typed Mss. from his desk. "I'd like your opinion. This came in yesterday by post, out of the blue. I know nothing about the author, A. B. Cabton."

The first sentence was arresting. He read on; the scene described stood out of the paper, the whole page was alive.

"It's good stuff, Anders. This chap can write."

"I'm so glad to hear you say that. As I said, I know nothing about the author. He sent it in from an address in East London. I thought of sending it to Coats."

"Yes, do. Edward Cornelian's the man to spot talent." Then saying "Au revoir, my pilot", he left Anders to his pile of letters and walked down the Strand to Savoy Hill to call on Piers Tofield.

It was a hot afternoon. He found Piers in a morning coat and trousers worn with a soft shirt open at the neck. He had been to a wedding; thrown upon a chair was a stiff winged collar, tie, slip, spats, and shirt with starched cuffs.

"I'm going home now, but will be back next Monday, Piers."

"Do come and stay if you've nothing better to do. We'll dine and go on to Channerson's party. One more won't make any difference, since it's a bottle party. I must leave you now, unfortunately, to prepare the first news bulletin. Archie Plugge was asking after you, he's down the passage, third door on right."

Ever since the first meeting Phillip had been awaiting a letter from Plugge, about broadcasting. He had thought out an original programme. Now was his chance.

"My dear Phil, I met a friend of yours the other night at the Game Pie, who knew you in the war." Plugge beamed through his enormous round glasses, awaiting a smile of recognition on the other's face as he announced, "Bill Kidd!"

"Bill Kidd? The only Bill Kidd I knew is dead. He was a Black and Tan, and ambushed by Sinn Feiners near Cork in nineteen twenty."

"This Bill Kidd told me that you served together in the second battalion of the Gaultshire regiment in the spring of nineteen eighteen."

"The last time I saw him he was standing outside a moviehouse in Leicester Square, advertising the film of *Shagbag the Tailor*, wearing a turban and the long white robes of a desert sheik. He was either the star, or the commissionaire in disguise; you know what British films are."

They were still laughing when the editor of *The Wireless Times*, a tall, thin young man, came in, was introduced, and left at once, murmuring 'Conference'.

"Horowitz says he is going to write a play around you. It's about a soldier killed in the war who comes back into ordinary life and tries to tell the truth, but finds it isn't wanted."

"Why, that's the theme of my new novel, *The Phoenix*!"

Plugge appeared to have forgotten about the broadcast.

London was exhausting, the pavements hot underfoot. He took a taxi to St. James Street, got his bag and went on to Paddington, where he had half an hour to wait. He sat on a bench near the clock, and started to make notes for a novel of scenes in Flanders in the late autumn and winter of 1914; but the face of Bill Kidd kept coming between him and the paper; Bill Kidd at his whisky-worst, arrogant, rude, refusing to obey the order to withdraw to the Peckham switch, resentful of having been passed over, as senior captain, for the command of the battalion after the March decimation. The withdrawal was a Corps order; Armentières had fallen; Bailleul in flames; Messines gone; the vital Hazebrouck railway junction almost within reach of the German heavy guns; and there in the Staenyzer Kabaret sat the half-drunken idiot, refusing to obey the order to withdraw, climax to near-insubordination ever since he, Phillip, had been in command. Through a chain of circumstances from Bill Kidd's whisky heroics 'Spectre' West had lost his life.

Bill Kidd dead during the past eight years had been a heroic-braggart figment in the imagination; Bill Kidd alive was—destruction of the character for his book. He sat there, the visual surroundings of the station unseen as he heard again the soft *floo-er-er-er* of yellow-cross gas-shells falling on Byron farm; the sudden *swish* of one striking at their feet; the crack of 'Spectre's' legbone; everything flaring, fading out as a spray of mustard gas met his face, his eyeballs burning red above a rough remote feeling, followed by infinitely faraway silence while he wondered if his face was blown away and he unable to feel it. The world had vanished, the earth pressing on his face through eyes clenched tight, face ragged in big knots burning in a world on fire.

Among his letters at home was one from Miss Corinna Arden telling him that the award was to be presented by Thomas Morland, O.M. Enclosed were half a dozen invitation cards for his friends. He posted one to Lord Satchville, who promptly sent a subscription for a copy of the limited edition of the book together with a letter.

> The award of the Grasmere Memorial Prize for 1928 really confirms what I divined of your talent during those days we shared together, my dear Maddison, and it is with the greatest possible pleasure that I shall come to the Aeolian Hall on the twelfth of June, during an interval of a debate in the Lords, to do honour to a fellow officer of the Regiment.

Phillip took this letter with him to Down Close the next morning, but before showing it to Pa he asked Ernest if they would care to go with Lucy and himself to London for 'a rather special occasion'.

"In confidence, Ernest, I've won the Grasmere Memorial Prize."

"Ah," said Ernest.

"It's to be given in three weeks' time in London. I'd like you and Pa to be my guests, if you don't mind staying at the Adelphi Hotel just off the Strand for the night. Do you mind if we all go in your car? I'll pay for the petrol and oil, of course."

"I'll think about it."

Ernest was deep in a problem of making a model of a crown wheel in mahogany, from which to cast, in yellow metal, a new wheel. The broken original belonged to an ancient Delaunay-Belville tourer which had broken down in the lane outside the Works. Ernest had observed the motionless car through the window and gone on with his work, which he had reluctantly left when one of the men had asked him how they could get to the station, and might he leave the vehicle under cover in his garage. The Delauny-Belville was pushed in, after which Ernest had driven the six men, on an outing with the driver, to Shakesbury railway station in his own car.

A week or two later he had set about taking down the broken differential. The various parts of this gear now lay neatly on a bench, with the chewed-up crown wheel exactly restored in mahogany.

"I suppose you're going to send that away to be cast?"

"I am."

"I can see you're pretty busy."

"You are right," said Ernest. "I *am* busy."

"It will only be one day up, and one day coming back, Ernest. Will that make much difference to this job? I mean, have you a delivery time to work to?"

"Not particularly."

"How about Pa? Would he like to come to London? It's a pretty good thing, you know, the Grasmere Prize for Literature."

"I don't know about Pa. At the moment he is watching his tomato plants for signs of potato disease."

"We'll be there and back within thirty-six hours. Will a plague be likely to spread in that time?"

"I—don't—know."

Phillip examined the ancient motorcar, upholstered in red Russian leather; but the body had been repainted in yellow and brown. It stood high on the concrete floor. Within the open body was a litter of paper and a number of dry ham sandwiches.

"Looks as though it were owned by a publican on an outing, Ernest."

"Ah."

Phillip went into the garden. Pa, having found his spectacles, read Lord Satchville's letter. "Ha," he remarked, giving it back. Then throwing up his head he said genially, "I'm quite willing to make the journey with you and Lucy if Ernest is."

"That makes two cards. Here's yours, sir."

"Ah, Grasmere Memorial, hey? Well done." Pa had read the otter book, and considered it somewhat fanciful.

"Who else have you sent invitations to, may I inquire?"

"Oh, I thought one to my Mother, one to Mrs. Chychester, one to Colonel Satchville, one to my Uncle Hilary, and another perhaps to the Duke of Gaultshire."

"H'm," said Pa. He reflected, then, "I suppose you know the Duke well?"

"Not very."

"Well, you've got one member of that family represented already, haven't you?"

Phillip took the hint. "No Duke. Thanks for the advice. Now I must be off, to revise the climax of my novel by Monday morning. Then I must take it up to London; there's not much time to be lost if it's to be published in the autumn."

"Ah."

"I'll be back in plenty of time for our visit to London, sir. I'm going up to meet Channerson, the war-painter."

"Ah. Well, I must spray my teddies with copper sulphate, I suppose."

Chapter 9

BOTTLE PARTY

Phillip delivered his packet at Satchville Street, and having a couple of hours to spare, went to the Tivoli cinema in the Strand; and thence, at 6.15 p.m., to Savoy Hill. Piers had left, so he walked to Blue Ball Yard, to be told by the porter that Mr. Tofield had asked him to give Mr. Maddison his apologies, but he had been called away unexpectedly and would Mr. Maddison dine with Captain Fox, Mr. Tofield's brother-in-law, at seven o'clock at the University Club and afterwards see Mr. Tofield at Mr. Channerson's party. Mr. Tofield was expecting to be there about 9.30 p.m.

"Not to bother about a bottle, sir, Mr. Tofield will bring one for you."

"May I dress here?"

"I'll show you to Mr. Piers' chambers, sir."

He waited until 8 p.m. at the University Club and then left, to eat eggs and bacon in the Café Royal; and afterwards got a 'bus to Haverstock Hill. He arrived at the painter's studio, which was behind a public house, at 9.20 p.m., and waited by a laurel hedge until Piers should turn up.

Half-past nine became a quarter to ten. People were arriving every few minutes. They came by taxi, and all were in evening dress.

Should he go in and look for Anders? Or go back to London. He imagined that a crisis had come about, between Piers and Virginia.

While he stood there, hearing a subdued hum through the curtain'd windows, a Rolls-Royce drew up, followed immediately by other cars, out of which sprang nondescript men with cameras. Magnesium lights revealed two men wearing opera hats and cloaks, with two ladies, one of whom wore a tiara and a white fox fur round her neck. They waited to be photographed again, while by the open door stood a man-servant in a white jacket.

Phillip followed the gay party, and gave his hat and coat to another servant after the flat opera hats and cloaks had been taken. Meanwhile the host—Phillip recognised his face from newspaper photographs—was waiting expectantly beside a young woman with a round smiling face and bobbed yellow hair. Channerson smiled broadly as he took the hand of the woman with the tiara.

"Ah, Princess!" as he kissed her hand. "Delighted you could come."

Other greetings; then it was his turn.

"I wonder if Piers Tofield has arrived? He was to have brought me here."

The painter said as though deliberately, "Really?" while giving him a keen look. "And who might Piers Tofield be?" The fair young woman beside him said, "The Crufts are bringing him. Virginia telephoned she'd be late, Dikkon. You must be Mr. Plugge?" she smiled.

"I'm afraid not. But I'm also a friend of Archie Plugge. My name is Maddison."

Channerson, smiling broadly, was now greeting other arrivals. Phillip moved away across a large room which was, he thought, the painter's studio. It was fairly full. He moved through groups of talkers to stand against a wall whence to keep watch on the door.

In front of him was a large table on which stood a surprising number of bottles, ranging from magnums of champagne to a solitary stone flagon of schnapps. The bottles covered the table as closely as troops assembled for an attack; behind the shock troops were the reserves: fat, thin, tall and squat bottles, rising from the back of the table on what appeared to a bookcase. Would they all lie sprawling after the battle? By the un-Bohemian looks of the guests—no. More and more people were now arriving; none carried bottles; perhaps they had been sent on in advance.

So this was post-war London semi-Bohemian society—face after face familiar from newspaper and magazine, faces patrician and elegant, bronzed male faces beside slender young women with extremely fair hair and straight, almost severe gowns; laughter and grace. He began to feel the ache of loneliness, and with relief saw the profile of Plugge bending over the table to examine the labels on the bottles. Archie's face was pink, as though much-washed by carbolic soap, above his tall white collar and thin white tie. His thick hair, inclined to kink, was brushed back and held in place by a mixture of oil, scent, and gum arabic. His dark eyes, enlarged by his horn-rimmed spectacles, showed delight on meeting Phillip's gaze.

"How good to see you here! I was only at this moment thinking of you. Have you seen Piers?"

"No. Have you?"

"Not since the 6 o'clock news bulletin. He told me he was expecting you later on at his flat."

"I was supposed to meet him there, but the porter said he had been unexpectedly called away."

"Did he say where?"

"No."

"Oh, my goodness. I think I need a drink. May I get you one?"

Plugge squeezed his plump body, with many winsome apologies, to the edge of the table and returned with two glasses and a bottle of champagne. They drank.

"The last I heard of Bill Kidd was that he had been shot outside Cork, after setting fire to a farmhouse, Archie."

"He told me he had to die officially, before he could do special work with Ironside's Force in Russia against the Reds."

"I hope he's not a friend of yours, because I had good reason to dislike the real Bill Kidd."

"I found him a little alarming myself, I must admit."

"He was a frightful bloody nuisance, and quite impossible when tight. But sober, he could be a very kind person, with his boyish enthusiasm. I'd rather like to see him again, come to think of it."

"He kept referring to you as 'My Mad Son'. I must get another bottle while the going's good. Do forgive me."

Plugge returned with more fuel. "I say, I say, I *am* enjoying this party, aren't you?" Plugge was looking round. "I *wonder* where Virginia and Piers have got to? I expect you've heard about them?"

"Piers took me to see them last week, when I was up, and we played cards."

"I suppose Piers has told you how Tony and I met Virginia Helston-Hood at Eleanor Metfield's party in the *Polaris*, and introduced her to Tony Cruft?"

"No."

"But *surely* you saw their wedding photograph in *The Tatler* last November, didn't you?"

"No, I haven't been to my dentist for eighteen months."

"Ha-ha-ha! Let me fill your glass, my dear Phil. This *is* fun, isn't it? I say, I am glad you're here."

Glasses were refilled. Plugge became most confidential. "*Surely* you know about the bogus marriage?" he almost whispered.

"No."

Plugge hunched his padded shoulders, and moved nearer to Phillip's ear. "Now where shall I begin? Well, about a year ago, it was last June, in fact, Tony asked me if I'd care to go with him to Eleanor Metfield's party in the *Polaris*. You know, that ship moored along the Embankment? Tony was then 'feeding' the Society columnist of *The Daily Trident*. It was his first *entrée* into Society, and when he saw me in a dinner jacket he refused to take me. We went in a taxi to Cahoon Bros., you know, that firm who run a night service during the London season. It may be worth knowing."

"Did you go to the party in *Polaris*?"

"Yes, as I was saying, having got myself fitted out, with these broad padded shoulders—they had only bandleaders' outfits for hiring out at ten o'clock—Tony gave me a lesson on how to pronounce certain key-words, as he called them."

Plugge paused before saying, with a conspiratorial air, "Tell me, old boy, how do *you* pronounce the word 'l-o-s-t'?"

"The cockney way."

"Have you noticed how cockneys and those in Debrett often have the same pronunciation?"

"Both resist compulsory education."

This set Plugge laughing loudly.

"Everyone spoke the same way in London until genteelisms arose among the superior middle classes, and their children were taught to pronounce words as spelt."

"I've never thought of it like that before."

Plugge looked as though he had received a revelation. "Now

isn't that interesting! Well, Tony certainly gave me a lesson in pure Cockney, to correct my middle-class pronunciation! The key word, he assured me, was 'girl'. Not 'gel' nor 'gal', which was Middle West American, he explained, but the 'gi' should be pronounced with the tongue close to one's upper back teeth, ha-ha-ha!' "

Faces were beginning to turn in their direction. Enthusiastically Plugge emptied his glass, and having refilled it, continued, warm with his story.

"Well, as I was saying, I found myself sitting in a taxi on the Embankment, in an actor's hired dress suit, being rehearsed before the gate-crash. I kept thinking what a funny shot it would make in a film. 'Go on,' Tony said. 'Say it! Gir—, not Gur—— Say it after me, Archie. Let your tongue lightly rest on your upper back teeth. Say it with your mouth partly spread, the position of the tongue is the same as when pronouncing the word 'cheese'.' "

Across the hot and crowded room came Channerson's hearty laughter. Phillip turned slowly to observe him. Channerson was about thirty-six, with prematurely grey hair above eyes which remained hard during his laughter. The laughter sounded hollow; behind the eyes which had looked at him at the door had been caution, irony, even despair.

"I suppose Channerson has had a fairly grim time. Most people loathed his paintings of the war—or did when he first painted them."

"He suffers from a simply frightful persecution complex, I'm told. On three occasions when he drove Tony to London, he stopped his car outside the Slade and cursed Tonks. I say, there's Virginia. Will you forgive me if I leave you? I must have a word with her. Well, I have so enjoyed our talk. You've simply made my evening."

"Before you go, Archie, what did you mean by *cheese*?"

"You know, surely? The debutante's smile of greeting, *cheese-cheese-cheese* all the way, but never before the camera."

Phillip watched him working a way towards the door, where Mrs. Cruft stood, looking around her without the least appearance of seeking anyone in particular. She was dressed in a tight gown sewn all over with silver sequins. Her lips were parted; her regular, white, elongated teeth were held ready to form the unspoken word *cheese* at the first sight of any known face. She had not yet seen

Plugge, whose padded shoulders remained politely fixed in the
press of bodies, waiting until some restless individual, seeking a
face more interesting than those around him, allowed a few
inches of progress.

With the arrival of the last of the theatrical and late-dining
people, the human density of the room was now at its greatest.
Suddenly Phillip saw Felicity Ancroft standing by the door. He
moved towards her. Young actresses gave him helplessly amused
glances as he insinuated his way past them, only to find himself
wedged in among elderly painters, musicians, actors, and Georgian
poets (to judge by their austere, aloof faces)—figures closely co-
hered all the way to the open double-doors leading to the adjoining
studio.

While he awaited a chance to move on, Felicity Ancroft saw him.
She waved a hand, and came towards him; in one flowing movement they met and clasped hands, he led her back to the comparative privacy of the wall where he had been standing.

"Will you have some champagne, Virginia?"

"Oh, thank you. I heard you were coming, Phillip. May I
call you Phillip? My name is Felicity, by the way."

"Of course. I'm so glad to see you. Are you at Savoy Hill?"

"I'm not on the staff, I'm a free-lance. I write things for the
Children's Hour."

"Do you live in London?"

"Well, fairly near. But I want to live in the country."

"Hullo, here comes my literary agent."

Anders Norse was pushing his way towards them.

"I've been looking for you everywhere, Phillip. Honestly, I'd
rather see your face at this moment than any other face in the
world. Hullo, Felicity. I didn't know you two knew each other."

"I'm waiting for Piers Tofield. Apart from Felicity, Archie
Plugge and you, I don't know a soul here."

"Why not go and introduce yourself to Channerson? He'd be
proud to know that the winner of this year's——"

"Let's all have a drink!"

By the look on Anders' face Phillip thought that he had been
drinking with friends in the Barbarian Club.

"I'll have a scotch. Have you told Felicity yet? Let's all drink
to the great news! Let everyone drink to it!"

"Oh please, Anders. I don't suppose anyone here has ever
heard of me."

"Then the sooner they know who's here, the better! Don't you agree, Felicity? After all, Phillip has won the——"

"Please, Anders!"

"But why not tell everybody?"

Alarmed by the other's earnest persistence, Phillip began to move away. "Do forgive me for a moment, I must speak to Virginia Cruft. She looks just like a mermaid. Perhaps she knows where Piers is."

At the far end of the room he saw Virginia looking about her. He moved on, leaving Felicity Ancroft by the wall. Anders, following, said, "Come and meet Anthony Cruft's wife, Phillip. Do you know Anthony Cruft's work? He's going to make a big name for himself, like you. Come on, Felicity!"

"Doesn't Mrs. Cruft look just like a mermaid?" repeated Phillip, allowing Anders to get past him; and then changed direction towards the door. There unexpectedly he met Plugge, who had worked through the press to intercept him.

"I say, Virginia is in a state. She thinks that Piers may have gone to Dover in his Aston-Martin, to cross by the night boat."

Anders reached Virginia, standing alone.

"Phillip Maddison says you are like a mermaid," he said. "If you're a mermaid, he is certainly an otter. Let me introduce my friend, Phillip Maddison. Phillip, let me—that's funny. I swear he was here a moment ago."

"Hullo, Anders," said Virginia. The skirt of her gown lay upon the floor, having formed itself into the semblance of an argentine fluke. "My dear, I am quite unable to move," as she put a delicate small hand on his sleeve. "What an idiot I was to put on this ancient frock." She smiled with sudden brilliance; she spoke, despite the awful doubt upon her diaphragm, in the clear, direct voice of a self-assured young woman.

"You have met Phillip Maddison, haven't you?" said Anders. "If not, may I introduce him?"

"Piers Tofield brought him to see us," she smiled. "I rather hoped I'd find Piers and Phillip here together when I arrived."

Anders had a puzzled look on his face. "Where's Tony? Didn't you come with your husband, Virginia?"

"I rather fancy he's looking for Piers," she said, with another wide smile. "Do be an angel and get me some brandy."

Phillip, having successfully dodged Anders, who had obviously had too much whisky to drink, made his way to Mrs. Cruft.

"Oh, I am so glad to see you," she said, touching his arm with a hand like a delicate small flipper with crimson claws. "I *do* apologise for not being able to come here before. Poor you. Piers was too, too naughty to leave you alone." She appealed to him with innocent round eyes. "Phillip—may I call you that? —Phillip, you *are* Piers' best friend, aren't you? He worships you. I *must* see him. I cannot explain just now—you *do* understand, don't you? But in case I don't see Piers before you leave, be an angel and ask him to be sure to telephone me tonight. I'm staying with Mama."

"He knows the address?"

"Oh yes. You *are* an angel, really you are."

Anders came back with two tumblers of schnapps. "It's all I could get, Virginia. Now I'd like to introduce you to Phillip Maddison. He's won the—— No! don't stop me, Phillip! Why not tell Virginia your news?"

"Anders is joking, don't heed what he says."

"Why do you say that?" asked Anders, his brow furrowed, his eyes unhappy. He swallowed half his tumbler of spirit. "Why not let everyone know the good news? No, don't move away." He held Phillip's arm and in a louder voice cried, "Tell Virginia, Phillip! Tell everyone! Let them know who's here!"

"No-one is really interested in my horses," said Phillip to Virginia. He went on, as easily as he could, "Well, I think I'll go and see what's happened to Archie Plugge."

But Anders the Norseman, the single-minded Viking, was not to be put off by the delaying tactics of a Celt.

"I really mean it, Phillip. I'm your friend, don't you know it? I'm *honestly* glad to know that you have won——"

"But my horse only won a local flat race for hacks, Anders."

"Tell Virginia——"

"At the Grand National," said Phillip to Virginia, as he tried to raise and lower his eyebrows in rapid succession, to convey a warning, "Staenyzer Kabaret, the colt from my Belgian stud, you know, may not be able to carry the weight of Captain Bill Kidd. Now there's a man, Anders. Bill Kidd! Can't you persuade him to write his memoirs?"

"Do you breed 'chasers, or for the flats?" asked Virginia, with

a brilliantly simulated interest in what appeared to be an entirely
bogus conversation.

"No, he doesn't, Virginia! It's *not* a horse," cried Anders, in
distress. He poured the other tumbler of clear schnapps down his
throat. "It's *not* a horse. It's an otter."

Phillip said, "Anders, will you kindly be quiet."

People around were looking at them.

"Tell Virginia, Phillip!"

Anders, who now had the expression of a man about to sink
for the third time, after appealing in vain for a life-belt, cried,
"Why not tell them, Phillip?"

"Virginia, please don't listen."

"But *why* not, Phillip?" came the agonised cry.

"Anders! *It—is—a—secret*."

"But why *let* it be a secret, Phillip? Tell Virginia. Tell everyone!"

"Don't believe anything he says, Virginia."

"I can't hear a word in this din," she smiled. "As soon as I
can get my skirt free—oh, thank you *so* much!" to a man who,
with many apologies, had found himself to be standing on her
tail. "Now I must powder my nose. Phillip, you won't forget to
tell Piers, will you?"

With a cheesy smile below unhappy eyes the brave, small mermaid moved away, dreaming of her new element.

"Phillip," cried Anders, gripping his arm. "Tell them!"

"Please do not hold my arm."

"For God's sake don't misunderstand me, Phillip!"

"I don't misunderstand you. Will you please not hold my
arm?"

His momentary anger induced a greater sense of being mis-
understood; and since by now a dozen or more faces were looking
their way he became alarmed lest Anders give away Miss Arden's
secret, and struck Anders' forearm a blow with his open hand.
The finger-clutch broke, he moved away; but Anders pressed
after him, begging him to believe it was only RIGHT that people
should know who he was and what he had done.

He pushed on through the crowd, apologising to one person
while thrusting past another; but Anders pressed after him. Disaster seemed imminent, for the way was closed by several of
Anders' friends belonging to the Barbarian Club. They stood
together to prevent what they considered might easily become a

brawl. One of them was a painter with a beard grown to hide the
scars of a machine-gun bullet which had gone through his cheek.

"Why not be reasonable?" he said. "I am a friend of Anders.
Now let us keep calm. Why don't you want to hear what he has
to say to you?"

"If you are his friend, will you ask him to forget about me? I'm
afraid that I can't explain."

"But that is being rather one-sided, isn't it? Surely Anders is
owed the explanation for which he has asked repeatedly?"

The painter's wife then tried to explain. She was a novelist,
and Anders was her agent.

"After all, you must admit that you are making Anders most
unhappy, and indeed, spoiling the party for him, not to mention
the enjoyment of others. Won't you make friends, whatever the
rights or wrongs of it, and shake hands?"

"Come here, Anders," said the painter. "And shake hands."

Anders held up a hand as though to make an announcement.
He stared straight ahead, and then slid down upon the floor and
lay still.

Channerson moved forward to inspect the only casualty so far
at his party which included, he considered, a hundred uninvited
people among the three hundred present. He called for help.
Phillip, Plugge, and two other men, each grasping leg or arm, bore
the body to the door. They waited while a taxicab drew up. Out
of it stepped Piers.

"I've been looking for you, Phillip. You're not going? I'm
most awfully sorry——"

"I understand, Piers. Do forgive me a moment. I must make
sure that Anders' head isn't bent too sharply forward. Help me
to put him on the floor, where he can't get any lower. Virginia's
inside looking for you. I think I'd better take Anders to the
Barbarian Club."

"Pickled?" asked the driver.

"He tried to make a speech."

Piers said, "Would you mind holding the cab? I won't be a
moment."

"Well," said the amiable voice of Plugge, "I wonder what it was
the poor chap was trying to say?"

"He was, like all prophets, a little before his time, Archie."

Piers returned with Virginia now looking extremely happy.

"D'you mind if we come with you, Phil? It's rather urgent.

Do you really want to leave now? If not, I can drop your friend at the Barbarian Club."

"I think I'd better say how d'you do to Channerson."

Piers gave him the latchkey. "It's awfully good of you. Do help yourself to anything you want—you'll find pyjamas in the drawer, drinks on the sideboard. I'll see you later."

Standing side by side, Phillip and Archie watched the taxi turning into Haverstock Hill.

"My dear Phil, it looks as though Piers is running off with Virginia. Oh dear. You see, it was *I* who introduced them to one another."

They went inside. As they inspected the débris of the buffet he said, "Have you had any dinner? I haven't." He salvaged the last remaining sandwich, and having blown off cigarette ash, opened it and saw a thin layer of potted meat within.

"I had some eggs and bacon before I came here."

"Oh, don't torture me."

Archie gulped down the sandwich, then continued his hunt round the table strewn with ashtrays, empty plates and glasses. There were some odd cheese-straws, and a squashed mince-pie.

"Well, I must go back to my horrible room in Old Compton Street, I suppose. I shall have a good dinner next Friday, which is pay day. What it is to be in Fleet Street and earning only four pounds a week, and thirty bob for my room. And dinner every Friday with Zorinda. I think I'll call on her tonight, and risk finding her with another boy-friend. Usually she's not at home to me on Monday. Not that I look forward greatly to Friday. I suppose one might call it one's social duty."

Having scooped up some crumbs of cake, an idea seemed to strike him. "I wonder if you'd like to meet Zorinda?" he asked, hopefully. "She keeps that hat shop at the Oxford Street end of Bond Street."

"I must go back fairly soon, thanks all the same."

"Well, I have so enjoyed seeing you, my dear Phil. We must meet again at Rookhurst, if not before. I'm quite a good cook— you know—plain, wholesome fare, should you ever want a house-parlourman who isn't above turning his hand to anything."

Felicity Ancroft was leaving, led by a small elderly man. She kept her eyes lowered, Phillip noticed, as she went towards Channerson, whose laughter was now coming almost continuously from the centre of a group of people. When the couple had gone, the painter's unlaughing eyes were turned on him as he approached.

"My name is Maddison."

"So you told me," replied the painter, with an air of ironic courtesy. "I have been wondering if you had perhaps mistaken our humble abode for an annexe to the Haverstock Arms next door? You didn't tell me you were a friend of Anders Norse. I thought you said that you were with the Crufts."

The young woman with a round smiling face came forward and took Phillip's hand. "I'm Dikkon's wife," she smiled. "Virginia has been telling me *all* about your lovely horses. *Do* come and tell me more about them. How good of you to come all the way from Belgium to our little party. Won't you stay and have some eggs and bacon and meet some friends of ours?"

She was charming with her joyous Saxon face, her warmth, her pleasure in being alive. She held his hand for a few moments and said, "I'd love a glass of champagne. And do get one for yourself as well."

They drank to one another. Channerson was looking at him gravely. "Who, or what, is Plugge, can you tell me?"

"He's a friend of the Crufts."

"He has such charming manners, Dikkon."

"He needs them," replied the painter, to his wife.

"Your husband's war pictures have the truth in them, Mrs. Channerson. They are beautiful."

"Beautiful?" said Channerson. "What is beauty?"

"Compassion. All beauty is truth, and all truth is compassionate. Few know that, fewer still can express it. You can, and do."

"Ah!" said Channerson, gravely. "But the problem remains, how to put paint on paint."

As Phillip was leaving, a man with black hair plastered on each side of his forehead like jackdaw's wings went up to him and said, "Have you by any chance a studio floor I could sleep on tonight? I was wondering if you would perhaps be feeling somewhat lonely after your boy friend left you so unhappily."

"I'm sorry, but I don't live in London. I'm a farmer, from the West Country."

"Fortunate man. You don't mind my asking?"

"Not in the least. I've spent hundreds of hours sleeping on billet floors in my time, and only wish I could fix you up."

Stars shone above the diminished tawny glow of London as he walked down the hill. He passed the Black Cat Cigarette factory

and came to the Charing Cross Road. In streets off Piccadilly pale
wastrel figures hovered in doorways. Poor darlings, he thought,
still elevated by the champagne in his blood, as he entered Blue
Ball Yard.

Which was his bedroom? The same one as last time? He
opened the bedroom door; snores came forth. He closed the door,
and composed himself on a settee. He was still awake when Piers
came in.

"I'm afraid it wasn't possible to explain at the party. Have a
drink?"

"I'd like some soda-water."

"Do help yourself."

Piers lit the gas fire. "Virginia likes you."

"I like her. She thinks with her head, and not with her feelings."

"I hope you can stay for a few days, I'd like you to meet her
again. Tony walked out tonight. He said it was no good remaining
with a wife mooning about the place thinking of someone else."

Phillip said nothing.

Piers went on, "Would it be asking too much if I came and
talked to you sometime at Rookhurst? In my Aston I can get
down in a couple of hours or so. I suppose it's asking rather a
lot, after the way I've behaved tonight. I've no excuse of course,
but it has been rather upsetting for Virginia."

"Do come, anytime, Piers. And bring Virginia if she'd care to
stay."

"What about Lucy?"

"I'm sure she'd welcome you both."

"Most generous of you. Must you go back tomorrow?"

"Yes, but I'll be up next week, for the Grasmere Award. I
hope it doesn't get to the papers prematurely. What sort of a girl
is Felicity Ancroft? She must have guessed, from what Anders
hinted."

"She does a thing for the Children's Hour on Tuesdays. I'll
warn her."

"Thanks."

"You found your bedroom?" Piers threw a dressing gown in
his direction. "You go first into the bathroom, will you?"

"I rather fancy someone's in my bedroom."

"Plugge, most likely. One never knows when or where he'll
turn up. I suppose he heard of the Channerson's party from someone. Have my bed. I'll sleep here. You've had too many rough

nights during the war, and deserve all the beds you can get. Sorry I can't supply a girl this time, but when you come again I'll ring up Felicity if you like. She'd be only too glad of the chance, I expect."

In the morning Plugge said, "I say, I'm most frightfully sorry, old boy, but I've no idea how I got into your bed last night. I went to the Game Pie, and had drinks with your late comrade in arms, Bill Kidd. I think I must have passed out afterwards."

"Oh."

"Was I very tight at the Channersons?"

"Sober as a judge."

Plugge sighed. "I always behave so badly, you know." He reflected. "I suppose I ought to send them an apology. I wonder if they saw that I arrived without a bottle? It must still be in my desk in the proof-reader's room. Oh dear, I feel as I felt after that awful floater of mine, the bogus wedding. You know about it, of course."

Plugge's face regarded him with blank eyes.

"You never got to it last night, Archie. Virginia came just at that point, if you remember."

"Well, Tony and I planned a bogus wedding to clear the way of any opposition to the marriage proper by Lady Donmaree. Virginia was eighteen then, and of course more minor than she is today, although whether a married woman can be a minor I don't altogether know." He groaned, and held his head. "It's horrible to remember one's past, don't you think?"

"You don't look bogus to me, Archie. You have a great sense of fun."

"Thank you. Yes, I was the bogus priest at the bogus wedding. We sent out engraved invitation cards. The press came. We were in all the papers. I had a job at a prep. school in Sussex then." He sighed once again. "I never went back—it was all too ghastly. My photograph was in *The People*. They even exposed me as a danger to young girls." He meditated before continuing. "I've often wondered whether Tony gave the story to the press, because *The Crusader* published a photograph of the bill for hiring my parson's rig-out from Willie Clarkson. You see"—he leaned towards Phillip and lowered his voice—"Tony suggested in the first place that I go to Willie's shop. No-one else knew."

"Still they were properly married afterwards, weren't they?"

"Yes, I suppose that can be put on the credit side, although it was a runaway affair in Caxton Hall. Even so, what will Virginia's lady mother think of me when she hears the too, too frightful news that Virginia has now bolted with Piers? You see, I am in a way doubly responsible"—the round unspectacled eyes were like a seal's out of water—"because it was *I* who introduced Tony to Virginia in the first place, at Eleanor Metfield's party."

Later that morning Phillip found Anders sitting a little diminished at his office table, a box of soda-mints before him.

"What happened last night, Phillip?"

"Nothing. Except that it was a jolly good party."

"Didn't I make an awful fool of myself?"

"No."

"I know I drank too much. I am a fool to drink."

"So am I. But I never drink whisky nowadays if I can help it."

"I seem to remember that you were trying to avoid me, Phillip. Was it anything I said that offended you?"

"No, of course not. I'm glad I didn't drink too much, because then I might very easily have told people about the Grasmere. If I had, and it got into the papers, I'd have had to withdraw my book. After all, it's Miss Arden's secret."

"I stayed at the Barbarian, you know. I've no idea at all how I got there."

"I think two people gave you a lift."

"Who were they, d'you know?"

Anders swallowed two soda mints with water.

"It was dark then. The moon had gone down."

"Perhaps Anthony Cruft brought me here. No, I don't think so, for he didn't mention it when he called earlier this morning. He's going off somewhere remote to write a novel, and will let me have his address when he knows where he's fixed up." He held out the box of soda-mints. "Are you sure I was all right last night? Not noisy, or anything?"

"Not in the very least, my pilot. You couldn't get a word in edgeways in all that chatter. Well, I must be off now, to catch my train. See you next week, at the Aeolian Hall. Keep mum about it meanwhile."

"You can rely on me, Phillip."

"I know I can, Anders. But keep away from the whisky bottle. It's the death of literature."

Chapter 10

GREAT DAY

They set out early, driving slowly into the golden silhouette of
morning above the downs, before turning north through the market
town and the road to Shakesbury. Now that the sun was out of
their eyes, Ernest went a little faster, the speedometer needle
showing 25 m.p.h. There was no hurry; eight hours lay before
them.

Phillip felt that life was good. He lay back against the leather
upholstery, his velour hat tilted over his eyes and one leg cocked
over the other. In his pocket were the letters collected at Colham
by special arrangement before the post-office opened. It was a
grand feeling to be driven by Ernest, a steady driver if ever there
was one. No ambition to show off the Crossley engine, or a fancied
skill in driving: there he sat, upright and unmoving, Pa beside
him looking about, approving what he saw of the natural world.
What a good idea it had been of Ernest's, after all, to buy a roomy
touring car, instead of some poky little roadster 2-seater.

"Happy, Lulu?"

"*Very* happy."

"Oh, I nearly forgot. There's a letter for you, from Australia.
From Tim, I think."

She read it eagerly, rich colour in her cheeks. It was good news,
she told them. The jobs Tim and Fiennes had in the coal-mine
were now more or less permanent. They had economised by living
in bivouacs made of sheets of newspaper stuck layer on layer with
flour-and-water paste until a hard stiff awning was secured,
stretched on rope between trees. A couple of coats of paint preserved
the surface, each had his own bivvy, they cooked their own food,
and were quite enjoying life, 'considering all things'.

"Good for old Tim."

Ernest was another matter. He recalled the talk they had had
that morning in the Works before starting off. There the Delauny-
Belville was, the parts of its transmission, accurate in every particular, laid out ready for reassembly. Ernest had done a meticu-
lous, a *beautiful* job, but——

"By the way, old chap, I suppose the owner knows you are
repairing this old crock?"

"Oh, I don't suppose so."

"But isn't this job going to cost a fair amount? These yellow-metal castings, aren't they phosphor bronze?"

Ernest had made no reply. It was hopeless: everything he did was a wastage of capital. There was Fiennes' brand-new Grindley-Peerless motorbike still standing in the garage, exactly as Fiennes had left it, except that now there was mildew on the saddle. And there, too, was the Tamp, its straight wooden mudguards green and rotting, the chassis hidden by nettles and brambles——

He picked up his letters. There was one in a slightly flourishing handwriting. He tore it open and saw within the signature Thomas Morland.

"We're invited to stay with them tonight, Lucy. In Hampstead. How about it?"

"Oh yes, if you'd like to."

"How about Pa and Ernest? Will they be all right in the hotel by themselves?"

She laughed, she coloured a little. "Oh yes, I think they'll be able to manage."

The next envelope was from Nuncle. He flipped it aside. "I think I can guess what he has to say. Open them, will you?"

A letter from Piers. "He sends his congratulations for the day and says he's afraid he can't manage to get to the Aeolian Hall, but hopes to see us later on at Rookhurst."

"Good."

"A letter from Mother. She says will meet 'Spica' under the clock at Charing Cross station as arranged. Who is 'Spica', Pip?"

"An old friend of mine, Tabitha Trevilian, a girl I was in love with in nineteen twenty, when I was a hack in Fleet Street."

There were two reasons for asking Spica to meet his mother: the one, he didn't want either of his sisters there; the other, that his mother and Spica would appreciate one another.

"I'd love to meet her."

"She's a fine young woman."

He felt optimistic enough to open Nuncle's letter. A glance at the two typewritten sides of the paper was enough: he refolded it into the envelope and put it in his pocket.

The journey proceeded in silence for a couple of miles before Lucy noticed that he was sitting up straight beside her, knees close together, arms folded across his chest. Thinking that he was cold she asked if he would like the side-curtains put up.

"Oh, I'm all right, thanks." Then he said, "You'd better read Nuncle's letter."

Hilary wrote that he would not be able to go to London for the presentation as he was temporarily indisposed. He hoped to spend a few days, if well enough, with them when the mayfly was up. It was now imperative that he, Phillip, make up his mind about what he intended to do with his life. A writing career was, at best, precarious; but apart from that, as he had said before, it demanded a life of comparative inaction, while farming was a constant involvement in practical affairs. He was not a rich man, much of his capital was locked up in the estate, and had charges upon it concerning the present and future welfare of others beside himself, namely the Aunts—Isabella, Victoria, and Theodora. In addition, there were burdensome tithes to be paid away. Agriculture at this period in its history was in the nature of a depressed industry, as he must have realised by now. In short, a decision must not be put off any longer; and he wanted Phillip's answer by midsummer.

When she had read the letter he waited for her to speak. When she said nothing, he clenched his hands and struck his fists together several times, while taking a deep breath. "Can't you give a lead sometimes?"

"What am I supposed to say?"

With an effort to control contrary feelings he replied quietly, "Would you mind very much if we gave up the farm?"

"I'm ready to fall in with anything you may decide."

"Can't you, for once, say what *you* would like? Shall we, or shan't we, give up the farming idea?"

"Perhaps if you will be happier writing, then it may be best to tell Uncle Hilary."

They were driving through a valley with a trout stream visible now and again. A gang of hoers were preparing to start work in a field. Coats were off, sleeves being rolled: obviously this was 'taken work'. They were their own masters, ready to work long hours up and down the pale green lines of seedling roots.

"Men work much better when they are their own masters."

"I absolutely agree."

This was a new Lucy. "But do you like living at Rookhurst?"

"Oh yes, very much. But then I don't mind much where I live, so long as you are happy."

A kestrel was hovering over an old, unbroached hayrick. Its black-streaked breast of chestnut brown was distinct in the eastern light, which revealed every slight curling of its pinion feathers. As the car passed, it half-rolled, like a scout 'plane before going into a dive, and glided away over the field of tillered wheat.

"I really want to write my war trilogy, Lucy. I see myself sometimes living in Scotland beside a trout stream and catching finnock, as they call the small sea-trout. I've never caught a sea-trout. In fact, I've hardly ever fished with a fly. In Scotland it would be fun, with the midnight sun."

"Yes," said Lucy, thinking that he had not fished once in all the time they had been at Rookhurst. Poor old boy, he had always been too tired after his work, particularly when he had been writing.

"Or Ireland. The coast of Connemara. Going about barefoot. Just fishing and writing."

"Oh, I would love Ireland. Pa and Mother used to go often, you know. Lough Corrib, wasn't it, Pa?"

"Hey?" said Pa, turning his head, so that the thin grey hair under his cap was stirred by the wind.

"Phillip was saying that he would like to go to Connemara."

"Ah, Galway. Those beggars burnt down cousin Roger's place in the trouble. Moorpark was a jolly place to spend the summer. Not much good for arable farming, I fancy, Phil. Horses, yes, if you like 'em."

"I'd like to write a book about fish."

"Plenty there still, in the loughs of Connemara."

Ireland; the wild and rocky coast; peat fire and white-washed cabin. The simple life, going barefoot. All the same, it was a bit of a wrench to think of giving up the downs, the beech hanger, the coppices, the brook, the Longpond. Also, it would be running away; deserting Uncle John, and his new lease of life. The poor old boy *lived* in Billy and the baby; and he and Lucy were so happy together.

If the dead lived on in their old places, would not Willie be rejoicing, and Barley too, that they were all there together?

And the thought was poignant; he relapsed, became heavy with a recrudescence of grief. No! He must not think of the past, he must hold on, and rise above his weak inner self. It could be done with a new routine. Be like Trollope; write by the clock—no more, no less. Oh, things would be much better now that he would no longer be dependent on Nuncle for money. Ideas for his novel sequence arose in his mind.

First, the general idea.

Illusion in 1914; chaos in 1915; disaster in 1916; deadlock in 1917 until the way was found at Cambrai in November; tremendous peril early in 1918, but the front held in balance—and so to the victories of the late summer: Passchendaele reached in a 5-mile advance *in one day*. All that had gone before had led to the smashing of the Siegfried Stellung, and the way open to victory. Haig had held on in the exceptional wet summer of 1917 at Ypres, according to 'Spectre' West, after being told by Pétain, in confidence, that over forty French divisions down south were in passive mutiny. *That* was why Haig had not broken off the battle of Third Ypres. Duty, duty, duty.

Before they had started out that morning, Phillip, fearing an unexpected delay, such as a traffic hold-up, had suggested to Ernest that they leave the car at Reading and go on by rail. This they did shortly after 10 a.m., catching a train to Paddington, and thence by taxi to the Strand, and the Adelphi hotel, seen in bright daylight to be a somewhat dingy sort of place, with its entrance facing north away from the Thames. Having seen Pa and Ernest settled, and made arrangements to pay the bill on the morrow, there arose a problem.

"Do you think we should take our bags to Hampstead now—or after the show? Where can we leave them?"

"Why not here?" suggested Pa.

"Ah, good idea."

That decided, there were four hours to fill in.

"Shall we 'spy out the land', Lulu?"

Saying goodbye to the others, they crossed Trafalgar Square, stopping to look at the pigeons, and then strolled up to Piccadilly, asking a policeman the way to Bond Street.

"We must reconnoitre the enemy territory."

There was a feeling almost of preparation for going over the top. He tried to find interest in various pictures in the windows fronting galleries, until unexpectedly he found himself outside the Aeolian Hall.

"The big dugout under the church at Graincourt, in the reserve Hindenburg Line. It was like a liner underground, with an electric light plant still being worked by the Germans. As soon as they knew they had to carry on, the engineers tactfully revealed that the whole place was mined, and the main switch was connected to the detonators."

"How clever of them to arrange that."

"When we arrived the sappers had already cut the leads."

They returned to the Strand where Lucy said she would like a cup of tea, so they went into an A.B.C. and shared a pork pie with *compôte-de-fruit* to follow. He picked up an evening paper left on a table and saw on the front page his own photograph with the caption that the prize was to be awarded that afternoon for *The Water Wanderer.*

"Someone's earned thirty bob by jumping the gun. I wonder if it is Felicity Ancroft, that girl I told you about, Lulu."

They drank coffee before leaving the shop to sit by the fountains in Trafalgar Square. Then, at 2.30 p.m., leaving the narrow light of Bond Street for the comparative darkness of the Aeolian Hall, where his 'civilised' nervousness—as he thought of it—returned. They were met at the top of some stone steps by a young man with a mass of hair like canary feathers who led Phillip into an ante-room where a number of people were standing. There he recognised J. C. Knight, the poet and editor of *The London Apollo*, who presented him to Miss Corinna Arden, a tall elderly lady with a bright, virginal manner; then to other members of the Committee —to a clean-shaven, rather bland-looking man with a square face in which was fixed a rimless eye-glass; a smaller dark man with a gentle, lined face and cleft chin denoting sensibility, and two other people whom he barely noticed, for by now he was wondering what had happened to Lucy; and as the minutes dripped away he began to feel she might be lost. And would Mother have missed Spica at Charing Cross Station? Supposing he had written *Victoria Station*, where Spica would arrive from her home in Folkestone?

J. C. Knight was talking to a Georgian poet who had won the Grasmere Prize some years previously, for a book of poems called *The Queen of Sumeria.* He now earned his living by reviewing books, writing critical essays, and anonymous contributions to Fleet Street gossip columns. It was he who had telephoned the details of the award to the evening newspaper.

The youth with canary-feather hair reappeared with Thomas Morland. Knight led Phillip to him.

"Do you know Phillip Maddison?"

Morland replied, "Oh yes, he's staying with us," and Phillip thought that Knight appeared to be momentarily abashed.

The next distinguished visitor to enter was an old man with

grey moustaches and keen friendly face. Phillip recognised the General who had spoken to him in the ranks of the London Highlanders during the final inspection before they had left to join the B.E.F. in Flanders in September, 1914. Dare he speak to him? He hesitated; then it was too late, many people were now passing through into the hall proper. He could not find Lucy. Dare he look inside the hall—or would his absence be discovered? Supposing they wanted to present him to the General? He returned to the ante-room, and saw Knight looking at his watch.

"Will you find yourself a seat at the edge of the gangway about half-way down the hall," he said to Phillip. "And come up to the platform when your name is called?"

"Yes, I understand."

"A press photographer for an evening paper wants to take some photographs of you now, with Thomas Morland."

Phillip repressed his anxiety about Lucy; and afterwards, his sight dazed by the camera flash, entering the hall, with its red upholstery and clusters of electric light bulbs, he made out Pa and Ernest seated with his mother and Spica about a dozen rows from the back; and there was Lucy in the second seat from the gangway.

"I've kept the end seat for you," she smiled.

"How thoughtful of you."

She replied, to his slight disappointment, "Oh, it was Spica's idea. She thought you might like to be free to go forward when your name was called."

Many people were now passing down the aisles. Among them, striding briskly, entirely buoyant, was Margot Asquith, with a beautiful, fair-haired young woman.

Spica moved to the back of his seat. "Well, my dear, I have always known this day would come."

He turned to see her brown eyes steadily upon him. What was she thinking, Could you but have trusted me? Or was this an idea from his own thought-grievance, distorting her simple gesture? He felt her brooding upon him; it was a relief when she moved back beside Mother: she cared too much, like Mother.

Now the platform was being crossed by members of the Committee. Was his regimental tie straight? Should his jacket be loose, or held by the middle of the three buttons? And the bottom button of the waistcoat undone? But he had nearly forgotten to twist the signet ring Uncle John had given him!

The round part must be inside the palm, the ring twisted as he had worn the ring given to him for his 21st birthday. He had reversed it before leading the raid into the German front line near La Boisselle in early June, lest the flat circle give a glint in the light of flares as they crawled to the wire.

People were clapping. Thomas Morland was walking to the centre of the platform, holding a sheaf of typed papers in one hand. Holding up his chin, he began to speak clearly, throwing his voice to the back of the hall, every word like a dart at a dart-board. He was speaking of the novels of Hardy, the work of W. H. Hudson, and Gilbert White of Selborne, and their concern for the preservation of wild life. A woman just in front turned to her companion and said, "I thought it would be a book about the sufferings of animals when I heard he was to give the prize."

Now he was for it. Morland was speaking about the book. Whatever was he saying... "The theme of *The Water Wanderer* is that the elements conspire together, on the face of the waters, to produce the species, with the force of love, to produce beauty: that wild animals are pure and heavenly, confined as they are within the limits of their instincts, that they are entirely loyal, thus preserving their pristine beauty; while Man, as the vehicle to contain the Imagination, is capable of flights of the greatest generosity, or descents to the most profound villainy and degradation imposed upon himself, his fellow men, and in the destruction of the essentially innocent species. This book is a work of stupendous imagination fortified by endlessly patient observation." The woman turned again to her companion and said, "I've never heard of him, have you?" as his name was called and he was on his feet and gliding down the gangway past side-turned faces and up the steps and across the platform behind the seated Committee to where Miss Corinna Arden was standing to give him an envelope, to shake his hand, and he bowed his head and thanked her, and still grinning went back the way he had come. As he recrossed the platform a hand stayed him; there was a whispered question from the dark lean man of the Committee, *Would you like to make a speech?* He knew that this was more than a suggestion, but now he was less than ever himself, and the 'stupendous imagination' was grief, despair, and longing to join her in the life beyond. They were clapping; they expected a speech; he must either speak or move away, not stand still, so he said 'Thank you' again to Miss Arden, who had moved to her chair, and was hesitating, and 'thank you' to the audience of hundreds of pink faces; and then he hurried away to the steps against a scatter of clapping and jumped down from the middle step and went back to his seat three-quarters of the way down the hall.

Miss Arden was now filling the hiatus, stemming the feeling of anti-climax among the audience: why, why, why didn't someone tell him before that he would be expected to make a speech. The fluttery voice of Miss Arden was speaking of a ghostly otter following ghostly salmon up an immortal river and it was all over.

So soon was it all over! People were getting up to go out. Then Spica over his shoulder was telling him that a famous war-poet was sitting just behind him; he sat still, hoping that the poet would not hear her words. When at last he looked round, as though casually, the poet was, to his relief, walking to the exit.

Then, seeing his old Colonel standing under the platform head and shoulders above all others, Phillip went down to thank him for coming. Lord Satchville moved to him to offer congratulations, saying from his great bearded height that he had managed to break away during an interval from the debate in the House of Lords to share in the honour paid to the Regiment. His cousin, the Duchess, he said, was much interested in wild life and he had given her a copy of the otter's story, and perhaps he and his wife would pay him a visit during one Saturday to Monday when he would take him over to Husborne to renew acquaintance with the Duke as well.

"Is your wife with you, Maddison? Perhaps you will introduce me to her?"

Phillip fetched Lucy; and while she was talking to Satchville his mind was a kaleidoscope of mind pictures—the summer of 1918 at the Duchess' hospital, blinded by mustard gas and walking in the park with his guide Lady Abeline; then it was the summer of 1908, and with his sisters and Mother, his cousins Polly and Percy and Uncle and Aunt, he was walking under tall fountains of gnats down a long grassy ride between lofty holly hedges, watched by keepers in brown livery and brown bowler hats. He saw again the lodge-keeper in his black claw-hammer coat and tall silk hat with the cockade at the side, opening the great iron gates through which they entered to see fallow deer and emus down the glades, gnus and emus and golden pheasants, and in the park the herd of bison and beyond them were very small deer, Père David deer, near the yaks, and Uncle was telling them that the domain wall was twelve miles round the park . . .

And he did not want to go back, to stay with Colonel Satchville, it could never be the same again, now that he had changed, and had begun to think; but he said, "Thank you, Colonel, it will be jolly to see Husborne again. I suppose all the hutments have long since been removed from the park?" No, no, he thought, I must not go back, never, never, never.

When Lord Satchville had gone a familiar voice, curt with a donnish minimum of lip movement, said in Phillip's ear, "I had no idea that you were on familiar terms with the greatest rowing blue my College has produced," and turning, he saw Martin Beausire, carrying as usual a pile of review books under one arm and, as usual, in a tearing hurry. "I've got to get back to my office to write a leader for my paper—walk with me down to Piccadilly where I'll get a cab—both Fifi and I expect you at Worthing tonight—bring Lucy if she's with you—you know the address, it's in the telephone book. What are you writing now—I hear you're farming near my old stamping ground. Then why aren't you writing about the Great Plain instead of writing about the Great War? All the articles I've seen of yours are about nothing except the war. Very good of their kind they are, too, but who cares a hoot about the war when your animal and country stuff is only as you can do it, you prize ass. Here's a taxi. Get in."

"I can't come tonight, Martin, thanks all the same, Lucy and I are staying with the Morlands."

"Then come as soon as you can. Fifi is always saying, 'When are we going to see Phillip and Lucy again'," and banging the taxicab door he cried "Fleet Street—*Daily Telegram*——" and off he went.

Returning to the hall, Phillip saw Archie Plugge, who came across an empty row of seats as though invisibly being impelled by a tall dark woman with brilliant dark eyes and red mouth. "First of all, *do* let me congratulate you, Phillip! Now may I present you to Zorinda—Mrs. Nembhard la Guardia. Zorinda wants to ask you how she can get a tame otter. Now, alas, I must leave you, if you'll forgive me. It *would* be press night for *The Wireless Times* at Watford, and I simply mustn't miss the van——"

He hurried away, leaving Phillip with the tall woman and her sparkling gaze upon him. "Yes, you *are* just like your book. I knew it. It is too, too divine. I *must* get a cub for a pet. How does one go about it? Archie has been telling me that they live in your river."

"Well, I've never actually seen one in the brook, but otters do roam about a good deal, I fancy."

"How perfectly fascinating. You tracked your beastie everywhere, Archie tells me. How does one see wild animals? Do tell me, is there an hotel near you, where one might stay? I wouldn't dream of suggesting myself, knowing how busy you must be," she said, her dark eyes open wide behind lashes sticky with lampblack. "The West Country must be simply heaven now."

He was wondering how to extricate himself when he saw Lucy. "This is Mrs. Nembhard la Guardia, a friend of Archie's," he explained. "My wife," he added, vaguely. "Do forgive me. I'll be back in a moment——" for he had seen Plugge beckoning him at the back of the hall.

"I'm most frightfully sorry, but Zorinda insisted—— What I wanted to say, although I couldn't for obvious reasons say it while she was there, was that my summer holiday begins next week, and as I'll probably be staying a few days with Piers, might I drop round and see you?"

"Yes, of course."

"You will forgive me, I know, but I simply must rush away to catch the press van. Don't for God's sake let on to Zorinda that I'm coming to you."

Phillip went back to the two women, arriving in time to hear Lucy saying, "Oh, we don't live in Devon, but Phillip has kept a cottage there."

"I suppose you wouldn't consider letting it for a period? One simply *must* get away from the mad rush that London is nowadays."

"It's rather damp," said Phillip. With relief he saw Spica approaching. She nodded cheerfully to the woman with Phillip, then said to him, "Some reporters from the evening papers want an interview with you. They say there isn't much time left if they're to catch the final edition."

"I don't awfully care for interviews."

"But you were once a reporter yourself, don't forget."

"Where are they?"

"Waiting at the back of the hall. I'll show you." She led him away. "Who's that awful woman trying to attach herself to you?"

"An object of mixed feeling to an undecided acquaintance of mine. I've never seen her before."

"Take my advice, and don't see her again."

Four young reporters, one of them Felicity Ancroft, stood in a row together. The man, speaking for the others, said, "Mr. Maddison, please will you give us a story?"

The three young women remained attentive. Felicity, he noticed, wore her hair in a different style: she looked like Barley about the brow, with two waves of fair hair growing back from the widow's peak. Conscious of her gaze upon him, he replied with ease, "I wonder if I waited so politely when I was on space with *The Sunday Courier*? There's not much of a story, I'm afraid. I left Fleet Street to live in a labourer's cottage in South Devon after the war—I lived with dogs, cats, and various birds. There was also—towards the end—a tame otter."

"Was that Lutra?"

He drew a deep breath. "One night he got in a rabbit trap, losing two claws of a front paw before I managed to release him. Then he ran off in fear. It took some months to track him, up and down the rivers of Exmoor and Dartmoor. I came upon him at last, towards the end of a hunt. He got down to the tide-head —salt water, as I expect you know, carries no scent, so hounds could not follow. That's the last I saw of him."

"But in your book the otter is killed by hounds. Was there any symbolism involved in its death?"

When he did not reply the reporter took another line. "Would it be true to say that you met your wife in the search for Lutra?"

"Yes."

"And she is a niece of Lady Kilmeston?"

"Well——"

"And since your marriage you have farmed an estate in Wilt-shire?"

"I'm a farm pupil."

"Does that mean that you will write no more books?"

"I can't really say. However, I've managed to complete another."

"May we know what the subject is?"

"A novel about an ex-soldier who rebels against accepted ideas."

"Would it be correct to assume that it is autobiographical?"

"I appear only as a minor character."

They thanked him, and three of them moved away. Felicity Ancroft remained, twisting white cotton gloves.

"I used to be diffident when I had to interview people," he said.

"Oh," she said, looking up at him. "I hardly like to say it—but—well—may I write to you about coming down to see you for an article on your work? I'm a freelance."

"Yes, you told me. I'll give you my address."

"I know where you live. I've actually bought a one-inch Ordnance Survey Map of your country. I mustn't keep you. Goodbye, and oh yes—congratulations." She went away.

He looked around for Spica. She was sitting alone in the last row. Moving down the aisle, he repassed the young man with feathery yellow hair who said, "I've just heard Sir Godber Hollins say, 'I discovered that young man', after receiving congratulations on being your publisher."

"Oh."

Phillip sat beside Spica. She took his hand.

"Well, Phillip, this is the day I've always looked forward to. Now you're a famous figure all right. What a very sweet person your mother is. You inherit your talent from her, you know." The large gentle eyes regarded him seriously. "You know I'm always your friend, don't you?"

"Yes, of course."

"And I've always said what I think. You know that?"

"Yes."

"Then don't be offended when I tell you to look after your beautiful, enduring, and tolerant Lucy. She's not Barley, you know."

"What makes you say that?"

She caressed his hand. "Because I'm very fond of you both. I'll say goodbye here. Bless you."

His mother was waiting with Pa, Ernest and Lucy. Hetty said gaily, "Well, Phillip, I am so glad everything went off all right."

"Thank you for coming, Mother. I'm sorry I've kept you waiting. It looks as if Lucy and I must find the Morlands now. They've asked us to stay the night with them."

"If you have time, do come down to see Father, won't you? I must go now, to be home when he arrives from the office."

"I wish you were coming with us to Rookhurst," he said, feeling sad that she was looking so old.

"Perhaps I shall come again, one day."

"Father must come, too. It is *his* country, really. Well, I suppose we must be going."

Thomas Morland and his wife were waiting in the vestibule. Mrs. Morland was a thin elderly woman with dark eyes looking as though she had been permanently hurt. Of course, she would be the wife of Morland's cousin, whom he put into *Possession* as the unsympathetic Evelyn Crouchend. He told her how startled he had been to hear Mr. Morland's praise of his 'little book'. She smiled wanly. They were driven to a house in Upper Brook Street, where, among a score of fashionable people, they listened to a string quartet playing in the drawing room, before having tea.

"I am so glad you like music," said Mrs. Morland. "We thought of going after dinner to hear *Hiawatha* at the Queen's Hall. There's a very promising young conductor named Henry Flashman."

It was a moving cantata. Whatever the modern attitude to lyric poetry, he said to Lucy, Longfellow was a true poet in Hiawatha. By the time the music had come to the death of Minnehaha he had withdrawn into himself, with a return of the very grief he had felt when Barley died on that winter morning when the fields of Malandine were white with rime.

The Morlands' house on the edge of the Heath seemed to be inhabited by maid-servants in uniform with starched caps. What a wonderful bedroom, he said to Lucy, wide and light, with white bathroom adjoining. The soft carpets, the furniture mellowed by aromatic wax, the whisky and brandy decanters and the siphon of soda at the bed-head. He did not help himself to a drink, even out of bravado: the luxury was a little depressive, everything was so correct: and yet, at the Copleston's house, he had tried to make everything correct. What was the truth about 'atmosphere'? Was it but a projection from a man's own experience? Had Tolstoi lived in such an atmosphere? While Lucy had a bath he sat in an envelopingly soft armchair and felt mean at his implied criticism of Morland. But the truth was he saw Morland as a writer inferior to himself. Even so, what a dreadful thing it was, to repay kindness, generosity, and *service* to another by assuming that, because Morland's books were not really in the rare first-class, Morland had only done his duty to a superior writer, by paying tribute to Caesar. And yet, Morland was faithful to his conception of the rich upper-middle class. How else could Morland write about his relations except truthfully? But *had* he? Were those old uncles true portraits? Had they really been mean and stupid in their lives? Had his own grandfather, Thomas Turney, been like that? As for Evelyn Crouchend, was any man truly like that—unless he were sensitive to the point of neurosis, and ineffectual in love. Was that famous character but a whipping-boy for the author's wife, who looked to be neurotic, possibly the victim of impotent rage? So, to her, he had grown to be a monster; and Morland had built up a 'character' that was not really human.

Was it not Morland's implied criticism of his characters that was his defect as an artist? But what about himself? Was he not a black pot criticising a slightly-smoked kettle?

And yet—and yet—it was all a little too much a conformation to the highest standards of gentility. David Torrence must have felt this extremely, when invited to Morland's house for a meal. For when he had asked Morland at dinner if he had met Torrence Morland had replied, guardedly, "I thought his eyes seemed to be dead," while Mrs. Morland had added, "He was probably very tired."

In the morning, thanking Mr. and Mrs. Morland for 'such a jolly visit'—feeling that was how the younger generations of Harrovian Crouchend nephews would have spoken—they left for Paddington, three hours before the train was due to leave. The blue rug was put round Lucy's knees by the chauffeur, there was a restrained wave at the door, and away they were driven, feeling relief. When the chauffeur held out his battered ancient portmanteau, Phillip gave him a ten shilling note, wondering if it should have been a pound. Would the driver, as in a magazine story, pause 'to give an icy thank-you' to show what he thought of so paltry a sum? But the Harrods' service-chauffeur bowed pleasantly as he told a porter to take the luggage to the Cloak Room and leave it there.

"They were awfully kind, weren't they?"

"Yes."

"Did you enjoy it all?"

"Oh yes. Did you?"

"Yes. But I'm glad it's over. Aren't you?"

"In a way, yes."

At the bookstall he bought copies of all the morning papers, and with the bundle went to the buffet room. Every paper had a

story, some with the photograph taken before the ceremony in
the ante-room. There he was, with slightly open mouth, holding
one end of a piece of paper shaped like a cheque in one hand
while Morland held the other and they were shaking hands.

"Look at this in *The Graphic*. 'Heir to more than a thousand
acres held by the Maddison family since the fourteenth century
writes work of stupendous imagination says Thomas Morland,
O.M.' Whoever put that in? Nuncle will strafe me to hell for
that."

He opened *The Mirror*.

" 'Otters sport in the lake under Wayland Down, where trout
exceeding six pounds in weight are preserved by the youthful
winner of this year's Grasmere Memorial Prize for Literature'.
Strewth! Where the devil do they get it all from?"

He opened *The Telegram*.

"Beausire wrote this, I bet. 'Mr. Maddison's spiritual search
for his lost tame otter is akin to that of Tristan for Isolde. Lutra
was the pet of his young wife, *nee* Teresa Jane Lushington, who
died giving birth to her first-born, a boy called William, in
January 1925. Mr. Maddison is now married to Lucy Amelia
Copleston, a niece of Lady Kilmeston'. What will your people
say to that, Lucy?"

"Oh, I don't suppose they'll see it."

He opened *The Crusader*.

" 'One day a struggling author in a remote labourer's cottage,
yesterday his work was hailed by all fashionable and artistic
London. Mr. Thomas Morland, O.M., declares the prize novel
(£100 and a gold medal) to be work of unquestioned genius'.
Let's leave this place, people are beginning to stare at us."

They took a taxi to the publishers.

The trade department of Mashie & Co., Ltd.—a small room
with a counter—was filled with pale young men and girls. After
peering in Phillip closed the door quickly and went upstairs by the
side-entrance, and into the typist's annexe adjoining Mr. Driver's
room overlooking the western end of Covent Garden market.
The telephone bell was ringing behind the closed door; so, leaving
Lucy, he went up to the sales manager's office. It seemed to be
full of men; so he climbed one more flight of stairs to the production
room, where sat a thin young man who had sent him the galley
proofs, and later the page-proofs.

"Well," he said, "how do you feel now that you've broken all Mashies' records for sales in one day since we published *The Crucifix* many years ago? The office is in a state of complete chaos! We've had orders for three thousand copies by post this morning— an entire sackful of letters from the booksellers! And ever since we opened the office we've been besieged by messengers. It's due to the broadcast in the B.B.C. news last night, didn't you hear it? 'Hamlet' is in a fume, asking why you didn't let him know, so that he could have run off a large impression to meet the demand. Now he can't make up his mind whether or not to have plates made and sent to several printers, or to run off ten thousand copies from standing type. The trouble is that our printers haven't the machinery to cope with such an order under a fortnight, even by working overtime."

"I think I ought to see Mr. Driver."

"You won't find him too pleased that Coats is to have your next novel."

"I did my best to get him to take it."

"I think you'll find that 'Hamlet's' chief gripe is that you didn't let him know in time about the Grasmere."

"It wasn't my secret."

Mr. Driver looked as though he had suffered a financial loss from which his firm wouldn't recover.

"So you've already gone to Coats, as all the up and coming young writers seem to go. Well, I suppose one should not really expect—how can I put it—that the artistic temperament should be fettered in any way by the—the—obligations that we ordinary folk consider to be the thing."

Mr. Driver waved a pencil, and looked at an overflowing waste-paper basket. "I suppose all that remains is for me to congratulate you on having such a great success. I suppose they've told you upstairs that we're literally overwhelmed with orders which we are not in a position to fulfil for some time?"

"Yes."

"And Coats is to do your next book?"

"Yes, in the autumn, Mr. Driver."

"I suppose you knew about the award some time ago?"

"Yes. I was asked to keep it to myself. I did try to get you to pay me £50 for the novel, you know."

"Well, it's done now. And your novels aren't in the same class as your animal books. By the way, did you tell your agent, Norse?"

"Yes, in confidence, Mr. Driver."

"But not your publisher? But there, I must not reproach you. And if I may dare to offer you some advice, such as it is, I think you should not regard yourself as a novelist. You have often told me about some of your adventures in your past life, and most amusing they have been, too; but when I have read of the same incidents, romanticised a little no doubt, all the vitality you showed while telling me, all the humour, is absent from the printed page."

At this point the Sales Manager came into the room and said, with a face almost woeful, "Mr. Driver, Harrods have just telephoned, they want an extra five hundred copies, in addition to their order by post this morning."

Mr. Driver sighed, and dropped his pencil on the desk. "There, you *see*?" he said to Phillip.

Pa and Ernest were waiting outside Reading Station, sitting motionless in the Crossley tourer.

"Ha," said Pa.

"Have you seen the papers?" asked Phillip.

"No," said Ernest.

"Thank goodness."

They drove back mile after mile upon the winding grey road that rose to the uplands of the Great Plain, past beech hangers and wilderness tracts of thorn and rounded barrows of the ancient dead. It was summer weather, and in coppice and brake the nightingales were in full song. Now the course of his life was running full. 'Young landowner awarded Grasmere Prize for finest book of the year by any British writer under 41 years of age'. 'Literary prize awarded to book of undoubted genius', says Thomas Morland O.M. 'Shy young man unable to make a speech, yet writes a book unsurpassed for clarity and truth to Nature'. And all that from a compound of suffering and regret removed from the page—an almost total refraction of light rays through the prism of the mind.

He sat beside a Lucy enjoying the sight of familiar fields and coppices, Lucy beginning secretly to glow with imminent warm thoughts of Peter and the little one within her, who would play through sunlit hours with their big brother, dearest Billy, the more cherished in her heart because she was 'Mummy' to him. The faces of children were still smiling in her imagination as the motor descended to the valley and climbed to the last ridge, whence fell before them a prospect upon the plain of Colham, and the distant

blue line of the hills above the Chase. Now they were descending
the winding lane sunken through the wreckage of Rookhurst
Forest and its wild growth of sycamore, elder, thorn and bramble
among its rotted beech-stumps—a perfect sanctuary for the wild
birds she loved; but to the man beside her an extension of a memory
of timber-tracks long since tipped and splintered by the shell-
fire of Third Ypres.

For Lucy, a happy cluster of thatched cottages of the village
around the church tower, the fields faintly green after re-seeding
with permanent pasture mixtures; for Phillip, the grave of Willie
under the churchyard yews, Willie who had not compromised, but
given his life for the truth as he had seen it. Perhaps, when *The
Phoenix* was published in the late autumn, people would understand.

Skirr Farmhouse; two excited little boys; broad beaming face
of Mrs. Rigg, Pa and Ernest having a drink before tea (Ernest the
teetotaller always drank port because, he said, 'it didn't count').
Then they had gone, Pa wondering about his tomato plants
because the sky was dulling over, and their going left no feeling of
absence behind them, because there had been no feeling of warmth.

"The childer was both so good as gold, ma'm."

As for the master, all the village had heard about the money
of the prize he'd won. And zum was zaying it was wonnerful,
my dear zoul, vancy winning a hunner pounds for writin' of a book
about a water-hotter.

"Vancy it happening to Mr. Madd'zn, whoever would have
thought it, but there it be, up on the paper. But what be I about,
forgettin' the post. There be scores and scores o' letters comed, and
several telegrams for the maister."

He left them unopened, and walked down to the village, hoping
that no-one would speak of money. He met no-one, and went into
the churchyard, to sit beside the grave of his cousin; and returning,
said to Lucy, "Would you put in some plants for me, when you go
there next? What grows best on chalk?"

"Oh, pinks and carnations, and love-in-the-mist. And there's
cornflowers, of course. Shall I get some in Colham? The 'bus
goes in tomorrow."

"Would you? Leave the wild poppies, won't you? They're not
in bud yet, but will be soon."

Part Three

STRAWS IN THE WIND

Chapter 11

A GIRL FORLORN

Phillip was up early, to walk as usual through the meadows beside the brook to the Longpond. The rainbows were feeding on some underwater nymphs, or perhaps minnows. Did minnows ever leave the shallows? Anyway, the trout were not feeding on surface flies. Swirls arose, little humps of water spreading out like shallow craters. The fish were after shrimp or minnow, perhaps.

He felt suddenly happy about the Longpond. The black overhanging, water-logged boughs of the willows could be sawn off, new trees and bushes planted. Peering into a shallow clarified by the low sun behind him, he saw the delicate lines on the oval shells of several large fresh-water mussels, some nearly six inches long. A kingfisher flew over the surface above its vibrating chestnut-and-blue image.

It was six o'clock. The water reflected patches of blue in the white of passing clouds. Swallows were flying high, sometimes letting out ringing cries. The morning mists below in the combe were lifting with the sun. Above slowly drifting nimbus could be seen motionless scales of cirrus.

He went on to the beech hanger, and looked down upon the vale. Far away a layer of smoke showed that kitchen fires had been lit. It was time to return and examine the letters and telegrams, most of which had been opened and glanced at the previous evening, while Lucy had gone to find out how Uncle John was. On her return she told him that they were invited to supper the following evening.

"He isn't very well, but he hopes to be better when we go there tomorrow. I knew you would like to see him, so I accepted. He sent his congratulations, and asked you to forgive him for not writing a letter."

About forty more letters were lying on the table. Most of them were from strangers, a few from old acquaintances. He flung them, read and unread, into the bushel measure he used for waste-paper, then swallowed his breakfast. Meanwhile Billy picked out the letters and arranged them in a linear pattern on the parlour floor, pretending to be the postman delivering one letter to each cottage. He gathered them up and went to the night nursery when Peter crawled over and started to post them in the bushel measure.

Phillip carried Peter up the stairs and divided the envelopes between those addressed by hand, which he gave to Peter, and those which were typed, to Billy.

"We must see what's inside them, so come down and I'll open them on the parlour floor."

Afterwards each boy had his packet to play with, while Phillip scanned the letters. One was from Anders Norse telling him that the galleys of *The Phoenix* would be sent to him direct from the printers at Plymouth, as Coats wanted to get the novel out in the early autumn. Anders went on to say that he had placed the short stories he had by him, seven in all, at forty guineas each. The English editors had agreed to hold them until American publication was arranged. He was confident of doing this through his New York agent, who was asking a thousand dollars a story.

Phillip calculated, and said to Lucy, "There's a possible thousand pounds from America, and a definite three hundred pounds from English magazines."

In the post next morning was a score of letters, one from his agent.

Further to my letter of yesterday I have just been on the telephone to Coats and they are prepared to draw up another contract for your next nature book, which is not covered by the options on their agreement with you for the novels. They offer you one thousand pounds now (£1,000) against a book on the life of a trout, half to be paid on signing the agreement and the remainder on day of publication. They are prepared to wait until you feel you are able to write the book. There is no hurry for a year, perhaps two years or even longer, as they don't want to rush you.

I don't know what you feel about journalism, but the *Sunday Crusader*, which I think you know is edited by Arnold Cressingham Brexell, offer fifty guineas each for a series of twelve articles, leaving the subject to you. Each article will be 750 words, more or less, but that is to be the average length. The payment will include all British serial rights, all other rights being reserved by the author. It occurs to me that you may like to consider these articles as a basis of a book about a trout, and

river life generally, which Coats wants to publish for you. Water seems
to bring you luck!

Perhaps you will think about these offers and let me know. There
is no immediate hurry. I saw you at the Aeolian Hall, but as you were
busy with others, I kept out of your way; but you know, I think, how
I have believed in your work from the early days. May I add my congratulations now, if only to affirm, once again, that I remain,

Ever yours,
Anders.

P.S. I have just heard that Coats has accepted the volume of short
country stories you looked at in my office recently, by A. B. Cabton.
Edward Cornelian wants Cabton to gain more experience, at first-
hand, of the countryside; as I think you know, Cabton has never left
London. He is going to write to you proposing that Cabton comes to
work on your farm, where, in his words, 'all will be grist to his mill'.
If you don't want him it doesn't matter, he says; Cabton will find himself a lodging somewhere. It's the starting point that is required. I
hope this won't put you out, but it will anyway give him a start, and
I can't think of anyone more suitable to whom to entrust a young man
of genius.

"Shall we invite Cabton?"

"Why not? It will be nice for you to have someone to talk to,
and go for walks with."

He opened more letters. After glancing at half a dozen, he
pushed the remainder aside.

"Fancy *me* having begging letters. Someone with forty-two cats
wants me to help pay for their food."

"Let me fry you some more bacon. Yours has gone cold."

"How ironic it all is. The Grasmere Memorial will make
Nuncle feel that I have betrayed him. No word from him as yet."

She flushed, and said, "I honestly don't see why he should
object to your writing in your spare time. After all, a farmer
shouldn't *have* to work all the time as a labourer."

"I quite enjoy working with my body. The trouble is, I can't write
unless I remain broody. And then I get irritable and over-sharp."

"Well, you deserve a rest now. Let Ned carry on with the farm
work. You have a holiday, now all the fuss is over."

"What about yourself?"

"Oh, I get along quite happily." She was big with a child due
in September.

He took the letters upstairs to his room, to reply first to Edward

Cornelian saying that he'd be pleased to put up Cabton, and show him the country. If Cabton liked the district, he would be able to get a room out. 'Or he can use our tent and camp beside the brook, while having his meals with us, as he prefers'.

By 7 p.m. all the letters were answered, except that from the woman with forty-two cats, who said that they were living in her house, like the otter she had read about who had lived happily with his dogs, cats, and birds; unless she could get money at once to provide food for them all, the order of the Court to have them destroyed would be enforced. Also her landlord had threatened to turn her out, as her rent money had been spent on the cats' food. Please would he send her £30 at once, and also advise her what to do?

Phillip made several attempts to reply, but as each degenerated into farce he threw it in the bushel measure, feeling guilty.

They had supper with Uncle John. Phillip noticed how thin he was getting. The old fellow complained of finding it hard to breathe, but did not speak of himself beyond saying that he had found the nursing home a bore. "Now tell me, Phillip, have you heard from Hilary?"

"No, Uncle John."

"Perhaps your success will make him reconsider his opinion of your abilities. Have you any ideas for future books?"

"I've a novel coming out in the autumn. That ends the tetralogy."

"What becomes of Donkin?"

"He comes to the end of his self-tethering."

Nothing more was said about the novel.

"I'm asked to write about a trout's life. But I know nothing about fish."

"Well, this is the country for trout, Phillip."

"Yes—it's all here, Uncle John."

The next morning, and the next, he walked beside the brook to the Longpond. Yes, it was the place for the story of a trout. He owed it to his work to 'be idle', to sit about and watch. Reaching the little wooden landing-stage, he saw that the row-boat from the barn was sunken, but secured by a rope to one of the posts which supported the fifteen-inch-wide elm plank. Obviously the boat required to be swelled, to stop it leaking.

As he lay on one elbow, feeling happy and free, he noticed that the water appeared to be sliding about. Fish were on the move.

A back-fin wavered above the surface, followed by the curled edge of a tail. As he stared he saw arising from the water the slow pale-green flutter of a newly hatched mayfly.

Kneeling on the bank and peering over the reeds he watched a grey, shrimp-like object crawling up a stem. It was about an inch and a half long. Then he saw others moving up the reeds. They remained still a few inches above the water, masked nymphs fixed as though glazed: but only for a moment: the celluloid-like sheaths split, and heads with bulbous eyes came forth, the bodies bent. He moved nearer, resting himself on his arms in water to the elbows, to watch one growing, as tremblingly it unfolded gauzy wings.

A swallow dived beyond the fringe of reeds, to dip its breast in the water and then, sweeping up, snapped a mayfly, and then it flew in a direct line to the farm premises down the valley. Was it going to call its mate? Many mayflies were now drifting all over the water, little spheres of pale-green light making scarcely any progress as they moved in a daze of a new and uncertain existence. Insect after insect rose slowly, each in a whirl of new wings, some to reach the willows and cling to leaf or twig. Their eyes were now large and dark, the three whisks from the end of the abdomen were upheld in anticipation of the climax of life, of love high in the air —later a drifting down the sky to drop the egg-burden on the mirror'd water—finally to fall spent into that which had given it life.

He lay on the bank, hands behind head, in a dream of sunshine until, hearing noon being tolled from the village clock—fitted into one face of the tower for a memorial to the dead in the war—he wandered home, leaving the Longpond to all kinds of small birds gathered to the feast.

"Billy and I were just going to look for you," said Lucy. "We thought you must have gone up to the downs. Two telegrams came with the post, one from Uncle Hilary, the other from that girl who wanted to interview you. I've left them on the table."

AM HAVING HOLIDAY AT SHAKESBURY STOP MAY I CALL ON YOU INTERVIEW PLEASE ANCROFT TELEPHONE SHAKESBURY 29

"Oh yes, the one I met with Piers in London. Shall we ask her over?"

Lucy telephoned, and left a message for Miss Ancroft to come over whenever she wanted to: and then dictated Phillip's reply to Uncle Hilary's telegram:

MADDISON POST RESTANTE HAVERFORDWEST
MAYFLY UP LONGPOND

After lunch, Lucy took the little boys to see Uncle John, leaving Phillip to reply to letters in his room, and feeling that he was wasting the light of the sun now beyond Whitesheet Hill in the distance. Remotely he was aware of an unsilenced engine muttering in the lane below, and then there arose a sequence of raucous noises on a klaxon horn. Was this some drunken cattle-dealer come to the wrong farm? He listened. There was an interval before the klaxon began its grating again. This time it seemed to have a rough rhythm of dots and dashes, like a contact observation biplane circling over infantry.

—— —.—— —— .— —.. ... ——— —.

There was a pause, and it began again. Phillip read the Morse Code.

—— —.—— —— .— —.. ... ——— —.

M Y   M A D   S O N

There was only one man who would announce himself like that —Bill Kidd. Phillip ran to the window. And there he was, extravagant moustaches and all, at the wheel of an open car, leather flying helmet on head, lifting a hand in salute. Beside him sat Archie Plugge.

"I'll come down."

Bill Kidd gave him the crushing hand-squeeze of the strongman of fiction, followed by a brushing up of his Kaiser moustache. After the greeting, Phillip had to think of what to say.

"This is an unusual type of 'bus, Bill."

"You're telling me, my Mad Son! Belonged to a bloke in the R.N.A.S. at Harwich during the war, who shot down a Zeppelin over the North Sea, after taking off into the wind at forty knots from one of Tyrwhitt's destroyers."

"What make is it?"

"I'll give you three guesses."

He went to the front of a Métallurgique radiator and gave the handle a jerk. At once there was a massive rumbling from four brass-bound Mercédès exhaust pipes serpentining through one side of the bonnet held down by a thick leather strap. On the off-side was painted a Union Jack; on the near-side the name in small red letters, *Otazelle*.

"French make?"

"Sneeze, old boy, your brain's dusty. Take a look at the front springs."

Phillip had to kneel, and peer under, because the space below the radiator was covered by a curved length of aluminium sheeting on which the registered number BK 1 was painted in white. He could see only that the front spring was transverse, and damped down on either side by André shock absorbers.

"What is it?"

"Take a squint at the body."

The seats of red russian leather were thickly padded, giving an impression of pre-war opulence.

"I don't know. It looks like one of those 'buses entered for the Gordon Bennett race from Madrid to Berlin in nineteen-nought-six."

"Getting warmer. The body belonged to a Richard-Brasier."

Bill Kidd opened the brass hand-throttle below the heavy mahogany steering-wheel; the exhaust thundered. He switched on a moveable lamp like a small searchlight beside the driver's seat, moved it about, until suddenly the beam was in Phillip's eyes.

"Sorry, old boy. But you see the idea? I had it put on for hunting rabbits at night. If you want yours kept down, say the word and Bill Kidd's on."

Avoiding the indirect invitation, Phillip pretended interest in the spot-light. "I suppose you run it off a dynamo?"

"Runs off the coil, with the headlights. Doesn't that tell you something? Look, I'll show you."

He undid the strap across the bonnet and there within cavernous space was the small rough block of a T-model Ford engine.

"Fools everyone," remarked Bill Kidd with satisfaction. "I could dine every night at the Piccadilly grill on the bets I've won about the horse-power of the old 'bus."

In the back of the car were two rods, a net, and a wicker creel holding reels, lines, and a box of flies. Had they come with the intention of staying the week-end? The trouble was that Nuncle was coming, too.

"I suppose you chaps are on your way to see Piers?"

"Well——" said Archie Plugge. "As a matter of fact, I've seen nothing of Piers since he resigned from Savoy Hill. One hears rumours, of course——"

"Who's this 'Piers'?" demanded Bill Kidd, as they went into the house.

"Oh, a neighbour who lives down the valley. Do come in. I'm sorry my wife is away just now." He went to the sideboard. Fortunately Nuncle's decanter of malt whisky was nearly full.

"Say when, Bill."

"Go on. What's his father's name?"

"Sir Roland Tofield. Piers is the heir to a baronetcy," said Plugge.

The level rose to the second half-inch, then to the third, when Phillip stopped pouring. "I'm afraid there's no soda."

"I chase it with water, old boy. Separate glass."

Bill Kidd threw half his whisky between his teeth, swilled it round his mouth before swallowing, then tossed back a splash of water.

"Old White Russian practice," he explained. "Kills the germs of cholera."

He seated himself in Nuncle's chair. "Now, my Mad Son, what about those six-pounder rainbows I've been reading about? Oh yes, I know all about reporters spinning a yarn, but let me tell you this. No rainbow can grow to that weight even in a chalk stream, let alone in land-locked water! And I'll tell you for why!" He admonished with a finger, "Rainbows, you may care to know, are migratory. They die if they can't get down to the sea to spawn. And a six-pound fish would be at least four years old, more likely five."

"Well, these rainbows *are* well over two feet long, and deep——"

"Then they're not rainbows. They're brownies. I was brought up on the Test. You know dam' all about fish if you talk about six-pound rainbows in England, my lad."

Plugge's face had a resigned expression. Kidd had talked fish all the way from London: he had borne with his boasting, awaiting the moment of arrival at their destination, when he and Phillip

could leave him to fish alone, and then perhaps they could go to
a pub, or call on some of Phillip's friends.

"Excuse me, sir, but there be a young leddy at the door, asking
for 'ee," said Mrs. Rigg, coming in from the kitchen.

A new edition of the girl he had known in London stood in the
porch. She was dressed in a tweed coat and skirt, and wore a
small hat of the same material, on which was the foot of a grouse
set in a silver pin. With a feeling of satisfaction that the two men
should see the young and pretty girl who had come to visit him,
Phillip led the way into the parlour.

"You know Archie Plugge, don't you? This is Major Kidd—
Miss Ancroft. Major Kidd comes straight out of *The Compleat
Angler*. What do you know about rainbow trout, Miss Ancroft?"

"Nothing, I'm afraid."

Bill Kidd, having inhaled smoke from his gasper, leaned forward. "Miss Ancroft, your education is about to begin. The
rainbow comes from California. Got that? There are two main
species of trout in the States where, incidentally, after I left the
Black and Tans, I spent some time on secret government work——"
His voice tailed off. He pointed at Phillip, who was laughing. In
a rasping voice he continued, "Now look here, my lad! I hear
that you've been casting some doubts on my having been with
the Black and Tans? In case you don't know, I was withdrawn
after a dead body had been substituted for my own, in order to
go on a mission to the United States." His voice assumed a drawl.
"All very hush-hush, old boy. As it happened, I spent quite a time
on the Coast—California, you know—and my host, the Earl of
Clyde—Ambassador and all that—showed me some sport. So I
know my stuff." He turned to Plugge. "As I told you on the way
down, *Salvenis* is the brook trout, the red belly. *Salmo*, the second
species, includes both rainbows and cutthroats. The rainbows,
Salmo gairdneri, are subdivided into various *genii*, such as the Kern
River whoppers, the Kamloops, the Golden Trout and the Steelhead. The steelhead is migratory, which means it goes to sea and
returns to spawn in fresh water."

He turned to Felicity Ancroft, "Now listen to me, my maid!
The steelhead and the rainbow are one and the same, *Salmo
gairdneri*. When the rainbow returns as the steelhead it has a pink
line on its flanks under its silver scales, which proves that it's
really *iridens*."

Plugge said, "Then it's a salmon-trout?"

Bill Kidd dismissed Plugge with a wave of a yellow-fingered hand. 'Salmon-trout' is a cook's word, a kitchen expression, a restaurant word. Don't let me hear you using it again. You're as bad as the Southerners in the United States—to hell with them. Those blokes below the Mason-Dixie line fancy themselves so much as soldiers that they are all born colonels. And what's more, they lump catfish, croakers and weakfish together as trout."

"May I help myself?" whispered Plugge, eyeing the decanter.

"Do, please——"

Phillip wondered what Nuncle would say when he found his special bottle empty when he arrived, tired, from Wales.

"It's a pretty thin malt whisky, this, Archie. Let's get a bottle of Haig——"

"You need reinforcements, my Mad Son? Then hold the line while I'm gone! No retirement to the Peckham Switch this time, old boy. You know you were wrong to go that time—however, let that go—I'll be back." He climbed out of the window, making a direct line to his car.

Plugge laughed deprecatingly. "I feel that we've rather landed ourselves on you." He turned benevolent owl-eyes on Phillip for a moment before continuing, "You know, one never knows quite how to take Bill Kidd." Peering round to assure himself that they were alone he went on, "On the way down he asked me if I was 'an old Wyck'. I didn't know what 'an old Wyck' was, and when I told him so he said he was at Winchester, leaving at the age of seventeen to go to Sandhurst. Then he kept referring to his uncle as 'Tiny Tinribs'. Does such a person exist?"

"All life is based on imagination, Archie."

Phillip was wary of saying much before the interviewer.

The hollow roar of *Otazelle* returned down the lane. Bill Kidd, climbing in by the window, announced that all the pubs were shut.

"Perhaps I can buy a bottle of this malt whisky, when they open in Colham, Bill. It really belongs to my uncle."

"I hear he's Sir Hilary Maddison? What's he, a bart?"

"No, a Knight of the British Empire."

"A profiteer, in other words. Sorry, I shouldn't have said that." He got up and salaam'd.

Soon the parlour was filled with tobacco smoke, and Bill Kidd holding forth on the glories of a dry-fly purist.

Eventually Plugge asked mildly, "Why exactly must a fly be dry? Is it anything to do with Prohibition?"

Bill Kidd wagged a wavering finger, "Now no funny stuff from you, my lad! A dry fly floats, if you want to know."

"But fish are sometimes caught on a wet fly, aren't they?" asked Phillip.

"Did Izaak Walton use a dry fly?" asked the girl.

Bill Kidd's reaction to this enquiry was unexpected. Swallowing his whisky rapidly he said, "Don't talk to me, my maid, about that faker! Izaak Walton didn't know what he was writing about. He pinched all his facts, and got some of them wrong, what's more, from an earlier book by a bloke called Franck. He dressed up his plagiarised piffle with classical tripe calling himself 'Piscator'. 'Piscator' my foot. Izaak Walton was so damned ignorant a hack that he had to pinch poems from John Donne to pad out his book." The finger waggled again. "I know what I'm talking about, mind. I was born and bred on the Test."

"What is the difference between a dry-fly purist and a wet-fly purist?" asked Plugge.

"You ignorant Savoy Hill wallah, there's no such thing as 'a wet-fly purist'! Look here, I'll begin at the beginning. A trout faces upstream in order (a) to breathe, (b) to watch for food coming down. The water stream to a trout is the same thing as the food stream. Got that? Well, in certain atmospheric conditions there occurs a hatch, or hatches, of fly from the surface of the stream. They swim up as nymphs to hatch into flies from the said surface, while the trout take position, some in echelon, others in line of companies, to await the food stream passing them. You follow me? If you see trout 'tailing', then they're taking nymphs below the surface. You see perhaps the tip of their tails only, as they make a bulging rise. Now take it from me, no dry-fly fisherman would do more than look at such a rise. He bides his time, standing well back from the bank, waiting for the main hatch, when many nymphs will have space and time to split their skins before flying up. A good trout doesn't waste energy tailing when he can just suck 'em in, you know."

"Suck what in?" asked Plugge.

"Fishermen's stories," suggested Phillip.

"The subimagos, you ignorant bastard, otherwise nymphs hatching into flies," replied Kidd. "They rest on the water, floating down while struggling to get their wings out of the pellicles, and then *bok*"—he made a sucking noise with his lips—"Trutta trutta has sucked one down, and in doing so leaves a wide ring on the surface. *That's* the time to fish! You've got to find out what's hatching, of course, Miss Ancroft—whether Olive Dun, Blue-winged Olive, Pale Watery, or even Fisherman's Curse, which fish seem to prefer to all other flies. Smut, in other words. You may as well pack up when the smut is up. After the smut has coupled you get then what we call the Knotted Midge. Fishing with the Knotted Midge is fishing—pure fishing—with a hook no larger than a match-head." He waggled a finger at Plugge. "You bring to the net a four-pounder on a Knotted Midge, on a 4-X tapered gut cast with a breaking strain of ten ounces dead-weight, and you're a fisherman, my lad!"

Phillip began to imagine the life of a trout in the crystal flow of a chalk stream.

"That's a very vivid picture you give us, Bill. How about dapping with a live mayfly, as they do in Ireland?"

"Why not shoot the poor bloody fish and have done with it?"

"Have you ever used a Wickham's Fancy?"

"That's an old-fashioned fly."

"In a sense, then, it's an old Wick?"

Bill Kidd stood up. Pointing at Phillip he cried, "Now look here, my lad, you're asking for it. One more word from you, and I'll snout you! Now let me tell you something. Never forget for one moment, my Mad Son, that you were the bastard who ordered, without my knowledge, all my boys to show their backsides to the Boche on the Wytschaete ridge on April the twelfth, nineteen eighteen, and thereby—now listen to me!—you left Bill Kidd in the Staenyzer Kabaret to face the whole Hun attack alone, after you'd softened up my boys. You put the wind up the whole battalion with your defeatist, pacifist, pale pink talk before we went into the line! *You* may have forgotten all about it, but Bill Kidd hasn't, not by a long chalk. You won't always get away with your Bolshie talk, and it's Bill Kidd who's telling you. Take a look at this, old boy."

He took out a pocket book and threw two photographs on the table. Then, saying "I need some fresh air," he climbed out of the window.

"He's escaping back to his native tree-tops," said Phillip. "Whisky always makes him frisky."

One of the photographs was of Bill Kidd in fur hat and coat standing beside a row of hanged men; the other, tinted, revealed him in blues with a row of ribands across his left breast.

"Do you think they're stills for a film?" asked Archie Plugge,

peering over Phillip's shoulder. "Perhaps he *is* a movie actor!
I rather fancy your remark about 'the Old Wick' was *touché*, don't
you think?"

"I shouldn't have made it."

Plugge examined the nails of his left hand before asking, "What
exactly did he mean about your pacifist talk to *his* men?"

"Oh, as acting second-in-command of the battalion, he was
supposed to look after training. There wasn't any time for training,
anyway—we were a mixed mob of young soldiers—less than a
hundred strong when we went north from the disbanded Fifth
Army, to rest and refit after the March retreat. When we joined
Plumer's Second Army in Flanders we got about five hundred
eighteen-year-olds straight from home. They were very frightened,
so I talked to them in the huts, telling them that we were all in it
together, and all equally apprehensive. So was the enemy, I said:
but it wasn't so bad in battle as it was before a battle. The Germans
had already mounted a second push in Flanders, and we all knew
it was coming. Just before the attack we were ordered to withdraw from the Wytschaete Ridge to conform with the line on our
right, after the Germans had broken through at Armentières.
We were to occupy the Peckham Switch, which ran down the
slopes of the Wytschaete–Messines ridge. Kidd refused to come
back, as I said, and stayed well forward in a pill-box, the Staenyzer
Kabaret, half-drunk. I went back to report to my Brigadier,
'Spectre' West, and while we were talking outside his dug-out a
gas-shell smashed his leg, and later he died of gas gangrene."

"Is it true what Kidd told me, that he got the Military Cross?"

"Yes. He was captured on the twenty-first of March, but escaped
and came back and did very well during the retreat to Albert. So
much so, that the Kaiser praised the way the division fought, to
some of the prisoners at Courtrai."

"Then what Bill Kidd told me in the Game Pie was true?"

"More or less. Felicity, I can't think why my wife hasn't come
back. Let me show you the geography of the place."

He returned to Plugge. "I'm awfully sorry, Archie, but with
one uncle ill in bed, and another coming to stay, I'm afraid we
won't be able to put you up. D'you know the Rising Sun in
Colham?"

"I've been there with Piers. 'Bosun' Tinker, ha ha——"

"Do you mind staying there as my guest? They're not on the
telephone, or I'd ring him up."

"Oh, I say, really—you must let me—— No? Well, it's most awfully good of you."

Felicity joined them in the garden. "I feel that you must have rather a lot to do just now, so shall I come back another day?"

"No, don't go. Just let me get these two base-wallahs settled——"

When the two men had driven away Phillip and Felicity sat on the lawn, which had been resown that year. There were many weed plants among the grass—plantain, daisy, dandelion. He began to feel frustration. The mowing machine needed sharpening. The first of the nature articles for the *Sunday Crusader* must be written. Nuncle was probably on his way. Where could he get a bottle of malt whisky? They walked to a cast-iron seat from which the Queen Victoria-Jubilee paint had almost wholly scaled.

"You won't include anything you heard indoors in your interview, will you?"

"Of course not. In any case I'll send you what I've written before I show it to anyone else. May I say that it really would be a pleasure to help you deal with all those letters I saw in the wooden holder."

"Oh, that's a bushel measure——"

He was a little discomposed by a feeling that he was being drawn to her. He knew that she felt this also when she said, "I thought your wife, when I saw her in the Aeolian Hall, was so beautiful. She had such a serene look."

"Yes, she is always composed, I've never been able to attain that condition, unfortunately."

"But you were happy when you lived at Malandine, surely?"

He said stiffly, "Yes I was so happy that I didn't do any writing in my last year there."

"But the year's rest ultimately produced the beauty in *The Water Wanderer*—— Oh, I shouldn't have said that."

"Why not? The book was an attempt, which failed, at resurrection."

"Oh no, not failed——"

The air was uplifting, butterflies and bees were on the garden flowers. The heat of the sun had cast the distant hills of Cranborne Chase in a warm blue leaden mould at the bottom of the sky. He looked at her; she was twisting a handkerchief in her hands.

"Couldn't you be serene again?" she said, her face pale.

"I really have a horribly critical mind. D'you hear that squeak-king noise? It's my wife coming with the baby's push-cart down the lane. I've asked for it to be oiled several times. I should lubricate the axles myself, of course. Instead, I prefer to criticise Lucy. I'm what the psychologists call, in condemnation, a perfectionist. My uncle is a perfectionist, too. That's why we don't get on together. A perfectionist is a neurotic."

Lucy appeared at the gate. She smiled and waved. They went to meet her.

"This is Felicity, Lucy."

"How nice of you to come. I'm so sorry I was out when you arrived. I'll get tea right away. I expect you're both hungry."

Leaving Felicity with Billy, who immediately claimed her, he went into the kitchen. "She's offered to help me with the letters. What do you think?" He added, avoiding the impulse of his real motive, "What will Nuncle say?"

"Oh, don't let that worry you. There'll be a bedroom if she wants to stay here."

"I'll insist on paying her, of course."

"Well then, I'll ask her to stay. Cabton will be here then, and it will be jolly with all four of us together. We won't bother Uncle Hilary, he'll be fishing most of the time."

Plugge had no intention of being landed with Bill Kidd for the week-end if he could help it. The problem was, where else could he spend the week-end? If the worst came to the worst, he could always get a bed at the Tofields', pretending surprise that Piers was not home: but the prospect of a teetotal week-end with two old people was too much. Better to go back to Town. There was always Zorinda, the Coal Hole whore.

"I'm afraid I may have to see someone about a proposed broadcast," he said to Bill Kidd as they approached the Rising Sun. "I do hope you will have some good sport during the week-end."

"Leave it to me, old boy. Wherever there's fish, I'll get them."

The landlord seemed to have been fixed in the same place ever since Plugge had last seen him.

"We are Mr. Maddison's guests," explained Plugge. "What will you drink, landlord? And you, Bill?"

When the glasses were empty, Mrs. Tinker took Bill Kidd to see his room. As soon as they had gone upstairs Plugge said, "Do you know if there are any local trains to Salisbury tonight?" He had remembered a Coal Hole acquaintance who had asked him to try to get him a job at Savoy Hill, and given him his card. Plugge carried a variety of such cards in his note-case.

There was a train leaving the station in twenty minutes. Asking the landlord to make his apologies to Major Kidd, Plugge picked up his attaché case, and left.

"Gone, has he?" said Bill Kidd, returning to the bar. "Still, at Eton he was a dry bob, so what can you expect? Have you seen my Mad Son lately? He's got some of the best fish in the county and never goes near the water."

"Your mad son, did you say?" enquired Mr. Tinker, looking subdued.

"That's right. We often talk about you as 'Bosun'. We served in the same regiment. Phillip did well, then goes and blots his copy-book after the peace. Think he'll make a go at farming? What are you having, 'Bosun'?"

"Thank you, sir, I'll take a drop of rum in me beer."

"There you go drinkin' again, you old toad, you!" cried Mrs. Tinker, appearing from behind a frowsy curtain. "Booze, booze, booze, that's all you do!"

"Now now, naughty naughty," said Bill Kidd. "Let there be peace between 'ee, midears."

Sitting in Phillip's study, Felicity was taking shorthand notes from dictation. It was difficult to keep calm: she kept telling herself that it was Phillip Maddison beside whom she was sitting, his soft voice sometimes hesitating, the mouth so gentle; the eyes, so deeply blue, sometimes giving her a sudden, half-timid, half-merry glance.

When she was left alone at his desk with the typewriter, she had to control the trembling of her hands with their bitten nails. Had he noticed them? She must stop biting them from that moment. She was beginning to sweat under the arms. If only she dare ask if she might have a cold bath, and then, as though accidentally, drop her blouse into the water. She typed on, after breathing deeply to feel calm again. She must be efficient in every way: she felt that her future—a new future at last—depended on how the work was done.

Felicity Ancroft barely remembered her father. He had left home when she was three years of age; later, her mother had told her that he had been killed in the war. As a fact Mr. Ancroft was still alive, with a family of natural children. His legal wife, on religious grounds, had refused to divorce him. Mrs. Ancroft herself had an admirer, but retaining her principles, had not accepted his advances lest, she used to say, 'the bright candle flame become smoky'. This admirer, 'Fitz', had diverted his attentions to the daughter, whom he had seduced at the age of fourteen, during one of the mother's absences from home. At the time Felicity had seen nothing wrong in this; to her mind 'Fitz', who from an early age had dandled her on his lap, was like 'Daddy Longlegs' in the play. The situation had remained during the past four years; but now the young girl's illusion, or fantasy of love, was transferred to Phillip.

Felicity had been typing for an hour when Lucy appeared at the open door.

"Can you spare a moment to say goodnight to Billy and Peter? They've had their baths, and are ready for bed."

The children came into the room. She knelt on the carpet, and kissed each boy in turn on the top of the head.

"Are you staying in our house?" asked Billy.

"Only for a little while longer, Billy. Then I must go back to Shakesbury."

Lucy said, "Oh, but won't you stay to supper? Phillip is expecting you."

"Oh thank you, Mrs. Maddison."

"Have you everything you want?"

"Oh yes, thank you!" She had to control her voice. "I wonder if I might have a bath when I've done my letters?"

"Yes, do. Let me know if I can lend you anything."

Felicity's face shone as she helped Lucy with the supper.

Phillip was sitting beside the wooden slip half-way along the southern shore of the Longpond, watching fish. A heron was watching him in a willow half way to the spring-head. The bird was well out of gunshot. Its thoughts were on the strings of eggs forming within the lower ribs of fish. It was an old bird, and knew when the eggs would be ripe; it had taken many a slender hen-fish trying to get up the side of the spillway of the weir in early autumn. Its main enemy was man, particularly the keeper with a gun; its lesser enemies, just before the spawning season, were carrion crows. They, too, liked the egg-strings of hen fish, and the milt sacs of cock fish.

Phillip imagined himself dictating the first draft of the trout book
to Felicity; the image in his mind was the outline of breasts under
her white silk blouse, the long neck, and fair hair growing, like
Barley's, in two waves up from the straight forehead.

His mind wandered, with a sense of irritation, to Plugge and
Kidd. How were they getting on at the Rising Sun? He regretted
that he had got rid of them rather abruptly; he ought to go over
and pay them a visit. He would go there after taking Felicity to her
hotel, and returning by way of Colham, buy a bottle of malt
whisky. He must get a motorcar, too. Perhaps he could drive the
combination to London and sell it there in part exchange.

After supper he drove her to Shakesbury, and having refused
the offer of a drink, said good-night after telling her that she was
welcome to come over the next day if she cared to.

"I enjoy being with your family tremendously. It's such fun
with the children."

"Shall I fetch you?"

"Please don't put yourself out for me. I love walking; and
there's always the 'bus."

"As you wish," he said quietly, before driving home to the
farm, wondering whether the slightly heavy feeling was—no, no,
he must never fall in love again. Lucy was sitting on the sofa. He
sat in the armchair, but could not rest. After awhile he got up,
and telling her that he would walk over the downs to Colham, set
out with dog and stick, to tire himself out.

In the bar of the Rising Sun the locals were enjoying themselves.
The stranger was, like many another on holiday from London,
'holding the cockpit', with free drinks all round. He waggled his
finger at 'Bosun' Tinker leaning on the bar, where his elbows had
made two shiny patches. "You're a friend of the dry-fly purist,
'Bosun', you old poacher, you get rid of the cannibals that won't
rise to a fly with your night-lines."

"Whippin' water," ejaculated the landlord, belching loudly.
"I've no time for they as whips water." He ejaculated skilfully
into the spittoon on the lime-ash floor.

"Don't listen to 'Bosun'", warned the voice of Mrs. Tinker
from the kitchen. "He's been at his capers all day long. Drink,
drink, drink, 'tes all he'm fit for."

"Quite right, midear!" Bill Kidd called out. Then to the
landlord, "My Uncle, 'Tiny Tinribs', has the best beat on the

Stour. I've told him that if he had any sense he'd have all fish over five pounds out of the water. Still got your night-lines, 'Bosun'?"

"Your uncle?"

"That's right. General Ironside, usually known as 'Tiny Tinribs'."

This produced another cackle of laughter among the beer drinkers.

"Fact, 'Bosun'."

"Whippin' water," remarked the landlord, taking a pull at his beer and rum.

"Don't take any notice of 'Bosun'," repeated Mrs. Tinker. "Would a fry do for your supper, sir? Mr. Phillip and Mr. Piers usually likes a fry when they comes yurr. I've got some green bacon, and a bit of pig's liver, and eggs."

"Splendid, midear. My favourite shackles. You an old soldier, Tinker?"

"'Im?" jeered Mrs. Tinker. "The nearest 'e got to the Army was sellin' fish to the sergeants' cook-'ouse when the Australians was yurr in the war. Yes, you, you old toad!" raising her arm for an imaginary back-hander at her husband continuing to grin good-humouredly at her.

"I be a Navy man, I knows nothin' about the Army."

"You know it be true! You took one of me best stackings for to put in that slaked lime you stole from they builders, and poisoned all they fish in the Longpond!"

Mr. Tinker's reply was to turn round, reach for the rum bottle, and pour another half-quartern into his beer. After taking a swig he said in a voice so low that it appeared as a plaintive murmur, "I'll tell 'ee what, midear, you be like this yurr noo factory cider, all gas."

"Now, now, 'Bosun'," said Bill Kidd in a warning voice. "Naughty—naughty. *Honneur aux dames*, shipshape and Navy fashion. I'll have another whisky, make it a half quartern. I never drink 'drops', which should be called 'drips'. And fill up all glasses."

The face of Mrs. Tinker reappeared beside the curtain. "'Bosun' did use poison, you know, major."

Mr. Tinker roared, "I nivver used poison, I tell 'ee! 'Twas burnt lime, and that be chalk, ban't it? And ban't the river full of chalk a'ready? So what's the difference?"

" 'Twas chloride, you know it was. You stole it from the camp, you told me you did. You spoiled one of me best stackings, you did. And you knew very well that in the war none was to be bought into market." The face gave way to the noise of frying.

"You can forget your lime, your stew-fed rainbows, your pitch-forks, gaffs, and carving knives," said Bill Kidd, waggling a finger at Mr. Tinker. "Leaning over the old bank and then saying you were *tickling* trout—yes, with a kitchen fork tied to a lump of wood! You can't tell Bill Kidd anything about poaching. Nor about dry-fly fishin'."

Holding up his wrist Bill Kidd made as if to throw a fly, crouching with elongated head sunk between shoulders, his dark eyes moving rapidly in the sallow face as he worked an imaginary split-cane rod.

"Watch this, midear! See that rise over there? He's sucking in olive duns just below the alder branch. I'll put a curl in the end of the cast. Don't move!" He leaned forward tensely. "Watch the fly riding down." He made a sucking noise with his lips. "He's taken it." With a jerk of the wrist Bill Kidd drove the barb into one bony corner of the trout's jaws. "Number fourteen hook, sneck-bend, in the yellow bone of the corner of the jaw, penetrating one-sixteenth of an inch. It's enough to hold him. Gently does it. Let him tire himself out, but 'ware that weed-bed below. Keep his head upstream—after a couple of minutes he's ours—now watch this, 'Bosun'—don't lift your rod point too far—gently, gently, does it. Now slip the old net forward from under the tail and lift him out."

"Whippin' water, that's all it be, whippin' water! Kids with bent pins an' worms do just as well."

Having swallowed his whisky, Bill Kidd said, "See this moustache? Shall I tell 'ee for why I wear'n like this, 'Bosun'? I'm by way of being a pal of the Kaiser, now in Holland chopping logs for his hearth. I was taken prisoner on April the thirteenth, nineteen eighteen. For an entire day our Division had held up the German advance across the old Somme battlefield. As far as I was concerned the Kaiser was still a Field-marshal in the British Army, and when he came specially to see my lads at Kortrai— that was after we'd been pinched through that yellow-bellied order to retire—never mind where it came from—as I was telling you, I was presented to the Kaiser, who shook hands with me, and congratulated us on our stand at Combles, three weeks before. Without a word of a lie, 'Bosun', he as good as said they'd lost the war then. Fact, my lad! So don't let anyone get away with any adverse remarks about Kaiser Bill."

"Square 'ead," replied Mr. Tinker, taking a draught of his special mixture. He added, as his nose emerged from the pewter pot, "I don't give a flip for no Kayser, see?"

The sward of the downs rising before Phillip was faintly purple with the setting sun. Out of breath after hastening to the summit, he sat down to rest; but, disturbed by his thoughts, soon got up to hurry onwards. Above the last red waves of sunset hung the evening star, a pearl left by the ebb of day. He must think only of his work.

Now for a plan. The first book of the trilogy must retain the original title of *Soot, or, The Irritable Man*. It must, as first conceived in 1919, be unflinchingly realistic. Never mind what the family would think, each one cowering within its little ego of fear. Once completed, the trilogy could be set aside for publication after his death.

First write the trilogy; then see. It must be entirely free of romantic fancies, or self-denying gentility. He would start after Nuncle's visit. Perhaps Nuncle would sell the estate to the War Department. Then he would be free. They would move nearer the sea and the Yacht Club. As he walked on, he saw himself lying on the banks of a trout stream, peering and watching; writing only in the mornings; enjoying the blue water of the harbour with Piers who had promised to put him up for the Yacht club.

The spaniel, who had not had a proper walk for a long time, was racing after a jack hare. It crossed the scent of another, and raced after it, giving tongue. His master stood still, listening. In the light of the moon half risen over the rim of the downs he saw the two hares moving in opposite directions. That had been like his life so far: the hares were two ideas and he was like Rusty, who after panting up to him turned away to hunt the scent of one hare backwards, hunting heel as the term was. In a way he himself was always hunting heel.

Other star-points were now visible in the deepening pallor of the sky. He was relieved to come to the cattle-track leading down to Colham. This walk was, he reflected, almost the only one he knew, and it was his third year in the district. He had walked

round the estate only once. Shades of the old days of walking at
least a dozen miles every day. Ah, Malandine, when the world
was young. He was now old: by next April he would be thirty-four.

Descending to the northern outskirts of the town, he came to the
Rising Sun just as eleven o'clock was striking from some clock in
the neighbourhood. Bill Kidd's car was standing in the stable
yard, near a lighted side-window. Figures were visible behind the
lace curtain. Voices. The same old cross-talk.

"Where's the skill in blowing the pools in the Stour with
acetylene and water inside screw-top cider bottles?"

"Whippin' water, I tell 'ee, that's all it be."

"Look here, 'Bosun', I'll bet you five pounds to a bottle of
whisky there isn't a trout in any chalk stream anywhere that I
can't take out with a dry-fly, and damn all your night-lines,
stockings of lime, and other novelties! One day I'll take you on
my uncle's water——"

"You mean Sir 'Ilary?"

"I meant 'Tiny Tinribs', General Ironside to you."

Craftily the publican said, "Thought you said you was a baronet's
son? I knows of only one wan round yurr, and that's Tofield, and
you ban't no relation, else us'd'v heard of it."

Phillip moved away from the window. What he had heard
settled every doubt concerning Bill Kidd. He lived his fantasies
instead of putting them on paper. What was the difference, funda-
mentally? None. He turned for home, feeling depressed.

The moon was up, he lingered with the voices of corncrakes, and
a solitary quail, coming through the milky light over the fields of
grass and corn. Lucy showed no surprise when he arrived home
about two o'clock. She was still up, sewing on the sofa drawn up
to the dying fire.

"Had a nice walk, Pip?"

She lay on her side to ease the weight of a kicking embryo. "I
could just make out the chalk quarry on Whitesheet Hill, from
the downs," he said, sitting on the end of the sofa. "I wonder if
there were ever any Saxons in Flanders. The troops always
pronounced 'Wytschaete' as 'Whitesheet'. And this was a Saxon
stronghold, wasn't it?"

"Uncle John will be sure to know."

"I must go and see him in the morning. How is he?"

"He looks rather thin, poor dear. Before I forget, I've left you
some cold bacon sandwiches on the kitchen table."

He returned with the sandwiches, and said, "What do you think of Felicity?"

"Oh, I like her. So do the little boys."

Soon after dawn a vehicle got up to look like a motorised farm van with a bundle of hazel spars tied to its bonnet strap and a wad of thatching reed beside the driver and two other wads covering the rear seats moved slowly and almost silently—the cut-out being closed—up the bramble-grown track to the Longpond. Near the spring-head it crossed over the small bridge which carried the original drive to the derelict house.

Within the hollow of the walls the driver parked his vehicle, and with a pair of field-glasses returned on foot to the bridge where, kneeling down, he leant his elbows on the parapet and examined the landscape.

The glasses were by Zeiss of Jena. These, with other souvenirs, had been looted from the Kommandant's office immediately British troops following the Armistice had arrived at the guard house of the *Kriegsgefangenenlager* where he and others had been imprisoned during the last six months of the war.

Satisfied that the valley was empty of human figures, Bill Kidd walked back to fit together the joints of an 11-foot split-cane trout rod, after which he threaded a fine plaited silk line through the snake-rings and attached to the end a tapered gut cast to which was tied a single sneck-bend No.10 hook.

Hundreds, thousands of mayflies were hanging upside down on branch and twig of the overgrown willows. He impaled one near the tail whisks so that it remained alive and fluttering upon the hook. Then pulling loops of the extremely thin magpie silk line, he let the gentle airs of sunrise float the lure over the water.

"Cor stone the crows," he muttered in his excitement of seeing a large black-fin and part of a tail near the descending lure. Allowing the fly to touch the water, he lifted the point of the rod again and again, dapping the insect until a large olivine neb arose and sucked it in. After a pause, the rod point was smartly lifted, and Bill Kidd told himself that he was into one of aldermanic proportions as the rod bent in an arc and the check on the reel screamed with line drawn out.

When Bill Kidd left about 7 a.m. nine large trout were concealed under the thatching wads at the back of the car. He sold the fish in Colham to a fishmonger recommended by 'Bosun' about

the time that Sir Hilary Maddison had finished packing for an
early start from Pembrokeshire.

Chapter 12

HILARY IS WORRIED

The London newspapers were on sale in the town of Haverfordwest every day after 10 a.m. On the morning following the news
of the Grasmere award on his wireless set Hilary had bought a
copy of every paper on the station bookstall—a small wooden shed
with lock-up shutters—and looked through them while sitting in
his motorcar. At first he had felt a little satisfaction in the prominent space given to the name of Maddison. There it was, in
the fourth leader of the *Telegram*. But when he came to the penny
papers this feeling changed to astonishment, then to exasperation.
The damned young idiot, posing as the heir to 'a considerable
estate in the West Country' and 'married to a niece of Lord
Kilmeston.' The Fawley property was little more than a holding
originally established by a scion of the family whose seat was in
Durham. The Durham estate had been sequestrated during the
Civil War, and later restored by Charles the Second. Master
Phillip was getting too big for his boots, evidently; and he was
not the heir: he was a probationer, to whom by now it should have
been perfectly clear that unless he made good within a stipulated
period he would not succeed to a life-tenancy.

Hilary called daily for his letters *poste restante* at the main G.P.O.;
he had collected them before buying the newspapers, but had not
yet opened them. They lay, neat and compact, within the cubby
hole in the dashboard of his second motorcar, the Wolseley
2-seater. Now he took them out, and with a feeling of constriction selected an envelope with a French stamp addressed to him
in surely too neat a handwriting—the dots between the letters
after his name so correctly placed, as though the writer had to
make up in added respect for adverse news within——

He sat back, overcome by dread, then by fear, and finally by a
pessimistic thought that he might as well be dead. Irene Lushington had refused his offer of marriage. He knew it, he knew it. He
had not asked for her love when last he had seen her in London;

only for her care, and, possibly in time, her affection. All he wanted, he had said, as they sat in his drawing room of Claridge's (usually when in London he stayed at one or other of his three clubs, the Voyagers, the East India, and the Flyfishers') was a home somewhere where he could feel that he really belonged. A man's home, he had said, meant the grace, the beauty, and above all the happiness of a woman.

He would prefer to live in the East, perhaps in China—Shanghai he had known romantically as a young man—but the choice would be hers; he would live wherever she wanted to live, and the marriage settlement should be on her own terms, subject to her grandson Billy inheriting the Fawley property.

Irene liked Hilary, up to a point. Beyond that point, she was shut-away from him. When driving her to South Devon, after the christening of her grandson, she had been drawn to his loneliness, for he had told her restrainedly about his long-ended marriage: being aware that to have put his ex-wife in a poor light might have aroused defensive or at least curious thoughts about himself in relation to Beatrice. And although he did not know this, Irene was already on his side; for Phillip had told her about the attempt of his aunt-by-marriage to get into his bed one night—the only night he had stayed at her Hampshire home after returning from Flanders early in 1915, while Uncle Hilary was at sea.

No; what had led Irene to have reserved thoughts about Hilary was his unfeeling attitude at her daughter's grave soon after they had arrived at Malandine. The weed-grown mound, set with a brief marble stone on which was carved a reaping hook encircling a rose-in-bud, had made Hilary critical of Phillip, whom she loved for his sweetness and sympathy towards others.

"If he cannot think to arrange an annual payment with the parson to have the grave kept in order, how can he look after twelve hundred acres and all that goes with the property? You see, Irene, I can never be sure of my nephew."

When he met Irene again in London, Hilary, after dining with her at the Savoy, had taken her to a play at the small and intimate Fortune Theatre. It was a comedy by Frederick Lonsdale. Hilary had wanted to see Cochran's revue, *One Dam Thing After Another*, but Irene had already seen it, so they saw *On Approval*; and afterwards they returned to sup at the Savoy.

At the next table sat a party of young men and women discussing a play about the war. Irene heard only words here and there, but among them, with a start, she heard Phillip's name mentioned. A man with a clean-shaven, meditative face, said, "If anyone can do it, it will be Phillip Maddison. That article in the *Crusader* on the opening of the battle of the Somme will be a classic. I heard him talking one evening in the Barbarian Club. There is something in that young man dead beyond resurrection, but he holds the entire war in the palm of his hand."

When the party at the next table had left, she had asked the waiter who they were, and learned that the speaker was Captain Reginald Berkeley, the author of a play called *The White Chateau*.

"Did you hear what he said about Phillip, Hilary? I read what he wrote about the Somme in the *Daily Crusader*. Someone cut it out and sent it to me at Laruns. It was deeply moving."

Hilary had replied shortly, "The sooner he forgets the war, the better for himself and his prospects."

"What they were saying was high praise, Hilary."

"Possibly; but have you looked at his novels? I found them an unreadable hotch-potch. In any case, it's too soon now to write about the war. Let him wait until all the history books have had their say. After all, I heard my father once say that Tolstoi wrote about the Napoleonic era in *War and Peace* more than fifty years after the event."

There had been a feeling of blankness when they parted that night, Hilary driving her to her club; but the next day when she had telephoned early to thank him for her evening he had offered to see her off at Victoria on the boat train. He was at his best, bringing her flowers and a light luncheon basket. As the time for the train to leave drew near, they felt that they were going to miss one another. Just before the whistle blew, without premeditation she leant down to offer her cheek for a kiss, while he reached up also without thought and kissed her gently. There were tears in her eyes as she sat down; while Hilary, having raised his bowler hat, turned away with the idea, enchanting and sad, that she must love him.

From that time he was preoccupied with the thought of what his sister Viccy would feel if he married again. Despite, or perhaps partly because of, their father's defects, and certainly because they had all loved their mother, the three Maddison brothers and four sisters had always been devoted to the idea of themselves as a family.

His sister Viccy might not live long. She had had one operation for the dreaded *carcinoma*, when her womb was removed. One could never be certain that the malignancy was no longer in the blood stream.

Hitherto Hilary had been fairly content to spend the summers in his caravan in Wales, 'far from the madding crowd of trippers', as he thought of it. Since the war, ribbon-building was increasing behind and along the coast centred on Bournemouth, a pleasant enough place to spend the winter, in his home efficiently run by Viccy. But should anything happen to her——

And now there was brother John. The doctor had said that he should be X-rayed to determine the condition of the chronic bronchitis.

These considerations had led Hilary to write to Irene and ask her to marry him. And now, within the envelope, was her answer. He dared not open it. He put it in his breast pocket beside his wallet, and looked at his remaining mail. Nothing from Phillip; and according to *The Times*, the mayfly was up all over southern England.

He returned to the post-office, and sent a telegram to his nephew; and then, going into the Mariners Inn, ordered a pint of porter, which gave him sufficient energy to open Irene's letter. At the first glance he was shocked; then depressed. He ordered a large whisky, and thus encouraged, read the letter in a different light. There was hope after all. She would like time to think it over: she was going on a cruise to India with a woman friend, and would let him know in the autumn, when she hoped to meet him and talk things over, because, she said, she had a persistent feeling that she might not be able to be all that she knew was expected of her.

The next day, on receiving his nephew's reply to his telegram, Hilary packed his rods and kitbag and set off for Colham.

On arrival there he went to see the family doctor about his brother's condition, to learn that there was some obstruction in the bronchus. A sputum test had revealed absence of tubercle.

Hilary went on to Rookhurst and made his first call at Fawley. There he offered to arrange matters with a London nursing home.

"Thank you, my dear brother, but I think I'll return for a spell at the Shakesbury home. After all, my old doctor has the case in hand. But I have little doubt that my time has come. We must keep it from the others. One does not want Phillip and Lucy to be worried."

"You're going to be all right, John. You'll pull round now that the weather is set fair, after all this wet we've been having. I'll come and see you again tomorrow, old chap, and hope to bring you a trout for your luncheon. Also, I would recommend stout, to build you up. It's about the finest tonic there is, when one is run down. I'll bring a bottle or two tomorrow from the farmhouse." If Master Phillip hasn't finished it by now, he thought.

As he was going down to the village Hilary passed a hatless young man with what appeared to be a walking stick carried under one arm like a gun, and an army valise on his back. Just before the car came level the man turned abruptly and held up his hand for the driver to stop. Hilary was put out by this, and when the young fellow, who had a swarthy face, asked him if he knew where Skirr Farm was, he replied shortly, "Yes. It's half a mile down this road, about a hundred yards past the church, on the left. Do you want to see anyone there?" He meant to add, "If so, I'll give you a lift"; but when the young fellow, who wore a pair of new brown leather leggings with ill-fitting khaki breeches, and a jacket he appeared to have outgrown, replied, "Yes I do, but I'll find it all right," Hilary drove on.

In preparation for Sir Hilary's visit, Haylock had asked the bailiff that the small boat, stored in the barn, be carted to the Longpond and there submerged near the pier. It was carvel built, and the seams needed swelling. As soon as the drakes were seen on the water, the keeper had the boat hauled up on the bank, there to be drained and cleaned before refloating.

Early the following day, on his rounds, he had thrown a pail of water into the boat, to keep the caulking damp.

Hilary arrived that evening; and after breakfast the next morning Phillip went with him to the pier, which consisted of a broad elm plank on sunken posts; and having seen his uncle aboard with Haylock, returned to the farmhouse.

The Longpond curved near its middle length. The boat, sculled gently backwards, moved towards the bend. Hilary sat in the stern, casting his fly on the water. Suddenly he said, "Haylock, I see a man up there, fishin'. Who is it?"

Haylock reversed one paddle, so that the boat swung broadside on. "No idea, Sir Hilary."

"Do you know if Mr. Phillip has given anyone permission to fish?"

"Not so far as I'm aware."

They both stared at the stranger, who continued to dap his fly as though unaware of the boat's presence.

"Take me to him. I made it plain that on no account was this water to be fished until I had paid my visit."

The fisherman was standing near one of the willows sprawling over the water. When Hilary looked at him again, to his surprise the fellow, whom he could have sworn had been without a hat when first seen, was wearing a deerstalker stuck with large salmon flies, of the kind fished in Norwegian rivers.

"How d'you do, Sir Roland," he called out. "You're just in time for the rise. I thought it was Piers at first. Is he comin' out this mornin'?"

"And who may you be?"

"I am Major Kidd, late of the Gaultshire Regiment, Sir Roland. I say, surely these rainbows are stew-fed?"

"I am Sir Hilary Maddison, I own this water, and no-one has been given permission to fish here."

"But this is Benbow Pond, isn't it, sir?"

"No. The Benbow Ponds belong to Sir Roland Tofield, my neighbour. They're three miles down the valley."

"I offer you my apologies, sir. It also explains why I've been puzzled. You see, Piers said the fish were brownies, but these big'ns are rainbows. And that fact's been puzzling me, for as you know, *Salmo gairdneri* usually dies off in landlocked water during the first spawning season."

"Rainbow trout grow quickly here, the food is plentiful. Have you killed any fish yet?"

The stranger was seized with a paroxysm of coughing. He bent double in apparent agony, a hand pressed into his midriff. "Gas," he managed to gasp. "Phosgene—got it in Oppy Wood——"

In his time Hilary had had to deal with lascars from East India, larrikins in the docks of Sydney, dagoes from Port Said, and bums at San Francisco: and in the attitude of the man before him he felt something of the underdog, the fly boy, the four-flusher.

"Did Sir Roland Tofield give you leave to fish his water?"

"Well, sir, I would hardly have fished otherwise? An Old Wyck knows his manners."

"An Old What?"

"I took my first trout from the Test at Winchester, sir, from the Common Water. On a dry fly, of course."

"You were in College at Winchester?"

"Yes, before the war, sir."

"And you served with the Gaultshire Regiment? In that case you know my nephew, Phillip Maddison?"

"He was my Commanding Officer in France and Belgium, sir."

"Did he give you permission to fish here?"

Bill Kidd thought rapidly: his mind prompted a divided answer. "Phillip did offer me a day on his water, so did Piers, when I met them together in London, and we talked trout. As a matter of fact, I intended to look him up after my day on the Tofield beat. I've just come down from London, as a matter of fact, and mistaken my destination."

Hilary decided to let it go at that. "Well, finish your day. I'll take the lower water, by the weir."

"That's most generous of you, sir, but I rather fancy I'll be expected at the Tofields' place." He wound in his line.

Bill Kidd had a dozen fish hidden in a bed of nettles: he didn't want the boat to land, so pulling off his deerstalker he bowed from the neck like a guardsman in plain clothes before Royalty; then with a "Good day to you, sir, I'll get my motor", he walked towards the site of the ruined house. There he shoved the wads of reed together with the spars or brooches through an empty window-space into the brambles and elderberry bushes below. Had anyone stopped him on the way there and asked what was he doing with them, Bill Kidd had his answer rehearsed. 'I'm an ex-serviceman trying to get a living. These are samples of the best wheat reed. Know any bloke wanting a thatcher? My partners and I can undercut local rates by twenty per cent.'

He congratulated himself as he returned slowly down the weedy drive. Near the farmhouse he met Phillip walking with a young man in creaking new leggings, together with the girl who had turned up the day before, whom he had seen several times at the Game Pie with a middle-aged man, who was obviously running her by the way he kept her from younger men.

"I've been looking for you, my Mad Son. I've just had the pleasure of meeting Sir Hilary, who was kind enough to give me permission to fish. But I don't want to take advantage of his generosity while he's here. How long's he staying, d'you know?"

"He may be here for the rest of the summer, or gone tomorrow."

"Blime, a fly-by-night. Seriously, I thought he was a decent old boy. A sahib, in fact. Who's this bloke?"

"Mr. Cabton—Major Kidd."

"Pleased to meet you, Major. What sort of car d'you call this one? 'Ot as 'ell. A joke, I perceive."

"What sort of walking stick do you call that one? Poacher's four-ten, what? You look out, my lad! Have you got a licence? Then watch your step! I've got a game licence, and that entitles me to ask questions, and don't you forget it."

Cabton replied in lazy tones. "What does your old iron do, if it isn't a rude question?"

"At thirty the engine rattles, at forty your ribs rattle, at fifty a gramophone plays 'Down Among the Dead Men'. Well, cheerio you blokes. If you, my little maid, can't be good"—with a finger wag at Felicity—"be careful! I spied you in the Game Pie, with my little eye. Naughty, naughty!" And with a roar of con- glomerate machinery Bill Kidd drove down the valley to the Benbow Ponds, thinking that what he knew about the little maid might one day come in useful.

Phillip and Felicity were walking up the borstal. His slight fear of her induced a satirical mood of defence. "In some ways, you know, Bill Kidd is a praiseworthy figure, if self-education be con- sidered a matter of praise."

"He didn't seem educated to me."

"He educated himself by telepathy at one of the three leading public schools in England."

"I don't understand."

"The fact that, in all probability, his name doesn't appear in the official list of 'Old Wycks', should be offset by the pride he must have felt before admitting himself at his advanced age, to Winchester College." He struck at nettles with his stick; a white- throat flew out in alarm. They peered for the nest. It was safe, thank heaven.

"Don't heed what I said. I was assuming my satiric, worthless self, Felicity, for I do really understand Bill Kidd's *persona*, or mask. I assumed an identical attitude when I became a temporary gent, and was attached for training to a territorial battalion whose officers were most of them from Cambridge. I had such a ragging for being a bounder—and I did behave like a bounder—that a little later on, when with another regiment, I found myself sud- denly saying that I was up at Cambridge University just before the war. I wasn't; I was a junior clerk in the City. I suppose it was a natural effect of fear, of wanting to conform in all respects. What in nature is called 'protective coloration', which after all springs from fear."

"That's a generous way to look at it."

"But isn't it the truth?"

"They say that truth is bitter."

"Why do you say that?"

"Well, isn't it?"

He stopped and looked at her. "What did Bill Kidd mean about seeing you in the Game Pie?"

"I've no idea. I've been there only three times, always with my guardian. The third time I saw you."

"But why do you think the truth is bitter?"

"I don't really. Blake said, 'Everything that lives is holy'. That's what I really feel." She concealed her bitten nails.

They sat down at the edge of the beech hanger. She longed to put her head against his heart, and feel his arms holding her. It was an aching feeling. But he merely spoke about Bill Kidd in Archangel. She burst out with "How can anyone *want* to be photographed beside a row of men who have been hanged?"

"They may have been dummies for a film. Tell me what he said in the Game Pie?"

She had looked flurried when she spoke about her 'guardian'. And also, there was Piers' remark about ringing her up the next time he went to London. *She'll be only too glad of the chance, I expect.*

What a hypocrite he was, pretending to Lucy that he thought of her only for help with his work. The days were drifting by, and he was not working. It had been the same with Barley—she had been between him and all thoughts about war. He *must* continue his book about the war. O, it cried out to be written: the historical truth of those years. How the war had altered not only the face of the land, with its hutment camps and practice areas, but also the faces of the people. Consider his own case—or, more obviously, the case of Bill Kidd. From being a frightened, evasive little fellow —his eyes in moments of quiet were still haunted—with moustache no bigger than one of his own eyebrows, Bill Kidd had developed, through fear and desperation, and in admiring imitation of his superiors, into a conglomerated man with a jargon improvised to fit the picture of himself as 'a bold, bad lad': full of ideas of his own potential valour; his old self, still the inner man, thrust behind that Kaiser moustache.

Felicity came to him with some shells of hill-snails in the palm of her hand.

"Are those ammonites, Phillip?"

"Aren't ammonites found only in water? Felicity, I feel I've been mean about Bill Kidd."

"Only because you understand him."

"You knew him before he came here, didn't you?"

"I've only seen him once before, at the Game Pie. But never spoken to him."

He felt warmly towards Bill Kidd.

"After all, every living creature strives to get on, by copying, that is learning from, others. Birds and butterflies imitate foliage—soil—rocks—to escape being seen. All the world *is* a stage, full of invented life."

There was a shot among the trees, the screaming of a blackbird. Cabton came to the edge of the hanger, holding up a bird.

"Ever had a blackbird pie? Not bad, eh? If I can get some clay, I'll bake it in the embers of a fire."

"I did that once with a sparrow."

"Did you eat it?"

"It was not only burnt, but burst."

"You should've taken out the guts first."

He took Cabton aside. "There are a lot of young birds about, pheasants and partridges included, so couldn't you watch them, without shooting?"

Hilary felt hedged-in when he saw two more strange faces in the garden. Phillip should have known better than to have his friends to stay at the same time as himself. After all, there was the rest of the year in which to invite them. However, he did his best to be pleasant, but got only monosyllabic replies from Cabton. He was finally repelled by the fellow cleaning his nails with a single-bladed penknife while sitting at table.

"Who is he?" he asked later, when he, Phillip and Billy were in the garden.

"Stick Gun," said Billy earnestly, looking up.

"A writer," Phillip hastened to say. "I've never met him before."

"Then why is he here?"

"Edward Cornelian, the critic and friend of Thomas Morland, thinks he has great talent."

"Then there was that other fellow who was poaching my trout."

"He just turned up."

"This sort of thing won't do, you know, Phillip. Who's the girl?"

"Miss Ancroft is staying at Shakesbury, and came over for the day. Lucy thought she could help with secretarial work."

"Well, don't get mixed up with too many people like Stiggun or Stiggin whatever he calls himself, and that other fellow, what's his name, Kidd. There's only one word for a man who claims to be a Wykehamist and tells you that the Test runs past Winchester. He hadn't even bothered to look at a map to find out that the river is the Itchen. I suppose it was you three who got rid of my whisky?"

"I must apologise for not telling you earlier, Uncle Hilary. When these people called, I offered them refreshment. There was also a man from Savoy Hill. I didn't drink any myself, by the way."

"I don't want to have to lock up my things, you know."

"I tried to get another bottle to replace it, but malt whisky isn't sold locally."

"Why didn't you drink any?"

"I'm trying to keep as fit as possible."

"Well, that's something. Good God, look at that child."

Billy had taken one of the table knives and was trying to clean his fingernails with it.

"You really must use your judgment about whom you allow in your home, Phillip. What does Lucy think about these people?"

"Oh, she's happy whatever happens."

Felicity came up to them.

"I'm going now. I have so enjoyed myself. I think I'll walk to Shakesbury. Thank you for letting me come here. Did you have some good fishing, Sir Hilary?"

"Oh, not so bad, you know."

Phillip said, "Well, thank you for all you've done for me."

"I wish I could have done more."

"Please let me pay you for the typing."

She was pale. "Oh no. It's been a great privilege to be allowed to come here. I'll find Mrs. Maddison, to say goodbye—— No, I love walking, really. Please don't bother about me——"

"Of course I'll run you back. I expect Cabton will like a ride on the carrier, too."

Hilary saw them off with a genial manner; he was relieved to think that now he would have the sitting room to himself before supper.

Lucy came downstairs, having put the boys to bed, to find Hilary standing by the fireplace.

"Will Phillip be long, d'you think, Lucy? I think it's time we came to some definite arrangement. I'd like you to be present, too."

"It takes about half an hour to go to Colham and back, Uncle Hilary."

"Perhaps we three can talk in another room? I suppose he'll be bringing that fellow Stiggun or Stiggin back with him? What's Phillip doing, anyway, to allow him to walk about with that poacher's gun of his?"

"I think he's supposed to be getting ideas for a book."

"Good God! Getting ideas for a book, with a Belgian walking-stick gun in June!"

"Anyway, I'll tell him we have some family business to talk over after supper. I'm sure he'll understand."

When the supper table was cleared, and Cabton had gone out, the brushwood in the hearth was lit. Sticks blazed against the back-log, they sat in the light of cheerful flames.

Phillip had feared the worst; he was therefore surprised when his uncle began by saying, "I've decided to follow my advisers, and go in for milk, and take a moveable bail to the fields. We'll build up a pedigree Friesian herd to begin with. The Government will be forced to subsidise milk sooner or later, and to build processing factories. Other downland farmers are going in for milk. It will mean getting rid of the ewe flocks. I want to do this at Michaelmas, before the slump really gets going. All the political signs point to a General Election in the Spring, and if the Conservative party has any sense it will let in the Socialists to show the country what a mess they can make of things."

"Make a mess out of a mess, you mean?"

"Exactly. If you have anything to say, now's the time to get it off your chest."

"Some of the men will be stood off, I suppose?"

"Almost all of them. We'll need five cowmen, including a head man, who will have had mechanical training. We'll require one horseman to look after five horses, the usual number for a teamsman. Lads can lead the pairs in waggon, tumbril, and watercart. In fact, there won't be any water-carts. Water will be drawn to the herds in hollow light rollers, which can also be used for those cultivations required for growing oats, hay, and other fodder for the cows."

Phillip asked about Joby the shepherd.

"He'll have to be given notice when the hoggets are finished off next spring. Hibbs will have to go, too."

"Poor Hibbs, he said to me that the farm should be all milk, with bails, nearly two years ago."

"I'm afraid it wasn't possible then, Phillip."

"What will I be expected to do under the new scheme, Uncle Hilary?"

"You'll have to make yourself responsible for everything generally, and particularly to see that the milk is got away in proper condition at the right time. That means early rising seven days a week, at least for the first year or two. Then you'll have to attend regularly once or twice a week at the agent's office, to get the hang of estate management." Hilary leaned forward, and held up a finger for emphasis. "It's the only way, Phillip. If you want to keep your head above water, you've got to learn the business from A to Z. Farming *is* a business, you know, and requires constant attention to detail. And as I've told you more than once, you'll have to chuck this writin' of yours. Remember the old adage—'No man can serve two masters'."

The next morning Hilary went back to Wales; and when Phillip rang up Felicity's hotel, he learned that she had gone back to London.

Cabton had apparently decided to remain, as a sort of detached member of the family. He did no work on the farm, nor any writing as far as Phillip could see.

He had the odd ideas of the urban amateur in the country. He collected horsehair from the gate-posts, made a plait of dark hair and tied it to the back of the chair where he sat at the dining room table. A row of old nests, taken from hedge and apple tree, adorned his bedroom window ledge. Mrs. Rigg complained of fleas. One day he brought back a trout which he had shot with his walking stick gun as it basked in the shallows by the cattle drinking place, and showed it to Phillip.

"Well, we don't usually shoot trout, you know."

"What's the difference between shooting a poor bloody fish and lugging it in on a line? Anyway, it's quicker my way. I thought you liked efficiency, you're always talking about it." He said this with a lazy, self-pleased air as he picked his teeth with a burnt match.

"I suppose it's rather strange being in the country after a town?"

"People are the same anywhere."

"You've got a fairly good idea of the country, I must admit, judging from your short stories. Where did you get your knowledge of birds?"

"From cigarette cards."

"Well, everything comes from somewhere, I'll admit."

"Have you only just discovered that?"

"It sounds pretty obvious, I agree. How do you get on with the chaps in the pub? Any ideas for a book?"

"They're all right, when I can understand what they're saying. Among other things, they laugh at you as a farmer."

"I'm glad they can laugh, there's been a lot of unemployment since the war."

"They all think your uncle is going to sell up."

"I never listen to village talk, so I can't say."

"Why not mix with the village people? It's the stuff of living, isn't it? That's your trouble, that's why you can't write. You're only interested in making money. Well, I'm going for a walk."

Phillip said, with an effort to be easy, "Don't you find it hot with those breeches and leggings?"

"There are snakes about, I'm told. Besides, I like the heat."

"Well, please don't shoot with your gun."

Cabton had something about him of the Levantine. He had the ease, almost the laziness, of the dark-skinned. One morning he showed Billy how to load the walking stick gun. It was done by twisting the handle to open the breech, and slipping in a cartridge. There was no trigger, only a small button just above the breech. Billy was standing in front of Cabton, looking up, when Cabton closed the breech by a reverse twist. The button was depressed under the grip of Cabton's right hand as he did this. There was a report with a kick of dust beside Billy's feet as the shot rebounded. Phillip saw it from his upper window and shouted out, "You bloody fool, Cabton. Give me that gun!"

Cabton merely grinned and held the gun behind him.

"A miss is as good as a mile, remember," as he walked away. Later in the day he said to Phillip, "Can you lend me some four-ten cartridges? I've run out."

"You've got a bloody nerve, haven't you? I've told you that I can't have you shooting indiscriminately, Cabton."

"Oh well, if you want to talk like that I'm off."

"Bug off, Stick Gun," said Billy.

"Huh, chip off the old block, I see," replied Cabton over his shoulder as he walked towards Colham.

The following morning the keeper came to see Phillip. "That man staying here is shooting at anything he sees with that collector's gun, sir."

"I've asked him to stop shooting, Haylock."

"Well, I won't have it, Mr. Phillip. I'm responsible to Sir Hilary, and I can't have my birds disturbed."

Phillip explained to Cabton that the keeper had to show a good head of game for the autumn shooting.

"Game is an anachronism these days, surely?"

"That's not the point. All birds have young at this time of year. And they're hardly an anachronism. Anyway, we don't shoot song birds in this country, whatever they do in France or Italy or the Middle East."

"You believe in convention, don't you?"

"All conventions are based on common experience."

"I believe in uncommon experience. Doesn't Shelley mean anything to you any more?"

"Shelley didn't go round shooting robins, larks, and blackbirds."

"It's not worth arguing about."

When Phillip went with some agitation to report this miserable encounter to Lucy she said, "Oh well, I don't suppose he can hit anything! Anyway, he'll be gone soon, I expect."

"If he doesn't go, I shall."

A chance to get rid of Cabton came the next day, when the thunder of *Otazelle* sounded in the lane. Bill Kidd was on his way home, and had come, he said, to pay his respects to the Mis'ess before returning to the Smoke. He told them a story of how he had met his old Divisional Commander who had given him a couple of days on his water. From a damp sack on the floor of his car he drew four trout, each about twenty inches in length. Cabton looked at them in silence.

"Not easy to take fish after the mayfly gorge, old boy. I got 'em on a red cock's-hackle put over them again and again until they slashed at it through irritation. That surprises you, doesn't it? Fact though."

"They committed suicide, in other words. I suppose you can't give us a lift to London, Bill?"

"Jump in, you bastards. Hullo, Billy boy, what are you, a stowaway?"

"Me come too, please, Daddy," the child pleaded. An awkward period followed. Billy had to be detached from the wheel, sobbing. Phillip tried to console him, while Lucy held him in her arms. Billy hid his face until the engine started, then with a last despairing effort he yelled, "Bug off!"

On the way to Stonehenge Phillip said, "Do you realise that at this time, exactly eleven years ago today, we had kicked off at Third Ypres? The Pilckem ridge was taken, and the counter-attack of the Pomeranian Grenadiers, the 'Cockchafers', smashed by the Machine Gun Corps. Then the blasted rain came down."

"I was in Oppy Wood then, old boy, gassed with green-cross —phosgene." Bill Kidd coughed violently, then lit another cigarette from the stub of his old one.

At Andover Phillip mentioned that he was thinking of getting a second-hand small car.

"I know the very 'bus for you, if it hasn't been sold. I'll take 'ee there, midear."

"I see you're already talking West Country, Bill."

"Sure thing, my dear. What's more, Bill Kidd and his missus are coming to live in these yurr parts."

"Yes, you told me. How about you, Cabton? Are you proposing to move in, too?"

"I'm going to Cornwall."

In spite of being squeezed next to the smells of Cabton, Phillip enjoyed the ride along the familiar route to Basingstoke and Staines. They drove to a place in Westminster, a yard with a number of coach-houses made into a garage, where many cars were lined up awaiting the weekly auction. Among them was a long, fairly narrow small French car, with a brown fabric body; a four-seater.

"There she is. Let me do the talking, my Mad Son. Now, not a word, mind," as a salesman approached.

"Good morning, Major," the salesman said brightly. "How did your conversion run? Nice little job, I thought."

"No soft soap, my lad. I've come to talk brass tacks. My pal here wants a small nippy car, with a roomy body, and a decent hood on it. But not that brown fabric Peugeot, no dam' fear. That crock was here the week before last. What's wrong with it, come on now, don't give me the old patter. What's it worth? Sixty pounds? Don't be silly. Sixty quid for that body, looking like a cockchafer on wheels? Don't tell me it didn't sell because they all want a saloon during the finest summer since nineteen twenty-one. Don't give me that line about saloons. Anyway"—with a wink at Phillip, "let's hear the engine."

The salesman pulled out the choke and charged the cylinders; then with a jerk got the engine firing.

"Four cylinders, six horse power, sir. Two years old, and only one owner." He smiled. "To be honest, the owner was a lady."

Bill Kidd pushed up the hand throttle. Blue smoke came from the exhaust.

"Any pistons left, old boy?"

"Like to try her?"

"Any saw-dust in the gear-box?"

"I'll have the lid off if you like."

"What's the compression like?" asked Phillip.

"Fairly good, sir. The scraper-rings may be a bit worn, but it's a simple matter to replace them. The engine doesn't smoke after she's warmed up."

"No bloody oil left, you mean." Bill Kidd drew Phillip aside. "Let me do the buying, I know these car copers. They're all bastards."

Phillip took the wheel with some trepidation. It was years since he had driven a motorcar. He started off slowly, and went the first hundred yards in bottom gear, then changed to second gear, driving on with more confidence. Seeing before him the Houses of Parliament, he turned in by one gate, meaning to try the reverse gear in the wide space beyond, but was stopped by a policeman.

They went down to the Embankment, and found a street leading off which was empty.

"How do you like the feel of her, sir?"

The blue smoke had now stopped. "Are we out of oil?"

"Ah, that little joke, sir. I'll show you the dipstick when we get back. Apart from that, how does she strike you, sir?"

"I like her very much."

The chief point was that the car would fit into the narrow space of the cart-shed; he had taken the measurements before starting out. After reversing in the empty street, they returned to the garage.

"She rides well, don't you think, sir?"

"Most comfortable."

"They know how to make springs in France. High clearance too—eight inches."

The dipstick was examined.

"I'll buy it."

Bill Kidd did not seem to be put out that the deal had been made without him. Phillip gave the salesman a cheque, telling him that he would leave the 'bus—already called Cockchafer in his mind—until the cheque was cleared. Bill Kidd had a talk with the salesman in the office before joining him; and while they sat in *Otazelle*, Cabton said, "Getting his rake off, no doubt."

"Well, why not?"

"Well, I'm much obliged to you, Bill," he said as they drove away. "You must let me pay you for the petrol for the journey up."

"Don't insult me."

"Well, I hope you got something out of the salesman."

"I don't make money out of my pals."

They drove up Whitehall, the driver moving the throttle of *Otazelle* up and down to create the illusion of a powerful racing car. "Where do you want me to drop you?"

"Where do you want to go, Cabton?"

"Oh, I'm not particular."

"Up the Strand and turn off at John Street, for Adelphi Terrace, Bill. I'd like you to meet my agent, Anders Norse. We'll have lunch at Simpson's. You'll be my guests."

Afterwards he said goodbye. "Anders and I have some business. Thanks for the lift, Bill. Good luck, Cabton."

Kidd took him aside. "Who's this dago who's planted himself on you? You want to watch out, old boy. First Plugge and now this bloke—they're nothing but bloody scroungers." He looked almost affectionately at Phillip. "Bill Kidd knows what he's talking about, you know. Well, so long, and thanks for the shackles. Remember our old quarterbloke, Moggers? See you at the regimental dinner in the autumn, no dodging the column this time, midear."

Anders Norse had a new office, and a secretary, in a side street off the Adelphi. When the contract for the trout story had been signed he said, "I have a feeling that there's going to be a revival of interest in the Great War. What about your own book?"

"Oh, I don't know, Anders. I'd have to go away somewhere, and live by myself for some months to finish it."

"What about your cottage in Devon? Have you still got it?"

"Oh yes."

"It's the only way to write, I think. But I suppose the farm takes up all your time?"

"Well—in a way. There are certain cross-currents——"

"Of course, writing is a whole-time job. D'you remember Anthony Cruft? He's left London to bury himself somewhere in the country and write a book. I expect you know that Virginia, his wife, has left him?"

Phillip nodded as though to himself. "Oh, before I forget, Anders, I've given a cheque for sixty pounds to Mews Motors, of Westminster, and would like to take the car away today. Do you mind if I give your name as a guarantor that the cheque is all right?"

"Of course. Ring them up from here, why not."

On the way to Westminster on foot Phillip called in at the Coal Hole, half hoping to find Felicity there. Instead, he saw Archie Plugge, pint pot in hand. He told him about the new 'bus, adding that he was going home by way of the South Coast to call on Martin Beausire; and left before he could be drawn into a round of drinks.

Arrived at Mews Motors, he saw that the body and windscreen of the Cockchafer had been polished.

"I've filled the tank and had the oil changed," said the salesman. "There's no charge, of course. By the way, you do understand, don't you, that this motor is not subject to guarantee? We are, after all, motorcar auctioneers only, and have so many vehicles passing through that it's not possible to do more than see that what comes to us is road-worthy. But the Baby Peugeot isn't a bad little 'bus. The second gear of this particular car is liable to slip out sometimes, so it may be advisable to hold in the gear-handle when going up some of those steep hills of the West Country."

It was a Friday, and being a fine day, there might be week-end traffic on the roads to the coast. He was advised to go by way of the Embankment to Chelsea, and over the river to Putney, then take the Dorking road through Leatherhead.

"It's a direct road from there to Horsham and Worthing. All the best, sir. By the way, you motorcar isn't licensed. There's time before Spring Gardens close——"

"Oh, I'll see about it when I get home, thanks all the same."

He soon got into the car's ways. The disc wheels drummed like

the flight of the July Bug, dumbeldore, or cockchafer. He considered what name should be used; and returned to Cockchafer,
emblem of the Kaiser's Foot-Guards. Cockchafer rode easily on her
large tyres and long springs. He had brought his goggles, and went
along with the windscreen open to feel the rush of air upon his
face. Many times he rejoiced at his luck in finding just the right
car for Lucy to drive. It's maximum speed was 42 m.p.h., but it
cruised happily at 35, battery charging 10 amps and oil pressure
steady at 20 lbs. Only the faintest suggestion of pale smoke behind;
and looking at the dipstick when he stopped in a valley between
tree-crowned hills along the South Downs, he saw that the oil was
up to the maximum mark and still clear. No blowing past the
rings! He held each cylinder's compression against the starting
handle. Gas sighed through the exhaust valves of each cylinder.
He would have the engine decarbonised and the valves re-ground
when he got home. He took off his coat and sang.

Martin Beausire liked having people about him while he wrote
at a large desk upon which stood many columns of books, rising
to three feet and more in height. He was confronted and flanked
by books—review books, reference books, encyclopedias, a hun-
dred-weight and more of books, constantly being consulted,
changed, lent, given away, and sold. There he usually sat, holding
a large fountain pen, one of half a dozen lying before him, mixed
up with pencils, bottles of ink, telephone pads, engagement pads,
and bookcases rising to the ceiling; pictures hanging in the otherwise bare spaces. Against one wall was a glass-fronted cupboard
holding silver trophies and mementos of a sporting life. Upon the
chimney piece—for Martin liked an open hearth—were hanging a
variety of miniature shields of school, college and family coat-
armour, the latter representing the millennium-old Saxon family
of Boocer, rooted in the West Country, according to Martin, before
the Norman upstarts arrived at Hastings.

There were photographs of bob teams, ski-teams, rugger teams,
tennis teams, running, high-jump, long-jump, rowing, cricket,
and curling; Old Boy dinners; skating in the Fens; Martin following hounds on foot; Martin swimming; Martin running. Martin
was no recluse; he lived a full life and liked his friends to be always
with him as he wrote at his desk.

It was after midnight on Saturday evening in Worthing. Phillip
had gone to bed. Martin sat, pen in hand, writing a word or two;

pausing before he added another word. It was a book about coal-mining sponsored by an association of young owners with the hope of promoting a New Idea of Industry: garden suburbs, swimming pools, sports' grounds; whippet races, underground skills, courage, comradeship—an entirely new conception of life for men who spent most of their lives away from the sun. In a phrase of Mr. Lloyd George, 'a land fit for heroes'.

Many of these young owners had fought in the war, from which they had returned with the burning idea of comradeship between men and management. In this they were opposed by the 'economic' ideas of their fathers.

Pinned half-way up one pile of books borrowed from the London Library was a curled photograph by flashlight of a dirty fellow with a black face and eyes like a sick eagle's under a leather skull cap to the front of which was fixed a small electric torch. In his hand this grimy fellow carried a Davy Safety Lamp. One side of his dungaree overalls were partly white from chalk dust thrown too vigorously from his left hand as he had walked along the gallery of a mine in Wakefield, sweating as he thrust himself forward in the low hot tunnel beside a track of miniature steel rails. The chalk was thrown out, as requested, to reduce the risk of a spark struck by nailed boot on rock-fragment, and liable to cause an explosion 2,000 feet below the surface of the ground.

Martin had worked a 4-hour shift below, at the end of a gallery. Most of the time was spent lying on his back and side at the crag-ging lip of a 19-inch seam of coal compressed between two layers of rock. He had crawled to the coal-face past pit-props which occasionally had given out sharp cracking noises; while all the time he had suffered because he was not at his home writing what he had seen. Now he was making up for time lost in travel-ling, prepared for a 20-hour shift at his desk.

Phillip, asleep in bed, heard a telephone bell ringing. He was immediately alert. Footfalls came up the stairs, a tap on the door. Horn-rimmed spectacles low on nose, Martin said in a very sub-dued voice, "Someone calling himself Piers Tofield wants to speak to you. He says it's rather important."

Phillip ran down to Martin's study.

"Hullo, Phil. I've been trying to find you, to give you some good news. Congratulations on having a daughter."

"Thank you, thank you! Is Lucy all right?"

"She looked extremely happy when I saw her an hour ago, after I'd taken her to the Shakesbury nursing home. A seven-pound daughter, dark hair, some weeks early."

"Thank you ever so much for telephoning. However did you know I'd be here? I didn't know myself until this evening."

"I've been telephoning to various people, and at last thought of Archie Plugge at the Game Pie. He told me you were going along the South Coast, and said you might call on Martin Beausire."

"Well done. Where are you telephoning from?"

"Skirr. Your home."

"What time was the baby born?"

"Half an hour ago. Virginia and I called here on our way down to Devon, and Lucy gave us dinner. It was unexpected—the baby, I mean. So I ran her into Shakesbury while Virginia looked after Billy, who was a little anxious, and asking for you. Mrs. Rigg's here, so don't worry."

"What made you come down?"

"Virginia and I want to find a furnished cottage near the sea, to spend the summer."

"You can have mine, at Speering Folliot. The Mules—he's postman and sexton—have the key. No water or light laid on, I'm afraid."

"May we take it? We'll rent it from you, of course."

"You won't. May I join you?"

"I'd like nothing more. Here's Virginia."

"Hullo, Phil. What a lovely baby. I adore her. Lucy looks too, too radiant."

"Stay the night, won't you. Take any bedroom. I'll be home for breakfast. Give Piers my thanks, and some to yourself of course. I must tell the others here. Au revoir, my mermaid. I'll start home shortly—it's a lovely night."

Cockchafer ran splendidly in the night air. Through Arundel and on to Chichester without a plug missing; past harbours and reedy inlets of the moonlit sea; up Portsdown Hill with its memories of Lucy and Billy lying in the sun on their way to Dover, all those years ago, soon after his marriage . . . he stopped the engine, and walked through the dewy grass. O world, O life, O time—but nothing of the past ever was found except in the mind; onwards, leaving Southampton on the left, and along the lonely road to

Romsey. Here is the New Forest, deep dark woods and a filigree of leaves above yellow headlamp beams. Through a ghostly town of sleeping houses, and at last open spaces on either side of the road, a road sinking but to rise again, second gear slipping out—engine slowing as though over-heated—into bottom gear—and only a gentle seeming rise. That woman driver hanging on too long in a higher gear, and slapping piston-skirts against the pots. Up to the crest—and dawn coming in the east. Larks were singing. Afar lay the dark sheen of Salisbury, he was within rejoicing distance of home.

Leaving Cockchafer in the lane, hood up lest it rain, he entered by a window and crept upstairs to the night nursery. The cots were empty, without bedding. He looked in Lucy's room, drawers were open, a pair of shoes left on the bed. He cried out; no reply; was going downstairs when he heard the key in the door and Mrs. Rigg's voice called behind the door held just open, "Anyone thurr? Ah, tes you, sir, I be very glad vor see 'ee!" She came in, breathless. "I've a-got thik childer auver to mine—they wor crying when Mrs. Madd'zn was took away by Mr. Piers—me an' that young leddy stayed yurr with them, dear li'l boys they be."

"Where are they now—the lady and gentleman."

"They'm asleep in your room, zurr. And the childer be to my place now, zur, they'm quite all right, they be slaping side be side together on two pillors on th' vloor, happy as kings they be, dear 'ms."

"Thank you, Mrs. Rigg, thank you. No, I don't want anything to eat, thanks all the same. I'll wait here, on the sofa, until breakfast. I've got a car, and tomorrow, no it's Sunday—this afternoon, if you like, I'll take you all in to Shakesbury to see Mis's and the babby!"

He walked up beside the Longpond, now rosy in the dawn rising above the black line of the downs. He had a feeling that he could accomplish everything. His euphoria increased when, returning from the crest of the downs, he saw Piers and Virginia strolling to meet him.

On returning with Mrs. Rigg and the boys from the maternity home in Shakesbury that afternoon, Phillip had a shock when he answered the telephone.

Hilary said that his brother John had had an emergency operation in order to examine an obstruction in the bronchus, and an advanced state of carcinoma was discovered. His voice was not steady when he continued after a pause, "It's a landmark gone, Phillip. My brother—hullo, you there?"

Phillip said with an effort, "If only I had taken him for walks. My damned writing's made me utterly selfish."

"What did you say?"

"I—I'm really most awfully sorry, Uncle Hilary. Please accept my sympathy in your loss. Yes, I'll tell Lucy. By the way, she had a daughter early today. I was going to telephone."

"A daughter, you say. Give her my love. And accept my congratulations, old man."

"Thank you, Uncle Hilary. I'm sure Lucy will want me to send you her love—with mine, Uncle Hilary. We loved Uncle John."

"It's the end of an age, Phillip."

"Yes, Uncle Hilary. I'm so sorry."

"We must pull together."

"Count on me, Uncle Hilary."

He went over to tell Lucy. "If only I'd gone for daily walks with John. Look how Pa recovered from your mother's death when you and the Boys took him into your lives. Poor old John must have been corroded right through with loneliness, like an iron pipe with this hard chalky water."

"He knew how busy you were. Don't forget that you always found time to go and see him, so there's no need to reproach yourself," she said, quietly.

"I must make it up by looking after my parents and sisters. I shall invite Father and Mother to live at Fawley."

Ever since Richard had retired from the Office at Midsummer he had been talking of finding a cottage in the country where he might end his days. Hetty, having him at home all the time, had felt more enclosed than ever. Yet during the journey from Paddington she felt she was on the way to freedom, with the imagined faces of Billy and Peter, and now little Rosamund, ever present in her mind.

It was Richard's first long railway journey for many years. He looked for old landmarks, murmuring now and again to himself, "God bless my soul——", feeling ravaged by the changes; but when the downs came into sight, his spirit settled upon the hills.

Lucy and the little boys momentarily restored his youthfulness. The burial service, the church, the coloured form of St. Christopher hidden behind plaster when he was a boy, were as spring-water to his being; the innocence of early life came back, with his tears. Happiness succeeded this restoration of faith: the years between were levelled with the sight of the open vault wherein his parents, and the grandparents he had known, were resting. And now John had joined them.

The will was read in the library, whence the dust sheets had been removed. Phillip was left the house and the furniture; there was little else. John William Beare Maddison had lived on an annuity purchased years before. Dora had been unable to come, so had Belle, who was living at Westcliffe-on-Sea in a boarding house, partly crippled by arthritis. Hilary had motored from Bournemouth with Viccy. She had kept her pale face and girlish voice with its clear tone; but she had little or nothing to say. They had tea in the farmhouse.

All thought highly of Lucy. In her presence the awareness of death gave way to a light, happy feeling. Phillip rested himself quietly among them, telling himself that never, never must he use satire, as Thomas Morland had used in describing his relations. It was the life within, human hopes and fears, and above all the tragic estrangement of love, which must be kept steadily in mind.

He went for a walk with his father to the Longpond. "Father, I shall be very pleased to offer you the house—your home really—for as long as you and Mother care to live there. Rent free, of course. I'll pay the rates, naturally."

Richard was inclined to refuse: the garden would be beyond him; but his son's thought for him must not be rebuffed. As for Phillip, he felt that his father was so used to not wanting presents that his offer had been made rather crudely.

"I know the house is rather large, but it seems to me a pity that the Aunts, I mean Dora and Belle particularly, should all be so far apart. Aunt Dora's 'Babies' are over eighty, and can't last for ever. You could have your own part of the house, and now I've got some cash of my own, I would like to put in an extra bathroom, and also central heating for the winter."

"I suppose you and Lucy will live in another part of the house, old man?"

"Eventually, yes, Father. My idea is that you and Mother, and the Aunts, shall all have your own quarters, and have a sort of mess together."

"But won't all that cost money, Phillip?"

"I can count on at least a couple of thousand coming in, Father. I've had all kinds of offers from publishers and editors. The alteration to the house will be done by an architect, of course, everything planned properly. In fact, if anyone in the family wants to live there, it would be a help to me, for then I would know it was being really lived in, instead of as it has been."

"Have you told Hilary of your plans?"

"Not yet, Father. I wanted to consult you first. There's no hurry, really."

"I suppose you know what is in Hilary's mind?"

"More or less, I think. But whether he gives up the idea of keeping the land, the house won't go with it. I know the War Department chaps have been down here. It's common talk in Colham."

"Yes, Hilary told me."

They watched a few rises of trout, then walked back. On the way Richard said, "I think, entirely between you, me, and the gatepost, that Hilary begins to feel he's taken on a bit too much. You'll keep this to yourself, won't you, but I fancy it's a millstone round his neck. He's losing a thousand a year at present, and the entire estate as a going concern is valued at under ten pounds the acre. And from all the signs a bigger slump is on the way, at least that is the feeling in the City. I needn't tell you what havoc would result if the Socialists came back into power. Still, house property is unlikely to depreciate in a comparable manner. The value of land at this present time has never been so low for well over a century."

When they returned to the farmhouse he said, "Well, I am most grateful to you for your offer, my dear boy, and I shall think it over."

Richard had planned to return by the evening train, which left the junction shortly after 7 p.m. There was time to look at the garden. He remembered the peaches and greengages along the walls, the espaliers of apples and pears lining some of the paths, the lavender hedges along others; the central lily-pond fed by a fountain; the hot-houses backed by the row of low buildings—apple-store, potting sheds, boiler house for vinery and orangery.

Beyond the acre and a half of walled garden lay the orchard, also within a lime-stone wall, of about an acre. It would require a great deal of work to keep in order, even with some of the men brought in to plough or dig, according to the season, as his father had done.

Richard found the postern half open. The gate must always be kept closed in his father's time, on account of roe deer living in the woods. He had to lift the gate up to get past; the upper hinge had dropped off. A rusty length of sheet-iron nailed to the foot scraped against grass on the path. He managed to squeeze between door jamb and post.

What he saw within reduced him to a feeling of helplessness. How long had it been like that? Docks, thistles, burdocks; roofs fallen in; skeleton glass-houses topped by elderberry bushes; espaliers gone to wild wood, canker, and hung with lichen. How many years had it been like that? He turned away, appalled; and was walking back when he met Phillip, who said, "I hope you won't allow the state the garden's in now to put you off. I meant to say that I had an idea to get it cleared, and then ploughed deep, to bury all the rubbish, as they call weeds round here, and the seeds. Also the cankered fruit-trees must be grubbed up, and new kinds planted. Not all at once, of course, but bit by bit."

He thought that his father looked very tired. "Anyway, there's plenty of time ahead in which to decide." He thought to add that he was going to ask his sister Doris and her husband to spend August with them, but knowing how his father felt about that marriage, forebore.

He spoke of it to his mother. "After all, they haven't much money, and there's plenty of milk and eggs now, and Lucy loves making butter. I'll be able to take Bob sailing, too. I've joined a yacht club, and one can hire boats there at non-racing times for ten shillings a day."

"Oh, I am so glad, Phillip. Country air will do Doris a world of good."

"Father needs country air, too. Look how he's different down here, from what he used to be at home."

"He's thinking of trying to find a cottage, you know, somewhere in Kent, now that he has thought of retiring. I hope it won't be too far away," she sighed.

"You mean from the girls? Oh, mother, why can't they live their own lives? I know how you feel about it, but I honestly think Elizabeth and Doris will be better on their own."

"Ah, my son, wait until your children grow up. Still, you have your own interests, you are fortunate, you are a man, and can do as you please."

When they had gone back to London he did not know what to

do with himself. There was now so much more to be done. He
went to look over the house with Lucy, but gave it up after going
into a couple of rooms. The aged house-keeper, what was to be
done with her? A telephone message from the solicitor awaited
him after his return. Would he go into Colham and see him at
his early convenience? He went immediately after a light lunch
of fish with red-pepper sauce.

"I think," said Mr. Grandison, "that I, as the executor of your
late uncle's estate, should begin to consider the matter of death
duties. Later on, perhaps you will tell me whether or not you
decide to dispose of any furniture. I ask because an auction of any
household goods that you may find surplus to your requirements
will not have to be valued for probate. The market value of such
household goods, as determined by an auction sale, will be accep-
table to the Commissioners. We shall, in any case, have to engage
the services of valuers for the property itself, that is, for the house.
If you decide to retain the house, I shall require to know your
assets, with a view of getting some idea of how we shall meet the
death duties."

"I've been offered a thousand pounds to write a book about
a trout, Mr. Grandison. Five hundred pounds down, and the rest
when the manuscript is delivered. I really must get down to it
after our holiday in Devon."

Chapter 13

BY THE ESTUARY

Now Lucy was back with baby Rosamund, and Billy and Peter
were happy again, Phillip motored to Devon. Piers and Virginia
were staying in the cottage, having their meals with the postman's
wife. For Phillip it was like old times; Martin and Fifi had stayed
there; even better times, for Piers was an ideal companion, and
Virginia had the candour of a boy, which she resembled with her
cropped hair and slight figure.

There was a boatbuilder's shed beside the creek leading to the
estuary. Various small boats, some decayed, others for repair,
were lying about. Among them was a long canvas canoe. The
paddles looked to be new under their varnish, so did the small

mast and triangular red sail. It had been lying out for a couple of
years, the canvas stretched over a wooden frame was not rotten,
but a coat of paint was needed. Was it seaworthy? asked Phillip,
thinking that it would be the very thing in which all three of them
might cross the estuary to the fishing village beyond the line
of sandhills.

It was all right for a short voyage, but to be in proper order it
needed a patch or two, and a coat of lead paint, replied the owner.

"How much is it?"

"Will five pounds be too much?"

While Phillip hesitated, the boatbuilder added that he would
make good any cracks and after the painting it 'would be tight as
a cup'. Phillip bought it, and asked him to paint it with two coats,
and the name, *Canute*, on the bows.

"I'll bring her back tonight for the painting."

They carried it down to the creek, getting black with mud
below the knees. It floated, they moved down to the estuary, and
thence close inshore to Point of Crow. The tide was flowing, gravel
barges waiting to cast off. They landed, and hauled up their
craft. Into pits whence gravel had been taken, discoloured sea-
water was pouring fast. It was a spring tide, a breeze blew up the
estuary. They watched while the paraffin oil engines were started
up. Crews sat on the decks, awaiting the rise of the tide to float
off their craft.

Phillip looked around. He felt clear and happy. The sun
glittered. Herring gulls were flying almost straight up from the
middle ridge of packed gravel which lay, an island in the rising
tide, between Crow Spit and the village across the water. The
birds spiral'd up a hundred feet or so before dropping down to the
stones below.

"What are they doing?" asked Virginia, sitting between Phillip
and Piers. All three were dressed in shorts and shirts, bare-footed.

"They prise mussels from the rocks, and then drop them to
smash shells."

"I've not seen gulls doing that before."

"I suppose a gull dropped a mussel one day, when pursued by
other gulls, and, diving to get it, learned the quickest way to break
the shell."

The wooden barges, gunwales awash, swung into the tide racing
up the narrow channel between Crow Spit and the black Yelland
rocks. Anchors were pulled up, drum-like engine-beats increased

as they wallowed away with the tide. Silence settled upon the
hot sands, save for the little wash of waves. They were alone on
the shelving shore in which were embedded ancient root-clumps
of riverside trees, wicker crab-pots, herring-boxes and other jetsam
of the sea. Piers lay back to enjoy the sun, Virginia stretched out
beside him. Phillip watched the Shrarshook, the middle ridge,
as it appeared to be shortening and sinking fast, while gulls flew
to the rigging of ketches by the distant quay-side.

At last Piers and Virginia got up to stroll into the sandhills,
and Phillip lay upon the hot sand, feeling to be dissolved in sunshine and air. When at last he arose on an arm the Shrarshook was
gone under the waves. He thought of *The Phoenix*, now being set-
up in type, and wondered if the story of Willie would stir and move
the public as it had moved him during the years it had lain upon
his life.

Footfalls purred in the loose sand, Piers' voice from the sky said,
"When is *The Phoenix* being published?"

"End of September. I was thinking of it at that moment. It
must be telepathy."

The footfalls purred away. He lay still, with eyes closed. He
heard quicker purring, and Virginia's voice said, close to his head,
"I ought to hate you." The words came so quietly that he replied
as gently, "Why should a mermaid hate me?"

"Because you tried to take Piers away from me."

"*Take?* Oh no! I remember saying something to Piers about a
girl I once knew, who was married, but it never occurred to me
that——" He sat up. "But of course that was what I *was* doing.
Trying to mind Piers' business for him. I am always interfering
in other peoples' lives."

"You have a great influence over Piers."

"I thought it was the other way about."

"Nearly everyone is against my marrying Piers. Before we
came down here my cousin Shetland asked me to luncheon to
talk it over. 'Take the fellow as your beau, but be discreet' was
the line he took. He has his mistress, and is *so* unkind to Angy,
who is such a sweet person. 'You know the one commandment,
don't you,' he said, 'Thou shalt not be found out.' Aren't people
beastly? When I told him that I loved Piers and we wanted to be
married, he said, 'My dear cousin, the heir to a baronetcy is the
lowest form of animal life.' People are such snobs and hypocrites."

"Perhaps the truth is best served by silence. I was foolish to say anything to Piers that night. I was thinking of myself and some-one else, long ago. Of course you are quite different, and I should have seen it, instead of laying down the law so stupidly."

She laughed. He was moved by her friendliness, and running down the steep slope of sand, plunged into the sea, to be carried fast up the estuary, but close in and parallel to the shore. Even so, he could not touch bottom, and struck out for the gravelly edge, since the current diverged a dozen yards ahead, streaming out from beyond the shingle tongue. He managed to crawl out just in time.

Piers returned and said, "The very place for a plunge. I'm going in."

"It's safe a hundred yards down, the tide runs parallel to the shore. But come out before the end of the shingle tongue."

"Yes, I saw you get out just in time."

Piers ran down to dive. Virginia followed. Phillip followed them along the strand, ready to plunge in; but both crawled out safely. After sun-bathing, they arose and walked hand in hand into the sandhills. He remained on the shore, beside one of the ancient tree roots embedded in the sand, while thoughts of Barley, who had walked with him on this very shore, pierced the ducts of his eyes. He got up and wandered away past the lighthouse and around Aery Point, whence was visible a prospect of three miles of broad sands.

The canoe was ready two days later. They carried it down to the creek on the last of the morning tide, finding an empty estuary of ridged sand around fresh-water pools. So they came to deeper water, almost still, through which the river moved slowly into the Pool beside the Shrarshook, and to the sandbank upon which lay petrol tins and other home-made buoys attached to salmon boats. Leaving the canoe drawn up, and walking bare-foot, they reached the rocks below the quay, and avoiding rusty bicycle frames, fish-heads, and other litter, climbed up a slip hung with sea-weed and walked down a narrow cobbled street between two rows of cottages to a pub at the far end, where Phillip had more than once had a lunch of beer, bread, cheese, and pickled eschalots.

Within the village were many public houses, or taverns: it was still the home of what were called mast-and-yards men, deep water sailors, while longshoremen lived in the small terraced cottages, get-ting a living from what they called rough-fish-catching. Then there were the crews of the licensed salmon-boats; and men working in the ship-yards. Phillip had been told that two out of every three children of the multitudes playing bare-footed on the rocks and in the little courts of cottages, tucked away among the streets, had been born out of wedlock. All this seemed to him to be a sign of vitality, he said to his friends as they walked down the narrow street; the pubs filled, at night, with laughter and the talk of far places; the scrupulously clean cottages, each with its threshold scrubbed and swabbed, and every third open doorway with a wooden barrier to stop babies from crawling out.

The doors had all been shut, the sea grey, the sky dull, the far hills white when first he had seen the village, on that winter day five years before with cousin Willie. Five years since they had walked across Dartmoor, in the frost and snow of winter.

If only he had re-created in *The Phoenix* but one part of that life —brought back but one image of life, then all would not be lost. Where else could old mortality find life again, but in the imagination of man—that illusive gift of the gods.

Piers divined the trend of his thoughts: and wanting his friend to be free, left him, to point out to Virginia the blue-painted figurehead of a woman fixed above a doorway in a little court beside the street, perhaps the home, he said, of some retired skipper of coasting ketch or schooner.

There was a gap in the narrow street; shadow yielded to sunlight. The open sea was visible beyond a low stone wall, on which nets were hung to dry. Fishermen, some still in the stiff leather thigh-boots they used in shallow water while hauling, were standing about, smoking; or leaning, calm and unspeaking, against the wall. They had fished, between lapse and flow of tides, in darkness, returning with the dawn; in an hour or two they would be going out for the next four-hour spell when the returning tide brought in the salmon.

"This is the place to live," Phillip heard Piers say to Virginia. "David, Brenda, and Elizabeth come and stay at a pub somewhere here. It may be this one."

Before them stood a lime-washed inn which overlooked the Pool, the lighthouse, and the sandhills across the estuary.

Within, the woodwork of bar, bench, and skittle table was dyed by tobacco smoke. The landlord, a grey-haired man looking like a retired soldier, was leaning on the bar. He recognised Phillip.

"Ban't you the gen'elman whose friend was drowned off the

Shrarshook the night of the big Fair tide five year back along? Cordarn, I wor' thinkin' of 'ee, zur, only this morning. Your face kep' comin' to mind. I zee'd ee on the sands of Crow when us took the poor young gen'leman in th' seine. I mind that someone made a beacon fire on Crow that night."

"Yes, that was my cousin who was drowned. I remember you well."

He shook hands with the landlord, who, like most of the inn-keepers, worked a salmon net to earn a living. He asked for three plates of bread, cheese, and pickled eschalots. They were hungry; the blend of ale and food was perfect. Skittles were fun, after he had shown Piers and Virginia how to swing the ball on its string in parabola or circle, regarding the post from the top of which the string swivelled as dividing the orbit.

Piers said to the landlord, "Do you happen to know where a number of people of my age from London come down to stay, usually four of five together?"

"They stay in my house, here, sir, if it's the same young ladies and gentlemen."

Piers mentioned names, and the landlord said, "That's right."

Phillip set up the three outside pins; Virginia swung the ball in a circle. The three fell, clipped on the outside. Her face showed her pleasure. "You're an awf'ly good teacher, Phil. I saw at once the idea."

He set up the nine pins. "Now measure the width of the top pin from the right of the post; then launch the ball to travel an equal distance from the *left* of the post. The idea is to strike the top pin on the left side, to make it scatt, as they say, the pins on the right side, while the ball travelling on scatts the pins on the left side. The nine go down together, and you have a 'floorer'."

Virginia leaned forward, to judge the throw; while Phillip heard Piers asking if anyone was staying there at the moment.

"Only one gentleman, sir. Ah, there he is, just coming up the slip." The landlord pointed through the east windows which gave a view of the sea-wall. "He's staying here while writing a book, name of Mr. Anthony Cruft, perhaps you have heard of him?"

Virginia dropped the ball. Phillip saw that the figure of Tony Cruft was only a few yards away, seen through the lace curtain over the lower half of the window.

"My God," said Virginia. "If he knows I'm here it will spoil his book."

This consideration for her husband's art roused Phillip to action. As the figure passed the window he said, "Out you both go, and down the slip. Double!"

Virginia hopped out, followed by Piers. Phillip closed the sash window. Any moment now Cruft would enter the side-door. He must not be seen, he sat with his back to the bar and close to the grandfather clock. He could observe through the gap between clock-case and wall. The door opened. "Any letters for me?"

"I'm afraid not, sir."

Phillip could feel Cruft hesitating; sinking a little in despair, after the hope that he knew was hopeless; fortifying himself by repeating *She will not write*, while remembering the tenderness of the flesh. His head was down, as for reflection; then with resolution his footfalls struck the treads of the stairs. Phillip tip-toe'd to the landlord and said, "Please do not say we have been here. Not a word, mind. I would never have brought my friends had I known who was staying here."

"I understand, sir."

He hastened to join the others on the rocks below, invisible from the tavern windows. While the two walked under the quay wall to where several masted ships were tied up, he got the canoe and hauled it up river. Which way to retreat? Either they cross the water to Instow, and leave *Canute* anchored at the top edge of the Pool, and so to paddle over to Crow on the flowing tide; or, pulling it up above the mark of high tide, leave it there and catch the next train to Barnstaple, and back to Speering Folliot by taxi.

Piers thought it best not to hang about, in view of a possible telescope; so they carried the canoe up the Instow beach and left it among the marram grasses.

Early the next morning Piers and Virginia made for Dover, and ultimately the mountains of Austria. Phillip went with them so far as Dorchester, where they said good-bye. He wondered about Piers as he went on to Rookhurst: that morning, when Mules brought in the post, there were two more letters for Piers, addressed in his mother's handwriting. All her letters which had arrived so far Piers had put between the bars of Mrs. Mules' kitchen range, unopened.

Piers had told him that his mother's letters begged him not to marry a divorced woman: if he did so, she pleaded, he would be excommunicated by the Church, and denied beatitude for all eternity. Lady Tofield had also written to Virginia, asking her if she intended to stand between her only son and Christ. Could she, Mrs. Cruft, take upon herself such a responsibility before God?

Virginia had replied that she believed that God was love, and she loved Piers, and would trust in God. This reply had broken the mother's heart.

Phillip considered it his duty to ask his younger sister and her husband to stay for their summer holiday. They came down in August with their baby son; and thinking that it would ease the strain of marriage if they did not see each other all the time, he suggested that he and Bob should go to Devon and stay in the cottage. Both Lucy and Doris readily agreed; it would give them a period of freedom during which they would be able to do what they wanted to do, go for picnics with the children and have a holiday together.

Phillip heard that the canoe had gone adrift on a high tide, and floating down half submerged, had been taken in tow by a longshoreman who had it stowed in the court where he lived in Appledore. The two crossed by the twopenny ferry and saw it. The frame was undamaged, but the canvas on the decks at each end was torn. Having paid £1 salvage money, Phillip arranged for it to be towed with the tide to the creek, and left at the boatbuilder's shack. There he and Bob ripped off the old canvas and fitted new material, tacking it with copper tacks before painting it white. Two empty petrol tins were stowed, one at each end under the new canvas, to act as floats should the long, unwieldy vessel capsize. The cracks in the old canvas of the hull were caulked, and painted. After an interval for the paint to dry, they carried *Canute* to the black mud in the creek, and slipped it down to the river-water running fast and shallow below.

At the creek-mouth they met the incoming tide, and then began a long and strenuous paddling against the froth and whorls of the current, Bob in the bows and Phillip in the stern. They managed to get to Crow Shingle, after some trouble to keep the bows straight: instead of paddling on the left or port side only, as Phillip had asked him to do, Bob sometimes dipped first one side and then the other, which threw out the steersman's efforts.

They waited until the tide eased, then crossed the Pool. The Pool buoy, green with weed and red with rust, now stood upright in slack water like a gigantic fishing float. They left the canoe in Appledore to be caulked. When this was finished—with putty only, Phillip noticed—the tide had turned. Grey-green water was gliding and swirling fast below the wet sands. The boatbuilder's son helped them carry it down from the yard, telling them to keep inshore in the riband of backwash and paddle up the Torridge so far as the dry dock, which was about half a mile up the river; then to shoot across the tide which would take them on a slanting course to the slackwater along the Instow shore. Still keeping well inshore, they must cross the String—which Phillip remembered as a fearful area where Torridge ebb battled with Taw ebb—and creep up past the Yelland rocks, now exposed, and continue on past them as close as they dared until they were well beyond Crow which they would see opposite the Yelland rocks. Then, a couple of hundred yards up-river they must turn and shoot across the tide racing between Crow and Yelland.

It seemed a difficult matter, with a narrow, 20-foot canoe. They set the small red sail; there was a breeze from the sea which would help them up the backwater and also keep the bows straight.

"You paddle on the port side only, this time, Bob. I'll take the starboard."

They got in, while the youth held the bows; they gripped paddles and were shoved off into the backwash, a ribbon of water about six feet wide travelling in the opposite direction to the ebb. The first thing Phillip knew was that they couldn't keep the nose straight, although the sail was being pressed hard against the little mast. He was comforted by the fact that Bob was strong, a stout fellow who had commanded tanks during the war. He had a bullet-splashed neck, where the steel-core of copper-sheathed Spandau machine-gun bullets had pierced the plates of his disabled tank. The enemy machine-gunners used to concentrate on one particular plate of a broken-down tank, while the crew inside watched the steel plate getting red-hot, then yellow-hot, to bulge and finally burst before the succession of steel cores which rang against the inside of the opposite plate and splashed off so that Bob got some molten steel globules in his neck.

Phillip saw the scars reddening as Bob drove his paddle hard against the greater thrust of the tide; and had to back-paddle to try to keep the bows straight, while seeing the thin crescent of the new moon sliding round the green western sky. The Shrarshook ridge, which was two feet above the water and growing every

minute, was sliding forward. He realised that they and their craft
were being taken down to the open sea.

"Don't waste your strength paddling both sides. You take the
port side. I'll take the starboard."

"Righty ho."

For several minutes they dug into the massive slide of water.
The dark stones and blue mussel clusters of the ridge were no longer
sliding forward; they were now in front of Bob's reddening neck
scars. He said, after some minutes of desperate paddling, "The
blasted thing's filling with water."

"We've got the empty petrol tins, remember, Bob. She'll float
if she fills up."

"Are you sure? You told the fellow to take them out and tar
them, didn't you?" He stove-in the brittle ply-wood of the bulk-
head with his heel. "He's left out the for'ard tin, any old how.
Water's pouring in. We're for it." He smiled to himself, and
fumbled for a cigarette. "Yo ho, and a bottle of rum on a dead
man's chest!"

Phillip felt the disintegration of fear. Below the lighthouse,
which they were now passing, lay the dreaded broken water of
the Hurleyburlies.

"Paddle, you bloody fool!" he shouted. "Don't waste time
singing shanties! Now then, for God's sake, together! Dig! Dig!
Dig! That's the idea! Keep it up like that. For God's sake don't
muck about!"

Water was slopping over his legs. They were sitting in three
inches. The gunwales, with their copper beading, were less than
six inches from the surface of the sea. The craft was heavy, deep
in the water. Their paddling could no longer control the steering.
They were moving down at seven knots with the tide. Phillip
heard the noise of water breaking over the rocks. He thought he
would be drowned. A frenzy arose in him; not from the thought
of Lucy left alone, or the children, but that now his book on the
war would never be written.

Unknown to his trembling self, men were running over the
sands a quarter of a mile away. He began to bale, using an old
rusty tin which he had picked up on a sandbank that morning
with the joking remark that one never knew when such a thing
would be useful. It was useless. The water was now spirting in
through those cracks in the painted canvas which had been stopped
by moist putty. Soon the canoe would pass the black-and-white

Pulley buoy, which was wallowing violently a few cables' length away.

"They're getting a boat," said Bob, pointing.

"Keep the head upstream! Paddle on the left! I'll take the right!"

But Bob had his own ideas; he dipped first one side then the other, causing the craft to rock with water slopping about inside. He ignored the shouting behind him. In his fear and rage Phillip wanted to strike him over the head with his paddle.

"I thought you were going mad," said Bob, when they were back on Crow Spit, having been taken in tow and the canoe left at Appledore. Phillip was ashamed of himself and resentful of Bob for his slightly contemptuous judgment.

"I thought we would both be drowned."

"So did I, but it was nothing to make a fuss about."

"Didn't you worry that you might never see Doris or your son again?"

"I thought that they'd probably be better off without me."

The two men went back to Rookhurst that evening. The holiday was a failure. A week later the Willoughbys returned to London— Doris and her son and their dog in the little sidecar.

After they had gone Phillip felt depressed. The baby was to have drawn his sister and Bob together. It hadn't altered the unhappy situation in the very least. Now the feeling between himself and Bob had ceased.

He walked to the Longpond. No fish were visible. They were dormant after the summer gorge. 'The sedge is wither'd from the lake, and no birds sing.' Piers and Virginia would be in the Austrian mountains by now, seeing through the open windows of some wooden *Gasthaus* the snow-peaks of the Alps.

From afar came the faint rattle of a reaper-and-binder. Ned was cutting the only corn on the farm, eight acres of oats grown for cattle feed in winter. He thought of Felicity: why had she left without saying goodbye? Had she started an affair with Cabton? Perhaps it was just as well: it would be pretty awful if he had had her, as he wanted to at the time. No; there could never again be anyone like Barley.

The next morning, an enlivening surprise—the galley proofs of *The Phoenix* arrived. In the post was a letter from Edward Cornelian

saying that he would like an opportunity of discussing certain points in the story, and did he know of any cottage to be let
furnished in his neighbourhood. Phillip thought to write at once
and offer him the cottage at Speering Folliot, but on second
thoughts decided that it would be unsuitable for such a famous
literary figure. There was nothing to be done on the farm which
Ned could not do; the old arable was now down to pasture,
being grazed by stock put there by a dealer, on the principle of
meat for manners. The manners being the dung dropped by the
bullocks. They were fed extra food from small circular iron bowls,
too heavy to be kicked over, each with a daily ration of crushed
oats mixed with broken cotton and linseed cake provided by the
dealer. Thus the fertility of the fields increased, while all Ned,
the one remaining man, had to do was to take up the 'cake', and
water in the iron cart to fill the drinking troughs once a day. After
the other two men had been given notice by the manager, Mr.
Hibbs, the rumour in the village was that the land had already
been sold by Sir Hilary to the military; but as Phillip told Ned, he
knew nothing about it.

"My uncle has not taken me into his confidence."

Many farms were being advertised in the columns of the local
paper, for sale as from Michaelmas. The unemployment in the
towns was increasing. Nearly all the workers said they would
vote for Labour at the next election.

"Why not tell Mr. Cornelian about the White House?" This
was a cottage on the sea-wall beside the estuary. "It's just the
place, and cousin Mary told me that the marshman's wife takes
in summer visitors."

"Let's all go on holiday to North Devon."

So they drove west, and stayed in Scur Cottage; and in the
evening went along the toll-road under the sea-wall to see the
marshman in the White House. Yes, they had two bedrooms and
a parlour to let. The charge was £2/2/- a week for the apartments,
and Mrs. Pedrick would cook for Mr. Cornelian and his friend
without extra charge, if they would supply their own food.

Mr. Cornelian arrived with an elderly woman friend, and said
that Cabton was coming to visit him, and did Phillip know of a
lodging in the village where Cabton might stay?

Lucy suggested that he might stay in the cottage, while she and
the children went to cousin Mary at Wildernesse. So Phillip lived
by himself, until the time for Cabton's arrival; and every day

went to visit the White House, taking groceries and provisions ordered the day before by Mr. Cornelian's friend.

On the fourth afternoon the critic said, coming out of the White House to greet him with galleys of *The Phoenix* in his hand, "I think you should be more reserved after the drowning. There is too much detail. You very nearly give the effect of sentimentality, like Morland in his novel *Possession* where Evelyn Groucherd's wife's lover commits suicide. And Donkin is not self-critical enough."

Phillip went on at once to see Lucy at Wildernesse.

"Before, Cornelian said that Donkin was too self-critical, so I toned down his remorseful outbursts. Now, he says Donkin lacks self-criticism. I based it originally on what you told me Mary had said to you. Do you think I might ask Mary? Or would it upset her?"

"I shouldn't think so, after all this time."

"All this time—five years? I can hear Julian Warbeck's lament as though it were last night. 'O sweet stray sister, O shifting swallow, The heart's division divideth us, Thy heart is light as the leaf of a tree, But mine goes forth among sea-gulfs hollow——'"

"I'll tell Mary you're here."

"Thank you."

He found her in the kitchen.

"Mary—forgive me—I keep remembering my cousin, as the equinox comes near——"

"Yes, Phillip, so do I."

"Will it upset you to talk about him?"

"No, Phillip—nothing you could say would upset me."

"Mary—surely he was self-critical?"

"Yes, he was *very* self-critical, Phillip. It was due, I think, to great sympathy for others, my mother included. When we are alone, sewing or reading at night, she still says sometimes, 'You know, I think I understand him better now'."

"Did Willie ever rant before her?"

"When he spoke bitterly, or in distress, it was always against himself, for his shortcomings, and failure to understand fully another's point of view. He even praised my mother to me for not liking his ideas, because they were too revolutionary and therefore outside ordinary living. He used to say, 'If anyone dislikes me, I feel that it is always my own fault for failing to understand. After all, other people's opinions should always be more important than one's own'."

"Yes, he said that to me once, Mary. I've tried to act up to it, but usually fail."

All that night Phillip was restoring the critical self-awareness of Donkin, putting back the former hard lines; and when the next day, having met Cabton's train, he brought over a corrected galley, Cornelian went in to read it. While tea was being laid he came to where Phillip was lying on the sands and said, "No, don't get up. I came to say that it's exactly right. Well done. Half a dozen galleys will have to be reset, but it will be worth it."

Try as he might, Phillip could induce no flow of *camaraderie* in Cabton. In Mr. Cornelian's presence he gave out a feeling of being slightly superior to all he beheld: not exactly from self-sufficiency, but of living independently of the feelings of other people.

"What sort of books do you like best, Cabton?"

"Oh, no sort in particular. Why?"

"I just wondered. Have you read Conrad's *Mirror of the Sea*, or *Heart of Darkness*?"

"Yes."

"What do you think of Conrad?"

"He's all right for those who like that sort of thing. But he's unreal."

"What about reality in Hardy? Have you read any of his stuff?"

"He"—with a jerk of his thumb in the direction of the white-haired Cornelian sitting on the sands with his flannel trousers rolled to the knee and exposing many varicose veins—"gave me *Jude the Obscure* to read. Hardy never knew a real working man."

"But it was a different age, surely? Hardy knew stone-masons and other working men at first hand."

"But he'd never been one himself."

This seemed ironic to Phillip: for according to Anders, Cabton wrote about country people and he had never been out of London. Still, the story was the thing, no matter how it came into being.

In the morning there was a letter from Anders, forwarded from Rookhurst, enclosing one from Coats with a report by Edward Cornelian on the earlier novels published by Hollins, which Phillip intended to rewrite, so that they would lead directly to the theme of *The Phoenix*.

These three novels are poor in construction, and if the publisher wishes to spoil a reputation likely to be consolidated by *Phoenix* he should set about republishing them at once.

Phillip showed this report to Cabton while preparing breakfast. Cabton merely glanced at it before saying, "I shouldn't take any notice of what that old fool says. Why, just look at those veins in his legs, obviously signs of gout. I saw bottles and bottles of port in his cupboard when I went to his house in Chelsea, and he used my visit as an excuse to open one as soon as I was inside, although I told him I don't drink."

"Aren't varicose veins due to thin walls of the veins?"

"Anyway, what does he know about writing? He tried to tell me what to write. I told him I never know what I'm going to write. It just comes, once I get an idea. He's all literary, trying to fit in everything."

"But sympathetic, surely?"

"Yes, to get letters from famous writers, and sell them when they're dead. He's got a lot from Conrad, he showed them to me —not that I was interested. Anyone can see that Conrad had to flog himself to write."

"But he produced passages of great beauty, don't you think?"

Phillip took the tent Lucy had brought down to the sea-wall and set it up in a hollow of the low grassy sandhills near the marshman's cottage. There he slept alone. The weather continued fine. The tent was among wild dogswood bushes. He cooked on a fire of driftwood dried in the sunshine. Lying awake at night he heard the wavelets of the high tide falling on the sea-wall. One afternoon Lucy and Billy came over to visit him, having walked barefoot through the sandhills. She and Phillip bathed on the incoming tide, while Billy paddled. Cabton hung back, not wanting to admit that he could not swim. Afterwards they all sat, Phillip and Lucy and Billy with bare feet, in the parlour having tea. Edward Cornelian said that Lucy's feet were most beautiful, reminding him of Jefferies' description of the young girl Amaryllis in his novel. Not that Lucy had 'thick, sturdy ankles', on the contrary, he said; but she possessed the serenity that was the ideal of all artists.

Lucy liked him, and under the stimulus of her smiles he began to joke, rather clumsily, on the vicissitudes of marriage to one with the artistic temperament.

"Arnold Bennett, you may recall, says somewhere that all great novelists 'begin clumsily, poor dears'. He was writing about Hardy's first novel, which has remained unpublished. Edmund Gosse told me, when he read it in manuscript, that it had a title something like 'The Lady and the Mason', and was full of comical errors about a social world of which the young Hardy knew nothing. And now your husband, who has written a very fine novel, wants to republish his juvenilia." He turned to Cabton. "You, my dear fellow, will never make the same mistake. Your talent is clear and direct, forthright."

"Ah, he is fortunate to have such expert guidance from the start, Mr. Cornelian."

"At least Cabton will never write the first thing that comes into his head, without practising the critical faculty, as you appear to have done in those early novels of yours."

"But surely one is practising the critical faculty in wanting to demolish them, and true them up, Mr. Cornelian?"

"Get on with new work, my dear fellow. Have you started your novel of nineteen fourteen and so through the war?"

"Well, as I think I mentioned when we met in Romano's, I want an earlier novel to lead to the Great War. So I think I should really begin in the early 'nineties——"

"It shows poor critical judgment to begin at a period which you cannot have known, since it must have been before your time. No! Start off in the summer of nineteen fourteen and plunge straight into the war. Or are you impervious to the voice of experience?"

"But surely 'the voice of experience' was not always right in the past? Even creative writers have gone hopelessly wrong at times. Look at Byron's opinion of Keats, sir. He wanted Keats to write like Byron. Keats wanted every line written by other poets to be loaded with ore. Yet both were creative writers, and if they could be wrong about other creative writers, isn't it possible that a non-creative writer, a critic, might be wrong too?"

"What do you say to that, Cabton?" asked Cornelian.

Cabton's face wore an expression of sardonic indifference. "Oh, I just get an idea and write. If it's no good, I tear it up."

Edward Cornelian went on to say that all writers had their blind spots, and if they did not take care, they would come to a poor end, usually on the bottle. He continued in this strain, humorously prophesying a drunkard's end for Phillip, until Lucy said it had been most enjoyable, but now it was time to go back to see to Peter and baby Rosamund. She blushed, because she had not mentioned the baby so far, when Mr. Cornelian showed pleasure and told her to be sure to bring the baby over one afternoon. When she was leaving she said to Phillip outside, "I'll try to come over and cook your breakfast for you, if you would like me too."

"Yes, come as early as you can. Do you think I went too far with Cornelian, with my simile of creative writer and critic with salmon and lamprey?"

"Oh no, he was ragging you, and you were ragging him back, that was all."

Lucy came over at half-past eight, and was crouched over the driftwood fire when Phillip saw Cornelian, with serious face, approaching over the crest of the sandhill. The old fellow returned a subdued good-morning to his greeting of, "Hullo, sir! Just in time for breakfast! Lucy has brought over some mushrooms."

"May I speak with you privately for a moment?"

Standing in an adjoining hollow, out of sight of tent and cottage roof, Edward Cornelian said, "Why did you insult me yesterday afternoon?"

"I'm awfully sorry, Mr. Cornelian——"

"Your remarks about the relationship of critics and writers were most offensive."

Lamely the younger man repeated that he was very sorry, but he had not been serious in his later remarks. "I thought we were ragging one another."

"Yes, but despite a superficial gaiety, there was, I felt, an undercurrent of dislike in all your remarks to me. This feeling culminated when you said that the creative writer was like a clean-run salmon in the estuary, and the critic was a lamprey which fastened on it and sucked its life away. Such a simile can hardly have a basis in anything but a grudge against myself. Is it because I, as was my duty, to both you and to Coats, advised against republication of those early novels?"

"But, Mr. Cornelian, how can there be any parallel?"

"That is what I am seeking to discover. All I know is that I have praised your recent work to a publisher, and highly recommended him to push it with all his resources. Why then did you insult me as you did?"

Phillip repeated that he was sorry that his words had seemed serious.

"There is another matter," went on Cornelian. "You spoke about critics making it their business to write to authors, and then

THE POWER OF THE DEAD

of selling the letters, when the authors were dead, for considerable sums. What made you say that?"

"Well, you had been telling us that it wouldn't be long before somebody—was it a Doctor Sidney Cockerell?—would seek my acquaintance with a view to getting letters from me, as he had from Hudson and Conrad. Really, I was just fooling about, saying anything."

"Yes, I notice that you say anything that comes into your head; but all the same, I feel that your remarks were based on a dislike of myself, because I wrote as I did about your early novels."

"I see now that I should have rewritten them, before sending them in. They will be quite different, I assure you, Mr. Cornelian. Well, sir, I do hope that you will not remain hurt by my silly remarks."

"Are you now suggesting that I am one to bear a grudge?"

"Oh no, no! I'd better say no more, the fact is I have a rather worrying decision to make soon, a family matter, which has been preying on my mind for a long time now. But I won't bother you with that. In fact, I rather fancy it has already been decided for me. Please let me give you some mushrooms, Lucy has picked some specially for you and Miss Beach."

"Thank you, but I dare not touch them. But do not let me keep you from your breakfast. Have you seen Cabton?"

"I lent him a fleabag, when he didn't return to my cottage, and he said he was going to make a shelter for himself in the bushes somewhere."

"He tells me that he has a young lady friend coming to visit him, whom he met at your house. A Miss Felicity Ancroft."

After breakfast Phillip walked with Lucy part of the way to Wildernesse. She had brought a letter with her from Mr. Grandison, the solicitor, in reply to one from Phillip, saying that he would go ahead with the details of the proposed autumn auction as soon as he knew what items had been selected for disposal.

"We'll do it at the beginning of September, shall we, Lucy? Grandison thinks that it should be held about Old Michaelmas Day, the tenth of October, when the weather is usually fine. By the way, Felicity is coming here, apparently. To see Cabton."

He left Lucy at a valley leading to the lighthouse. The sun was over the mainland, and in the eastern light the village buildings across the water looked to be sharper, greyer, while the tide at flood was a mirror in which a second village, spectral and distorted, hovered wanly. He moved along the jetsam line, making for Aery Point, where the coast curved to the north and the open Atlantic was before him.

It was a haunted shore, it belonged to the past, because all was now safe in print. He felt that he must never return; all was now gone into ancient sunlight.

He sat by the seaward line of the sandhills, and made a fire for companionship, while past him floated the restless hollow mutter of ocean lapsing under miles of wave-sounds. He lay on his back, letting loose sand slip through his fingers, while the sun swung up into the southern sky, and the air was filled with the roar of the ebb tide becoming more tumultuously broken upon the gravel banks of the North Tail. Melancholy deepened in the vacuum of his heart. The sea was empty, so were the sands stretching under a mirage to the northern hills. He had thought that when *The Phoenix* was written the ghost of Willie would find rest. All began, all ended, with oneself. There were ghosts, aye there were ghosts: but they lived in the human heart. There they had their dwelling, to leave it with the coming of love. *I am all your friends,* he could hear her saying. O Barley, bright vision with Michael and All Angels, come to me.

The breaking moment passed. Bruce's spider had more reality than 'a poet's tearful fooling'. He thought of Flecker's play *Hassan* he had seen in London soon after the war. The music of Delius had been beyond resignation, a serene acceptance of immortal longing, of beauty accompanying the lovers who had rejected life, and chosen death, for one hour of love. Then, leaving Death the antic behind, the caravan setting out for Samarkand. 'Always we must go a little farther.'

James Elroy Flecker, dead of consumption: all that was left of him were his poems, some learned by heart in the Malandine cottage before the coming of Barley.

> West of these out to seas colder than the Hebrides
>   I must go
> Where the fleet of stars is anchored and the young
>   Star-captains glow . . .

Georgian poetry died on the Somme. The young star-captains —Sorley, Butterfield, Thomas, Ledwidge, Brooke, Owen, Rosenberg, Grenfell—now glowed phosphorescent in the wood of wild willows in the unclaimed areas of Flanders, Artois, and Picardy. Their poetic race was run. Modern verse now surveyed the waste land of Civvy Street; but no urban poet of alley-way and coffee spoon could speak with the authority of the phoenix—which had no real existence. The fleet of stars was burnt out and black.

A feeling of wildest desolation arose in him; he searched the immeasurable legions of the sand—rock, bone, tree reduced by air and water ever fighting for creation. He stared along leagues of empty wave, sky, and shore, longing to see one human figure. Had Wordsworth felt that—life a vacuum, once filled by what he had, in youth, been able to put into 'nature'?

The far prospect of sand lay under its dilating shimmer of blue. When he stood up the mirage dissolved, releasing three small specks in line. Lowering his head to the level of the sea-shore, he saw the specks crumble and melt once more in quivering heat.

He ran up a sandhill, marram grasses pricking his bare legs, and surveyed from the crest. A man and two women were walking there. He awaited their coming, his mind buoyant once again as he watched them getting nearer. He decided to go towards them and see who they were; and running down the slope of sand came upon a number of blue butterflies among flowers of sea-rocket growing with yellow-horned poppies above the tide-line. He wondered if, there being no scent in the sea-rocket, the butterflies had been drawn by the colour of the flowers. His footfalls purred past them, and as the group came nearer and the man waved, his heart leapt: surely it was Martin Beausire? It was; and with him were Fiona and Felicity.

"We've been looking for you," cried Martin, approaching with a hand held out. "We met Lucy in the village and she told us where to find you."

"Where have you sprung from?"

"We're staying with the Mules."

He wondered about this, since Martin's novel published two years before, with its caricatures of the Mules family, had been read in the village.

"Hullo, Felicity. This *is* a surprise."

"But, Phil," said Fiona, "surely you knew Felicity was coming?"

Seeing the girl's downheld eyes he replied quickly, "Of course I heard from Cabton that she was coming. Only I'd forgotten the exact day."

Martin wanted to bathe.

"It's dangerous at the ebb, particularly at Aery Point. When the tide has run out we'll be able to cross over the Hurleyburlies to the Shrarshook, and swim in the old gravel pits there."

"It's your line of country."

They put on bathing dresses and sat in the sun before wandering down to Aery Point to look at a salmon boat which had just put in to shoot a draught. The ebb was still running fairly fast; but the main volume had lapsed. The fairway was two hundred yards distant. Salmon, cruising along the coastal shallows, just clear of breaking waves to find the river, were now moving into the estuary, he told them.

In the fairway two other boats, each with its crew of four men and piled net, were making for the sandbanks of the South and North Tails, now marked by white confused waves. Each of the fishing places, or pitches, he explained, were visited in rotation by the licensed boats, on the basis of equal chances for all.

Phillip and Felicity walked down wet shingle towards a whale-back of gravel where a shallow stream was rushing fast and noisy.

"Here the ebb is checked by the sea-mass, Felicity, and so the shingle piles up."

They crossed the stream, the whale-back was loose with draining water. Each step up caused a slide of pebbles, so he gave her a hand. They descended the seaward slope, to walk upon the sand-bank which lay beside the deep and narrow channel of the fairway. Marking buoys were lying nearly flat on their sides as though exhausted by resistance to the weight of the ebb.

"Cabton is in the camp. We'll go there after the bathe. I expect you'll be glad to see him."

He left her, to follow or go back to Beausire, as she wished. No, he thought: I must stand alone. I belong to the dead. This is the North Tail, and across the narrow channel is the South Tail. There, on that late September morning the body of Willie's spaniel was found. Did Billjohn follow his master to the Shrars-hook in the darkness of that awful night? Did they meet? Did the spaniel find Willie and were both swept away together on the rising tide?

He heard the crunching of gravel behind him.

"Phillip, do you really think I came down to see Cabton?"

He looked down at her, as she stood before him in her black bathing suit. He saw the swelling breasts, the slope of her legs, the soft curve of the thighs foreshortened in his downward glance to the feet standing as though obediently before his own. Only with Barley had he felt the lure of a girl's feet, seen past brow, nose, breast, and soft diminishing curve of thigh.

"How is the free-lancing going?"

"I can't work in London any longer." Pale blue eyes appealed to him.

Lucy, so kind, so sympathetic, so trustful; Lucy so often set aside in his mind because she could not share his world—his memories. No: he must not allow his feelings for this young girl—— No: Lucy had come to rescue him, after Barley had died.

"Why shouldn't you come to see Cabton?"

He felt his lust rising; and plunged down the loose shingle. Each step broke away a hundredweight and more of white, brown and blue pebbles; he arrived in time to help haul on the heel rope. Seven fish were in the seine. She turned away as one after another was clouted on the back of the neck with a wooden club.

"Phillip, didn't he give you my message?"

"I heard indirectly through Edward Cornelian."

"I wanted to write but I felt I might not be wanted——"

In his happiness he said, "Come and look at these salmon. Can you see the dreamy hues of ocean on them? The colours of the sea, silver of the scales: a suggestion of pale green of shallow water on ribbed sand: the faintest coralline of the paired fins. I suppose it dreams of homecoming to the river of its birth, after the long sea wilderness."

Martin asked one of the crew how old were the fish.

"Maidens," said one.

"Four-year hen-fish," said another.

"They ban't true spawning fish, they come later," said a third.

"That's right," said the skipper. "They be maiden summer fish."

"If they don't come to lay their eggs, why do they come into the river?" asked Fiona.

"They'm rinnin'."

"I don't understand."

"They'm playin'."

"When is the spawning season in the rivers?" asked Martin.

"They fish spawn on the Shrarshook."

"Why don't they stay in the sea, where it's safer," persisted

Fiona, "until it's time to lay their eggs. What makes them come into the river?"

"Dream," said Phillip.

Chapter 14

INCOMPLEAT ANGLER

Felicity proved so companionable to Lucy that she was invited to return to Rookhurst with them. One morning the three went to look over Fawley House, to decide what furniture should be sold at the forthcoming auction. Felicity carried pencil and note-book.

While the two women were examining furniture, Phillip wandered away. What a place of dark tunnel-like passages the 'big house' was, beyond the living quarters of the family which once existed with its many children. Surely one half of the occupants, in the south-facing, tall rooms, had not known how the other half in the coving attics had lived. As for the kitchen, it was like the engine-room of a small tramp-steamer, without the engines and without the electric bulbs.

Feeling that the desolation of the house was too much for him, he climbed the stairs to the attics in order to see the view from the upper windows. The servants' quarters, approached by steep and narrow steps, were crossed by papered beams. The wide but shallow eave-windows barely permitted the entry of direct light. During the years of silence up here only wandering butterflies and queen-wasps had found their way in, to add to the wreckage of wings and masks in ancient spider webs. He sat down in an attic bedroom to lose himself in a dream of past life. Sometimes from below came remote voices and footfalls as from another world. After some minutes Lucy's clear voice floated up. "Are you still there? Can you come down and look at what we think might be sold?"

He went down the stairs and along a narrow passage to a baize door opening into the main gallery, and so to the tall bedroom where they were.

"What's this, Pip?"

Lucy had seemed more affectionate since Felicity had come, he thought. Was it because some of the load was taken off her mind?

"I've seen something like that before, where was it, now?"

He could not remember. "My memory isn't what it was. It may have been here. Yes, it was, Willie showed it to me. We bumped up and down on it. It's a dandy horse, for shaking up the liver in the morning after two bottles of port and all that went with it into the belly of a glutton."

It looked like a squat bellows, it was square and heavy with leather; toad-like; a row of five boards inside a square bellows, five rows of brass-headed nails, the brass held on by lead, along each board: coiled wire or springs between the boards to give the glutton a bounce and jerk each time he sat, stifling groans at aching eye-balls, fingers clutching scrolled wooden arms, sweaty feet on foot-board so that each pressure of his fat behind on horse-hair-stuffed top board, leather-covered, squeezed the fat of the belly-muscles.

"What a thing. Put it on the list to be sold, girls."

He looked at other queried items: an oak sideboard, carved with scenes of the Crimea, a present to his grandfather; a wine-cooler by Sheraton (although he did not know this); several chests riddled by the beetle, and rotten underneath from long standing on the stone floor of what used to be the servant's hall; large black coach-trunks in the loft, together with uniforms in japanned boxes. Other trunks of women's clothes looking to be well over a hundred years old.

"Oh, they're beautiful gowns!" said Felicity.

"Do you want them, Lucy?"

"Well no, I hardly think so." She looked at some of the clothes with an eye to cutting them down for the children.

"They should go to a Repertory Company," said Felicity, wondering who had worn the one she held up, with its tiny waist. She saw herself in it, beautiful for Phillip.

Seeing this with some satisfaction, he left to look elsewhere about the house. The dust-sheets had been removed from the drawing room, which was on the first floor. Now revealed was a conglomeration of Georgian and Victorian furniture—chairs, tables, lamp-stands on the marble shelf of the fire-place beside an ornate German over-mantel framing a tarnished mirror. Below was a brass fire-basket, green with verdigris and loaded with sticks and frayed feathers. The chimney seemed to be solid with jack-daws' nests. He thought of setting fire to them, but resisted the impulse and went downstairs to a tall room, dark with beams to the roof, which was the dining hall of the original barton around which other rooms had been built in Stuart times, according to Aunt Dora. The uneven oak-slab floor carried a refectory table with carved bulbous legs, around which were placed oak chairs with tall straight backs hung with tapestry, and the seats covered by flat, patchwork cushions. He hit one seat with his stick; dust fell from the chair frame, with dead moths and fragments of woollen fabric from the chair-back.

At one end of the hall, under the minstrel gallery, was a great open fireplace, above which was to be seen a square of sky. Bits of burnt paper, discoloured by damp, lay on the hearth, with rusty bully beef tins and ends of charred furniture frames. Here in the war soldiers had evidently been billeted. Initials were scratched in pencil on the plaster walls, with dates, most of them in the summer of 1916. Seeing these relics, the dead life of the hall became momentarily alive with khaki phantoms—only to recede into the viewless past.

Some candle lanterns, on posts wrenched out of missing wooden pedestals, lay along one wall. Every pane of glass within the rusty frames was broken. He could imagine what had happened—the pedestals had gone into the soldiers' fire. Had Uncle John claimed compensation? Probably not: too much had lain upon his spirit before, during, and after those days.

"Don't worry," said Lucy, seeing Phillip's face. "Felicity and I will gradually get it all tidy."

As he climbed to the downs above the borstal, he thought of the house soon to be altered to let in light and air; and striding along the ridge way to Colham, felt optimism returning. There he saw his solicitor, and told him his ideas for renovation. He was given the address of an architect. Having talked to that individual, he went round to the Rising Sun.

Outside in the yard stood Bill Kidd's motor-car. And from within the bar-room came the familiar voice.

"Seriously, 'Bosun', my lad, and without the word of a lie, I took that fish, all of five pounds on the spring-balance, on a cast tapered to 4-X and ending with the single hair of a Percheron stallion's tail knotted to my special fly, the Crystal Killer."

The reply of the landlord was a belch, followed by a squirt into the brass spittoon on the floor near Bill Kidd's feet. Then Bill Kidd's voice called out, "Come on in, my Mad Son. I know you're there. I'll tell you for why," he added when Phillip was in and the door closed. "See that knot-hole down there? Now watch it when I'm outside." He went out and closed the door. There on the floor was a dwarf image of Bill Kidd, surrounded by a faint halo of light.

"The old pin-hole camera, Phillip. It only happens when the sun's east-south-east. Have a drink. Where've you been all this time?"

"In Devon."

"Done any fishin'? Well, blow me down. And in the best season since nineteen fourteen! Did 'Bosun' tell you that I've moved into these parts, and got a cottage not far from your place? Near Uncle 'Tinribs' water, too, you must come with me and I'll show you how to catch fish. See this little fellow?" He lifted the lapel of his coat and revealed a small crushed artificial fly. "The Crystal Killer, old boy. It will take any fish anywhere at any time."

Phillip took the page-proof copy of *The Phoenix* from his pocket. "Some bits here and there might interest you, Bill. Would you care to borrow it?"

"Thanks, I'll let you have it back. Well, chin-chin, old boy. See you tomorrow."

'Bosun' became ruminative when Kidd had departed.

"Blest if us knows what to make of 'n. Funny sort of feller; 'a saith so many things. One day 'tes this, t'other day it be that. He be all fly this an' fly that," went on 'Bosun'. "Now can you tell me where a blofly comes from? I knows, see, but 'a don't. I seed one come out of a she-maskell, it flipped out in a flash, and not a feather on 'm. The maskell was up in thik corner." He pointed to a chrysalis on the wall.

"If that's a she-maskell, what does a he-maskell look like?" asked Phillip.

"Aw, like any other booger, I don't trouble nought 'bout he, midear."

"Yurr," Mrs. Tinker whispered, beckoning Phillip. "Last night Farmer Mock and Butcher Dellbridge was in yurr, discussing yaws, and the Major must say something, so 'a zaid he once had a yaw-flock on his uncle's estate. Was they two-toothed or four-toothed yaws Farmer Mock asks him, taking the major up, and the Major, I sees'm hesitating before he replies, 'Three teeth'. Of course us all laughed, and the Major looked proper dark, sayin' 'a had lost his memory after the wound 'a got, while rum-runnin' off 'a Long Island for the bootleggers in America."

"Funny sort of rum-runnin' it was too, I reckon," said Mr. Tinker.

"When I asked 'im afterwards he told me it was Booth's High and Dry Old Gin, and I told'n there wasn't no such gin, noomye!" and this time 'Bosun' spat so violently that he straddled the target.

"But you know'd'n in the war, didden you, Mr. Phillip? 'A saith 'a knowed 'ee, di'n 'ee, 'Bosun'?"

"Oh yes, he was a major all right, Mrs. Tinker."

The next morning Lucy and Felicity were continuing the list of surplus furniture to be sold, so Phillip again walked to the Rising Sun.

Something had happened before he arrived; Mrs. Tinker drew him behind the curtain and said, "Yurr! Have 'Bosun' told 'ee? 'Bout the Major's cheque what comed back? He asked us to change'n for'n, and it comed back this morning. What should us do? They do say that Malkin the butcher have got one comed back, too."

"Shouldn't be surprised if that be Malkin now, sounds like's bike," said 'Bosun', coming into the barrel-room. "'A comed yurr earlier on and zaid if he caught the Major 'a'd break his bliddy neck. There 'a be, comin' in. Say nought about nothing, missus."

The door opened and a man came in. He wore a jacket over blue-striped butcher's apron, below the hem of which were revealed a pair of brown boots and natty leggings. He was a man of about thirty, and already his face and hands were assuming the meaty hue which butchers have from handling meat the juice of which, Phillip had heard, entered the body through the pores of the palms. He was partly bald, his forehead and dome of head gave the idea that the roots of his hair had refused to continue growing in the suet or fat which, like the juices of meat, were ever trying to press through an oft-wiped brow.

"That feller about?" he enquired, abruptly. "Half a pint o' fourpenny, 'Bosun'."

"You mean the Major?" asked Mrs. Tinker. "'A cometh yurr sometimes 'bout now. P'raps he's working. I know 'a gets a cheque about this time of the month, for us changes it for'n, don't us, 'Bosun'?"

"It goes through all right," murmured the landlord. "Missus, draw me a pint."

"I'll give he 'major'," replied the butcher. "How does he make his money?"

"Yurr, I'll show 'ee, Mr. Malkin." Mrs. Tinker returned with a handful of crude pen-and-ink drawings. "The Major did all of these," she said, a little proudly.

Phillip asked to be allowed to look at them. They were based on the simple kind of proposterous joke-cartoon repeated year after year in the comic weeklies of the Conglomerated Press.

"Yes, the Major did all they," said Mrs. Tinker.

"I'll give he 'major' when I zee'n," repeated the butcher. "Twice I've had to leave my business to come yurr after my money. The bloody cheek of the feller!" He spat violently. "He comes to me, asks me to cash a cheque for five quid, and I obliged him. When it comes back from my bank I was after him, and he says he's sorry, but his account was overdrawn and he'll bring it down next day. Well, I was away to market when he calls at the shop to pay the money he owes me. He gives my boy a cheque to pay for the first cheque, then has the damned sauce to ask him to cash another for five pound, then makes the cheque out for ten pounds, and asks for t'other back. Then that one comes back also. I told'n if he didn't pay me back by this mornin' I'd put it in the hands of my solicitor and take him to court. And if he's not here by one o'clock that's what I'll do. Wait till I gets my hands on him. The rotten booger!"

"I'm sure it be a mistake," said Mrs. Tinker. "For 'a hath money be'ind'n, you know. The Army Paymaster gived he a pension—tes nearly thirty pound a month, too. I sees the envelopes to the Major, on His Majesty's Service they be. Wait a minute, I've got one here."

She went into her dark kitchen and returned with a much-folded envelope, on the back of which was a list of spirits—whisky, brandy, rum. "My eyes ban't what they was. That's what the Major ordered, perhaps you can read'n."

"I don't want to see no envelopes," declared the butcher. "I wants my money, else I'll take him, major or no major, to court."

"Perhaps you can see it," said Mrs. Tinker, passing the envelope to Phillip.

"It seems all right," he said. "Addressed to Major William Kidd, M.C., and this envelope was forwarded from the United Services Club in London."

"It will have to be all right," said the butcher grimly. "What does he think I am? He's one of the bloodsucking parasites, and I'll make him sit up."

"Such a shame the Major's so careless," remarked Mrs. Tinker. "And his wife, nice and quiet she is, going to have a baby."

"Then why the heck does he go about doin' things like this?" cried the butcher.

He had another beer, and when the grandfather clock struck one he got up, his face set, and said that they could tell the Major he'd be up for false pretences and swindling. Phillip heard the excessive noise of his engine—the valves obviously had too much gap—going away down the road.

"Major be a fool to 'isself," said 'Bosun' reflectively.

"It's his poor wife I'm thinking of," said Mrs. Tinker. "You men!" she cried suddenly, with a feline look at her husband.

"What have I done, tho'?" shouted 'Bosun', his shoulders hunched under his blue jersey. "What you always tacklin' of me for?"

"You're all alike, you men. Booze, booze, booze, and the poor women have to put up with your ways. Go on with you!" She made as though she would fling the water-jug, its base green with algae, over him.

"Gor' booger!" yelled 'Bosun', good naturedly. "Anyone'd think I'd give misself a bad cheque, to listen to you."

"It's a shame, I call it," retorted his wife, relapsing into herself.

"Course it's a shame, woman, but I harn't the bliddy fool what's done it, be I?"

"Aw, go on, you'm all mouth."

"Bring me a pint then, and I'll stop me mouth with that."

"Draw it yourself, you lazy old toad, you."

"I don't care if I have to."

"Well, I will this one, then don't you have no more midday! You know you can't eat your dinner properly if you take too much. You be all wind and water as it is."

Phillip found his way to Bill Kidd's cottage. He was sitting on the scruffy sofa of his furnished room, a soiled towel round his neck. He was unshaven, the room full of cigarette smoke and stubs squashed on plates and the dry earth of a withered geranium in a pot. He looked haggard. The towel round his neck only partly concealed the fact that he wore his pyjamas under an old jacket and a pair of shapeless flannel trousers. It was usually about sunset that Bill Kidd got dressed.

"The gas has got me," he wheezed. "I got a whiff of phosgene at Oppy Wood, and it recurs at intervals, as you know, old boy."

"Malkin is after you, Bill. About a cheque."

"That bloody ruffian. I was to have met him in 'Bosun's' today, but I didn't want a scene. I'd have laid him out. Jujitsu you know——" he caught Phillip's thumb and bent it so that he was forced to throw his body back with the sudden pain.

"What the hell are you doing?"

"Sorry, old boy, it's the phosgene——" cough, cough, paroxysms of coughing, piteous eyes in Phillip's direction—"it gets me like that, and I don't know my own strength. I've got t-b rather badly, you know. Eighty per cent disability pension, paymaster's warrant due any day now. In fact, those Pay Corps wallahs at Hounslow have slipped."

"Why not open the window? This smoke is enough to make anyone cough."

Bill Kidd looked at Phillip narrowly. "Are you inferring that I'm a liar?"

"Because I suggested that you open the window?"

Bill Kidd pointed at him a hand on an elbow tensed as for boxing, accompanied by a hard stare. His sallow face narrowed until it seemed to Phillip that an intelligent low-running animal was looking at him. "Some day, old lad, you're going to get what is coming to you! You think you're Jesus Christ, don't you, all that Donkin stuff? Yep, I've read your new book, with its pale pink philosophy, its Little England defeatism. Well, old boy, if you can get away with that sort of stuff, good luck to you, but be careful how you go!"

The voice took on the exaggerated semi-nasal drawl of a hero of a Conglomerated Press sevenpenny magazine. "You may consider yourself a damned fine writer, old boy, but when it comes to narking the British Empire, then look out. Sob-stuff for the Huns is fashionable for the moment, but let that pass; but when it comes to praise of Lenin and the Bolshies, then—well, don't say I didn't warn you."

"Malkin the butcher is after your blood. He says he's going to take you to court. I've come only to warn you."

"Well, old boy, thanks for your good intentions. I want to help you too. And my advice is, write about trout! Forget that Donkin salvation stuff, you can't do it. Donkin's all fake emotional stuff, anyway. Now you come with me tomorrow, and I'll show you a bit of dry-fly fishin' on the Stour, and see if I don't give you a subject for a book. It's Bill Kidd tellin' you, mind! I can give you all the dope, and you can write it down, and make it up into dramatic form, and we can go halves. No, I won't take anything, I don't want to make money out of trout. I love 'em too much, as you will, too, my Mad Son, when you find out what I am going to show you."

A young woman entered the room. She was heavy with child and, Phillip thought, afraid.

"Phillip Maddison and I are just going up to the Rising Sun to have a quick one, darling," he said. "This damned phosgene is working off, thank God. I won't be long. Come back and take pot luck afterwards, won't you, Phil?"

"Thank you, but I'm expected home, and am already late, but may I come another time?"

"Course you can, midear! Can't he, Molly? We don't stand on ceremony here, do we?"

They stopped outside the Rising Sun. Phillip saw no motorbike there. Nor did Bill Kidd, for he said, "I hope Malkin isn't inside. I should hate to have to sling him out on his ear."

Phillip didn't want another pint; he was becoming more and more unpunctual, and this day Lucy had asked him to be home at one o'clock, as there was a roast duck for lunch; and now it was a quarter to two. He followed Bill Kidd up the stone steps into the bar-room, intending to have half a pint of cider, and then to run home; but as they were standing there, 'Bosun' joining them in a drink, he heard the clatter of an old motor-bicycle engine stopping outside. Bill Kidd heard it, too, and his eyes darted from the door to the opening of the barrel room, and then to the window, while his face went the hue of sea-sickness.

The next moment the door opened, and the butcher walked into the room.

Phillip half expected a brutal exchange of blows, grunts, thuds and cries of pain; with himself intervening and perhaps being slugged. But no, the butcher went to the bar and asked for a half-pint. Bill Kidd, in the silence of the room, demanded when the butcher's glass was set before him, a brandy. He invited Phillip to have one with him.

"No thank you."

After swallowing half his glassful, Malkin turned to Bill Kidd and said, "You know what I be here for, I want my money. I've been fooled about enough, and have my living to earn."

"Quite," replied Bill Kidd. "I came here specially to see you, as a matter of fact. I'm expecting a telegraphed money-order from the Pay Corps wallahs this afternoon, which will pay you the loan you so kindly advanced me."

"I don't see it that way," said the butcher. "Nor will the county court judge, I reckon. Now I'm telling you, major you be, or say you be, but that's neither here nor there. If you don't bring thaccy money to my place by noon tomorrow, I'll expose you for what you be. And that's my last word." He went out of the door.

"He didn't leave a moment too soon," remarked Bill Kidd, as he brushed up his moustachios. "Something was coming to him, and would have come to him, too, if he had said one more word! Just one more word, my Mad Son, and he would have got it—Hook —line—and sinker! *Wough.*" He hit the palm of his hand with a fist. "Have a drink, old boy."

"I'll tell you what, Bill. You show me how you fish, and I'll settle your account with Malkin."

"Done! Shake, my Mad Son."

That afternoon he went to the butcher's shop and offered him ten pound notes in exchange for Bill Kidd's cheque. Malkin was suspicious at first, and seemed not to want to accept his offer. Phillip told him bluntly that he could take it or leave it when Malkin began to expostulate, "But what about my expenses? I had to make three journeys here!"

"You'll incur more expenses if you don't have your engine looked at. Your valves are late."

Grudgingly the butcher took the stumer from his till, and gave it to Phillip while looking at him as though he were the cause of the trouble.

That afternoon he posted the cheque to Bill Kidd, in an envelope with a short note. Soon afterwards the familiar roar of *Otazelle* sounded in the lane. Almost with tears in his eyes Bill Kidd thanked him, saying he was a white man, a pukka sahib, and he would for ever remain in his debt. (Phillip took this remark literally.) Meanwhile, declared Bill Kidd, he was only living to take his Mad Son to the river the next day, to show him the best occupation in the world, bar none, and when he said bar none, his Mad Son must understand he meant bar none.

Phillip concealed his half-amused, half-supercilious attitude to-wards Bill Kidd as he watched him changing the number plates of his car from BK1 to FU2. Obviously Bill Kidd was chancing his arm, he thought; and was therefore the more surprised when they stopped by a lichened oaken gateway and Bill Kidd said with satisfaction, "Here we are, Phillip. When we've taken the regulation brace-and-a-half, I'll take you up to Uncle Tiny's house and we'll have poached eggs on muffins for tea."

They pressed through purple loosestrife and tufts of foxtail grass from which arose spear-thistles four and five feet tall, to the river. There, beside a notice board declaring that the fishing was strictly preserved, and that trespassers would be prosecuted, Bill Kidd put his rod together, greased a tapered enamelled line, fixed a damp gut cast taken from an aluminium box containing other casts curled on wet flannel, and tied to the end of 4X gut a minute and glistening imitation of a fly, in feather, silk and steel, and hardly larger than a mosquito. After stroking and arranging the filaments with fingertips which he had touched with odourless paraffin wax, he crouched forward, and with the expression of an intent dog upon his face and a whispered "Keep on my left side," began to pull line from the reel and to throw it forward and back, a heavy gossamer, from the tip of his split-cane rod; a wavy gossamer growing longer and longer as it travelled backwards and forwards from the rod-tip: until suddenly it was curling out over the river and straightening along its length and then lying upon the gleaming waterflow, the fly alighting last by the far bank where the ripples of a rise were scarcely smoothed away by the gliding current.

Then, even as Bill Kidd had demonstrated in the bar-room of the Rising Sun, there was a jerk of the wrist which tightened the line, and with a swift flicking away of the cigarette from between his lips with his left hand, he muttered, "Got him", and wound in the reel rapidly until the rod was bending in an arc and the check making a noise like a grasshopper warbler.

A brown-tail waggled near the surface, making a bulge in the water streaming with sky and cloud in reflection.

"Phillip, I ask you! Every time the Crystal Killer does the trick! Three pounds if he's an ounce. I've marked that fish there since April. Here, take this." He gave him the landing-net to hold.

"Gently does it, old boy. Lean over the grasses and dip it under the fish as it comes up on its side below the bank. Gently now, gently midear. Got him. Take the rod, hold the point well up."

Bill Kidd beside a river was a different person. Phillip began to think of him as a natural man who just didn't fit into ordinary life—the kind of conventional life, based on money, that he himself was, alas, beginning to conform to. This image was soon dissipated.

"Bill, there's another fisherman walking fast towards us from downstream."

The shifting eyes of Bill Kidd, observing the approaching figure, assumed the hunted look they had shown when Malkin the butcher had come into the bar of the Rising Sun.

"Damn, my luck's out. That bloke is my uncle's solicitor, and for reasons I won't go into now, I don't want to see him. Bit of trouble with his daughter, as a matter of fact we were once engaged, but there were family objections. Grab that fish, shove your fingers through its gills, quick's the word. Now follow me, and don't look back, walk up the bank as though we haven't seen him."

A voice behind them called, "Hi, there. Hi!" They walked on, while Bill Kidd gave a running commentary out of the side of his mouth.

"Listen carefully. I'll go on, while you go back and keep him talking while I start the old 'bus. Kneel down as though you're doing up a shoelace, and shove the bloody fish in the runner we're coming to. Damn good job we didn't stick a spike through its head. I'll meet you later on the road. Say you just met me and don't know who I am. Here's the hatch. Shove the fish in."

Phillip let it slip through the thistles and grasses fringing an overgrown dyke into which jets of water were falling from a half-rotten hatch.

"Don't forget—say you don't know who I am, you just met me, while doin' a bit of nature study on the bank. You see, old boy, I'm on remittance while I keep clear of England, and if he knows I'm here, there will be no more allowances from the old avuncular purse."

Phillip thought the best thing to do was to walk back and meet the probable owner of the beat. He saw a gentleman with a clipped grey moustache and the curt cold manner of a second-rate soldier, to whom he must appear as a hatless cad in overlong plus fours.

"I am Colonel De 'Ath. This is my water. What are you doing here?"

"I was looking at the river, sir."

"Just 'looking at the river' were you? I have taken the number of your car by the gate, and shall report the matter to the police. Your companion caught a fish."

"It was put back, and swam away."

"Where do you come from?"

"I live near Colham."

"What is your name?"

"Phillip Maddison."

The other looked keenly at him. "You're the nephew of Hilary Maddison? You are. Then don't you think it's an underhand thing to do to spoil another's sport?"

"I hope it isn't spoiled. We've only just started to fish."

"At least you have the honesty to be straightforward. Did your companion take any more fish?"

"Only the one that was put back, sir. It was caught in the corner of the mouth, and the tongue wasn't injured."

"What fly was your friend using?"

"I think it was a home-made one. He calls it the Crystal Killer."

Colonel De 'Ath looked at Phillip keenly once more. "Your friend doesn't suffer from the supposed effects of alleged phosgene-gas poisoning, I suppose?"

Phillip thought that this might be a relation of Bill Kidd's after all; and that he must be cautious.

"He has an eighty per cent disability pension for a tubercular lung, I think, derived from gas in the war."

"Is the fly he uses anything like this?" He lifted his rod, and pointed to the fly stuck in a minute ring near the cork handle.

"Well yes, it did look something like that, sir."

"Then his fly is an ordinary Badger. I think I recognise your companion. Last year I caught him poaching this beat, and he began coughing when I spoke to him, telling a tale about gas at Oppy Wood. I gave him the benefit of the doubt, and told him that he might finish his day's fishing. And I happen to know that he has returned many times during the past spring and summer and moreover has not only claimed to be related to my cousin, General Ironside, but in addition to that has brought his friends here, including the editor of *Countryside Life*, who wrote an account in his journal of the fishing on this water, illustrated by a photograph. Tell him from me that if he comes here again he will not only be apprehended, but lose his tackle as well. Good-day to you."

Phillip returned to Bill Kidd.

"Well, my Mad Son, what did the lawyer bloke say? Rusty old Tory stuff, to which you quoted Lenin and the New Testament?"

"How did you guess, Piscator?"

"What were you two jawing about?"

"Oh, among other things an article in *Countryside Life*——"

"That silly bastard Frank Spinnaker went and advertised this beat to every poacher within a hundred miles. Now, here's my plan. We'll wait till this bloke's off the map, and then you can have a few casts. Pity we didn't hold on to that fish, she was a beaut. Hen fish, not such deep shoulders as a cock. Not an ounce under three pounds."

"I really think I ought to go home now. I've quite enjoyed this outing, and my first adventure in fishing under a master."

Chapter 15

INCOMPLETE GIRL

Phillip motored to London and left the Cockchafer under the Adelphi arches, a series of caverns faced and arched with London Brick once yellow but now dingy with soot. These had been built when a wharf lay beside London river and small shipping bore up with the tide to discharge wine and other merchandise for storing in the great cellars.

The Barbarian Club was a place of good-fellowship among writers, actors, painters, lawyers, and doctors of distinction. There were small bedrooms in the garrets, a library, billiard and card rooms, and on the first floor a large supper room and an adjoining bar. It was near the theatres, and the supper room was a place of convivial talk which often went on after midnight.

The new member found much kindliness at once. He did not know who the older men were, except those with internationally known faces—two pianists in particular, men with hard eyes in austere faces set to concert pitch, as it were, before attentive mankind. To escape from mental, spiritual, and physical devotion to their art, such men were to be found in the card room, playing poker. That, and golf some week-ends, appeared to be their only relaxation. They never drank and made merry like other Brother Barbarians who lived mainly on hope—the comets and shooting stars below the established constellations.

Phillip felt that this was his home in London. Within the Adelphi Terrace house was warmth, light, and joviality; below, along the Embankment, the leaves of the plane trees were falling; the Strand was a hurrying place of people, near-homeless most of them, transients or inquilines as Compton Mackenzie had called them in *Sinister Street*—men and women like himself, conscious of the appalling loneliness of the soul as they hurried to find, to meet, to hope for—what?

Whom could he see, or go to? Was the best of life to be lived only within the spirit, the mind which was made up almost entirely by memory? He walked along the crowded Strand, wondering how Piers and Virginia were getting on in Austria and Germany, or would they now be in some *pension* or *auberge* on the Riviera; wondering what his mother and father were doing, and his sisters—Doris now on her own, for Bob had disappeared: simply gone to work one morning as usual and never returned. No letter, no card: nothing. A week after returning from Devon he had vanished. Doris had given up her school-teaching to marry him; now she was left with a small son and a baby soon to be born.

Should he take them in, and look after them? Lucy was willing. That generous, kind, and tolerant woman, what was she doing at that moment? Sitting in the parlour at home, by the fire, knitting or sewing in the light of the oil lamp, perhaps making herself a cup of tea, happily absorbed by thoughts of her children sleeping in the room above her, having seen them all tucked up and settled for the night. And he was so regarded: one of her children, sitting in his room listening to the wireless, or trying to write—and nothing beyond sketches or articles, mere journalism, ever attempted nowadays. One could not write in that house; one was no longer self-sufficient, no longer a writer. It required a space continuing, a wilderness extending for hundreds of consecutive hours of imaginative living to begin, continue, and finish one real book. The artistic imagination must be free, unhindered, and never adulterated by material life.

He turned back at Waterloo Bridge and hurried to Adelphi Terrace. There was the old porter, Flanagan, in his small lodge, the old soldier of the Chitral campaign, and other small wars on the mountain passes of Empire. Lucy's grandmother, Mrs. Chychester, had told him that what was 'colonial exploitation' to many stay-at-home critics, was 'service' to those who helped to keep the peace, and improve the living standards of the natives.

"Where may I telephone, Flanagan?"

"Box over there, sir."

He asked for a trunk call to Lucy. After a while the soft voice said, 'Hullo'. It quickened when he asked about the children.

"I think I'll remain up for a few days and start my trout book."

"Yes, do that. But don't work too hard. You deserve a holiday. Oh, I'm quite happy. The little boys ask after you every evening, when I put them to bed. Rosamund is a pet, *so* good, and putting on weight nicely."

"Any news of Nuncle?"

"Only that he's coming in October. Oh yes, before I forget. Shall I invite Irene to stay here for the shooting week when Uncle Hilary comes with his friends? I think it would help things along, don't you? I heard from her yesterday. She's coming over from France at the end of the month—goodness, it's nearly that now, isn't it? She'll be staying at the Ladies Carlton Club, she writes, her usual place in London, in case you want to see her. How do you like *your* new club?"

"It's rather romantic, in a way. I have an attic room and can see the lights on the Thames when I turn my head on the pillow."

"I am so glad. Do you know anyone yet?"

"Oh yes, there's Anders, Channerson the war painter, and lots of other famous people. I've met Archie Plugge here, but I don't think he's a member. I must invite him to supper one night. Poor old boy, he hasn't got much money."

"Yes, do. Remember me to him, and to Mr. Cornelian if you see him."

"I'm going to see Edward Cornelian tomorrow at the Soho restaurant where they all go to on Fridays. I wonder how he'll regard me."

"Oh, I expect he's forgotten all about *that*. Have you seen Felicity?"

"Do you think I ought to?"

"Why not? She's not very happy, and you might be able to help her."

Phillip laughed. "In what way, do you mean?"

"Well, she doesn't have much fun, I imagine, in the circumstances."

"What circumstances?"

"Oh, I don't know. I rather gathered from what she told me that she feels a bit out of it, with her mother having her own particular friend. What Felicity wants, I think, is to meet young people with tastes similar to her own."

There was a pause, then he said, "Young people, yes. I'm not young any more."

She replied, with a light laugh, "Well, if you see her, give her my love."

"By the way, do you think I ought to have a secretary?"

"I certainly do."

"Felicity?"

"Why not?"

"You really *do* like her?"

"Yes, I do. The little boys do, too—very much."

"Well, au revoir. I'll let you know when I'll be coming back."

He looked at the London directory, and found the telephone number; hesitated; then went upstairs to the bar to drink whisky. A little man with a long head was standing there, swaying on his feet several inches clear of the counter, his eyes half-closed, his hands hanging down by the seams of his trousers, which were crumpled like his coat. His starched collar was frayed, he was without a tie. An empty port glass, which had been full when last Phillip had seen him standing in the same place like an upright mooring buoy in slack-water, was turned down before him on the counter.

He had been a gag-writer for a number of music-hall comics since 1902; he was still a gag-writer, spending nearly all his conscious hours trying to think of new jokes. For five years he had lived with despair and self-ridicule; and port wine, his only tipple, gave him some sense of what he thought of as Nirvana. The moving pictures had reduced the halls; now talking pictures were the coming thing, and he had sudden flashes of hope, and with each flash as he stood at the bar he asked for a small port, and slipped back into Nirvana.

Phillip said to him, "Will you honour me by having a drink with me, sir?"

The little man did not move.

"He don't hear you," said the barman.

Phillip swallowed his whisky and said, "Well, I must go," and running downstairs went to the telephone box and asked for the Ealing number.

"Hullo, Felicity?"

He heard a sibilance; then an 'Oh!', as of relief. "I thought at first it was someone else." He could hear her breathing irregularly.

"Lucy sends her love."

"I was just thinking of her. How is she?"

"Oh, very happy with the children, as usual. Did you get back from Rookhurst all right?"

"I should have written to thank you—I did mean to——"

"The Beausires are fun, aren't they?"

"I stayed three days with them. I see Coats is advertising your novel. I'm keeping my fingers crossed for tomorrow."

"I suppose you'll be too busy to meet me."

"Where are you?"

"In London. At the Barbarian Club."

"Oh! Yes, of *course* I'll meet you."

"How about tonight?"

When she did not reply at once he said, "Perhaps you're busy? How about lunch tomorrow?"

"I'm trying to think. It's all so sudden. Yes, of course I can come tonight. I'm alone here, Mummie is away for the night. So it doesn't matter when I come home."

"Good. Where shall I meet you?"

"I'll be at the Underground at Charing Cross in half an hour."

"I'll meet you there."

"It's by the Embankment—not the Southern Railway station."

She could think, she could anticipate; she would help him in his work. They met gladly, and walked arm in arm along the Embankment to Cleopatra's Needle.

"This is where I collapsed eight years ago. I had a groggy lung."

"You poor dear," spoken with almost the same intonation of voice as Irene's.

"I'm all right now. Devon and long walks cleared it up."

"I dream of Devon, and our walk on the Whale Back."

"I've never really realized how beautiful London is at night."

"I thought I was never going to see you again."

"I'm an icicle whose thawing is its dying."

"You're not."

They looked at the Zeppelin bomb holes in the Sphinx.

"My father was killed in the war," she said in a shaky voice.

"I'm sorry. You must have been very young."

"I just remember him."

A string of barges was going with the tide down-river: dim red lights, shadowy figures on the bridge by the big brass funnel of the tug.

"They have to go so fast, to keep way-on in order to steer. It's as swift here as the spring tides past Aery Point."

"What happened to your canoe?"

"I abandoned it."

"I'm so glad."

"I abandon everything—before it abandons me."

They walked under the gas-lit Adelphi Arches.

"Quite Dickensian, isn't it? The Cockchafer is up here some-where. But no-one would want to pinch her. There she is. And up above us the bright Strand, where my grandfather was run over by the brewer's dray—let me see, it was in the winter of 'ninety-four—I was born the following April. So you see I am very old—thirty-four—and you are eighteen—a child."

"I'm not a child."

They climbed steps to Adelphi Terrace and stopped outside the Barbarian Club.

"Ladies are allowed in. Would you like a drink? Coffee?"

"May I have some beer?"

"Better still."

Within the hall was a small divided space, the ladies' room. Here sat Channerson, the war painter, with other men and a thin pale-faced girl whose continuous remarks in a pert Cockney voice were making him bellow with laughter. His hard eyes recognised Phillip, he said gravely, "Come and join us. May I introduce you to the Virgin of Soho."

The Virgin of Soho waved a hand, and said to Felicity, "Hullo darling, what fresh cheeks and wind-blown hair. Stars in your eyes, too. Hope they get a rise out of your boy-friend," at which Channerson's hearty-hollow laughter again filled the hall.

Phillip concealed his feelings by playing the part of a West End *roué* of fiction.

"We're going to drink champagne. Anybody wearing gilt dancing shoes? I've got a book coming out tomorrow, so let's all drink to it."

The bottle came with a plate of ham sandwiches. Felicity appeared to be hungry. Other men from upstairs attracted by the liveliness, joined the party, ordering more bottles. At eleven o'clock

the actors began to come in, some accompanied by women friends.
Phillip told himself that this was life.

"What time is the last train to Ealing?"

"About twelve. But I'll go now if you're tired."

"I was thinking of you. I'll see you catch the train, anyway."

The door opened and a tramp with a raggedly forked white
beard and beaky nose entered. He stared with the tragic eyes of the
very old, then with battered silk hat still on head went up the
stairs. The next to enter was a heavy clean-shaven man who looked
like a retired pugilist. He also stared at their faces before going to
the lavatory. When Phillip went there the man was cleaning his
shoes. He looked up and said, "You're a new member, aren't
you?" His voice had a metallic accent.

"Yes."

"Don't you want to insure your keys?"

"Keys?"

The bald man took a ring from his pocket. The metal label
attached to the ring was numbered, he said. For half-a-crown a
year anyone finding the keys on that numbered ring would be
rewarded by the insurance company when they sent them back.

"I'm an agent," he said. "Ain't it worth it, gettin' your keys
back?"

Phillip gave him half a crown and took the ring.

"Aren't you going to put your keys on it?" asked the agent.

"I haven't got any keys."

The bald man explained that he had insured the keys of over
ten thousand people in Australia, New Zealand, and London.

"I'm Zorago the contortionist," he said. "I'll lay an even dollar
that you've never even heard of Zorago the Human Python."

"Yes I have."

"A long time ago?"

"No. Quite recently."

At half-past eleven Channerson got up to leave with the thin
Cockney girl called the Virgin of Soho. She came over to kiss
Phillip, putting her lips on his and waggling the tip of her tongue
in his mouth. He concealed his distaste. "What can you do with
an elemental force?" said Channerson, chuckling. "Isn't she a
marvel?" Then he said in a quiet voice, "Do you know what it
is to be poor?"

"I saw the slums die in Flanders."

"Do you know my picture in the National War Museum?"

"It is immortal."

The painter looked at him doubtfully. "Do you think so?"

"I know."

Felicity had not heard what was said; but when Channerson held out his hand with the words, "We must meet again," and added, "Give my regards to Piers Tofield when you see him," before bowing to her distantly, she wondered if there had been perhaps some quarrel over Piers Tofield, of whom she had often heard, as the man who had run away with Anthony Crufts' wife. According to Fleet Street many famous men, and women too, were homosexual and lesbian.

While she was in the ladies' room Phillip leapt up the stairs three at a time to the bar, first looking in the supper room. Among the many faces were outbreaks of gaiety; he half-wished that he had not telephoned her, but had remained to join the fun. He went across to the bar, where the gag-writer was standing in the same place, a glass of port before his closed eyes; while at the other end of the counter stood the old tramp wearing a silk hat. Before him were ranged, in two rows, eight medium-sized khaki cigars —cheap Dutch ones—and six glasses of Irish whiskey.

Phillip ordered one for himself, and the barman said, "Club Special, sir?"

"Yes please."

While he was sipping it a man even smaller than the gag-writer came in, and going up to the aged man in the seedy frock coat said, "Hullo, Old O'Damn. How are you tonight?"

"Go to hell."

Phillip thought this funny, and began to laugh silently to himself.

"Be a sport, Old O'Damn, I'm not on the free list like you. You'll only be ill if you drink all those drinks. You remember me, don't you? I'm the librarian."

"You're Tom Fool."

"Well then if you can drink all that whiskey, you can't smoke all those cheroots."

"Go away, bloody boy."

The odd thing was that the librarian went away. Laughing weakly, but inaudibly, Phillip sat down in a chair with a short rounded back. Immediately the ancient man tottered towards him, and pointing a finger with a long and dirty nail at him, quavered, "You are sitting in my chair."

"I beg your pardon, sir. I thought it was club property."

"*I* am club property!"

Phillip hurriedly left the bar, and went laughing down the stairs. What a wonderful place London was, when you knew people.

Felicity was still away. He spoke to Flanagan, the porter, who told him that Old O'Damn was a famous character, one of the original members of the club founded in the middle of the last century.

"He must be very old."

"Due for his century next year, sir."

"Does he live in the club?"

"Some say he kips under the arches, others that he lives in a disused sewer what is bricked up and forgotten and what runs under the vaults of the Bank of England."

"All life is fiction, anyway."

He leapt up the stairs three at a time to the bar. The second little man exclaimed, "Ah, I was looking for you! You're a new member, aren't you? You didn't come in for your month's trial, did you? Doesn't matter, you can stand me a drink now. I'll have a Club Special. I'm the honorary librarian, you know. That"—he pointed to the ancient figure apparently asleep in his chair—"is Old O'Damn, I expect you've heard of him? I wish they'd also put me on the free list, I've been a member for over thirty years, and have looked after the library all that time. Here's to your very good health. Welcome to the Barbarian Club. Oh, must you go? Isn't it funny, everyone has to go whenever I come into the bar."

They walked hand in hand to the underground station. The Thames sparkled with lights. A bright train roared in. How quickly it arrived at Ealing.

"Let's go this way, then we can walk home on the grass. Oh, but you'll miss the last train back."

"I feel like walking all night."

They came to a short terrace of Victorian gabled houses. She switched on the light in the hall, and opened the door of the sitting room.

"Oh." She put her hand to her mouth.

A man was lying on a sofa. He got up, a smallish man, with a clean-shaven face and grey hair brushed back from his temples.

"This is my guardian, Mr. Fitzwarren," she said to Phillip. "I'll make some coffee."

"Felicity stayed with us in the West Country this summer," he said to the smallish man.

"So I heard. You're farming, aren't you?"

"A pupil of sorts."

The older man removed a silk handkerchief from the breast pocket of his grey cashmere suit, opened it to blow his nose loudly, then having folded the handkerchief carefully upon the ironing marks, replaced it in the pocket so that it showed a straight line. Then saying, "Excuse me," he left the room, closing the door behind him.

Phillip wondered why she hadn't mentioned her guardian. *I'm all alone here, Mummie is away for the night.* Perhaps he lived there, being her mother's friend, and she had not thought it worth mentioning. Yet she had been shocked to see him there: she had turned pale. And when he had telephoned, *I thought at first it was someone else.* He felt dull, and thought to leave, but stood still, listening. He could just hear the man's voice, a full continual growl. It went on and on. At last he went down the passage and tapped on the door of the kitchen.

"I feel I mustn't keep you up, Felicity. It's after midnight, I think I ought to be going."

"I'll see you to the door," said the man.

"Oh, don't go," she whispered, touching his sleeve, as the older man led the way to the front door.

"Felicity hasn't been very well lately, and her mother asked me to keep an eye on her while she was away. Mrs. Ancroft likes her to be in bed by eleven."

"I'm not tired, Fitz, and coffee won't take long," said Felicity.

"Very well. Would you mind waiting in the sitting room, Mr. Maddison? I'll bring the coffee. I have a small matter to discuss with my ward before she goes to bed."

He returned down the passage and found himself in the wrong room. A gas fire burned in the grate, on the shelf above were photographs; one of a smiling R.F.C. observer, others of school scenes, girls in gym clothes, and on the hockey field. There was a reproduction of Shelley's face tinted with girlish colours, pink cheeks, brown curls, and blue eyes. A man's black pair of silk pyjamas lay on the bed. On the dressing table was another photograph, of an elderly woman. *To My Darling Girlie, from Mumsie.* Evidently it was Felicity's bedroom.

He switched off the light hurriedly and re-entered the sitting

room with relief. So that was the set-up: Felicity had left before
'Fitz' was due to telephone his arrival, to make sure that the
coast was clear. It explained the sad look on her face at times.
What should he do? Obviously she had transferred her feelings to
himself—an escape from the frying pan into the fire, because he
didn't love her. Or did he? In any case it would be the same
situation for her.

'Fitz' came in carrying a tray. She followed, her face was
powdered. She gave him a timid smile as she put down a plate of
petit beurre biscuits.

"It was good of you to see Felicity home, Maddison. It seems
that, as the last train has gone, you'll have a long walk before you,
unless you can find a taxi at this time of night."

"I wonder if I might wash my hands?"

Felicity jumped up, "I'll show you," and led the way up the
stairs.

"Please come back when he's gone," she said before returning
down the stairs.

"Do you want to get rid of him?"

"Oh, yes!"

He drank too-hot coffee and arose to go. "Mr. Fitzwarren, if
you're going my way, perhaps you'll show me the road to Shepherd's Bush? It's fairly straight once one is there."

Standing behind 'Fitz', Felicity shook her head at Phillip. He
waited.

The other man blew his nose, refolded the handkerchief, and
tucked it back into his breast pocket.

"I understand you are a married man, Mr. Maddison? Then why
do you come here after this young girl when her mother is away?"

"I merely brought her home. I'll go now. Goodnight, Felicity."

The other man said, with a change of manner to the gracious,
"I'll come with you, and put you on your way."

The morning papers were on sale in Piccadilly when Phillip
arrived there. He bought copies and with a bundle under his arm
walked down to Adelphi Terrace. The old man in the top hat was
wandering about the main room.

"Everyone goes to bed early nowadays," he complained in
woeful tones. "There are no Bohemians left."

Big Ben tolled three times as Phillip went up to his bedroom.
In most of the newspapers there was a prominent review of

The Phoenix. Nearly all the critics had taken the book as he had felt it. A few gave it the highest praise. I knew it would happen, he thought: Edward Cornelian was right.

He looked in *The Daily Telegram*. Martin Beausire's notice was disappointing. He wrote that he longed for a magic wand to wave and change all the human characters into animals.

In the morning the hall porter said he was wanted on the telephone. Felicity asked if he had got back all right.

"Oh yes, thanks. We said goodnight at Marble Arch. Did he come back?"

"I don't know, I went for a long walk by myself. Do you still want me to come to lunch?"

They met outside Swan and Edgar's in Piccadilly. Thence they walked to the Commercio in Frith Street, hoping to meet again Edward Cornelian. It was Friday, the day for the literary gathering at luncheon. The *literati* usually sat at a big table in the corner of an upstairs room, by a window. When they went into the room Edward Cornelian was already seated at the table, which was laid for a dozen places, alone. Phillip said good-morning, and was about to bring Felicity forward when the critic remarked that the table was reserved. So they sat at a small table for two. It so happened that on that day only three others came to the big table.

Phillip remained in London. He was invited to dinner by Felicity's mother, who rejoiced that her daughter seemed so happy, where before she had been moody and restless. A country life was the very thing for her, she said.

The new book was a success. Ten thousand copies of the first edition had been sold, another ten thousand were at the press, and a further five thousand ordered from the printer. He met Felicity every evening, going to cinemas, the opera, and promenade concerts in the Queen's Hall. He stayed for another week; his pockets were stuffed with Press Clippings, which came with every post. While nine out of ten were entirely favourable, two were bad. A North Country novelist reviewing for *The Evening News* wrote that Donkin was half-baked, while *The Ecclesiastical Times* declared that the book was an almost uninterrupted sequence of bad taste, wrong thinking, and blasphemy. It demanded to know what the publishers were doing in issuing the book, and reminded them, and the author, that there was such an office as that of the public prosecutor.

"Excellent," cried Edward Cornelian, at the round table. "You are in the tradition, my dear fellow. Hardy had the same sort of thing written about *Tess*, and again about *Jude*. Such critics, their senses repressed by pavements, are full of pretentiousness masking itself as religious sincerity."

He stayed on for his regimental dinner. In the morning they walked on the Sussex downs. The year had entered the season of calm following the equinox: rest for cloud and air, an unshadowed sun. They lay on their backs above Beachy Head.

Her hand sought his, and held it. At length he said, "Felicity, I must tell you something. I feel I can never love anyone ever again."

Ocean drew down the blue of the sky. She raised herself on an arm and said, "Your eyes are a deep blue, and O, so kind. Let me be your hand-maiden, if ever you want one."

She took his hand and kissed it before sitting up to look at him. She patted her lap, inviting him to lay his head there, and rest. Her face was shining, she was all sweetness, smiling expectantly. How Richard Jefferies would have loved her, he thought: Felicity in *The Dewy Morn*, inviting love, dreaming of a child perhaps.

"You're a nice girl, Felicity. You deserve a fine young man for a husband. You're a kind girl, too."

He sat up and examined her face, intrigued by the tiny gold hairs on her upper lip.

"I've never really looked properly at you before. Now turn your head sideways."

She had a straight brow, her profile was Grecian. He turned her chin to full face. The fair hair grew back from the forehead like Barley's; but where Barley had been direct and clear and forthright in manner, Felicity was a little withdrawn, hesitant; appealing, under a subdued but continuous longing, for safety: to be lapped in loving kindness.

"Which do you need more, I wonder? To be loved—or to love?

"Both of course."

"But if you merely fell in love with me you might be in a worse position than you are with 'Fitz'."

"Oh no, I couldn't be. Anyway, I've done with him."

"Well, that's honest anyway. Did he love you?"

"He says he did, now."

"Did you love him?"

"In a way, I suppose I did."

"Did you mind him forcing himself on you when you were fourteen?"

"I thought I might as well make the best of it."

This frankness shocked him. He got up and walked down the sward towards the Cockchafer. She followed slowly. He waited for her, they walked on side by side unspeaking. When she could no longer contain her feelings she stopped, and staring at the ground said as though to herself, "If you don't want me, I think I shall commit suicide."

He knew that feeling; it had in the past been his own. He held her in his arms, knowing that she was wounded to be needing love so desperately. He must be her friend and not abuse her.

"Don't worry, pet. We'll always be friends."

"You'll see me again, won't you, before you go? And don't forget your regimental dinner tonight."

She was happy again, so was he. They walked down to the Cockchafer hand in hand.

The dinner was in the Connaught Rooms. After the meal and the toasts the Colonel of the Regiment moved around, talking to men who once had worn khaki, and had been such great friends, and now saw one another but once a year, for an evening.

It was a quiet occasion, for all remembered too much. Phillip, as a war-time acting lieutenant-colonel, sat at the high table, between two friends, one of whom had won the Victoria Cross in the penultimate month of the war, in the advance through the forest of Mormal. Ditchings had gone forward with a sergeant and a Lewis gun when the battalion was held up by a German rear-guard, consisting of a line of machine-gun posts. The two men had worked their way down a flank of the German line, knocking out one post after another—for the flanks had been left in the air, and so it had been almost a text-book exercise. Even so, it had opened the way for the Division to advance. Phillip asked Ditchings what he had felt afterwards, and Ditchings wrote on his menu card, *Sleep-sleep-sleep*. He had been sweated out, emptied away. No fear, no broken sleep—the German boys it was who died.

When Lord Satchville came round to speak to those who had once been his senior officers, he asked Phillip about his new book, saying he must read it, and what was the title. Phillip felt embarrassed, and began to stutter, for he knew that it held to a point of view that the Colonel would consider alien to the spirit of the Regiment: so he said it was only a novel, and then thinking what he ought to say, felt that words had gone from him. Ditchings spoke up and said it was a very fine book: then he too became silent; for he knew the gulf of suffering between the spirit of the Regiment and what actually occurred before, during, and after a battle; and of the two diverse things, which was of the greater truth? Service to England and Empire, that was the spirit of the Colonel; service to mankind, which meant the poor man, that was the spirit of cousin Willie, the theme of *The Phoenix*.

"I must get your book," said the Colonel.

Hoping to ease the inarticulateness of himself, Phillip said the book was about an ex-soldier he had known, who had tried to bring a new vision to people—and he mentioned the name of a soldier-poet who had written some of the few truthful poems of the war.

"Oh," said Lord Satchville, "I'm afraid I don't much care for the fellow."

"It's rather a difficult thing, to be truthful about actual warfare, Colonel."

"He isn't English," said the Colonel, musingly. "His father's family are Parsees, from Bombay."

"He was a very good regimental officer, Colonel, so I understand from those who knew him, and soldiered with him."

Lord Satchville was stroking his Viking beard, now turning grey, and looking sideways with his fading blue eyes at Phillip, who could feel the Colonel's disappointment in his own diminishing sensations. The Colonel knew, he thought, of how he had failed after the war: that black period in his life when he had spent some time in prison. The Colonel changed the subject and spoke to Ditchings, asking after his family; he was the benevolent patriarch once more. Phillip began to wish that he had not gone to the reunion dinner: for the truth was, he could not bear to disappoint anyone, and yet knew well how his weakness or incapacity too often led to another kind of disappointment. For this reason he had made an excuse not to accept the invitation to stay with Satchville, and to revisit Husborne Abbey, although Lucy's grandmother, Mrs. Chychester, had advised him to accept, saying she was sure that Lucy and he would find the visit enjoyable. How would the great man—great because of the strength of his simplicity—feel about a young man who "ceaselessly blasphemed against all the values a Christian holds dear," according to *The Ecclesiastical Times*? He could think no further—the views of 'Donkin', the hero, were more in keeping with those of the outcast heir to the historic name and ducal estates of Husborne, the socialist Marquess who since youth had been alienated from his father, the Duke of Gaultshire, cousin to Satchville. A few pages of naturalistic prose and dialogue—how could they maintain themselves against the vision of the Abbey, with its immemorial traditions? How could his complicated consciousness fit in with the simplicity of such established assurance of life?

"Ah, I must read your book," the Colonel murmured affably, as he left the top table. "I have your otter beside my bedhead, and read a few pages every night before turning out the light. For me, it is part of England."

At these unexpected words, Phillip felt himself to be on the verge of tears.

Afterwards he walked with two friends of the Regiment, both holders of the Cross—Colonel Vallum, and Captain Ditchings—to the Barbarian Club. They sat together over a drink at the bar; they parted, saying they must meet again at the dinner next year. He felt sad seeing them go. He walked on the Embankment for awhile before returning to his garret bed with the near-cardboard walls through which travelled many sounds. Two of the dining-room maids slept up there; the floorboards creaked as footfalls went slowly past his door. He lay in bed, wondering how bad a man he was becoming, having failed Nuncle, and then Lucy, and now it looked as though he had spiritually seduced Felicity. Why hadn't he gone before it was too late. Yet he wanted her, as she wanted him. No: he must never betray Lucy.

Midnight struck from Big Ben, down the river. One o'clock —two o'clock—

It was ten years since the Armistice: the war seemed deeper and darker in the imagination than during the actual days of that lost time: the faces of friends in uniform, against the smoke and intolerable crash of bombardment: faces around the piano in the ante-room: ever-gay, laughing faces round the table on guest-nights—these phantoms were more real to him than the living. One must never go back among the living: one must, for ever, say goodbye to old comrades, so that one might always see them with young faces, gay and carefree, in those scenes of the vanished world of the Western Front which could only be entered in silence and alone.

Chapter 16

ALL SOULS' EVE

Autumn moved serenely into St. Luke's Summer, as the early days of October were called—that period before the moon begins to wax, before its full shine brings the first woodcock over the North Sea to the downs and the beech hangers; before the woodland leaves begin to drift upon the winds and gather in the waving weeds of ranunculus swelling the trout-streams of the meadows.

The sheltering woods still showed the colours of autumn among their dark massed foliage.

All the village came to the auction at Fawley, and a surprising number of people from the towns, as well as from neighbouring houses, and of course the farmers drove up in their gigs and traps behind cobs. Phillip was surprised to see Piers and Virginia: his friend in a grey Tyrolean felt hat and red-chequered shirt and *Lederhosen*, Virginia more conventionally dressed in tweed coat, skirt and blue beret. Piers had sold his Aston-Martin and bought an old £5 bull-nosed Morris two-seater, which looked as though it had been standing out in a field for a couple of years.

Phillip spoke to many of the farm-hands—Joby the shepherd, Ned the baliff, Mac the forester, Haylock the keeper. He saw also Captain Arkell, and Mr. Tinker of the Rising Sun. There must be nearly two hundred people present.

For the village people it was a holiday: at last they could see inside the 'big house' they had known, distantly and with awe, all their lives. There they were, clumping up and down the pale wooden stairs of the servant's quarters, deal once scrubbed with sand, water, and perhaps home-made soap of fat and potash, until the grain stood out in lines. Now they were prying into empty rooms; moving in loose procession up the wide oaken stairway from the hall, to sit on Mr. John's bed and try the mattress. As for the village boys, they were having the time of their lives, playing hide and seek down the dark passages.

Sitting on one of the higher stairways he tried to assemble, in orderly procession, what tasks he had set himself for the immediate future. The accepted estimate was £1,450 to put the place in habitable condition. There were to be three divisions of the house, each self-contained. In addition, and before his parents came to live there, the gardens must be made ready for spring planting.

After that, all decaying boughs of oak and walnut in the little park must be cut, the stubs painted with Stockholm tar. All rotten wood, and shreddings from the uprooted fruit trees burnt for potash to be added to the compost heap, or heaps, ready for those cultivations.

The reconditioning of the game-house, on the north side under the big walnut tree, was not included in the architect's specification. Perhaps in his spare time—perhaps with Father's help, it might be converted for a study for himself—a place apart, where he could write? It was an octagonal building with a roof rising to a point. The walls were lined with lead and spiky with a thousand rusted nails set in rows, whereon game in the remote past had been hung. Ivy darkened the broken hand-made perforated zinc sheets covering the windows. The pitch-pine wood-work was sound.

He must work at his writing. The money made that way must flow back to the estate. That was just. The heart of the land must be restored. He had many detailed ideas for the future, including a map of the estate to be painted on plaster to be rendered on the breast of the chimney piece of the original barton hall; an electric light plant installed, with points (put in by Ernest?) for irons, small heaters, and of course a vacuum cleaner. A new septic tank was included in the estimate, also an artesian bore to be drilled. Captain Arkell had suggested a water-softening plant, and central heating by hot air. For the children, vita-glass in the nursery windows. Say £2,000 in all. Could he manage it?

The prospect made him a little tremulous. First, the trout book must be written. But before that, he must study the ways of fish. He knew nothing about them, really. He could read books, of course. Perhaps he could write a short novel, all action contained within a confined space, like James Joyce's *The Dead*; the story of one small maid at a New Year's party in the servants' hall—a girl based on Felicity. He began to imagine the young girl in cottage-made carpet slippers, dreaming of love; and being betrayed by a cold hearted fornicator. He must write it as soon as he could see a clear space before him. But the thought of all that must be faced

before he could attain such a space gave feelings near to suffoca-
tion: he clattered down the wooden steps in nailed shoes into the
sunshine to avoid his thoughts; for he must think only of his duty to
the land.

Already a start had been made. In the courtyard, flanked by
stables, coach-house, brew-house, and adjoining laundry-house,
were heaps of fine gravel and a stack of bricks. As soon as the sale
was over and cleared away the builder was to start. In fact, he had
already begun. Wandering into the house, Phillip saw that the
tapestry panels of the drawing room, shut up for so long, had already
been stripped, showing the wooden framework nailed against the
wall of chalk-blocks. Through the open windows he watched the
crowd moving about on the lawn outside, among the parallel heaps
of worn bedding, puffed up by feathers, beside rows of uncomfor-
table-looking attic beds with rusty, chain-harrow-like mattresses.
The prevailing hue of the bedding was suet-pudding grey, but unlike boiled puddings, the masses of ticking and feather-bedding
were shapeless, giving the effect of having long been moribund. It
seemed that innumerable repressions and sighful thoughts still
hovered over them.

"Isn't it exciting?" said Lucy, moving to him. "And won't it
be fun when it is all over, and the place done up? I'm so glad it
isn't very big. I remember how relieved Pa's cousin Maude was,
when she had the house left to her by her father pulled down, and
she went to live in a small modern house by herself. 'O, why
didn't I have it done before?' she said to me. 'I feel now that I'm
an entirely different person.'"

Wandering around, Phillip saw Bill Kidd talking to the landlord of the Rising Sun. Kidd was there to buy furniture for the
house he had rented.

"When you want a trout for your breakfast, send for me, my
Mad Son."

"Ah," replied Phillip, in imitation of Ernest, who was somewhere about.

They talked together until Bill Kidd saw Piers approaching,
and saying that he wanted a word with the auctioneer, made off
into the crowd.

The auctioneer began at the collection of odds and ends, then
passed to the bedding. This was quickly disposed of. By half-past
twelve he was half-way; they broke off for lunch, the auctioneer
saying that he would begin again at a quarter past one sharp, in

the raftered dining hall, where some of the more cumbrous furniture from outhouse and side rooms had been brought.

Phillip was dismayed by the price some of the pieces fetched. Most of them went quickly; there was a group of hard-eyed men in city suits and bowler hats who appeared to have arranged to bid in turn, he thought. Only afterwards did he realise that he had been too hasty in his desire to make a fresh start with the house.

The oak sideboard, carved with scenes of the Crimea, a wedding present to his grandfather from the Regiment, went for 17/6; the wine-cooler for 8/-; a pair of Jacobean cast-iron fire-dogs, half-buried under the ashes of the original hall, went to a scrap-dealer for eighteenpence, with the fireback.

"Now we come to a relic of the past, gentlemen. A genuine Georgian chamber-horse to reduce your weight. I don't suppose there's many left like this one throughout the entire British Isles. Anyone wanting to start a museum, now's his chance. Who'll open for me?" The auctioneer looked around. "Come on, where will someone start me? Shall we say a fiver?"

He looked down at the row of bowler hats.

"If this was in London, you'd get the Victoria and Albert bidding against some American gent," he remarked conversationally. "Now who'll give me a start? All right then, make me a bid! A shilling? Be serious, please; we've got a lot to get through this afternoon. Who'll bid me a crown? You will, sir? Thank you. A crown I'm bid, a crown. Anyone want a valuable piece of furniture, the 'Chamber Horse' as the first one was described nearly two hundred years ago by the inventor, a Londoner called Marsh. I shouldn't be surprised if this was made by Thomas Sheraton, at the beginning of the nineteenth century. Now then, who'll say seven and six? You sir? Going at seven shillings and six-pence—for the last time—any advance on seven-and-six—going, going——" he struck the top of his rostrum, and nodded to Bill Kidd.

"That will sweat the whiskey out of him, Lucy."

"Well, we didn't really want it, did we?" she whispered.

"I might need it one day."

For a shilling or two went uniform trunks and japanned cases. Then heaps of dull pictures, most of them of horses with their riders or grooms; followed by the servant's wash-hand-stands and towel rails, which made a little more.

"Perhaps things will be better in the drawing room."

Felicity spoke quietly, conscious of many eyes upon her; she determined to remain aloof, lest people suspect her for an interloper. They followed the crowd through the tall white door.

The same gang ruled in the drawing room. Once the auctioneer stepped down and had a quiet word with Phillip: would he like him he said, to buy in some of the better lots? Phillip shook his head, unable to decide otherwise.

Again the name of Thomas Sheraton was mentioned from the rostrum.

"Some call it a supper canterbury, others a music canterbury, gentlemen, but Sheraton describes it in his *Cabinet Dictionary*, published in eighteen hundred and three, as a supper tray. You might call it a dumb-waiter. Who'll say ten pounds to start me?" He sighed loudly. "Why, what's the matter with you? Here we are in one of the original West Country bartons, and . . . what's come over everybody? Are you all afraid of the slump? Then now's the time to buy! And hold for a rise when the Americans come over!"

It went to a bowler hat for five pounds. A Sheraton mahogany secretaire bookcase went similarly for ten pounds; a 1745 gilt-wood carved upright mirror for two pounds. A parquetry dressing-table, style of Louis XV, and a mahogany pedestal writing desk of a decade later, made six pounds each. The bowler hats got all the lots—Dutch marquetry cabinet, 1760, £4: mahogany sofa table £3; eight Hepplewhite mahogany chairs £9; ironstone china flower-painted dinner service of 120 pieces £3.

Outside the room Phillip saw Pansy. She asked if he was busy. No. During the year and a half since Tim had left for Australia she had written regularly to him, but had had no answer.

"I haven't heard from Tim, either. Nor has my uncle, who arranged the passages for those two."

"Do you think Tim is waiting until he gets a good position before sending for me, Phillip. May I call you Phillip?"

"Of course. Yes, that may be Tim's idea, Pansy."

"Oh thank you, you have given me new hope!"

Another of the spectators at the sale was a lean and spare man who had a severe military appearance offset by a tweed hat in which several flies were stuck. Reading of the forthcoming auction, at

the home of a Phillip Maddison, Esquire, Colonel De'Ath had
motored over to find out if this was the same fellow he had caught
poaching on his beat. Having confirmed this, his next thought was
for the Dynawurkur vacuum cleaner which the fellow's brother-
in-law, Copleston, had tried to sell his wife a couple of years back.
He recognised Ernest, and putting on an amiable one-sahib-to-
another manner spoke to him about the possibility of getting a
machine.

Ernest said that he had one at home, but it was second-hand.
This was the same machine which had been the object of a judge-
ment summons and several delaying fees to stay execution, and
had finally cost about £40. It had never been unpacked, beyond
examination by a pawnbroker when Tim had popped it for £4,
since leaving the factory. Ernest let Colonel De'Ath have it for
thirty shillings.

When Phillip heard of this from Lucy he said that he had
behaved in the same dud manner over the furniture, as Ernest
had over the Dynawurkur: how then could he, even in his mind,
criticise his brother-in-law?

Lucy went on to say that the owner of the Tamplin had turned
up, on leave from Africa. After staring at the wreckage in the
bramble bush 'Bongo' had gone away without a word, to return
with a scrap-metal diddecai, who gave him £1 for the engine,
leaving the skeleton behind.

The same diddecai was at the sale. He had looked over the
Delauny-Belville in the workshop. Ernest had made a sound
job of crown-wheel and differential, the motorcar was in running
order. The late owner, disclaiming responsibility for unauthorised
work, had already sold it to Ernest for £5.

"What'll you take for the old crock, guv'nor? Five pun'?"

"All right," murmured Ernest, glad to get rid of the beastly
thing.

Phillip thought, these Coplestons are England in decadence,
yet, O God, I am part of this decadence. I do not really care
for this land. I am a book-worm feebly channering one of
those leather-bound books of dead sermons I have tipped out as
rubbish.

Other eyes had looked among the rubbish besides the diddecais.
Billy was accompanied by his best friend, Artie Rigg, a boy with

yellow hair hanging over brow and neck, who owned a wooden
box mounted on a pair of old perambulator wheels. Billy had
been scrounging, a word he had learned from his father, from
bits and pieces left behind by the diddecais. Thus Billy had
salvaged half a dozen pink chinese lanterns, each made in the
shape of a lotus flower and bearing a tiny candle. These paper
lamps had once belonged to Hilary, who had brought them back
from his first voyage in the China Seas.

Piers and Virginia were staying at an hotel in Milborne, for
Lady Tofield would not receive a divorced woman, or one about
to be divorced. They invited Lucy and Phillip to tea with them
the next day. Lucy could not get away, so she proposed that
Felicity go with Phillip. When she came down, having dressed
for the occasion, Felicity wore rather noticeable clothes, he considered. She had on a blue woven fibre cloche hat to match the
colour of her eyes; her frock showed off her figure rather too
prominently, while the slender umbrella and high-heeled shoes,
together with an embroidered and beaded silk handbag with a
large silver mount was not quite the thing for the country. She
knew his feelings, and seated beside him in the Cockchafer said
that her mother had bought all but the hat for her, saying she
must look her best when taking up her new job.

"Nice girl," remarked Piers, when they were leaving to return
home. "Hope you manage to get some work done. I thought once
of having her myself."

"There's nothing like that between us, Piers."

"You mustn't be cruel to the girl. She loves you."

The south-west gales streamed away leaves from the trees;
beaters went *tap-tapping*, in smocks, through the coverts, to the
screechings of cock-pheasants and their rocketting wings. Then
the shooting was over, the guests departed, including Lucy's
father and brother. Ernest did not shoot; but Pa had been in
fine form. It was agreed that the shoot of the day was the bringing down of two high pheasants from the Hanger while standing
in Lobbett's, two cocks travelling at well over forty miles an hour
with the wind.

'Mister' had come over to lunch of steak-and-kidney pudding,
potatoes in their jackets, cheese and burgundy, a 'spread' in the
keeper's hut at the edge of one of the coverts, afterwards wobbling

back to Ruddle Stones with a cock and hen tied to the handlebars of the 'Onion'.

Once again the farmhouse was redolent of the scent of burning joss-sticks.

'Mister' had brought with him a copy of *The Ecclesiastical Times* to give to Lucy. She left it on the parlour side-board and Hilary took it up the next day. He had already heard of the 'attack' on Phillip's novel in a letter from his sister Viccy. After glancing at it his first impulse was to put it down; then he read it through . . . 'Donkin's communist propaganda . . . extolling Lenin . . . bathing naked with children . . . attacking patriotism, soldierly virtues, and the sacrifice of the dead; sneers at parsons in uniform' . . . 'a hero who is ceaselessly blaspheming against the Established Church and attributes the birth of Our Lord to purely physical causes' . . . he put the paper back on the sideboard while telling himself that while he did not share the religious beliefs of others, there was such a thing as good form, and to give needless offence to his readers was the act of a fool.

He wanted to discuss it with Irene, but hesitated. How far was she in sympathy with such ideas? Surely not with Phillip's book, which, according to the Editor of the paper... He read it over again. What in God's name was the young idiot thinking of? Whatever induced him to follow in the footsteps of his cousin Willie, who had also gone off the deep end, according to what brother John had told him in the past. What was the purpose of it? Where was the sense? Unless—and here Hilary thought he had seen the light—Phillip was indeed what they called in *The Morning Post* 'a pale-pink communist'. His socialist ideas had been bad enough, but this latest thing was beyond the limit.

He was still fuming over the review when Lucy came in.

"Did you know Phillip was writing this sort of thing, Lucy?"

"Oh yes, I think so."

"What is his idea, d'you know?"

"I think he wrote it as a sort of memorial to Willie."

"Good God! Have you read this?"

"Not yet. It only arrived here from 'Mister', yesterday."

"Have you read the book yourself?"

"Yes."

"What do you think of it?"

"It made me feel rather sad." It was an effort to add, "I thought Donkin was rather a poor one."

"'Donkin' is based on my nephew William?"

"Well, not altogether, Uncle Hilary."

"I'm glad to hear that. My brother John would turn in his grave."

He pulled down his waistcoat, the bottom of which had ridden up. He had not had a new suit since before the war.

"Have you seen Irene? She was here before I dropped off for—" he looked at his watch, "ten minutes."

"I think she went with Phillip to see the spruce scions grafted in the nursery."

"Did they take Billy?"

"No, Billy went with Felicity to play with the rector's children."

Hilary walked up and down for awhile before saying, "I suppose you wouldn't care for a walk? You do far too much, you know. Can't you get a woman to live in, a cook-housekeeper? That's what Viccy has."

"I did think of it, but it's a question of the bedrooms. And now that Felicity is coming to live with us—"

"Who is this girl, Lucy? Oh, a nurse for the children. She seems a cut above the usual run of nannies."

He noticed that Lucy blushed as she answered, "Well, she is going to help me a little, but really she's a secretary for Phillip."

"Then he's going to continue writing this sort of stuff?"

"Oh no. I think he wants to write about fish."

"Has your father seen the new book?"

"Oh yes. Phillip sent him a copy from London."

Pa had read the copy all through to the last page, and then closing the book had remarked "Ha," as he removed it from his reading stand, to replace it with a detective story, with a remark to Ernest, reading on the sofa, "Phil's an ass." Ernest had told Lucy this, as a joke, and Lucy had repeated it to Phillip soon after his arrival from London. She had expected him to laugh; instead, he had remained silent. Then she had changed the subject.

"What did your father think about it, Lucy?"

"Oh, I don't know. He's getting on in years, and prefers detective stories."

Phillip was standing beside Irene in the nursery, which occupied a couple of acres of land behind the keeper's cottage. The area had been reclaimed from wilderness in the year following the Armistice. Plots were laid out in rows of seedling beech, oak, larch, and spruce. Adjacent plots carried rows of 4-, 5-, and 6-year old trees, which were ready for transplanting. The area was wired against rabbits with galvanised netting 4-feet high. Occasionally a squirrel was shot, since their teeth cut the sapling conifers, he explained.

"But these clones in this row were topped by the forester, Irene. I helped to graft the scions on them nearly two years ago."

He pointed out the scions, which had been collected during the white winter when Piers had taught him to ski.

"What exactly is a clone, Phillip?"

"It's a grafted sapling. The scions are from one of our few remaining sixty-year-old spruces. We shot them down with swan-shot. They're old, and can produce fruit—as the forester calls the cones—while the sapling stock, being young, rapidly pushes out the scion into branches. The idea is to get fruit quickly, near the ground."

"How long will it take these clones to produce fruit?"

"Oh, some years yet."

Irene had been wondering how her acceptance of Hilary's offer of marriage would affect Phillip's future. She saw that the present complication might become simplified by her answer; she had given it much thought. Hilary was not normal; he had suffered, he was still suffering, from loneliness. It made him a little over-bearing, and unkind to Phillip. He had spoken of his wish to travel again—to visit the places of his youth, particularly China —in her company. 'Alone, I shall feel entirely lost, dear lady.' He had written to her of his future hopes of making over the estate to a trust, to provide for her present living, as well as her future. He had no wish to be one of the trustees; he wanted all to pass out of his hands, it was time that he gave up his burden.

'I'll be only too glad to wash my hands of the entire matter, once I have evidence that Phillip is prepared to devote his whole energies to management, as tenant-for-life. I'm prepared to add a capital sum to ensure a life-income for Lucy. I believe that farming will come back in this country. As a nation we cannot afford to neglect the land for long, with signs of German resurgence. And I'm not alone in my opinion that the neglect of agriculture will not last very much longer —ten years at most. Germany should have been broken up into states and principalities as she was before Bismarck. The Prussians ruined my mother's family, they've caused one world-wide war, which wasn't properly finished, as it should have been, by carrying on with the

Americans through 1919 after refusing the German request for an armistice as soon as they saw the game was up. This is an unpopular idea at the present time, I know; but I am prepared to back my judgment. There'll be another war within ten years, and when that happens the land will be of supreme importance to the nation. Your grandson will be growing up then, and ready to take his place in the production of food for the nation.'

Phillip was explaining that timber-growing was a long-term business.

"The stands, that is the mature trees, take about half a century from seed to timber-hauling."

"That's more than a generation, isn't it?"

"Yes, provided there isn't another war, which there may be unless the die-hards like Nuncle don't change their ideas. Look how Germany was treated during the occupation of the Rhineland! Willie was there, six years ago, and told me a lot about it, how the French allowed the rival political parties to meet, and fight it out. 'Divide and rule', of course. Our blockade caused much starvation and suffering among the poor—their bread, he told me, was half sawdust. He saw small girls of six and seven years offering themselves to sailors at the ports, for a cake of soap. I've put all he told me into the mouth of Donkin, the half-deranged ex-soldier in my novel, *The Phoenix*. In it, Donkin, who is based on Willie, prophesies another war in a few years' time, arising from the hard faces of what he calls 'the old men of Europe'."

"I must read your book, Phillip."

"Will you? Oh thank you. I'll give you a copy."

They left the nursery, and went homewards. Before they went into the parlour, where Hilary was erecting his wireless set, Phillip gave Irene a copy of *The Phoenix*; and after she had gone to her room he went to see if he could help his uncle.

"With luck we might get Hoover's speech tonight, and hear how things are over in America, Phillip. Our economy is tied in with that of the United States."

"Yes, I realize that it's the international money system which rules the world."

"Why do you have to talk like that?"

"Well, it's the truth, isn't it?"

"You make it sound like a conspiracy to dominate world trade only for the sake of making money."

"But aren't slumps and booms engineered by international

speculators, Uncle? The markets are rigged—bullion transferred —sterling finances Bombay cotton mills to put Lancashire on the dole——"

"A slump is the effect of over-production of certain commodities, a boom is the effect of under-production."

"Isn't there a slump coming in the United States—where the dollar rules solely——"

"If America undergoes a slump I agree that it will affect our economy. If it comes, it might very well put paid to farming in this country for a year or two."

To change the subject, Hilary went on to talk of the effect of shooting stars at that time of year, and how they might cause wireless interference. "They usually come from the constellation called Berenice's Hair, you know."

"What a beautiful name, Uncle!"

"In any case it will be about eleven o'clock before we can hear Hoover, owing to the five-hour difference between Greenwich and Eastern Standard Time."

"Oh good. I rather wanted to hear *Parsifal* on my own wireless set tonight, but it'll be over by ten-thirty."

"By the way I heard from Colonel De'Ath that you and that ruffian Kidd had been poaching his water——"

At this point Lucy came in with Billy helping her to push the tea-trolley, and Phillip took the opportunity to go up to his room.

After tea Irene retired to continue her reading of Phillip's novel. At six o'clock, Greenwich Time, Hilary switched on the B.B.C. news. This was followed by the Stock Exchange prices, a message of gloom to Hilary, but a joy to Billy, whose enthusiasm was echoed by Peter. Hilary cheered up when Flotsam and Jetsam came on, the one a squeaky tenor, the other a *basso profundo*, to sing their usual commentary on the news in verse, to the tinkle of a piano. Everyone enjoyed this brief turn before the owner of the set switched off with the remark, "There's nothing interesting until the nine o'clock news."

He was left alone to read his newspaper, but his attention wandered. Why was Irene avoiding him, by going to her room again? He felt hurt that she had gone for a walk with his nephew that afternoon without even letting him know that she was going. Surely she realised that he, too, was interested in the tree nursery, and could have suggested to that selfish nephew of his that he ask him to go along with them?

When Phillip ran down the stairs from his writing room, Hilary said, "I'd like a word with you later on this evening." He saw hesitation in his nephew's face before Phillip replied, "Yes of course, Uncle Hilary."

"You speak as though you weren't sure, Phillip."

"Well, I was rather hoping to hear the second Act of *Parsifal*; but it doesn't matter."

There was an hour to supper—cold birds, the remains of a ham, and the Stilton ordered by Hilary from London. He opened two bottles of claret, and having stood them behind one firedog on the hearth, prepared to continue reading his paper.

Sometime later Lucy went upstairs to tell Philip that supper would be ready in twenty minutes. She found him looking at *The Wireless Times*. He told her that *Parsifal* was being broadcast that night from a German station, the second Act was starting in a few minutes. There was an interval after Act Two, couldn't they have the meal then, since it was a cold supper?

"Well, Uncle Hilary wants to say something to us after supper, you know."

"Why can't he say what he has to say now? Either he's going to carry on, or he isn't. All right, I'll be down in twenty minutes."

Left alone, Phillip corrected this attitude: he knew that the responsibility for the decision lay with himself. But must there be a decision? He had done his two years, and more, of apprenticeship, such as it was—and now he was a mere walking-stick farmer, looking at cattle which didn't even belong to the estate. The milking herd was apparently as far off as ever. The fields, down to grass, were a mere cattle range, bringing in half-a-crown a week for each agisted beast. The bullocks belonged to a dealer, who was virtually tenant of the fields. Soon the bullocks would be in the yards, treading straw to make muck to cart back to the grass. Joby the shepherd had his ewe and hogget flocks, and was always complaining about insufficient feed for them. That was all the farming of Fawley Estates, Ltd. The fishing and shooting were to be let if Nuncle wanted to travel again. As Ned the bailiff had put it, "This land won't walk away, even if Sir 'Ilary do do."

Phillip was sitting in his room beside the little crystal-cum-valve Cosmos set, his ear close to the four-inch flare of the loudspeaker, when he heard tapping on the door. Thinking it might be Felicity returning from the Rigg's cottage, come to tell him that supper was almost ready, he shouted out, "Come in!", and switched off the feeble reception.

Irene's voice said, "Am I disturbing you? I do so want to hear *Parsifal*. It is such heavenly music."

"I'm saving the battery at the moment, Irene, for when the Grail appears."

"Then it won't disturb you if we talk for a little while?"

Every time Hilary had started, hesitatingly, sometimes cold with fear, to ask for Irene's decision, she had tried to avoid hurting his feelings. She had listened with outward sympathy. She had done her best to keep him buoyant; but she had not said what she could not help feeling—that he and she were so different in their outlook on life. At the same time she realized that he needed help: and if he had that help, it would bring his mind to a balance, perhaps, over his doubts concerning Phillip. It was all so involved, and she felt also that she had a duty to help Phillip to come to a right decision.

Irene had confided her own personal feelings to Lucy. She was alone in the world, she said, but not lonely. She was a Roman Catholic; while Hilary, dear and generous man as he was, could not understand the reasons that had led her to the Faith. She realized that he had absorbed this aspect from his mother, who had come from a Protestant Swabian family which had suffered much in the religious struggles of the past; and particularly— though it had not been a religious war—in 1866 when Prussia had fought against Austria, with which Württemberg had allied itself, and been conquered: a war in which the *Baronin* had lost father and brothers on the battlefield.

Irene could allow for the idea of a son being loyal to his mother, she told Lucy, but not for continued prejudice in a grown man who, in himself, had no feelings for any religion.

All that Lucy could say was that perhaps things would settle down in time, like most things. Irene had begun to realize why Phillip felt lonely with Lucy. She had had a quarter of a century of experience beyond that of the gentle young mother. She did not believe that men and women could change their natures, as Phillip appeared to believe. And since the death of her daughter she had felt more and more that her life must be one of service to others, perhaps as a lay sister in the convent at Pau near her home in the Basses Pyrénées.

Irene and Phillip sat before the fire in the small room with its leaded casements which shook in the winds. Now all was quiet outside. The rising moon showed up the leaded panes to be small crosses.

"I was reading your description of Donkin coming upon all those tarred crosses in the German Concentration Graveyard at La Targette, Phillip. I suppose you felt the same shock when you suddenly saw them?"

"Oh yes. You see, Willie worked with the War Graves Commission there. He wrote an article and brought it into the newsroom of the *Sunday Courier* one Saturday night. Bloom, the editor, said he couldn't print it, but it was good. Ironically Bloom wanted it when Willie was 'news' two years later, just after he was drowned. But I couldn't find it in his cottage. I walked over the battlefields after Barley died——"

He recovered his voice and continued, "My description is much inferior. I remembered what Willie said about Jesus walking on water. He said that a poet walks on air when inspired, and Jesus' disciples must have felt that Jesus could walk on water in his finest moments of inspiration. He *did* walk on water, because his imagination could go through all things with clarity. He was *all* spirit. I made Donkin say that it wasn't intended as blasphemy."

"Yes, my dear, I know—but you did rather trail your coat, you know. But the book is *so* compassionate. Perhaps it would have been better to have omitted some of Donkin's wilder sayings, such as the bit about the bishops blessing naval guns——"

"I feel now that I've maligned Willie."

"Don't, whatever you do, allow shallow critics to affect you. You are going on with your writing, aren't you?"

"I don't know if I'll be able to."

"But you must follow your star."

"But if I give up the estate, Billy and Peter will be deprived, won't they?"

"My dear, how can one tell? They may both turn against a farming life. One may want to be an engineer, another a painter, or a sailor, like their great-uncle. Do you really want to be a farmer, Phillip? Really and truly, cross your heart?"

"I like living here."

"You can still live here, if not in this house, another like it."

"But supposing Billy or Peter *do* want to farm?"

"Then they can learn, and if they show real aptitude, and are keen, nothing will hold them back."

"But this land has been in our family for generations."

"That idea may be the root of the trouble. Hilary does not really *care* for the land, he wants to impose upon himself, and in a way upon you, too, a duty which is really what psychologists call a compensation-complex. He has never forgotten the failure of his father, your grandfather, who apparently had a writing talent which was never properly developed, I suppose, because in those days young men went either into the army, the church, or the law. They were disposed of by their fathers like that, while the heir was trained to take the place of his father in due course. The land was then the basis of the family; today the basis is rapidly changing to commerce. Hilary admits that, indeed it was he who explained it all so clearly to me. But a writing career isn't altogether respectable, unless one writes to the current convention, with just a little 'advanced thought' to stir people. But such authors aren't the real ones, are they?"

Irene said all this so gently that he felt considerable relief, and taking her hand, he shook it with affection; and when she said, "An angel is watching your progress, you know," he got up and looked at the moon through the lattice, then opening a casement, drew in a deep breath, feeling that he could never turn from the pathway on which his feet had been set, not through egotism or conceit, but because he was a trustee of a talent inherited from the spirit of that which had brought life upon the earth.

"Phillip, I'm longing to say something else, but I hardly dare——"

"Please do, Irene."

"You still love Barley, don't you?"

"I can't forget her," he replied hoarsely, with sudden tears.

"Oh, Phillip—— I'm so sorry. I *do* understand. But, Phillip, can't you turn your feelings to Billy—and Lucy?"

"I've tried," he said with more tears.

When he was calm again she said, "I think that perhaps we should go down now. Thank you for being so frank with me."

"But it is you who have made everything clear, Irene."

"Tell me one thing more, Phillip. Are you falling in love with Felicity?"

"I'm trying not to."

"If you do, you will be kind to her, won't you? She's still very young, you know."

After supper all were quiet while Hilary listened to the 9 o'clock news. Lucy and Felicity were playing Mah Jongg. When the news ended Hilary turned the switch and lit some more joss-sticks. Lucy noticed after some minutes that he was no longer doing his cross-word puzzle. Phillip and Irene sat on the sofa. Lucy was about to invite them all to join in the game when from up above there came a cry, the noise of a stumble, and the nightgowned figure of Billy, clutching his teddy bear and one of his pink lotus lanterns, tumbled down the stairs. He picked himself up, and staggered into his father's arms, muttering 'Find real Mummie dead', and then settled to sleep.

"He often gets like this when the moon is full," murmured Lucy. "In his dream Billy always comes down to Phillip. Don't you, darling?" she whispered to the boy, as she smoothed back the hair from his forehead, which showed a red mark where he had fallen. But Billy was already at peace; dreamlessly asleep.

Hilary said, "Does he sleep with his head to the north? The moon on the face can keep one awake. Dora as a child was affected by the full moon, but she grew out of it when her bed was changed round."

"Ned the bailiff says that corn sown on the growing moon chits quickly, while on the waning moon it takes weeks. I wonder why, Uncle."

"Light is light, Phillip, and seeds respond to light. The moon's light is growing, so the pull is stronger from a waxing moon than from a waning moon. The light comes from the sun, weak light I grant you, but light all the same."

"I'd never thought of it like that, Uncle Hilary!"

Billy sighed and opened his eyes. "Hullo, Mummie. Where's Dad to?"

"Daddy's here, darling."

Holding the child, Phillip picked up the pink lantern from the floor. "Where did you get that?"

The voice was sharp, imperious. It did not sound like Nuncle's voice.

"Billy and his friend found them. I put them at the bottom of the gun-cupboard, Uncle Hilary."

Hilary went down on his knees before the gun-cupboard. He remained on his knees, silent, until he said in a low voice, "I brought these lotus flowers back with me from China after my first voyage to the East."

It was a gentle night; frost had not yet faceted the dew; earth worms, their whole bodies sensitive to light, were out of their holes in the garden beds, and on the lawn, drawing leaves to their tunnels, where in darkness those gentle priests would perform the annual miracle of changing dead tissue into living soil. In May it was petals of apple blossom which they sought: each worm, wholly defenceless lay with its tail in its hole, ready to draw back at the tremor of an enemy. But undisturbed, they gathered petal after petal, sliding each to its entrance with its prize; and when six or seven petals were laid there, the worm withdrew all but its head; then seizing the pad, took it down to scent and sweeten the soil which had fed the tree. Billy had been shown the worms by candle-light, and had loved them ever since; later, the sight of a thrush hauling one from the lawn in the early morning had brought tears

So mild was the night that they stood outside the french windows, Hilary between Lucy and Irene. A calm lay under the moon's golden haze dissolving the downs. An apple dropping in the orchard made a thud. A flock of lapwing flew across the path of the moon, one uttering its wild cry for reassurance. Phillip opened his jacket and covered Billy's legs and buttocks.

Felicity stood apart, wishing that she belonged to these people. She felt herself to be an intruder, except with the children whom she looked upon with love in which was always a sub-feeling of fear, near to hopelessness that they could never feel for her as she felt for them.

"I wonder if you'd care to see how the Chinese set out their lotus lights on what is their All Souls' Eve, Lucy? They believe that certain spirits of the departed hang about where they lived while on earth."

"Are you feeling cold, Felicity?" said Lucy.

"Oh no, no."

"The Chinese call this the Seventh Moon of the Homeless Ghosts," remarked Hilary to the girl in an effort to be genial.

"How it all comes back to me," said Irene, as she took the girl's arm, and led her to the others. "Have you ever been out East, Felicity?"

"No, Mrs. Lushington, but I'd love to travel."

The girl was trembling. "Let me lend you a coat, my dear."

Hilary said to Lucy, "I remember when I was a young man, on my first voyage to the Far East, being deeply impressed by what I saw outside Peking one night of the full moon. The Chinese believe in the moon's influence, you know, and hold various festivals at different seasons. Some were very impressive——"

Phillip held the small pink objects, more like paper flowers than lanterns of paper and bamboo, and stood by quietly while his uncle continued speaking.

"The New Year festivities started with the full of the First Moon, and went on for several days until the New Year, Lucy. Everyone paid their debts, shops were shut, fire-crackers were set off, strangers in the streets bowed to one another, saying, 'The New Year has come'."

"How wonderful. Everyone makes a fresh start in the release of the social spirit!" exclaimed Phillip.

Hilary ignored this remark and said, "How do you feel about it, Irene? It's a warm night, would you like to see the lights on the Long Pond? Good heavens," he said, half relenting towards Phillip, "it must be all of forty years since I brought these back from Peking, intending, with my brothers and sisters, in the presence of our parents, to float them off under the hunter's moon."

Coats were put on. 'Billy's haystack friend', as Phillip called Mrs. Rigg's child, was allowed to go with them. The Riggs followed at a distance.

By the shallows of the Longpond the yellow stubs of tapers were lit by Hilary. There was no wind; the faintest of airs in motion carried the floating papers away from the shore. Standing alone, a little apart, Phillip thought of friends now faceless under the dissolving rains of Flanders and Somme. The Chinese Feast of the Homeless Ghosts was inspired by love; Hilary had been inspired to see again his parents, and the faces of his young brothers and sisters with the hopes of nearly half a century before . . .

The lotus was the flower of immortality; the tapers were symbols of light offered in darkness—the homeless spirits helped away from haunting the minds of the living . . .

He felt upwelling love for Hilary.

Lucy felt the harmony come upon all as the glims of light moved away into the track of the watered moon. She heard Hilary speaking to Irene in a low voice—it seemed impossible that anyone could speak otherwise on such a still night. She moved away with Billy to leave the two together, whispering to the boys that they could see the little boats from another place, where they would be out of the path of the moon.

Hilary was saying, "We could take a couple of years off to visit the places we both knew out there, Irene. I've had a hard life. I've done my best here, but it's been no good, you know. Phillip will never settle down to what we older ones have hoped for him. I've tried, times without number, to bring him to a level-headed view of things. He's in the clouds all the time, I can see that. Well, as you know, the War Department want to acquire this land. I've fought against the idea of chucking my hand in, time and time again. Now I've come to the point where I can't stand any more. Please help me, Irene, I love you, I need you——" His voice had a guttural sound, he was crying.

When they went in, Phillip thought that his accumulator would have picked up a bit, so that he could hear part at least of Act Three, where the chalice bearing the blood of Christ gleamed in the forest—symbol as alive as any work of the spirit, truly a celestial manifestation revealed through the imagination of Wagner· to those with ears to hear. All life, save of the spirit, was weariness: this was the Kristos of Willie, the music was Truth.

"Phillip, I'd like a word with you."

"Uncle Hilary, do you mind if I go up to hear part of the last act of *Parsifal*? It won't take long."

"It doesn't do you, or anyone else, any good to brood on that kind of thing, Phillip."

"Man does not live by bread alone, Uncle Hilary."

"Now look here, Phillip. I've been in India, I've been in China, I've seen tens of thousands dying of starvation, and their religious fancies didn't save them. Only hard, organised work can do that."

"Yes, I realise that, Uncle Hilary. I'll be back in a minute."

He went to the kitchen where the two women were making coffee.

"Irene, there's just a chance to hear a bit of Act Three. The accumulator may be good for five minutes. We'll hear the part where the chalice glows in the wood. Can you keep back the coffee, Lucy?"

"Yes, of course go up and hear it, you two. Where's Felicity?"

"I don't think she came back with us," said Irene.

Hilary sat at ease before the parlour fire, deeply relieved, entranced. He saw Irene and Phillip going up the stairs, and felt contentment that he was no longer alone in the world.

Phillip and Irene sat side by side on the couch, the small tin trumpet between them. Reception was now better, the music flowed with the pilgrims through the dark forest. Soon the vision would be revealed.

Left alone in the parlour, Hilary stared into the flames. After a while, hearing no sounds from above, he went upstairs to see how they were getting on. Just in case, he tapped on the door and opened it at the same time. Their faces looked at him a moment before Phillip got up and said, "The accumulator is giving out at the very moment we wanted to hear."

Remaining by the half-open door Hilary said, "If you'd asked me, I'd have switched on my set for you. Why not come down and hear it? I'll go and tune into the wave-length."

When he was gone Phillip said, "I think I understand him now. He was thinking of his mother and father, and of the break-up of the family, while launching those lotus-lights." He got up and walked to the casement. "I, too, have been thinking, all these years, that my 'homeless ghosts' were in my care, and that I must do for them what they didn't survive to do. But they were in God's hands all the time. Yes, I can see now that I've been wrong. My double life has hurt Lucy; it has made me impatient and irritable like my father with my mother. My father has always lived in the past, in dreams of this very country."

He paced up and down the small room, to stop at the place where he had been standing in the light of the moon, to hold up a finger as though in warning to himself.

"I see clearly my duty to the estate from now onwards. After all, it is the land which remains. Not even our bones do that." He was shaken by thoughts of cousin Willie. "What is a mere writer, when he sheds his conceit—and in the course of time his dream dies with him? A scatter of black compost in the chalk." His voice quavered. "I'll go and tell my uncle that I'll never write another word that is not entirely practical——"

"Dearest Phillip, I think you should know something. Promise you will say nothing until Hilary tells you? He has made up his mind to sell to the War Department."

He stood with a feeling of being riven before going downstairs to face what was to come.

"*Parsifal* appears to be ended, Phillip. It was on the Rhine-landsender."

"Thank you for trying to get it for me, Uncle Hilary."

"Now look here, old man. You've had some success as a writer, haven't you? In fact I'm told you've done quite well. And having fully considered the matter, I've come to the conclusion that your writing is what you are most fitted to do."

"Yes, I understand, Uncle Hilary. Thank you for telling me."

He left the house and started walking towards the moon, thinking of the same moon shining in the sky while he and Barley were walking from Queensbridge to the cottage in Malandine on the white night of their marriage. With deep emotion he repeated aloud the lines which he had quoted to her then:

Thou movest me . . . as the innocent moon, that nothing does
    but shine,
        Moves all the labouring surges of the world . . .

Felicity, standing by the Longpond, heard the words. They sat together on the wooden pier. He told her the news. She saw a tear glistening on his cheek, she took him in her arms, she held his head against her breast while giving small nervous kisses on the greying hair of his head.

Christmas 1961—Midsummer 1963. Devon.